# SHADOW & FLAME

# SHADOW & FLAME

## MINDEE ARNETT

BALZER + BRAY

*An Imprint of* HarperCollins*Publishers*

Balzer + Bray is an imprint of HarperCollins Publishers.

Shadow & Flame

Copyright © 2019 by Mindee Arnett

www.epicreads.com

ISBN 978-0-06-265269-0

Typography by Torborg Davern
Map illustration by Maxime Plasse
19 20 21 22 23   PC/LSCH   10 9 8 7 6 5 4 3 2 1

First Edition

*For Lori Miller, a true wilder*

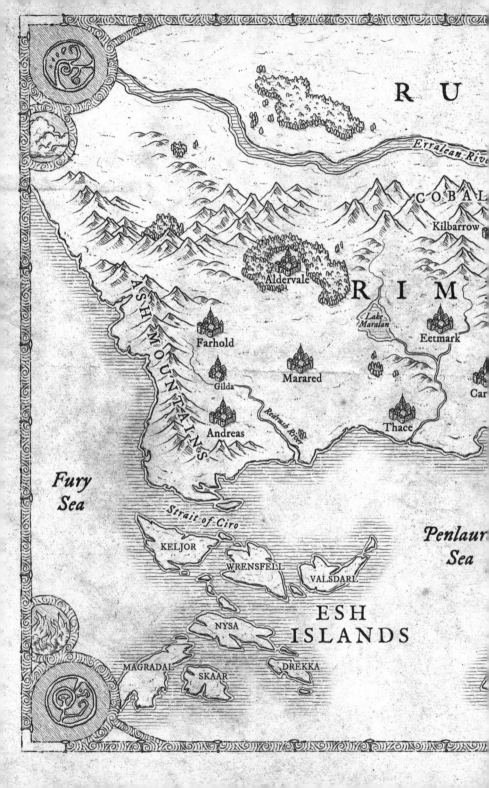

# SHADOW & FLAME

# PROLOGUE 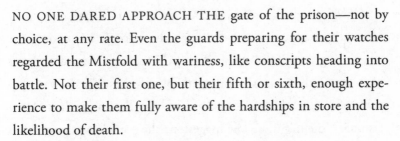 KATE

NO ONE DARED APPROACH THE gate of the prison—not by choice, at any rate. Even the guards preparing for their watches regarded the Mistfold with wariness, like conscripts heading into battle. Not their first one, but their fifth or sixth, enough experience to make them fully aware of the hardships in store and the likelihood of death.

Kate Brighton couldn't blame them for it. The fortress was as foreboding as any she'd seen. Its red mud-brick wall, the color of dirt mixed with blood, stood more than thirty feet high, the top hidden by the thick, undulating mist that gave the prison its name. That mist was as vast and imposing as the sea, obscuring everything beyond it, even sunlight. Not that there was much of that to be seen yet, only a vague brightening from black to gray. Another dawn was here, and yet again Kate hadn't sensed it, her magic, once stirring to life with the rising of the sun, dead inside her. She pushed away the reminder and the wave of homesickness it brought.

*Almost time*, she thought, raising one hand to touch the revolver belted at her right side. A sword hung from her left, hidden by her long cloak. It was a heavier, more impressive weapon at a glance, but far less deadly. If fighting broke out, the revolver was all she would need. *When* it broke out. Despite their planning, violence seemed inevitable. There was too much they didn't know about what awaited them beyond the wall and beneath that unnatural mist. The only thing she knew for certain was that her little brother was being held in there, along with dozens of her fellow wilders.

"It's almost time." Corwin spoke from beside her, and hearing him echo her thoughts sent a trickle of warmth through her, easing the tight knot in her chest.

Craving a glimpse of his face, Kate turned to him, only to be met with disappointment. Although the voice was Corwin's, the face staring at her from the shadows belonged to a stranger. It was a plain face with features so unremarkable that Kate's brain was incapable of remembering it. But that had been the point when Harue fashioned the disguise. The magestone she'd made was perched in Corwin's left ear, the telltale glow of its magic hidden behind a gold plate. Fortunately, Harue had the foresight to create it before they'd left Rime a few weeks ago. The very next morning after setting sail for this gods-forsaken country, her magic had vanished, same as Kate's and the others'. It stopped Harue from making new magestones, but at least the ones she'd already made had retained their normal level of power and duration. An advantage of magist magic over wilders', it seemed.

"Yes," Kate replied, glancing away from that unfamiliar face. She wished Harue were a little less skillful at her craft. The magist might've left some trace of Corwin in the masklike glamour. Then again, such precautions were warranted. Corwin Tormane, high prince of Rime, was a wanted man. Both at home, where his older brother had labeled him traitor, and especially here, in Seva, the longstanding enemy of Rime. King Magnar Fane of Seva would sacrifice six of his seven sons to capture him.

"You hate this face, don't you?" Corwin said, a tease in his voice.

Despite herself, Kate smiled. Here was her Corwin, for certain—the one who could always see her hidden truths. "Not at all. It's better than your regular face, honestly."

"Well, in that case, I will make sure Harue remains in my employ indefinitely so that I might wear it for you each night."

"Moderation, my love." She patted his check. "Once a week at most, otherwise I'll surely grow bored with it."

"Is that so?" He arched an eyebrow, or at least tried to, but this face wasn't made for the gesture and so both brows rose, making him look surprised instead of playful. "Does that mean you'll grow bored of me as well?"

A smirk lifted one half of her mouth. "Let's survive this rescue first and discuss the rest of our lives later."

Corwin grinned back at her, a hint of himself flashing in those false, dark eyes. "Tonight then. Soon as we're on the ship for home."

*Home.* Kate longed for it. Despite the troubles waiting for them in Rime, she missed the land itself with a physical ache. The rolling hills of Norgard, covered in lush green grass and everweep flowers, the towering trees of Aldervale, the blue skies over gray mountains in Farhold, and the crystalline waters of the Penlaurel River. The life and color of Rime made Seva seem a withering wasteland by comparison. And her magic, of course. She missed that most of all. Even though she'd always heard that magic didn't exist outside of Rime, it had been a shock to discover her abilities were so conditional to her location.

She returned her attention to the gate where the change of guard was just finishing. Although she admired Corwin's absolute certainty about the outcome of this rescue, she didn't share it. Too much of their plan relied on luck and chance, both in short supply. If only she were able to use her ability to influence the minds of others; then they could get in and out of the prison with relative ease. Without it they were forced to rely on stealth and tricks like ordinary bandits.

Remembering those tricks, Kate reached into her pocket and pulled out two small pieces of cork, which she gently slid into her nostrils.

"Good luck." Corwin handed her a small glass vial.

She accepted it with a quick nod, hiding its smoky contents from view with her clasped fingers. Then, stepping out from the alley, she approached the two guards standing by the gate.

The one on the left looked up at the sound of her footsteps and raised a hand to the hilt of his sword. "What goes here?"

Kate smiled warmly, counting on these men misjudging her based on her size and sex. "Pardon me, but I seem to have lost my way." Her voice sounded strange with the cork in her nose, but neither guard seemed to notice. "Would you be able to tell me how to get to Merum?"

At the mention of the nearby pleasure district, both men's expressions shifted, and Kate seized her chance. Before either could respond, she took a quick step forward, squeezing her mouth shut as she flicked off the stopper on the glass vial, setting its smoky contents loose. The poison rose up in a thick cloud, enveloping the guards. The one on the left tried to cry out, but the smoke filled his mouth, rendering him silent. A moment later, they both fell to the ground, unconscious.

Kate dispersed the remnants with her hand, then beckoned behind her. Corwin and the others appeared in the courtyard, stepping out from their hiding places in the alleys surrounding the Mistfold. The prison was located on the farthest northern point of Luxana, the capital city of Seva. A strange place for a prison, although rumor claimed it had been a temple long ago.

There were eight of them in all, counting herself and Corwin, a small but deadly band. Dallin Thorne and Tira Salomon appeared first, both of them former mercenaries: Dal from the legendary company known as the Shieldhawks and Tira from their sister unit, the Shieldcrows. Dal flashed a grin at Kate, teeth bared in his eagerness for battle. The cavernous scars on the left side of his face gave the expression a sinister edge. Next to him, Tira yawned broadly, as if bored. Kate supposed she might well be. In the four months Kate had known the woman, she'd never seen anything faze her. She greeted every danger with the same unflappable indifference.

Walking a few steps behind them, Tom Bonner appeared more subdued and somehow far more dangerous than either of the mercenaries. Given his ability to manipulate metal, there wasn't any doubt of his potential for deadliness, at least when they were at home, but still Kate didn't like thinking of him that way. His countenance these days made her more uncomfortable than Corwin with his stranger's mask. She missed the old Bonner, gentle and optimistic, but that version of her friend seemed to have died along with his father, the elder Bonner murdered nearly half a year ago now by the same man responsible for putting the prisoners inside these walls.

The remaining three were wilders, too: Yvonne, an aerist, with control over air; Vander, a pyrist, with control over fire; and Francis, another earthist like Bonner. Only unlike him, Francis had a greater affinity for stone than metal. If he'd had access to his magic, Francis could've torn a hole in the Mistfold's wall and given them entry that way.

Remembering her own weakened state, Kate brought her focus back to the task at hand and stooped toward the nearest guard, relieving him of the ring of keys belted at his waist. Then she turned to the manway door off to the side of the gate and unlocked it. Dal and Tira headed in first, weapons drawn, while Bonner and Francis picked up the sleeping guards and hauled them inside.

Corwin, Yvonne, and Vander followed with Kate coming last, shutting the door behind her. She turned in time to see Tira bend toward the guards and slit their throats, one after the other, as easy as if she were harvesting wheat with a scythe.

"Dammit, Tira," Kate said. "What's the point of putting them to sleep if you're just going to kill them?"

Corwin touched her shoulder. "They are our enemies, Kate, and we couldn't be certain how long the sleep would last."

She shrugged him off and turned away, trying to regain her composure. Corwin was right, of course. These were Sevan soldiers, oath-bound to a king who'd been trying to conquer Rime for years and was now closer than ever to accomplishing that goal—that could be the only reason why he'd been imprisoning wilders, to use them against Rime in some way, magic or no. Though surely their magic would return once they came home. Yvonne, who had visited Seva as a child, claimed it would. *And these people are holding Kiran prisoner.* The thought of her little brother was all it took for Kate to steel herself against the guilt.

Quickly, the group discarded their cloaks, revealing the Sevan uniforms beneath, each one painstakingly acquired these last few weeks. Kate freed the helmet from the strap on her back and slid it over her head. The nose guard and cheek pieces hung too low, half obscuring her vision from all sides, but at least they would hide her face from onlookers. She was less certain about the uniform. The last time she'd tried to pass herself off as a man, it hadn't gone well.

"Yvonne," Corwin said, inclining his stranger's face toward the aerist, "you stay here and silence anyone who comes this way."

"With pleasure," Yvonne replied, her eyes bright with anticipation. She was one of the few wilders with them who didn't have a loved one caged somewhere here, but her mother had been killed by Gold Robes, the magist order that had secretly been kidnapping wilders and sending them to Seva. Rescuing those wilders was Yvonne's chosen method of vengeance. Kate often wondered what kind of person Yvonne would've been if her mother had never been killed. She seemed born to be an assassin. Even without her magic, which she could use to squeeze the breath from a man's lungs with a single, silent thought, she was just as deadly, her knives more like extensions of her hands.

Corwin addressed the others. "The rest of us will move on in groups, staggering our approach. Try to blend in as much as possible. Our goal is to free as many wilders as we can without discovery." He turned and headed down the corridor searching for the nearest exit out of the gatehouse and into the prison itself. They'd been able to gather ample information about the gatehouse, but little about what lay beyond it, other than that the wilders were being housed in an area called "the pit." The dreadful name had kept Kate up late at night, especially the thought that her six-year-old brother was imprisoned there. No—Kiran would be seven by now. She clenched her jaw at the realization.

They reached the exit without incident, and Corwin opened the door and stepped outside onto a dusty, sunlit field encircled by the prison's walls. Kate blinked, her eyes slow to adjust to the sudden change. She hadn't expected this. From outside the mist seemed to enfold the entire prison like a dome, but glancing up she saw clear sky. The mist was still there, but it went no deeper than the wall itself. *Magic.* Only, Kate couldn't see how it was possible. No wilder could do this, not in Seva.

Lowering her gaze, she scanned the rest of the field, searching for prison barracks, but there were no structures in view. Instead, a massive hole sat in the middle of the field. *The pit.*

Kate and Corwin approached it quickly, hoping they appeared like nothing more than two guards going about their duty with the others following some distance behind. But when they reached the edge, Kate forgot her role completely.

"How?" she gasped, eyes drawn downward into the pit.

This place couldn't be. It was like looking through a window that opened onto another world. The bottom lay several hundred feet below, over a sheer vertical edge. Grass so green it was almost blue covered the pit floor, even though Seva was an arid place, water scarce and the flora rough and colorless.

But the grass wasn't the only thing that didn't belong. There were everweeps, too, thousands of them scattered across the floor thick as a garden. The sight of those flowers, with their perpetually dew-drenched petals of every color, sent an ache of homesickness through Kate, as if Rime itself waited for her below. "What is this?" Kate said. It didn't look like a prison at all, despite the presence of several structures down below. There were few walls and even fewer guards.

Corwin shook the question off. "Come on. There's a stairway down." He hurried toward it, and Kate followed half a beat later.

She swept her gaze over the pit as they descended the steep, narrow steps carved into the cliff's side, still trying to make sense of it all. More than a dozen long, low-ceilinged buildings squatted in a pentagonal formation in the middle of the circular pit. At their center was an arena-like structure formed by a short, crumbling wall. It might've been the ruins of an amphitheater. *Or a temple*, Kate thought, as her mind at last made sense of the most startling object in the pit, one so incongruous that her eyes had at first slid right over it.

A massive stone face lay in the center of the arena, the head of some long-decapitated statue. The statue rested on its side, part of it buried in the grass so that only a single eye and ear remained visible. That and half of the crown encircling its brow, fashioned in the shape of a serpent or perhaps a dragon. Kate supposed if the statue had a body to go with it, it would've reached the top of the pit and then some.

Although they descended the stairs as quickly as they could, it still took several long minutes to reach the bottom. Kate did her best not to think of how hard the climb back out would be. At least she wasn't tired. Just the opposite. She felt more awake, more alive, than she had in days.

Given the early hour, there was little activity in the pit, only a handful of guards walking scattered patrols. When one of the nearest spotted them, Kate instinctively reached out with her magic. *Go away*, she thought. *You don't see us.*

To her surprise, she sensed the man's mind clearly, and the sudden desire he had to turn back around again. Her magic. It was back! She nearly swayed on her feet at the realization.

"What happened?" Corwin grabbed her arm, steadying her.

"My magic. I can use it again."

"How?"

"I don't know." She peered around, prickles running down her skin. Some of it from the joy of having her magic again, but more of it from fear. Fear of this unnatural place, and the certainty that if she could access her magic again, so could everyone else. Including all the wilders imprisoned here. What was Magnar doing with them?

"There's no time to speculate," Corwin said. "Come on. Let's count our blessings while they come." He made for the nearest building, testing the door and finding it locked.

Kate reached for the keys, which she'd belted at her waist, but Corwin stopped her. "There's no need for that." He turned and waved to Bonner and Francis, who'd been following closest behind them. "Is your magic back, too?" Corwin asked Bonner.

Bonner started to frown, then stopped, a shocked look spreading across his face. "It is. I don't understand how—"

Corwin cut him off. "Can you take care of this lock?"

Pressing his lips together, Bonner raised his hand toward the lock, melting it open with his magic. Corwin clapped him once on the back, then stepped inside.

Kate followed, the smell of too many bodies in too small a place enveloping her. She peered around at the murky darkness, her eyes making out the human shapes covering the floor. For a second, she thought they were dead, but a simple sweep of her magic told her they were only sleeping—and that Kiran wasn't among them.

She and Corwin began waking them one by one, soon helped by the others joining them. Sluggishly, the wilders stirred. Although they looked well fed, and there was no visible sign of abuse, they remained dazed long after waking, men, women, and children alike staring up at their would-be saviors with expressionless gazes.

Kate motioned Bonner over to her. "Can you remove this woman's collar?" She indicated the nearest wilder, who'd managed to sit up but hadn't yet tried to stand. She wore a collar studded with glowing magestones designed to stop a wilder from using their magic. Bonner waved his hand at the woman's neck, and the metal melted away like ice.

"I can't believe this is happening," Kate said, encouraged by how easily he'd performed the magic.

"I know. I feel nearly myself again," Bonner replied, unsmiling.

If only that were true, Kate thought, watching as he removed the next collar, and the next.

She turned back to the woman. "Can you use your magic?"

"Magic?" The woman stumbled over the word, as if Kate had spoken in a foreign language. But then she glanced down at her palm, and water appeared as if she cupped a miniature fountain in her hand.

"Good, you're going to need it." Kate closed the woman's fingers, and the water disappeared. "How long have you been here?"

She blinked slowly. "How . . . long?"

Dismayed, Kate plunged into the woman's mind. A small, quiet voice in the back of her head admonished her for the invasive act. Once, not long ago, she never would've combed through someone's mind like this, as if she had a right to these memories, these thoughts and feelings. But there was no time to consider the morality of what she was doing—her desperate need to find Kiran outweighed everything.

The woman's thoughts were dull and hazy, as if she'd been drinking. The effect was so powerful that for a second, Kate nearly forgot herself. Then she pushed through the haze to find what she needed. This woman had only been here some four weeks, and she hadn't been out of this room much at all. She hadn't seen any young boys who looked like Kiran. Kate withdrew, impatient to move on with her search.

Corwin approached her. "Everyone's free of the collars, but we're having a hard time making them understand what they need to do. They must be drugged or something. Can you help?"

Kate nodded, knowing at once what he wanted her to do. A few moments before, it would've been impossible, but now her magic swelled inside her, making her feel both full and light and complete all at once. Closing her eyes, she stretched out with her sway, pulling all the minds toward her like kites on a string. In an instant she conveyed the plan—that they were all to wait here, silent and still, and when the time came to leave they needed to be ready to use their magic on the guards.

She withdrew a moment later. "It's done."

Leaving Tira and Dal to stay with this group, Corwin and the rest moved on to the next house. Instead of a single, large room, this one held a long hallway lined with doors on each side, locked and windowless. Individual cells, Kate guessed. They wasted no time opening the first few doors, Bonner using his magic with careless ease.

When one of the doors opened to reveal Kiran inside, Kate couldn't stop the shout of joy that escaped her throat. She dashed into the room, reaching for him.

With a startled look, Kiran jumped back from her, fists raised to defend himself. Then recognition lit his face. "Kate!"

She pulled him into her arms, hugging him so tight he gave a grunt. Her mind reeled from the shock of how different he looked, how much older, bigger.

"Come on," Kate said, loosening her grip. "We've got to get out of here."

"No," said a voice from the other side of the room. Kate looked up to see Vianne, Kiran's mother, standing in the far corner and watching Kate with bloodshot eyes. Her face was bruised with fatigue.

"What do you mean, no? We're getting all of you out of here."

Biting his lip, Kiran took a step back from Kate and shook his head.

"We can't leave, Kate," Vianne said. "You don't understand—"

She broke off at the sound of a commotion outside, voices raised in anger. Kate turned to the door as Francis stepped through it, dragging a woman behind him—Anise, one of the wilders captured at the same time as Vianne and Kiran.

"Kate!" Francis said through gritted teeth. "Make her stop fighting me. Make her come."

"Let go of me, Francis." Anise tried to jerk free of his grasp, her face purpled with anger. "I'm staying. Let go!"

Kate gaped, confused that Anise, Vianne, and Kiran would refuse to be saved. What was going on? She began to ask, only to be silenced by the sound of gunfire. She and Francis exchanged a startled look. It could only be one of their people—revolvers were as rare as magic outside of Rime.

"Let's go." Kate grabbed her brother by the arm. He pulled back, but Kate didn't let go. Not until Vianne stepped forward and sunk her nails into Kate's forearm.

Anger cut through her disbelief, and without a second thought, Kate reached into Vianne's mind, grabbed hold of her thoughts, and forced her will into submission. A moment later she did the same to Kiran and Anise. She didn't understand what made them want to stay, but she wasn't going to wait around to find out with armed guards on the way.

Kate stepped out into the hallway, dragging her wards behind her. She felt them fighting against her at each step, their minds like eels, slippery in the hands of her magic.

Corwin dashed down the hallway toward them. "Go . . . go . . . go!"

"What about the rest?" Kate ran her gaze over all the open doors.

"They won't come," Bonner said, joining them. "Can you make them?"

Kate reached toward the other wilders, sensing them, but the moment she tried to engage, she almost lost her grip on Kiran,

Vianne, and Anise. They fought her so relentlessly it took all her concentration and strength to hold them. She shook her head.

"Watch out," Corwin said, as several Sevan guards came through the doorway. He pulled out his revolver, but before he could fire, Bonner crushed the guards' swords with his magic, rendering them useless. Then he and Corwin mowed them down.

Turning away from the carnage, Kate moved toward the exit with her captives in tow. Outside, Tira and Dal were leading the first set of prisoners out of the house. As before, the wilders remained sluggish and dull-witted, only a couple of them using their magic against the attacking guards.

The entire prison was aware of their presence by now. Still, with the help of their revolvers, they were able to keep the danger at bay until they reached the steps. Dal led the way up with the wilders following behind him. Vander went next with Tira quick on his heels. Behind her, Francis dragged Anise along by the arm. Reaching the steps, Kate sent Vianne and Kiran up first. Corwin and Bonner brought up the rear after her. Bonner paused several feet up the stairs and turned around long enough to destroy the stone steps with his magic, preventing the guards from following that way.

They climbed as fast as they could, the stairs steep and treacherous. On the ground below, a dozen Sevan guardsmen had formed a line, bows in hand. They nocked arrows and drew back to fire.

"Bonner!" Kate shouted. "Stop them!"

Bonner raised his hand as the guards loosed the arrows. They took flight, only to be halted by Bonner's magic. But already the bowmen were drawing again, even as more guards swelled their numbers. It seemed if they couldn't prevent the prisoners from escaping, they would kill them instead.

"I can't stop them all!" Bonner shouted, his face contorted from the effort.

A loud crack echoed over Kate's head, the sound like lightning striking the ground. She looked up to see a huge chunk of the pit wall being wrenched away. Another glance showed her it was Francis, his arms outstretched as he guided it, his face strained with the same effort Bonner had shown. The huge slab of stone hovered beside them as a shield.

"Keep going," Francis yelled through gritted teeth.

They charged onward, their steps punctuated by the sound of arrows bouncing harmlessly off the stone. Kate's legs began to burn, and her breathing grew labored. The top loomed far above them, an eternity away. But they only needed to get out of reach of the arrows.

"Kate," Tira called from ahead of her. "You've got to kill those guards before they kill us."

"I can't!" She didn't have the breath to explain how Kiran, Anise, and Vianne struggled against her even now, worse than before. Kate could feel their panic—their terror—at leaving the pit. If she let go, she didn't know what they would do.

"Please, Kate," Francis said, his face purpled from the effort of holding the stone.

Glancing down at the guards below, she knew she could kill them with her sway, easily and quickly, and likely not risk losing the wilders' minds completely. But she didn't want to. She'd killed that way only once before and it haunted her still. She could just put them to sleep instead, but that would take longer. Indecision taunted her. *They are our enemies*, she heard Corwin saying to her once again.

Reaching the limits of his magic, Francis let out a strangled cry and stumbled to his knees, arms dropping to his sides. The stone slab fell as he did and struck the side of the steps with a noise like a mountain being rent in two. Below, the guardsmen seized their chance, bows raised for another volley. At once, Kate reached out with her magic to subdue them, but she was slowed by the strain of holding Kiran, Vianne, and Anise. Before she could reach them all, one guard let loose an arrow. It flew toward Kate, so fast it was almost invisible. A heartbeat later, she felt the pain tear through her mind, realizing too late that it wasn't her pain.

But Kiran's.

Turning, Kate saw the arrow protruding from his chest, his features already slackening, his body going limp.

"NO!" She reached for him, but her hands found only air as he slid off the edge. It was over in a moment, his body crashing to the floor below. Before Kate could even scream, she watched another body plummeting to the ground after Kiran. In Kate's distraction she'd let go of her other wards, and Vianne had jumped, compelled both by her son and whatever force had been working so hard to draw her back to the pit. With a sickening lurch in her stomach, Kate turned to see that Anise too was trying to leap off the edge, held back only by Francis's tight grip on her.

"Stop her, Kate." The muscles in his arms rippled from the effort to hold her.

Kate grabbed Anise's mind with her magic. As before, the

woman fought her, but Kate wrestled her under control. All the while the terrible truth beat in her brain—*Kiran is dead. Kiran is dead.* She hadn't saved him. She'd hesitated and he'd fallen. *Oh gods.*

"Move!" Corwin shouted from below Kate. His voice cut through her thoughts, reminding her there were other lives at stake. Staving off her grief, she renewed the climb with the others.

They didn't make it far before there was another crack like lightning hitting ground. A violent tremble rocked the stairs, throwing Kate forward onto her hands and knees. The crack sounded again, louder and nearer than before. She glanced behind her toward the source of the noise and saw Corwin and Bonner were on their knees as well, but farther away then they'd been. A rift had appeared in the steps, dividing her from them.

"Corwin! Bonner!" she screamed. "Jump!"

Corwin scrambled to his feet, but before he could make the leap, there was a third crack, and this time the rest of the stairs beneath Corwin and Bonner fell away, a landslide of stone and dirt that dragged them both down, slowly at first, then faster, until they both plummeted toward the ground as Kiran and Vianne had done moments before.

Kate lost sight of them in the cloud of dust and didn't know where they'd fallen. But she didn't need to. She'd seen Kiran's. It was a fall no one could survive, and the truth of it made the world shatter around her, her heart seizing in her chest.

"Come on, Kate." Hands grabbed her shoulders, pulling her up, forcing her to stand.

"No," she said, reaching for her love and her friend, as if she could will them alive by her mind alone. She stretched out with her magic as far as she could, but she couldn't sense either Corwin or Bonner down below.

Dal knelt beside her, mouth to her ear. "They're gone, Kate, but Corwin would want you to survive." Dal's voice was like steel, hiding his own pain beneath it. Corwin had been his best friend for years, same as Bonner had been hers.

*Dead dead dead.* The truth filled her mind, overwhelming her until nothing else existed.

"Come on," Dal said, hauling her forward now. "You can't give up, Kate. Signe is counting on us."

At the sound of her name, Signe's face appeared in Kate's mind, through the black of her despair. Signe, another close friend, someone she loved. If Kate died here, Signe would feel the same pain Kate felt now. Dal was right. They needed to escape, to live.

Blinded by tears, Kate finished the climb. Once up, they crossed the field back to the wall and out into the city, sneaking their way down alleys and side streets until they reached the harbor where Signe waited on the ship to carry them back to Rime.

*Home.* Just as Corwin had promised.

Only he'd been wrong. He wasn't there to tease her with his stranger's face as she lay down for sleep that night. She was alone. And when the ship reached Rime's shores at last, she stepped onto her home soil feeling like a person rent in two. For a part of her remained in Seva, lying dead in that pit with Kiran, Bonner, and Corwin. Three parts of her heart, torn asunder.

# PART ONE

*The Prisoner and the Wilder Queen*

# 1                            KATE

*One year later*

KATE SURVEYED THE NEW RECRUITS with a critical eye as they practiced their sword drills. In a single glance she could tell which of them would die first and which might last longer.

It was an old habit, one she needed to break now that the worst of the fighting was over. The war hadn't even lasted that long, less than a year from when the Rising first took control of the city of Farhold until High King Edwin finally agreed to an armistice. Taking the city had been a strategic move. The wilder rebels and rogue magists that had made up the Rising were powerful but few in number, enough to hold a single city, so long as that city was self-sustaining, as Farhold was. It had been a modest goal, a modest desire—a single city where wilders could be free to live without fear of being hunted down for their magical powers, a safe haven for any wilder in Rime or anyone else who wished to support them. But the cost had been high. Edwin, with the backing of the Mage League, refused for months to concede the city, forcing the Rising to attack as well as defend. So many dead. So many wounded, so many lives changed forever.

Unconsciously, Kate's gaze slid off the recruits and onto the tattoos of flames running down her right arm, bared in the sleeveless jerkin she wore despite the chilly spring air. Trailing from her shoulder to elbow, each one represented a life of a lost loved one.

The next moment, her hand was rising of its own accord to touch the first and largest of those flames covering the point of her shoulder. Her mouth opened, the name of the dead man on her lips. But just before she said it, she came back to her senses and dropped her hand away. This too was an old habit she needed to break. There was no point in reciting the names of the dead. Of dwelling on a past that could never be undone.

*At least their sacrifices have proven worth it*, Kate thought, taking in the familiar sprawl of the training fields and stables on the edge of Farhold that had once been owned by the Relay, the royal courier service of Rime. Now that they were occupied by the Rising, their purpose was to train soldiers. Armistice or not, the conflict was far from resolved. Wilders had fought and won their freedom. Now they needed to defend it from a world that still hated and feared them. And there were other threats, too, like the wilders still imprisoned in Seva, waiting for whatever purpose King Magnar intended. But Kate never let herself think of that too long, the memory like a wound that never healed.

"Are you attempting to look frightening or something?" said a voice from Kate's right.

She turned toward the speaker, a bemused smile crossing her lips at the sight of Tira's wry grin. The two of them stood side by side on top of the training tower, which gave them the best vantage point to oversee the training activities below. "I learned the tactic from you, you know."

Tira snorted, brushing back the two long braids of her hair behind her shoulders. "I wouldn't dare take credit for it. You surpassed my teachings ages ago. And my reputation as well. I heard

Jonas over there refer to you as Saint Kate only yesterday."

"Saint?" Kate leaned against the railing to stare down at the cadet in question.

"Indeed. Saint Kate, the Wilder Queen."

*Saint Kate . . . Wilder Kate . . . Traitor Kate . . .* So many names she'd worn. The realization made her weary. "I think I'm ready to be known as Hermit Kate, thank you very much."

"You're too young." Tira rested her arms on the railing. The hilts of the two swords she wore strapped across her back perched above her shoulders like pet birds.

"Not nearly so young as that one." Kate motioned to Jonas, a sandy-haired boy with a long neck that gave him a swanlike appearance. He looked hardly older than a child, despite being sixteen, the minimum age to serve in the Rising. *Now, that is,* Kate reminded herself. During the worst of the Wilder War, as they'd now begun to call it, boys and girls much younger wielded what weapons they could. The sight of children maimed and dead was a horror emblazoned on her brain, fueling her nightmares.

As Kate took in the boy's stance, she wondered if he was one of those who could make it. The clumsy way he handled his practice sword didn't inspire confidence. He scraped the tip of the blade against the ground as he did an upper strike, and when he went into the left fade afterward, the sword shook like a flag blown in the wind. He was so clearly unaccomplished that the other cadets were giving him a wide berth in the formation, as if afraid he might accidentally wound them. Although they carried mere practice swords for now, the dull-edged steel could still hurt.

But, Kate knew, he had the mind to be part of the Rising. With a single touch of her magic, she sensed the resolve in him.

At the sound of snickering, Kate's gaze slid off Jonas and onto David, the boy standing next to him. By contrast, David's technique already bordered on perfection, and he was making sure that everyone knew it. Especially Jonas, to whom he was muttering snide remarks. Annoyed, Kate touched David with her magic, finding at once that her suspicions were correct. There was cowardice in David's heart and frailty in his mind. At the first sign of true conflict—the blood and screams and stench of death—he would tuck tail and run.

For a moment Kate considered using her magic to put David in his place, but then she passed over the idea for a better one. Descending the ladder, she stepped out onto the training field. At her appearance, the drillmaster called for a halt, and the cadets lowered their swords to stand at attention.

Kate walked down the line of them until she reached Jonas and David, eyeing them both in turn. The latter stared back at her defiantly, while the former kept his gaze on the ground, a slight tremble in his hands. Kate reached over her shoulder to grasp the hilt of the sword strapped across her back. She used to wear it belted at her waist in the Rimish fashion, but Tira's influence had taught her better. With a quick, easy movement she pulled the sword free, the sharp-edged blade winking in the late afternoon sun.

"Cadet Jonas," Kate said, holding the sword straight before her, "step forward and prepare."

With an audible clack of his teeth, Jonas did as she commanded. The moment he held up his blade, Kate attacked, but as she did, she called out the name of one of the forms they'd just been practicing, the best response to her attack. It was a common enough training method, but usually one reserved for cadets a little less green. By all rights, Jonas should've failed this test. And yet almost at once, he raised his sword in the exact form she'd called for, his blade catching hers with a screech of steel.

A surprised look crossed Jonas's face, as if even he couldn't believe what he'd done. Kate didn't give him a chance to enjoy it—or to suspect that she'd in fact reached into his mind and willed the correct action with her magic. She twisted the blade in her hands, freeing herself from his block, and the next moment she struck again. As before, Jonas responded to her called form, catching her strike with his own front guard. Startled gasps swept through the assembled cadets, and Kate sensed its effect on Jonas, the way it bolstered his nerve—just as she'd hoped it would. She called for the next form and the next, slowly easing back her influence until finally he responded to the last command perfectly, and completely on his own.

"Nicely done, cadet," Kate said, lowering her sword at last.

He beamed at her, a boyish grin alighting his features. Kate pressed her lips together to keep from returning the smile. Best not to overdo it.

Sweeping her gaze over the rest of the recruits, she said, "In battle it does not matter how perfect your form was in drill. Technique is more than mimicry. What matters is execution—your ability to wield your sword against a living, breathing, *thinking* opponent, and not mere air." At this, she shot a quick glance at David, making sure he'd been listening. Pleased to see the incredulity on his face, the seed of self-doubt planted in his mind, she turned to the drillmaster. "As you were."

The drillmaster bowed to her, then shouted at the cadets to get back in formation. Tira, who'd come down to watch the demonstration, shook her head at Kate in dismay, but she waited until the two of them had walked away from the cadets before speaking.

"It's only false confidence you gave that boy just now."

Kate shrugged. "Maybe, but he doesn't know that. Besides, isn't that how most of us start? With false confidence? Until time and experience turn it true?" That was how it had been for her when she was just a girl, certain at every swing she took with her practice sword that nothing could hurt her, nothing could best her. How wrong she'd been. She didn't mention that shaking David's confidence had also been her purpose. It was best for the boy to accept on his own that he wasn't cut out for this rather than learn the truth at the tip of an enemy sword.

Tira opened her mouth to argue, but broke off at the sight of a page running toward them.

"Madam Councilor," the page called to Kate. "Chancellor Raith requests your presence at the gate. The caravan has arrived."

"I'll be there shortly."

With a quick farewell to Tira, Kate headed for the stable yard to fetch and saddle her horse. There were several other horses already saddled she could've taken, but she never passed on an opportunity to ride Nightbringer, no matter how short the trip. Besides, he would make the biggest impression on the new arrivals. The black warhorse nickered at her as she approached his stall. She stroked his nose, touching his mind with her magic while a flood of memories rushed through her. Although the horse didn't remember his previous rider, she did. Just as she remembered Firedancer, her mount before Night. The red chestnut mare had died in a skirmish on the road between Farhold and Marared, taken down by a pistol shot to the chest. All that remained of the horse was one of the flame tattoos on Kate's arm.

A few minutes later, she rode out of the stable yard onto the streets of Farhold. People stepped out of her way as she passed, some of them bowing, some staring at her with a mix of surprise and awe. Saint Kate, she thought, an unpleasant shiver sliding down her spine. Nothing could be further from the truth. She held all gods in contempt. As she saw it, they were either cruel schemers meddling in the affairs of mortals, or uncaring, impassive observers. Those were the only explanations for the evil and injustices she'd witnessed, tragedies that any such being could've prevented.

*Unless they do not exist at all.*

Whatever the truth, they were of no use to her.

The Farhold city gates were already opened when she arrived, but a squad of foot soldiers blocked the way. As with the people in the street, they stepped aside at the sight of her, allowing her to pass through their ranks out onto the open road where Chancellor Raith waited astride his own horse. Two clerks stood beside him on foot, one bearing parchment and pen, the other a leather satchel.

In the distance, a caravan was slowly drawing near the city. A dozen or more wagons rode nose to end, each flanked by soldiers on horseback. White flags flew on the left-hand side of the drivers. On the right waved the blue and white of House Tormane, the ruling family of Rime. High King Edwin's banner. The sight of it brought a lump to Kate's throat, and once again she had to resist the urge to touch the topmost tattoo on her shoulder.

Raith reined his mount over to hers. "Hello, Kate. So glad you decided to shirk only part of your duties this day." A cordial smile crossed his face, the wine-colored birthmark spread over his cheeks and nose contorting at the gesture.

"Don't start, Raith," she said, not bothering to use his title, even though he was the head of Farhold—or the Wilder City, as it was now sometimes called in these parts. "I've told you a hundred times I've no interest in governing. It doesn't matter how many council meetings you summon me to. Nothing will change that."

Raith smiled again, less cordially this time. "You're mistaken, Kate. It's not me who wants you there. Our people elected you to the position."

Kate shot him a glare, not bothering to hide her anger, always so close to the surface when discussing the subject. "I didn't ask to be elected, and you know as well as I do that my skills are best put to use training the cadets and for moments like this." She gestured to the approaching caravan.

"Yes, so you've claimed many times before." Raith gave a dry cough. "Although you'll understand why it bothers me that you're so content to be a glorified statue rather than a real player in the game."

Kate gritted her teeth to hold in a retort. This was an old argument between them, and it was a day for new beginnings. She forced her jaw to relax. "Did the caravan send the list of names ahead, and a summary of their patents?"

Raith nodded. "The Relay rider arrived late yesterday. The council reviewed it this morning. All the new citizens check out."

"On paper at least," Kate said, ignoring his implied rebuke. Yes, if she'd gone to the stupid meeting she could've reviewed it as well, but it would've made little difference. A name written down on paper would tell her nothing about the person themselves—or their intentions in coming here.

She returned her gaze to the caravan still inching its way closer. Those wagons carried human cargo, either wilders or wilder sympathizers. As part of the armistice, High King Edwin had agreed to allow any wilder found living in one of the other eleven cities of Rime still under his dominion safe passage to Farhold. In exchange, the Rising agreed not to lay siege to any of them. Live and let live was the current political attitude. Kate wasn't ready to embrace it as truth yet, though. This was only the second such caravan to arrive, far too few for her to trust that Edwin would keep to his word and not attempt some treachery beneath the veil of peace.

Though, she thought, he should know better by now.

When the front of the caravan finally drew close, Raith and Kate rode out to meet it, the clerks trailing behind them at a slower pace. Two of the riders at the front of the caravan also came forward, a soldier wearing the blue and white of the royal city of Norgard along with a captain's insignia, and a magist wearing a gray robe trimmed in white—the full, bone-white mask on his face marking him a master.

At the sight of them, Kate automatically reached out with her magic and probed their minds for any hint of treachery. She found none, although she sensed plenty of animosity, especially on the part of the magist whenever he looked at Raith. Kate didn't let it alarm her though. Before becoming one of the key leaders of the

Rising, Raith had been a magist, like this one a master in the Mage League, a group determined to eradicate wilders and wild magic from Rime. Raith had seen the evil and hypocrisy of it, though, and dedicated his life to freeing wilders instead. The irony, of course, was that wilder and magist magic was the same at its heart, both subject to the rise and set of the sun and both tied to the elements. But magist magic could be used only to imbue objects with spells, making it easier to control and less dangerous than the more unruly wilder magic.

Kate could sense this magist's resentment went deeper, however—that Raith's perceived treachery was personal somehow. *It's all your fault*, the man was thinking. Kate didn't understand it at first, seeing nothing in the man's memory that connected him to Raith.

Then she realized that it wasn't the political strife for which he was blaming Raith. It was his gray robe.

Withdrawing from his mind, Kate took in the sullen color of his garb. Before the war no magist would have ever worn such a color. A magist's robes used to identify the order of the Mage League to which they belonged, one of six: blue, green, red, brown, white, and gold. Now, Grand Master Storr, head of the League, had disbanded the orders—or rather, unified them under the gray in an attempt to undo the damage caused by the gold order's treachery. That order had been secretly sending wilders to Seva in order to create an army. Given the animosity Kate sensed here in the ranks, she assumed the single-order strategy wasn't working. At least, not as Storr hoped.

"Greetings," Raith said, smiling at the captain and the gray robe in turn. "I am Chancellor Raith, and this is Councilor Brighton. We will be overseeing the transfer of the hopefuls."

The captain's lips tightened at the use of the word "hopeful," as if he couldn't imagine why anyone would hope to be granted admission to a city full of wilders. Disgusted by his attitude, Kate tuned out his thoughts.

"Very well," the gray robe replied. "We already verified that each of them has their patents as agreed. Will you collect them now or later?"

"Now." Raith gestured to the clerk carrying the leather satchel. "Mr. Jennings here will accept them."

The gray robe frowned as he glanced at the sun already making its descent toward the horizon. "Will you be reviewing them all here?"

"That won't be necessary," said Raith.

Now the gray robe raised a questioning eyebrow. He'd expected more of a fuss, Kate knew. That was good. It meant that he didn't realize her true purpose in being here—to probe each of the hopefuls with her magic. If any of them intended to do harm, she would know long before they were allowed to set foot inside the city. The patents they carried—documentation of their place of birth and any significant family history—were a mere formality.

The captain and magist returned to the caravan to oversee the unloading of passengers. Kate waited patiently, clearing her mind of all distractions. As the hopefuls came forward one by one to give their names and patents to the clerks, she carefully slipped into their thoughts, gently gleaning their intentions and memories.

Although she had never come across another wilder with the gift of sway, she was always on the lookout for one, the gift rarest but most dangerous of all.

First was Mary Pierce, a widower from Eetmark, accompanied by her two young daughters, both of them wilders. Her husband had been a wilder too, although Mary didn't know that until her daughters were born and old enough to start showing signs of their abilities. Even now she harbored an underlying resentment for the man—both for deceiving her and also for foolishly dying in an ill-advised attack on a magist order at the start of the war and leaving her to raise them alone. But beneath that, Kate sensed the woman's love for her children, one that transcended her fear of what they could do, what they were.

Next came Austin Thatcher, an orphan from Kilbarrow. He too was a wilder, a pyrist with control over fire. He wouldn't be sixteen for another year, but once he was settled in Farhold he planned to lie about his age in order to join the Rising army, get some revenge he sorely desired. It wouldn't work—Kate vetted the recruits same as she was doing with these hopefuls—but there was no reason to dash his hopes just now.

There was Declan and Sara March, two siblings from Andreas. Neither of them were wilders, but they came from a poor family and hoped for a better life here, behind the more tolerant walls of Farhold. They had no fear of wilders or ulterior motives beneath their naive hopes.

On and on it went, so many people with so many thoughts and memories that after a while they all started to blur together. Kate felt her magic draining and longed for it to end. She would need a large meal and a lengthy nap after this.

As the line dwindled, a young man from Norgard stepped forward, giving his name as Colin Davies—a lie. Kate sensed the deception immediately, and at once a surge of adrenaline went through her, sharpening her sluggish thoughts. If he was lying about his identity, he could be trying to hide intentions more sinister.

She entered his mind searching for the truth, only to find his thoughts murky. At first he seemed glad to finally be here, but behind that she sensed anger and resentment. Disconnected images flashed through his mind. She saw a Norgard soldier lying dead on the battlefield—this young man's father. Killed in one of the many battles during the Wilder War. *So why come here?* she wondered, but hard as she tried, she couldn't find a clear answer. It was possible he meant no harm . . . but the opposite was equally possible, and Kate wasn't here to take chances.

"Not this one," she said inclining her chin toward the young man.

Raith turned a questioning look on her, but she only nodded, certain in her conviction. Raith let out a sigh, then said, "This one is denied entry."

At Raith's words, the man's face clouded first with fear—then with rage. "You can't do that. I want to be here. I've nowhere else to go, no one else . . . !"

His shouts of protests continued as the soldiers dragged him back to the wagons. Kate did her best not to listen, even as the doubt niggled inside her. He'd been lying about his name, but his desperation in being denied entry was real enough. *It is not my concern*, she reminded herself. She was charged with protecting this city and its people. There was no room for leniency or doubt.

The vetting process resumed until the last of the hopefuls finally approached them. The old man walked stooped over, his back curved like a shepherd's crook. His bald head shone brightly in the fading sun, and he wore a tattered green robe.

*A magist's robe.*

No sooner had the realization struck Kate then she heard Raith draw a sharp breath. She turned to see the shock alight across his face, disbelief and wonder surging through him.

"Master Janus?" Suddenly beside himself, Raith leaped from the saddle and rushed toward the green robe.

Kate watched with her mouth open, stunned by Raith's behavior, like a giddy child on a festival morning. In all the years she'd known the man, through all the hell they'd been through together, she'd never seen him like this. So . . . *vulnerable.*

The old man looked up, his pale eyes squinted. "Who's that?" He reached for the spectacles hanging from a cord around his neck.

"It's Raith, Master Janus." Raith took the magist by the hand.

Janus's lips parted into a smile, one made ghastly by the number of gaping holes in his mouth where there should've been teeth. "Raith, Raith. So good to see you."

They embraced. The gesture—and the emotion bolstering it—was so intimate that Kate had to look away, reining in her magic lest she start feeling the same affection. She didn't need an introduction to know this must be the magist who saved Raith's life when he was just a baby. Afraid of the ill omen of their child's birthmark, Raith's ignorant, superstitious parents had left him to die in the snow. But Master Janus found him just in time, using his healing magic to keep him alive before bringing him to an orphanage. After that, the magist had made it his personal duty to ensure Raith grew into manhood, eventually becoming a magist himself. And now they were both here, Janus evidently choosing to join Raith in living among wilders.

Once the emotions lessened some, Kate turned back to the two men. They'd broken the embrace, but Raith hadn't let go of Janus's arm.

"I didn't know you were coming," Raith said. "Your name wasn't on the list."

Janus scowled, reaching into his pocket to withdraw his patents. "I'm not surprised. Any magist who dares defect here is treated like vermin. I suppose someone decided to conveniently leave me off the registry in the hopes I might be denied entry."

"Utter foolishness." Raith accepted the patents and handed them off to the clerk just as quickly. "You are welcome here. Let me call for a litter to take you into the city."

With a scathing look, Janus waved him off. "I can walk fine. It only requires a little patience on your part."

If Raith had a mind to argue, he thought better of it. "As you wish, but I will find a place for you in the governor's house."

"You mean your house, if the rumors are true? It's Chancellor Raith now, no?" Janus squinted up at Raith, who nodded once. "I always did know you'd ascend to the highest . . ."

"Miss Brighton," the Norgard captain said, suddenly appearing next to her, close enough that Nightbringer bared his teeth at the man's horse. In her distraction over Janus's arrival, she hadn't noticed his approach.

"What is it?" she said, annoyed more with herself than anything.

"Ambassador Thorne asked me to deliver this to you."

Kate stared at the brown paper package in the man's hand, guessing it must be a gift for her best friend, Signe. Dal had left Farhold nearly two months ago to serve as the Rising Ambassador in Norgard. He'd been the best person for the job, but the decision to leave hadn't been easy on him and Signe, the two of them practically husband and wife, even if they hadn't yet made it official. Accepting the box, Kate glimpsed Signe's name written in Dal's carefree script across the top. She wondered what was inside, feeling an old familiar ache of jealousy at their love, one that remained unbroken even now.

"Thank you," Kate said, aware she'd been silent too long.

The captain bowed his head, then turned away, heading back to the caravan to muster his men for the return journey. Despite the threat of nightdrakes—the deadly, dragonish creatures that prowled the land of Rime from sundown to sunrise—they were not welcome to stay in Farhold. They would have to rely on mage magic to keep them safe. At least there were no more daydrakes for them to worry about. With her own magic, Kate and her small team had managed to hunt down and kill them all. Or rather, force them to kill themselves. *Drake Killer* was just another of her titles; at least she'd earned that one.

Distracted by the unruly flow of her thoughts, Kate nearly forgot that she hadn't vetted Master Janus. Despite the old man's slow pace, he and Raith were halfway to the gate. For a moment she considered not doing it all, having no wish to intrude on the reunion, but she remembered her argument with Raith earlier—that ensuring no one who meant harm to Farhold be allowed entry was the best way she could serve the wilders living here. She couldn't make exceptions in that duty.

Reaching out to the man, she at first felt his affection for Raith, as she'd known she would, though it seemed far less than what she still sensed in Raith. The knowledge gave her pause, but not nearly so much as what she sensed when she went deeper.

Nothing. There was nothing there. She couldn't sense his thoughts or memories behind the introductory ones she'd already gleaned, vague recollections of Raith as a young man and various memories of his service as a green robe, the order of healing. Puzzled, she tried to delve deeper, but to no avail. It was as if there wasn't anything else to him besides these fleeting memories.

Concern fluttered in her stomach, and she opened her mouth to say something, but stopped. How could she explain this? It wasn't as if she'd sensed deception in the man, uncovering some plot to overthrow the Rising. And yet, it wasn't normal either. She'd never encountered anything like it before.

"Master Raith," she said, forgetting for a moment that he was chancellor now, and no longer the master magist he'd once been.

Nevertheless, Raith turned at the address, the smile remaining fixed on his face. The joy he was feeling struck Kate anew, the power of it taking her breath away.

"What is it, Kate?"

She started to answer, then stopped, a warning sounding in her mind. She knew enough about the strength of feelings to understand that Raith wasn't going to believe her, no matter what she said. Love and affection this strong was blinding.

"Nothing," she said. "It doesn't matter."

Raith turned back to Janus, the moment forgotten.

Kate followed behind them as they entered the city, her nerves prickling. She decided to let Janus inside her city for now, but she would keep watch on him. He might be old, but he was still a magist, and that made him a threat. If he showed any sign of betrayal, she would kill him. Simple as that. No hesitation. That was the greatest lesson of her life, one learned in the failed rescue attempt in Seva. If she hadn't hesitated, if she'd simply done what she needed to do without fear or self-doubt, things would've ended differently. And her arm might bear fewer mementos of the dead then it did now.

With her resolve made, Kate at last gave in to her old habit, unable to resist any longer. She raised a hand to the tattoos on her arm, starting near the wrist this time. Then slowly, one by one, she touched each flame and spoke the names of the dead. Firedancer . . . Bonner . . . Vianne . . . Kiran . . .

Finally, she reached the topmost one, and for a second she allowed herself to think his name.

*Corwin.*

THE PRISONER HAD FORGOTTEN HIS true name.

It wasn't surprising. He'd forgotten many things. The color of a blue sky on a cloudless spring day. The sound the wind made as it passed through the trees. The way the sun felt on his face, or the soothing caress of warm water as he sank into a bath,

The sleepy contentment of a full belly. What it meant to laugh without care.

He'd forgotten what it was to be alive.

The guards and his fellow inmates called him Clash, a name he supposed he'd given them when he first arrived at the prison, although he didn't remember much of those early days. His injuries had been greater than anyone realized or cared, particularly the blow he'd taken to the head, one that left him feeling like he'd been cleaved in two. Months had passed before the fits finally stopped. At least, he thought it had been months. It could've been years, or mere days. Time seemed to pass differently down here, in the bowels of this Sevan work camp. Most days it didn't seem to pass at all, an endless loop, day after day.

He'd been called the name often enough that he answered to it, but no matter how many times he heard it, it always felt like something he'd lost a long time ago and had unexpectedly found again.

Hearing the name now, he glanced down at the man who had

spoken it, hunched on the ground next to him. Dirty rags clung to a body so thin the bones of his spine protruded through the flimsy fabric. Henry looked up, his eyes glistening black points above the tangled beard on his face. "Did you hear me, Clash? Said I found it. A new deposit. I'd bet my last teeth it's a dragon's share of nenir."

Clash lowered his pickax, the muscles in his shoulder giving a quiver of relief. It amazed him that, despite wielding the ax day after endless day, it still had the power to tire him. He would've expected the tool to feel like an extension of his own arm by now, like the way the sword he once carried had felt. Instead it was more like the chains he wore, something alien and cold.

He bent down next to Henry to examine the find, his eyes already aching from the bright glow of the nenir crystals protruding from the rock Henry had just dug through. Godtears, they were often called. A sweet, musky smell wafted off them. At a glance, Clash saw that Henry's assertion was true. It did indeed look like a large find. The color of the rock surrounding the area was just a bit lighter than the rest, suggesting more glowing crystals beneath. Despite knowing better, he felt his spirits lift a little. For ages now, neither of them had found any nenir, not so much as a shimmering speck of dirt. Already their overseers had cut their food allotment, threatening to stop feeding them altogether unless they made a successful contribution soon.

"It's a lot, ain't it, Clash? Ain't it?" Excitement rang in Henry's words.

"Keep your voice down," Clash said. This was the sort of treasure men would kill for, although he doubted Henry realized the danger. He couldn't see or think beyond his excitement. Needing to get across the point, Clash added, "If Foster hears, he'll try to claim the find as his own."

Henry's eyes widened, and he moved his frail body in front of the find, as if he could block it from view, but nothing could hide that glow. No one in the prison seemed to know what the godtears were used for—they were too fragile for jewelry and other such ornamentation—but they must be worth something for Magnar Fane, the Godking of Seva, to imprison so many to mine for them. *Killing us would be far less costly,* Clash knew. Even the little amount of food they did receive added up. Not to mention the wages paid to their overseers.

"No, no, don't want that." Henry grabbed Clash's hand with a snakelike movement, the chains on his wrist clanking. "Will you fetch the warden?"

Clash frowned, although he doubted Henry could see it through his own considerable beard. He'd worn it for so long he no longer remembered what it was like to be clean-shaven. Clash suspected that Henry had forgotten that Berit was the warden in charge of their sector today, the cruelest of the prison foremen. The man thrived on spreading pain and misery. Every chance he had, he instigated fights among the prisoners, goading them into petty rivalries for the sheer enjoyment of watching the violence play out. A newly discovered deposit of godtears, especially a large one, would fuel his game for days.

Of all the damnable luck. If it had been any of the other wardens, Henry might've been rewarded for the find. Given a day's rest and an extra meal. Maybe more if it was deemed big enough. But not with Berit in charge. Somehow or another, the man would find a way to twist the reward into punishment.

"Won't you go, Clash?" Henry squeezed his arm harder, surprisingly strong despite his thinness. He cast a furtive glance over his shoulder, in case one of the other inmates was already listening in, but it appeared he and Henry had been alone in the narrow shaft, one of the deepest offshoots in the mine. Few of the prisoners came down here willingly, fearing a collapse or sudden release of poisonous air. Clash preferred it, though. It was cooler down here, the interminable darkness just beyond the reach of their lanterns a welcome distraction, a promise of oblivion, if he could just get there.

"All right," Clash said, holding in a resigned sigh. There was no point warning Henry about Berit. He could tell by the crazed, desperate look in the man's eyes that he wouldn't be able to keep the discovery hidden until tomorrow when they stood a chance of having a better foreman. Desperation was as much a companion as the darkness in this place. "Stay here. I'll be back as soon as I can."

Clash retrieved his lantern from the peg on the cave wall, one he'd hammered in a few days before, when he and Henry first started to mine this section of the shaft. The tired flame flickered at the movement, threatening to go out. The cheap oil that fed it sent a thick stream of smoke rising up from its top, cloying the air and burning Clash's eyes.

He headed down the shaft to the lift, the first of many that would finally bring him to the main shaft at the top of the mine. While the mine itself was old and deep, the apparatus here was new, all the lifts in perfect working order.

"What are you doing back up so early?" Berit's voice struck his ears before the lift's basket had even breasted the floor. "Your shift only just started."

There was something eager about Berit's tone, and when Clash finally spotted the foreman standing beneath the light of one of the torches hung from the wall, he didn't fail to notice the way he stroked the leather handle of the bullwhip he wore strapped to one hip, eager at an excuse to wield it. A phantom ache spread through the webbing of scars on Clash's back at the sight of the whip, the memory of the way it felt when the glass- and stone-encrusted leather struck his skin. It was like being eaten alive, one agonizing bite at a time.

"Henry has found a new deposit," Clash said, keeping his eyes locked on Berit. Most of the prisoners were too afraid to look at him directly. Not Clash. Fear was a luxury for the living. The dead had nothing to fear.

*You don't really believe that*, a woman's voice spoke in his mind, both comforting and cold at the same time. *If you did, then why remain? Why not lie down and accept defeat?*

It was a fair question. He supposed he just didn't see the point of actually dying. But he knew better than to respond. That voice haunted him enough as it was without such encouragement.

"Is that so?" Berit's eager look intensified, his eyes gleaming in the flickering light of the torch. The two guards sitting at the small wooden table next to where Berit stood exchanged a look, one full of the same greed so palpable in the foreman. A new vein of nenir would mean a boon for them as well.

Clash nodded, preferring not to speak unless he had to, especially to the likes of these men. He'd learned early on that silence was his best weapon in this place. When the other prisoners screamed or cried or pleaded, Clash held his tongue, undermining their power over him.

"Well then, take me to it." Berit shot a glance at the other guards. "You two keep an eye on things. I'll be back."

Clash turned and entered the basket, leaning against the edge to make room for the warden. The journey down was faster than the journey up had been. They hurried to the next lift and then the next, heading deeper into the mine. Clash's shackles jangled as he shuffled along, the weight of them tugging at his wrists and ankles.

The moment the final lift came to a stop, the sound of raised voices reached them. With a mumbled curse, Berit pushed past Clash and down the shaft, already pulling the whip off his belt. Clash followed the warden, aware of the dull thump in his chest.

"Whatever is going on, it'd best be over by the time I get there!" Berit called as he hurried his pace. His breath came in hard pants, his lungs unused to the air down here. His bulky frame nearly filled the space in the cramped tunnel. Despite his warning, the shouts continued. He rounded the corner into the offshoot with Clash trailing just behind.

"What's going on here?" Berit's voice boomed against the walls.

"It's my find, mine, mine, mine," Henry shouted. "You can't take it from me."

"That's a lie," the deeper, heavier voice of Foster shouted back. "I found it first."

As Clash navigated the corner, bringing the scene into view, he realized at once what had happened. Against all reason and chance, Foster had stumbled into their shaft, seen the glow of the godtears, and decided they were his.

And Berit would let them fight for it, knowing full well it belonged to Henry. He enjoyed watching them suffer more than anything.

*Then why don't you do something about it?* the voice said again, and as before it was female. It was always female, the voice of a woman he'd known and loved. And forgotten.

*Have you?*

*There is nothing for the dead to do*, Clash thought, pushing her from his mind.

He stepped into the shaft to see Henry lunge at Foster, fingers curled into claws as if he meant to gouge the man's eyes out. Foster reared back, avoiding him by an inch.

"That's enough." Berit swung the whip over his head, its short length brushing against the low ceiling. It landed across Henry's shoulders with a loud crack, and he shrieked. The whip struck again. Crack, crack, crack. Henry ducked, arms shielding his head and neck as he crouched down in submission.

Berit struck once more for good measure, then let the whip fall to his side. "There now. That's better." He turned to Foster. "Why don't you tell me what's going on."

Clash listened from a few feet away as Foster told his lie.

"It's not true!" Henry screamed. "I found it. Clash was with me. That's why he went to fetch the warden."

Foster shook his head, casting a pleading look at Berit. "He's lying, sir. They planned it together to try and cheat me."

Berit tsked, his gaze alighting on Clash for a moment. "This is a dilemma." Clash saw everything he suspected confirmed in Berit's look. He would make them play the game. *Although in the end we all lose, we dead men.* He was weary of it.

Berit turned back to Henry. "I'm afraid I have no choice but to let fate decide." He reached into his pocket and withdrew a bronze coin, one side emblazoned with the image of the Godking, the other bearing the red bull insignia of House Fane. "Heads it's Foster's, tails it's Henry's." He tossed it into the air, nearly bouncing it off the low ceiling before catching it again. "The dead gods have spoken," Berit said, revealing the image of Magnar Fane.

"It's not fair," Henry said, in a voice small as a sigh. He looked up at the warden, his eyes wide and watery.

Ignoring him, Berit motioned to Foster. "We'll need to call the surveyors down to examine it. Depending on what they say, you might have a hot meal tonight." He sniffed toward Foster. "And a bath."

Henry's howl of rage seemed to shake the very walls. Clash felt the pain of it like a nail shoved in his eardrums. Leaping at the warden, Henry grabbed him by the throat before the bigger man could so much as raise an arm to defend himself.

"It's mine. You can't take it. Mine! Mine!" Henry tried to force the warden to his knees as he squeezed and squeezed, the grubby stubs of his nails pressing into Berit's thick neck.

Clash didn't move. Neither did Foster. Whatever they tried to do, it wouldn't matter. Berit hadn't become a warden because of his brains. He grabbed Henry's wrist just above the shackle and squeezed, driving his fingers into the tender spots beneath the heel of Henry's hand. Henry let go of Berit's neck with a shriek.

But that wasn't enough to satisfy the warden. Keeping hold of

Henry's wrist, he raised the whip again and struck the man across the legs. Henry stumbled sideways and fell, his head smacking the side of the shaft. Berit rained down more blows on the man's head, shoulders, and back, tearing through the already tattered fabric of Henry's clothes. Red welts appeared on his pale skin, soon breaking open to weep blood.

Clash watched, silent and still.

"Mercy!" Henry cried, the word nearly incomprehensible around his sobbing. "Mercy!"

*Help him*, the woman spoke in Clash's mind.

*We're already dead men*, Clash replied.

*No, not yet. Not if you choose . . . remember who you were . . . who you are.*

Something stirred inside him, a feeling as long forgotten as his name. *Anger.*

"Help me . . . mercy . . . help . . ." Henry's voice was weakening as he shrank further and further down in a futile attempt to escape the blows. He would pass out soon, and it would be over. But the shock might kill him. Or the infection that would set in after.

The scars in Clash's back ached. Anger throbbed in his chest. Emotions he'd long buried crawled up inside him, pushing their way to the surface. Like a floodgate opening.

*Crack, crack, crack—*

Clash, with lightning speed, reached out and grabbed the end of the whip before it could strike Henry again. Pain prickled across his palm, but he barely felt it through his calluses. Clenching his fingers, he yanked, pulling the end of the whip free of Berit's hand with stunning ease.

Berit gaped at him, shocked by the sudden change.

"He's had enough." The sound of command filled Clash's voice.

"Why, you—" Berit sputtered as he grabbed for the sword strapped across his back, pulling it free in one quick movement.

At the sight of that naked steel, some long-forgotten instinct came over Clash, and he stepped toward Berit, out of the sword's reach in the cramped quarters. Clash seized the warden's wrist and wrenched the blade out of his hand, letting it fall uselessly to the ground. Then he swung, the punch landing square against Berit's stomach and sending him into a stoop. Clash followed with an uppercut, landing it on the underside of Berit's jaw. The big man stumbled backward, teeth clacking. Clash moved in for another strike, but Berit had overcome his shock and managed to duck, the blow glancing off him. He countered, but Clash was ready, side-stepping the punch with ease.

They began to fight in earnest, trading blows—Clash hindered by the small space, Berit hindered by his size. Then at last Clash saw his opportunity. Berit charged toward him, and Clash ducked and rolled, sliding past the warden to come up just behind him. He'd snatched the whip on the way, but rather than strike the warden, he swung it around Berit's neck before he could turn around. He pulled it taut.

And squeezed.

"Help . . . me . . . ," Berit said, his eyes fixed on Foster, who still hadn't moved. He watched the man dying with an almost eager look, the kind Berit usually wore at the sight of others' suffering. The warden had taught his charges well, it seemed.

Berit sank to the ground, and Clash went with him, pulling

harder on the whip. A kind of frenzy had come over him, the desperation he'd long battled rising up to seize control.

*Not so dead after all*, the woman said inside his mind, the sound like a contented purr.

*No*, he thought, feeling the last of the warden's life slip away.

Clash let go of the whip and stood, his sides heaving from the exertion, his head spinning. Foster glanced at Berit's lifeless eyes bulging in his skull, then he turned and fled up the shaft, screaming at the top of his lungs. Clash considered going after him, but saw no point. He couldn't escape, no matter how many guards he killed. The only way out of the mine aside from the lifts was a ladder built into the sheer side of the mountain, one with rungs set too far apart for any prisoner to reach with the shackles on their wrists and legs. And none of the guards carried keys to those shackles either. No, there was no escaping the three hells of trouble he would have to pay for killing the warden.

*I'm ready*, Clash thought, and he stood there, arms resting at his sides, while the guards came and seized him.

He expected for it to end right there; when they didn't kill him, Clash assumed it could only be because they wanted to make an example of him instead, lest the other prisoners get ideas. But he didn't fight. The anger that had seized him was gone, leaving him a dead man walking once more.

They brought him to the yard, the vast room in the center of the mine where the inmates ate and slept. The guards lowered the metal cage hanging from the ceiling in the center of the yard like some macabre chandelier and shoved him inside it. The gibbet was small, the metal bars pressing against him on all sides, preventing any movement.

As they hoisted the cage back into the air, the guards below began making bets on how long he would survive.

"Serves him right," one of them said. "And it'll keep the rest of them from daring."

"Yeah, but we'll all have to suffer the smell once he finally dies and starts to rot," another replied.

"All the better to drive the lesson home, if you ask me."

"I wonder how long it'll take for him to beg for us to just kill him. That's Clash, ain't it? I've been looking forward to hearing that one scream just once."

*You'll look forward to it still*, Clash thought. Silence remained his only weapon. He would wield it to the last.


Still, as the days went by, it became more and more difficult to maintain his silence as the agony spread through his body from lack of water and being trapped so long in one position. His throat burned, tongue swollen and aching. Then the cramps started, first in his legs but slowly spreading throughout his body. His head pounded with every breath he took. His thoughts started to slip, until he could no longer tell the difference between waking and sleeping. For the first time, he prayed for death, for release.

*You're too stubborn to die*, the woman spoke in his mind. She refused to give him peace, even now. But it would come in the end. *Death comes for us all*. It was the one thing he could be sure of in this wretched life. Still he lingered. Until one day, he noticed voices speaking down below, the words rising up to him through the silent yard like a prayer. The prisoners were gone, off to their worksites for the day.

"Who is that up there?" The speaker had a strange, melodic voice, unfamiliar. But the man's accent tugged at Clash's memory.

"No one, my lord," a guard answered. "Just a prisoner who got it in his head to kill a warden."

"A prisoner managed to kill a guard?" The speaker sounded both amused and incredulous. "I thought they'd be too weak for that. Was he new to the prison?"

"No, sir. Been here nigh over a year. And he's Rimish, so he got the very best of treatment, if you know what I mean."

"Yes, I do," the man replied, sounding cold now. "The very worst, you're saying."

"No offense intended, my lord. I know you're on our side, but still I hate Rime and all those that come from it." The guard spit on the ground in emphasis.

"Hated enemy or not, it seems wasteful to let an able worker die. You know how important the nenir is. How old is the prisoner?"

"Beats me. Youngish, but it's too hard to tell once they've been here awhile. They all start to look the same."

"Let him down. I wish to find out. I sense something . . . unusual about him."

Clash closed his eyes as the cage began to move. Pain lanced through his body, and he kept his lips pressed together to hold in the scream.

"How old are you?" the speaker with the strange voice said once the cage had reached the bottom.

Clash didn't respond, his eyes and mouth still closed.

The speaker sighed. *How old are you?*

This time Clash heard the question *inside his mind*. His eyes flashed open, shock bringing him back to his senses for the first time in days. It had been so long since he'd felt something like that. *Magic, wilder magic.* He stared at the man beyond the cage, not recognizing him. He was short and broad-shouldered, his shorn hair colorless and his eyes like black beads on his face.

"My name is Clash," he said, his voice reedy and dry. He started to cough.

*That's not what I asked.* The man, a lord judging by his velvet tunic, stared at him, not speaking, but Clash could feel him inside his head. Rooting around, digging. He wanted to push him out, to scream at the violation, but he didn't have the strength for it. Just speaking his name had robbed him of it.

"Show me your hand," the lord said.

Clash frowned and shook his head. He didn't want to show this man anything. What he wanted was to be left alone, to die, to know peace at last.

*Show me your hand.* The voice rang like a gong inside Clash's mind, and against his will he felt his hand slip through the bars of the cage, muscles protesting.

The lord grabbed his fingers and pulled down, exposing Clash's grime-blackened palm. Refusing to be deterred by it, the man spit on Clash's hand, and then, using his own sleeve, scrubbed his palm clean.

"In the name of all the gods both living and dead," the lord said, exhaling in disbelief.

"What is it?" The guard leaned in for a closer look. "What . . . what is that?"

Clash stared at his palm, seeing the symbol branded there, a wheel with eight spokes set inside a triangle.

"Get the keys to this cage," the lord said, letting go of Clash's hand and motioning to the guard. "Get it now and get him out of there. Call for a healer."

"But why, my lord? Who is he?"

The man drew a breath, his chest expanding as if he needed the extra space to hold his astonishment. "This, my good man, is none other than Corwin Tormane. The high prince of Rime."

KATE FOUND SIGNE IN THE solarium of the governor's mansion, as she'd known she would. Her friend spent nearly all her time there anymore. Today Signe rested on one of the recessed benches in the windows of the circular room, her face raised to the glass and the hazy glow of dusk in the distance. The padded benches offered loungers a comfortable and unimpeded view of the city beyond, stone buildings surrounded by cobbled streets crowded with people heading home for the night. A large table occupied the center of the room, glass vials filled with various powders as well as instruments for weighing and measuring scattered across its surface, all of it covered in a thin layer of dust.

Signe didn't look up from her position on the bench farthest from the door as Kate entered. "Hello, Kate."

She rolled her eyes, not bothering to ask how Signe knew it was her and not someone else. It wasn't magic. Signe wasn't a wilder or magist, only a woman from the Esh Islands of unknown birth and background. Still, she possessed many talents, including senses keen enough to provoke envy in any assassin or spy—and one secret that made her the most important woman in the Rising.

"Package for you," Kate said, crossing the room. "From Norgard."

"Dal?" Signe looked over her shoulder, her languid position on the bench tensed into excitement. She swung her legs over the edge and made to stand up, but Kate waved her back down, reaching her before she could rise and shoving the parcel into her hands.

"I'm not an invalid, you know." Signe's reproachful look was sharp enough to cut.

Kate sighed, inwardly scolding herself. No, Signe wasn't an invalid, but walking hurt her, even though she tried to hide it from everyone. With her magic, Kate felt every painful step her friend took—all thanks to the irreparable damage done to the bones in her foot by a madman who fancied himself a god. *No, don't trivialize it,* Kate reminded herself. Rendborne, the Nameless One, did indeed have godlike powers. He was something to be feared—especially as he was still out there, somewhere. She glanced at her flame tattoos but didn't touch them. Rendborne wasn't responsible for all of them, but certainly for the ones most important to her. Every day she renewed her vow to kill him, to make him pay for what he'd done. There had been no sign or word about the man since before their journey to Seva.

"He sent it with the caravan," Kate said, her throat tightening at the longing look on Signe's face as she traced a finger over her name written on top of the box by Dal's hand.

Signe nodded, not looking up. She also made no move to open it.

"Don't you want to see what's inside?"

Scowling, Signe set the box on the bench next to her and leaned back on the pillow tucked into the window nook, her golden-blond hair framed about her face. "What does it matter? Dal isn't inside it."

Kate drew a slow breath, her sympathy fleeing her in an instant.

*At least he lives*, she wanted to say, then chided herself for it. She would feel the same in Signe's position.

Signe looked up at Kate, her gaze cutting once more. "And neither is there a key to help me escape my prison."

Kate arched an eyebrow, not needing her magic to sense that Signe was spoiling for a fight. "How can you be sure if you don't open it? There are magists in Norgard. Maybe there's some bit of magic that will turn you very, very small and you can sneak out beneath the door. Just make sure no one steps on you on the way out. Or that the cats don't make you their plaything."

Signe stuck out her tongue, a little of her old spark coming back to her. Kate was glad to see it. The past few months had dampened the life in her, smothering it slowly, until her old friend was almost unrecognizable. Signe's so-called imprisonment was mostly by choice and certainly by necessity—she was the only person in the world who held the secret to the black-powder formula essential for the bullets used in the revolvers. The guns were Bonner's legacy, an invention that, fortunately, some of the other earthists in the Rising had finally been able to replicate since his death. But not the bullets. Ordinary black powder, the kind used in the single-shot rifles and pistols so common in the rest of the world, didn't work in the revolvers. Without Signe's knowledge, the Rising would never have been able to hold Farhold and win this peace.

Wilder magic could do a lot of damage, it was true, but the nonmagical population far outnumbered them, and a wilder was just as vulnerable to a sword thrust, arrow strike, or bullet as anyone else. And when magic met magic, whether wilder or magist, the two forces effectively canceled out, rendering the armies essentially magic-less against one another—and thus at the mercy of conventional weapons. In the end it was simple math. The Rising had revolvers and the bullets necessary to fire them. The high king's army did not.

Now, with peace looming, Signe's knowledge was more important than ever. They couldn't risk the enemy capturing her—or worse. Already there had been more than a dozen attempts on her life. So many that now she had no choice but to remain here, inside these chambers, under the watchful eye of an entire squadron of soldiers and wilders.

Kate shuddered, not needing to sense Signe's feelings to understand them. She would hate it as much as her friend did. Then again, she'd rather see her friend miserable than dead.

"If there was any magic in there, you never would've let me have it," Signe said, resigned. "So no, I'm not all that interested in what might be inside."

"Suit yourself." Kate turned and sat down at the table, pushing back some of the accruements as she did so and sending up a cloud of dust. It had been weeks since Signe had needed to mix her black powder. With the fighting at an end, the storerooms were brimming over with ammunition. Kate supposed the lack of work was making Signe's situation even harder to bear.

Hoping to salvage this visit, Kate said, "Dal will return, you know. In time." The moment she spoke, she regretted it. She'd said it like there was some kind of guarantee, but there weren't any guarantees to be had in a world at war. Despite King Edwin's promises, Dal's life was in danger every minute he spent in Norgard. All it would take was a drop of poison placed in his cup during a meal or a quick dagger to the throat while he slept. Of course, the Norgard ambassadors here at Farhold faced the same threat, and indeed, if anything happened to Dal, they would be killed quickly in response, but what would it matter? It wouldn't bring Dal back. Just as nothing would bring back Corwin. Then again, she supposed, killing Rendborne would still bring her great satisfaction—and closure. Or so she hoped.

"Was there anyone interesting among the new arrivals?" Signe asked after a moment.

Kate nodded, her thoughts turning to both Colin Davies and Master Janus. She told Signe about the former first and then confessed her worries about the latter.

Signe let out a sigh as Kate finished and slowly got to her feet. "Perhaps it's best if you just leave the man alone. For Raith's sake if no one else's."

Bewildered, Kate frowned up at her friend. "How can you say that? Janus could be a magist spy sent to bring us down from the inside."

"Or he could be the kind and generous man Raith always describes him to be." Signe made her way across the room to a side table where a bottle of wine waited. She managed to hide most of her limp, but inside she cringed each time she set the foot down, the sensation like walking on shards of glass. Kate looked away, trying to cut off her magic, but it was no good. She was too attuned to Signe to ignore the pain. The guilt ate away at her. Just another reason to find Rendborne and end him. She'd been content to wait until rumors of him resurfaced, too busy fighting the Rimish armies to make it her primary concern. But with peace settling around them, that contentment was quickly fading.

Looking back at the sound of Signe uncorking the bottle, Kate said, "If he is, then fine, but I need to make certain. I've never felt something like it. His mind was so empty."

Signe shrugged. "Perhaps it's nothing sinister. He's not young— maybe his memories are going? I've seen it happen often among the elderly."

Kate frowned. "I suppose it's possible. I've never used my magic on someone with an ailment like that." The closest she'd come was the day she probed the mind of High King Orwin, Corwin's father, dead nearly a year now. That experience had been very different. *And Orwin was suffering from a magical ailment,* Kate realized, which seemed to support Signe's idea that maybe this was a natural ailment. Still, Kate wasn't ready to embrace the theory.

"Even if it's possible, there's too much at stake for me to make that assumption."

Rolling her eyes, Signe downed the contents of her glass in a single gulp. She wiped her lips with the back of her hand. "Maybe the problem has nothing to do with Janus at all."

Kate stood, her temper sparking. It seemed if Signe insisted on a fight, she was willing to give her one. "What are you getting at, Sig?"

"It makes me sad, is all," Signe said, her shoulders drooping and a forlorn expression replacing the earlier fierceness. "You used to be capable of believing in the good of people, of giving them the benefit of the doubt. But now all you see is deception and deceit."

"Can you blame me?" Kate walked over and poured her own cup of wine. "You don't know what it's like, to see into someone's mind. To know what they truly are, even when no one else does. Even when they don't know it themselves."

Signe set down the wine glass, doing it slowly as if she feared slamming it. "That's my point. These truths you're seeing weren't meant for you. They're private. You used to be careful about using your magic, only invading a mind when there was cause for it. Now you do it at will. All the time. To everyone."

"That's not true. I never eavesdrop on your thoughts, Signe." *Not intentionally*, Kate silently added. She couldn't help the unintentional things she gleaned. Her magic was a highly developed sense inside her—she couldn't simply turn it on and off at will.

"Well, thanks to Aslar for small mercies," Signe said, pouring herself another drink. "If you did make a habit of it, you would see my thoughts can be just as vile and unworthy as any one of our enemies."

Kate scoffed. "That's nonsense."

"Is it?" Signe cocked her head, birdlike. "Are you always so innocent in your own thoughts then? Are there not times you're glad no one knows what you're thinking?"

"Of course," she admitted, tight-lipped. Just a few moments ago, she'd been glad Signe couldn't sense what she was thinking about Dal still being alive when Corwin was not, her jealousy a vile, disgusting thing. Selfish and wrong. But private, at least.

"I'm relieved to hear it," Signe said. "The difference is that around you, the rest of us risk condemnation for those thoughts, even if we never intended to act on them."

Kate folded her arms across her chest, awareness striking her at last. "This is about that follower of Bellam again, isn't it?"

"Yes," Signe said, blunt as ever. "His name was Jonathan Bailey, in case you've forgotten."

"I know his name," Kate said through gritted teeth, her anger returning in full. Even though the incident in question had occurred months ago, just days after peace had been declared, she would never forget it. She knew more about the man than Signe could ever learn. She'd delved into his thoughts and seen the black heart of him; she'd *felt* it. Bellam was the god of war, one of the few deities of Rime without a patron city to his name—and for good reason. He was a god of violence and destruction, and those who worshipped him were of the same ilk. As Jonathan Bailey had been. He'd come into Farhold claiming to be a refugee from neighboring Aldervale. Instead, he was a part of the cult of Bellam, a group that believed that the god of war would be reborn only when Rime was in chaos, city against city, brother again brother. They abhorred the newly settled peace and meant to overturn it.

Kate saw Jonathan's plan when he was sneaking around near the storeroom where they kept the ammunition, the black powder inside it highly combustible. A single spark could send half the city into oblivion. That was what he wanted—to see them all burn. He just needed to find a way inside. The moment Kate had probed his mind and seen his intent, she'd drawn her revolver and sent a bullet through his skull, ending him.

Signe had been there. She'd witnessed the execution—and it had bothered her ever since.

Kate drew a breath, warning herself to remain calm. Signe

deserved her patience. "I've already told you a thousand times that he intended to kill us all."

"No, you've said he *thought* about killing us all. He was only there that night to see if he could break in. But he might not have gone through with it."

"I felt his desire to hurt us, Sig. There was no mistaking it."

"Yes, but he was afraid, too, Kate. I saw it. So did you before you ended him. He might have changed his mind once faced with the reality of what he was doing. Doesn't that count? Should we all be condemned for our thoughts over our actions?"

Kate could see her point. But she refused to embrace it. *No hesitation. No doubt.* "I know what I saw, and that is the end of it."

Signe's nostrils flared. "And I suppose if you uncover such thoughts in Master Janus you will kill him, too?"

"Yes," Kate said with no waver in her voice.

"And what about Raith? What will that do to him if you cut down the man who saved his life?"

Kate hesitated. It would hurt Raith, for certain, but it didn't matter. She couldn't let it matter, not when the lives of others would be at risk. "Raith will see it as I do. We can't afford allowances likes that. There is no place for such mercies in the world we're living in right now."

"You sound like Rendborne. He believed in such absolutes as well."

Kate flinched and took a step backward, sucking in a shocked breath. "I can't believe you said that."

"Just because something is difficult to hear does not make it any less true."

Kate drew another breath, this one steadier. She felt her anger draining away, replaced with a despair so heavy she could barely breathe. All of them bore scars after the war, but the worst were on the inside. She could feel the corruption growing all around her. Destroying friendships and lives.

Averting her gaze, Kate turned and headed for the door.

"Kate, wait." Signe's voice broke as she spoke. "I'm . . . sorry. That was uncalled for."

Kate stopped, debating whether or not to turn around. The comment about Rendborne had wounded her, cutting deeper than she would've imagined possible.

"I shouldn't vent my frustrations on you," Signe said. "It's not your fault." Slowly, Kate turned and faced her friend. Signe drew a ragged breath. "I hate it here. I hate living like this." She gestured to the table, full of the accoutrements that made her so valuable.

Kate exhaled, unable to hold on to her anger. Not against Signe. "I know. I hate it for you." *Just as I hate the things I must do to keep you safe.* And the things she wouldn't. They both knew Kate could use her sway to convince the council to let Signe go free, but Signe had never voiced the request aloud. She despised it whenever Kate used her powers like that, and would never ask her to do it.

*Not that I would*, Kate thought. Signe was the last of her friends still alive, her true friends, the ones who had known her before she'd become Wilder Kate, war hero and figurehead of the Rising. Bonner was gone. As was Corwin. *I will not lose you, too.*

Signe took a deep breath. "Shall we see what Dal has sent?" she said, as a peace offering.

Grateful for it, Kate smiled. "Knowing him it will be something either amusing or dangerous. Probably both."

"Only if we're lucky." Signe grinned and retrieved the box from the window nook. She sat down, balancing it on her legs as she peeled off the wrapping and pulled open the lid. She froze at once, her expression going blank.

"What is it?" Kate joined her by the window. When she peered into the box, she fell silent. There was a doll resting inside, peering out at them with an expression so familiar it sent a shiver down Kate's back. Whoever crafted it had captured Dal's likeness completely, everything from the deep rivets of scars along one side of his face to the way his right eye crinkled whenever he was about to laugh. That was what the doll appeared to be doing now—laughing.

Kate smiled down at the doll, finding it charming despite its eeriness. "Dal must think you're soon to forget what he looks like. He had to have spent a fortune on it." She reached into the box.

"Don't!" Signe tried to pull the box away, but Kate's fingers had already closed around the doll. It felt wet and slick to her skin, coated in some unknown substance.

A bright flash erupted in front of Kate's eyes and pain seared her hand. With a yelp, she let go as flames covered the doll. Kate watched in horror as the miniature Dal's face melted away. It was so real she could almost imagine the sound of its screams.

"Get something to put it out!" Signe said as the flames spread to the box and she dropped it. Kate dashed to the table and returned with the wine bottle, upending it over the fire. The flames sizzled and went out.

Kate and Signe exchanged a look, neither of them speaking. Kate didn't understand it, or have any idea who had really sent it—but the message behind it was unmistakable.

Dal was in trouble.

VOICES CALLED HIM OUT OF the dreams.

They'd been good dreams, or at least welcome ones. Full of people and places he knew but hadn't seen in a long time, fueled on memories long forgotten. They filled him with a deep and desperate yearning. For, in the way of dreams, he knew they weren't real. He knew they would end.

The voices lured him back to wakefulness, but he didn't open his eyes. He didn't want to be awake yet. He wanted to keep dreaming, to avoid the work that waited him. The mines were always so damp and cold. Empty. Nothing like the soft warmth surrounding him here.

*You're not in the mines, not anymore.*

With the recollection slowly coming back to him, he became aware of voices around him and kept his eyes shut. They were strangers' voices, just as this was a strange place. He knew it without looking, the bed beneath so soft it felt like he would fall through it if he dared move. Such softness did not exist in the mines. He felt the change in his body as well, his face freshly shaven and all the dirt and grime scrubbed from the rest of him. Someone had dressed him in soft linen, a loose pair of trousers and a shirt, his feet left bare. The feel of being clean was so welcome he almost drifted off again. Still pretending to be asleep, he listened to what they were saying.

"Is *that* really him?" a woman asked.

A man replied, "Lord Gavril says it is, and this young man has the mark to prove it."

Clash heard the rustle of skirts as one of the speakers approached. He willed his body to be still even as he felt soft fingers touch his hand, gliding over the mark on his palm.

*The uror mark.*

"I don't see how that makes him a prince," the woman said, this time with a note of petulance. "Any fool can go and get himself branded."

"They say the brand comes from the gods."

"The gods are dead."

"Our gods, yes, but Rime is a different place." Again Clash heard steps, and a new set of fingers touched his palm, these callused and hard, where the woman's had been soft as down. "Gavril says the mark is magical."

She scoffed. "He thinks everything is magical, or at least has the potential to be so. But this is stretching things a bit much, even for him. I mean, look at this man. He's so thin and so . . . so scarred. I refuse to believe this is Corwin Tormane."

The name struck Clash with the force of a thunderclap, and he had to stop himself from sucking in a breath.

*Corwin Tormane.*

*My name is Corwin.*

The truth came rushing into him, like a second awakening. A

rebirth. *I am Corwin, not Clash.* Clash was the name he'd used when he'd been a mercenary, one of the Shieldhawks. Corwin was the name he'd been born with. How had he forgotten?

*I chose to,* he realized. It was the only way to survive his imprisonment. To stay sane. But he remembered everything now. He'd come to Seva to free the wilders imprisoned by the Godking as soldier slaves for his army. They'd broken into the Mistfold, but everything had gone wrong. The wilders didn't want to leave. Kate couldn't make them.

*Oh gods, Kate.*

Remembering her was like a wound reopening. Where was she now? Did she live? Had she escaped the Mistfold that day? He didn't know. *She must think me dead. Like her brother is dead. And Bonner.* Only he wasn't sure about the last. Corwin had survived the stairs collapsing, after all; it was possible Bonner had as well. Or maybe it had been because of Bonner, some bit of magic he'd worked before the impact. He didn't know. Sevan soldiers had found Corwin buried in the rubble, but they didn't recognize him beneath his magestone disguise. All his captives knew was that he was from Rime, and not a wilder, all of which made him suitable as a worker for the mines and little else.

That was when the forgetting started—once he realized there was no escaping the mines. He tried three times, only to fail the moment he attempted to scale the ladder out. As the awful, bitter truth of it came to him, he began to bury everything deep inside. He'd pretended to be Clash until he'd become the man, a prisoner and nothing more. By the time the magestone wore off, he'd already been lost to the mine, beyond the reach of anyone who would know him as the high prince of Rime. He comforted himself knowing it was better that way. He couldn't risk falling into the Godking's hands.

*But here I am.*

The voices were still speaking, still unaware of the transformation he was undergoing, the slow becoming of Corwin and letting go of Clash.

"Do you really think Father means to go through with it?" the woman asked. She and the man both spoke the Sevan language, but Corwin had mastered it in his long imprisonment.

"Lord Gavril has made a good case. Besides, I'm certain once he recovers, you'll learn to make the most of it."

"Have I told you how much I hate you, brother?"

"Not today, sweet sister."

Corwin opened his eyes, just enough to judge where his captors stood—both of them on his left, the man nearest. He wore an ornamental dagger at his waist, the golden hilt fashioned into the head of a bull and polished to a high sheen. Corwin closed his eyes again.

"If only I could trade places with you," the woman said. "Then I wouldn't have to hate you quite so much."

Inhaling slowly, Corwin gathered his strength. He was weak from his captivity, but he wouldn't let it impede him now. His need to escape was too great. This was worse than being in the mine. At least there, he suffered in isolation. But with his identity known, much greater damage could be wrought.

His chances were about as good as he could've hoped for. There were no shackles on him now, no wall to climb. He had the element of surprise, and these two weren't soldiers or guards, but wellborn and likely soft.

"Do you really believe so?" the man said. "At least you will serve some purpose. That has to be better than to be a mere extraneous part in the machine."

"Oh, yes, you're quite right." The woman's sarcasm was as thick as honey. "Because being used as a—"

Lurching upright, Corwin grabbed the dagger and yanked it free of the man's belt in one quick motion. Then he kicked out, the blow striking the man in the hip and sending him sprawling. With a yelp of fear, the woman tried to move away, but Corwin grabbed her by her long brown hair hanging loose nearly to the floor and jerked her toward him just as he gained his feet.

Pressing the dagger to her throat, Corwin whispered in her ear, "Be still if you wish to live." He coiled his hand around her hair twice more, tightening his grip as he glanced about the room. To his surprise he was in an ornate bedchamber, the kind to be found in any castle or palace. It was large enough for several people to lounge comfortably—the four-poster bed alone was thrice the size of the cell he'd shared with Henry. All the furnishings were lavish, from the elaborately carved chairs and trestle table to the plush sofa upholstered in red velvet. A wardrobe bedecked in golden handles stood near the doorway to another chamber beyond. Corwin glanced through it, thanking his good fortune that there was an antechamber. Any guards posted outside would've been too far to have heard the disturbance.

Sensing movement, Corwin glanced back at the man he'd attacked slowly rising to his feet, hands held out from his sides.

"Be careful, princeling," the man said. "My father may intend for you to remain alive, but if you harm my sister I will kill you myself."

The woman stiffened in Corwin's grip, her head craned back as far as it would go to avoid the knife. Even still a thin line of blood appeared on her pale skin as she said, "Don't provoke him, Eryx, for the dead god's sake, he's been in the nenir mines. He could be mad."

"Eryx?" Corwin laughed, recognizing the name. Good fortune was his boon companion, it seemed.

"See, I told you," the woman said. "Madness."

Corwin laughed again and gestured at the man with a quick flick of the dagger. "If you are Eryx Fane, then that makes your sister here Eravis. The only daughter of King Magnar, the Godking himself." He gave her hair another tug in emphasis.

Eryx made a sound like a hiss. "And you are Corwin Tormane. A dead prince come back to life. I do wonder how King Edwin will take the news once he finds out."

Corwin flinched. *King* Edwin, not *prince*. His brother had been crowned? But that was impossible. It would mean . . . "My father is dead?" He hadn't meant to voice the question, but it came out of him before he could stop it.

A tight-lipped smile crossed Eryx's lips. There was something almost unnatural about his features. They were too perfect, his skin so fair it was almost translucent. Or maybe it was just how closely he resembled his sister. He had the same brown hair that fell to his shoulders. "Apparently, yes. Our spies in Norgard witnessed King Orwin's funeral pyre. They say it was a grand affair with the coronation taking place right after, a feast that lasted four days."

A tremble slid through Corwin. His father was dead. Edwin had been named king. He felt the brand on his palm, pressed against the dagger's handle. The uror mark. Once it had been a thing of magic, a sigil so powerful it had repelled the Nameless One, a man far more a god than King Magnar could ever hope to be. But that had been a long time ago. He hadn't felt that magic in the mark since his feet first touched ground on this barren, miserable land. Perhaps the magic had never been real at all, but a trick conjured by the priestess who had placed it on his skin.

Corwin shook his head, forcing the questions to the back of his mind. He had to focus on escaping. With Eravis Fane as his captive, he just might stand a chance. The Godking had many sons, but only the one daughter. No one would risk harming her.

Belatedly, Corwin realized Eryx had stepped closer to him, taking advantage of his distraction in the news about his father.

"Don't come any closer," Corwin said, a warning in his voice. Adjusting his grip on the dagger, he edged his way toward the door, keeping Eravis in front of him as a shield. She went along meekly, her arms loose at her sides, the only tension in her neck and shoulders as she fought to keep a distance between her skin and the blade's sharp edge.

Once past the threshold into the other room, Corwin angled her to the side, meaning to shut the door and bar it. For half a second, he eased the dagger away, not wanting to harm her as he reached for the handle. Quick as a startled cat, she grabbed his hand holding the blade and pushed it away from her. At the same time, she stepped down hard on his bare foot.

With a yelp of pain, he let go of her hair to grip the dagger with his other hand, wresting it away from her easily. She was tall but slender, arms like willowy branches. Her brother came charging through the doorway, head down like a battering ram. Corwin tried to sidestep but failed to get entirely out of the way, and the two of them careened to the ground. The dagger popped out of Corwin's hand and skidded across the floor, where it disappeared beneath a heavy wooden chest. Corwin thrashed, trying to free himself from Eryx's weight, his tired, abused body screaming in protest. Ignoring it, he made a fist and landed a punch to Eryx's temple. Stunned, the man rolled to the side, the shift in weight just enough for Corwin to slip free.

He scrambled to his feet, then kicked Eryx in the side. Without shoes on, Corwin was hurt nearly as bad as the Sevan prince, but nevertheless he kicked again, desperate to keep the man down long enough to retrieve the dagger.

"Stop it!" Eravis screamed from behind him. He turned in time to see her rushing at him as her brother had done, outrage on her face. He raised his hands to defend himself. She wouldn't catch him off guard again, although he was glad she chose to attack rather than run for help. As she reached him, Corwin spun to the side, snaking out an arm to grab her by the waist. She stumbled sideways, nearly falling, but Corwin hauled her upright. Pulling her against his chest, he slid his arm around her neck and squeezed.

"Stay down or I'll break her neck," Corwin said, his eyes fixed on Eryx, who had pulled himself up to his knees. The prince went still, but in the next moment, the door to the chamber opened and several guards rushed in, drawn by the noise at last.

"Stop or I'll kill her!" Corwin shouted, and the guards halted. All but one—except this man wasn't a guard, Corwin saw, but a nobleman, richly dressed in a maroon waistcoat trimmed in white silk. He was of average height, average build, his most striking feature his strangely elegant hands, which he held folded in front of him. Something about his face was familiar, but it took Corwin a moment to place it.

This was the man who'd discovered him in the prison.

"I said stop." Corwin tightened his grip on Eravis's throat, squeezing her hard enough that she began to wheeze.

"I believe that's enough of that," the man said. Although he spoke in Sevan, his accent was Rimish. "Let her go."

The words were like a clanging gong inside Corwin's mind, and a shudder passed through his body as he realized what that feeling meant. This man, whoever he was, was a wilder, one born with the gift of sway. *Same as Kate.* Corwin shuddered again at the thought. He trusted Kate like no other, but sway was a dangerous power, utterly devastating in the wrong hands.

And this man was wrong. Corwin felt it in every fiber of his being.

*Let her go*, the voice said again inside his mind, only this time Corwin felt the force in it, the deliberate pressure on his will. As in the prison, he was powerless to resist. His arm slid from Eravis's neck. The moment she was free, she spun away from him, rushing over to her brother, one arm thrown about his waist to help him up.

"Keep him away from me, Lord Gavril," Eravis said, glaring at the wilder. "Or I will kill him no matter what you or my father says."

Lord Gavril smiled at the princess, his voice and expression soothing. "Now, now, my dear Eravis. Is that any way to talk about your betrothed?"

"My betrothed just tried to kill me. How else should I talk about him? He's a madman, wild and dangerous and unfit to marry anyone."

Lord Gavril shook his head, still smiling.

Corwin stared between them both, not understanding. He *couldn't* understand, the words making no sense in his mind. Betrothed? Married? Him . . . and this woman?

No, not any woman. But the princess of Seva.

Realization struck him with the force of an earthquake, his legs threatening to buckle beneath him. A marriage union between Rime and Seva. Edwin might have been named high king, but it didn't matter, not once word spread that Corwin was still alive. He glanced at the uror mark on his palm, sensing that there was still magic in there, despite how it felt. He was Corwin Tormane, high prince of Rime, and until the uror trial came to an end, he had a claim to the throne. The gods willed uror. No decrees of men could stop it.

But before he could return to Norgard to complete the uror challenge, he would have a wife forced upon him, daughter of the Godking, a man who for the last fifty years had been doing whatever he could to claim Rime for himself. A man who had a wilder gifted with sway in his employ.

And if Corwin did indeed win, it seemed Magnar would finally have found a way to make it so.

ALTHOUGH SHE WAS A MEMBER of the wilder council, Kate felt like a child as she stood before them now. Perhaps Raith was right, and she should've been attending the meetings all along. Maybe then she would've felt more like an equal and less like an interloper.

Then again, she doubted she would ever feel a part of this group. They were seven in all, counting herself and Raith, and the others were far older than she. For the most part, they'd been elected because of their wisdom and experience. Like Talleen, an aerist from Eetmark who had single-handedly orchestraed the escape of twelve wilder orphans to Farhold, whom she'd kept hidden after their parents had been executed by the Mage League. Or like Jiro, a pyrist who'd had the foresight to guess that the loyalist forces in Farhold would attempt to destroy the food stores once the city had fallen, and had been there to stop the fires they'd set. The only nonmagical person among them was Deacon Lewis, former Relay foreman of Farhold. During the fighting, he'd overseen the care of the wounded, even taking on the difficult task of triage, determining which lives could be saved and which could not.

Kate had been elected simply because everyone knew her name and what she could do with her magic. They'd heard of her victories in battle during the Wilder War, the way she used her sway to turn the tides again and again. But the wilder council was not about winning in battle, but about ruling in peace. She had no business being here.

She felt it keenly now as she awaited their response. She'd just finished telling them about the doll bearing Dal's image and her and Signe's certainty of what it meant.

Francis was the first to speak, as usual. He was the only member of the council whose judgment Kate sometimes doubted, due in no small part to how strained their relationship had become in the aftermath of their journey to Seva, but he'd been a leader among the Rising nearly as long as Raith. Clearing his throat, Francis leaned forward in his chair and draped his heavy arms on the table. "Did anyone else see this doll before it erupted in flames?"

Kate's toes curled inside her boots at the sound of his skepticism. Not that she expected anything else from him. He'd never cared for her much, but since their return from Seva, he'd come to despise her. Kate hadn't known about Francis's love for Anise when they'd gone into the Mistfold to rescue her and the other wilders, but she'd learned of it since. Although they'd freed Anise, she remained a prisoner still, trapped inside her own madness by whatever had been done to her in there—the same affliction that had driven Vianne to throw herself over the edge of the pit to her death. Francis blamed Kate for failing to cure Anise with the strength of her sway. But she couldn't even understand what was wrong, let alone how to make it right. As it was, they were fortunate the wilders they'd freed from that first building had eventually recovered from their lethargy.

With an effort, she forced herself to remain civil. "Are you suggesting that Signe and I are lying?"

Francis drummed thick fingers against the table. "It's no secret that Signe isn't happy with her circumstances here, and if rumors are true, neither are you. A threat to Ambassador Thorne could be an excuse to change her situation, and I wouldn't put it past either of you to invent one."

With her temper sparking, Kate opened her mouth to respond, but fortunately Councilor Genet saved her from saying anything regrettable.

"Come now, Francis. Don't be absurd." Genet pinned him with a shriveling look. "Kate would never deceive the council, by magic or otherwise."

Kate gave the woman an appreciative glance, which Genet acknowledged with a slight nod. Of all the councilors, Kate liked her second best, after Deacon, who had been her ally long before she joined the Rising. Genet was a hydrist, with a personality to match, her attitude perpetually calm and steady like a smoothly flowing river, never ruled by her emotions like Francis.

"Genet is quite right," Raith said, speaking for the first time since the meeting began. He sat with his hands tented in front of him, worry creasing his brow. He'd come into the meeting wearing the expression, and Kate couldn't help but wonder what was troubling him. She hadn't had a chance to discuss her concerns about Master Janus with him. Raith lowered his hands. "So let's not waste time debating whether or not the threat is real. We will accept Kate's assessment of it as truth. The only question now is what exactly has happened to Dal, and what to do about it."

Kate inhaled her relief, grateful that Raith believed her without question. Even more, he would understand better than anyone what a threat to Dal would mean to her and Signe. Turning her gaze on the other councilors, she said, "We must send someone to Norgard to find Dal."

"I do hope you don't mean sending someone in as a spy," replied Jiro. Although he was a pyrist, he didn't have a temper to match. Never blustery nor easily angered, he was a man of caution and reserve. He was so thin that it seemed a strong breeze might scatter his bones like leaves.

"Not with any sort of clandestine mission," Kate said quickly. "Only to ensure Dal is safe. Sending someone we trust is the only way to be sure."

"Our treaty with Norgard is quite clear," Jiro said. "We are permitted the two ambassadors and nothing more. If we're discovered sending in anyone else without permission, the war will resume. I am as fond of Lord Dallin as you, but we can't risk that even for his life."

"I'm afraid I must agree with Councilor Jiro," Deacon said, casting Kate a regretful look. "We owe it to our citizens to keep them safe, and that means abiding by the terms of the cease-fire."

A knot formed in Kate's stomach as she saw Talleen's nod of approval, one quickly taken up by the others.

"I agree as well," Raith said with his own nod. "The armistice must be preserved at all cost. Nothing is more important than peace at present."

Through gritted teeth, Kate said, "But if Dal is being threatened, so then is the very peace we all wish to preserve."

Raith shifted his weight in his seat. "That very well may be true. Which is why we will address our concerns openly. I will send a letter to King Edwin about the doll and request that we be allowed to send another ambassador to ascertain the situation and ensure Lord Dallin is safe. It seems to me more likely the threat to Dal is of a personal nature. That would explain the doll's likeness and the fact that it was sent directly to Signe."

Kate shook her head. "We can't wait that long. It will take a week or more just to get the message to Norgard, and who knows how many weeks after that to get approval for the exchange." It had taken nearly six weeks for Edwin to agree for Dal and Laurent, the other ambassador, to come into Norgard. Not that the wilder council had been any quicker to accept Norgard's ambassadors in return. "If he even agrees at all," Kate added. "He hasn't been very cooperative so far." Dal's reports made that clear. Several times Dal had tried to get Edwin to discuss the situation of the wilders still imprisoned in Seva—a situation the Rising was in no position to affect right now without help—but Edwin refused to listen; he considered Seva no immediate threat to Rime.

"I'm sorry, Kate," Raith said, offering her a sad smile. "But the delay can't be helped."

"Yes, it can. If we send someone in secret. Right now."

"And who would we send that we could be certain wouldn't be caught?" said Raith. "Dal is living at court. If we're being realistic, it would take a spy weeks just to gain access. We can't send someone claiming to be a noble—they are all known at Norgard. The person would have to go in as a servant, but those positions are being carefully vetted. Again, it would take weeks. No, the best option is to request the exchange."

"And are we to just hope that nothing bad happens to Dal in the meantime?" Kate folded her arms in front of her, fingers clenched around her biceps.

"Kate could do it," Genet said, speaking before Raith could reply. "With her sway, Kate could convince anyone to let her in anywhere."

Kate hid her relief behind a frown, glad someone else had made the suggestion. That was her hope from the beginning—that she be sent to investigate it. No one else could do it better.

Francis barked a laugh. "Ah, to be sure. And I suppose no one would recognize Saint Kate, the Wilder Queen, sneaking around the court of Norgard."

Kate flushed, embarrassed by the title and surprised it had spread far enough to reach Francis's ears.

Again, Genet came to her rescue. "She would wear one of Harue's disguises, of course. They are nearly undetectable."

"No," Raith said, his voice as hard as a mallet striking steel. "It is out of the question. Kate is needed here. I will dispatch a rider to Norgard with a letter to King Edwin immediately. In the meantime, we need to consider who we will send as Dal's replacement. I will expect your nominations by morning."

And, just like that, the debate was over. With nothing further to discuss, the councilors quickly departed.

Kate waited until everyone had gone before leaving herself. She didn't want any of the other councilors to witness the fury bubbling up inside her. Once again, she felt like a child, told to be quiet while the adults made the decisions. It wasn't that she didn't understand their concerns, just that their plan would solve nothing in the end.

Not if whoever meant Dal harm got to him before they could.

If there was one thing she missed about the war, it was the expediency of it. Decisions were made quickly and actions followed at once. The bureaucracy she found herself surrounded by now was just the opposite. Every decision was questioned and requeried, modified, changed again, and then finally, if they were very, very lucky, something would actually happen. She didn't have the stomach for it anymore. Not with Dal the one dangling over the fire. She couldn't get the vision of that flaming doll out of her mind.

"I take it things didn't go well," a voice said as she stepped out into the corridor.

Kate turned a glare on Tira. "Getting the council to do what needs to be done in situations like this is like trying to shepherd cats."

Tira, who was particularly fond of cats, grinned at the analogy. "At least you didn't get scratched." She eyed Kate up and down as if to be sure. Kate rolled her eyes and started walking toward the exit, Tira falling into step beside her. "So what did they decide?"

"To call him home and send another ambassador in his place." Kate didn't have to explain all the problems with that plan to Tira. In her service to the Shieldcrows, the mercenary had experienced her share of politics and all the time-wasting involved. She claimed it was one of the reasons she'd left the company to join the Rising.

"Yes, and what have you decided?" asked Tira.

Kate cast her a sidelong glance. "What do you mean? The council has chosen that course of action, and I'm oath-bound to honor it."

"Are you?" Tira arched an eyebrow.

"What do you—" Kate broke off, aware of listening ears in the vicinity.

"Fancy a stop in the gardens?" Tira said, head cocked to an exaggerated angle.

Silently, the two women made their way to the walled garden that abutted the backside of the governor's mansion. This time of day, Kate hoped it would be mostly deserted. Besides, she never passed on an excuse to visit the garden. There was no other place in Farhold quite as beautiful. Several earthist gardeners kept all the trees and flowers in the height of summer bloom year-round. It reminded Kate of the gardens in Norgard where she'd grown up. Hours she'd spent with Corwin wandering through rosebushes and beneath clematis-lined trellises. Aside from the stables, it had been their most frequent rendezvous.

As she and Tira stepped past the entrance into the garden, Kate reached out with her magic. To her relief, she sensed only one person near the fountain at the center of the garden. It should be easy enough to avoid them.

Kate led the way to one of the benches built around the trunk of an oak tree near the western wall and plopped down onto it, weary from defeat. Tira, always as graceful as one of her cats, eased down next to her.

"All right," Kate said. "What are you proposing? That I sway the council into action or something? I'm not doing that."

"Of course not," Tira replied, examining her fingernails. "I'm saying you just go anyway. What's a little defiance between friends?"

Kate waved away a fly buzzing around her face. It seemed a great irony that the earthists could keep the flowers in bloom but could do nothing to stop the bugs. "I'm a member of the council, Tira, I can't just . . . And even if I weren't, there would be consequences in defying them and breaking the accords."

"Yes, of course. There are consequences in everything we do. Good and bad." Tira rested her elbows against her legs, the dual blades on her back preventing her from leaning against the bench as Kate did. "What will you tell Signe?"

Kate sighed, closing her eyes. "The truth, I guess. And hope she doesn't have something sharp on hand to stab me with."

"I'm sure she will understand your position. It's so . . . understandable."

Kate opened her eyes to glare at Tira again. "Even if I were to defy the council, I couldn't get to Norgard without their help." Kate sat up, only to lean forward and drop her head into her hands. "It's impossible to travel that far without magestones to protect against the nightdrakes, and none of the magists will disobey Raith."

"Harue might. Seems to me she's made a career out of defying Raith."

Kate harrumphed. "Only when his orders interfere with her latest obsession." For Harue that meant one thing—pursuit of what she called the science of magic. Before joining the Rising, Harue had been a white robe, the magist order dedicated to the study of the high arts. It was a posh position, and she was great at it. Kate sometimes wondered why she sided with the Rising in the first place. Perhaps because the consequences of her disobedience were so much less here than with the League. "And she only gets away with it because she's brilliant and ends up stumbling across some new spell that makes everyone's lives better," Kate added. Not that she was driven by any kind of altruistic intent. Quite the opposite, Harue interacted far more with her books than people.

"That's my point," Tira replied. "It should be easy to come up with some reason why helping you get to Norgard will help her solve whatever mystery is currently preoccupying her thoughts."

"Knowing Harue, that could be a hundred different things at once."

"Even better. So many to choose from." Tira bared her teeth in a grin. "And I will come with you, of course. I've always wanted to see Norgard."

*Norgard.* Kate allowed herself to picture the city of her birth, the place she'd called home for nearly sixteen years. The towering white wall surrounded by green fields. The statues of Niran and Nelek, the two horses carved from onyx and ivory, standing watch at the gate. Mirror Castle glinting in the sunlight as if it had been draped in stars. And all the pastures filled with the finest horseflesh.

Yes, it was a place worth visiting. Beautiful beyond words. But it was ugly too, for Kate at least. Home to all of her most painful memories—the execution of her father, the decree of her exile, Kiran's abduction, and her battle with Maestra Vikas, the woman who orchestrated her father's death for treason.

*Her and Rendborne.* It was also the last place the Nameless One had been seen.

Kate shook her head, driving the memories away. "You could go anytime you wished," she said, trying to hide her bitterness at the thought. "No one would recognize you there."

"Nor you, with one of Harue's disguises. And no offense to Chancellor Raith, but exchanging Dal will solve nothing. Even if whoever is threatening him isn't able to act before we get him out, the threat will still exist, and this person's plot likely doesn't end with killing Dal. You're the only one with any chance of uncovering the secrets behind this."

"You mean by using my sway," Kate said, remembering her argument with Signe earlier. Not everyone was so worried about the morality questions associated with her gift. *You're siding with a mercenary about the morality of using your magic*, Kate thought, finding humor in the irony. She was about to point out that Genet had suggested the same thing, but stopped at the sound of commotion. The noise was like a pig being slaughtered, and Kate and Tira rose at once and headed toward it.

They rounded the corner toward the fountain in the center of the garden. Anise was there. The healers must've brought her out here for some fresh air—and left her unattended. Kate's teeth clenched at the stupidity of it. No matter how many times she told the healers never to trust Anise by herself, they didn't listen. They let the woman fool them into thinking she was getting better. She wasn't. Kate sensed the truth every time she saw her—Anise was determined to die, and nothing could stop it. It consumed Anise's every thought, her every moment, a cancer planted by whatever had been done to her in the Mistfold that had spread throughout her entire being.

Looking at her now, Kate gave an involuntary shudder. Once stately and attractive, Anise looked like a corpse whose flesh had not yet rotted, her skin ashen and stretched taunt over a starved body. She wouldn't eat or drink, not voluntarily, and what little nourishment the healers managed to force on her was only enough to keep her alive.

Anise screamed again as one of the healers attempted to wrestle her arm away from her neck, where she'd been clawing at her own throat, ripping away skin until it bled. Pushing past her horror, Kate summoned her magic and grabbed hold of Anise's mind. At once despair and pain flooded her, the woman's misery becoming her own. For a second it was so powerful, Kate almost reached out to snag a sword off Tira's back in order to end both of their pain.

"Obey me or seek death. Obey me or seek death!" Anise chanted, the refrain as familiar as it was chilling. She said it so often Kate sometimes heard it in her sleep.

*Be quiet, be still*, Kate thought, forcing her will on Anise. It was hard, the woman's mind slippery in Kate's grasp. *Be quiet, be still!* Kate increased the force, feeling her magic burn inside her at the effort, like the straining of a muscle. Slowly, fighting her at every step, Anise lowered her arm enough for the healer to refasten the leather strap around her wrist. How she'd gotten free in the first place, Kate didn't know, and she had no desire to find out. She wanted away from Anise's mind as soon as possible, the death the woman longed for like an infection Kate risked catching herself.

The moment the healer stepped back from the woman, Kate let go of her mind and drew a ragged breath. The healer glanced at her, muttering an apology. Kate nodded, too tired to bother telling the healer once again that Anise was a danger to herself every moment she wasn't being restrained. Besides, the damage Anise had inflicted on herself this time would be enough to convince the healers to be more careful with her. For a while at least.

"Go fetch something to staunch the bleeding," Kate said. "I will stay with her until you return." The healer darted away without a word. Tira, who had kept a safe distance, said nothing, although Kate could sense her eagerness to depart this unsettling scene.

Anise watched Kate with the dull, hooded eyes of a reptile, hatred etched into every careworn line on her face. The first time Kate had met the woman, she commanded respect with her mere presence. She'd been impeccably dressed, her gray hair coiffed with not a single strand out of place. Now, her beautiful hair was long since shaved off, to keep her from trying to choke herself with it.

"Have you come to let me go at last?" Anise said. Eerily, her voice was the only thing unchanged. She sounded like the commanding madam of a brothel she'd been when Kate met her. Anise showed no other signs of mental illness—she could talk and reason, recall facts and memories, and she never spoke of seeing things or hearing voices. She was herself completely. All except for her desire to die. And the fact that whenever she tried to tell Kate what had happened in the Mistfold, she would instead start chanting . . . *Obey me or seek death.*

"You already know the answer to that question, Anise," Kate said with a sad shake of her head.

The woman shrugged, the gesture causing the collar on her neck to rise up and brush against the still-weeping wounds on her throat. It was a magical collar, studded with magestones designed to keep Anise from accessing her magic. Once, she'd been a hydrist, but it was a power she couldn't be trusted with anymore, not after she'd used it to drown one of the healers who'd made the mistake of trying to stop her from cutting her wrists open with a dull spoon.

"Yes, I do," Anise replied. "But that doesn't mean I don't still wish for mercy."

*Mercy.* The word was like a knife to Kate's gut. She understood that it would be merciful to give Anise the death she craved. She suffered worse than anyone Kate had ever seen. *And yet it's not her,* Kate thought. That will to die had been placed inside Anise somehow, just as it had Kiran and Vianne, and the other wilders they'd been unable to free from the Mistfold.

It had been placed inside her by *someone.*

*Rendborne,* Kate thought. He might not have done the actual work, but he was responsible for them ending up there in the first place. Hatred swelled inside her, her need for vengeance like a physical ache. But in order to have her vengeance she had to find him first. *Where is he?*

Norgard. It was the last place he'd been seen, at the Hellgate inside the Wandering Woods north of the city. She hadn't been back there since the battle where she killed Isla Vikas, Rendborne's lover and second-in-command, but it seemed the best place to start tracking him down. She'd waited long enough.

Kate held silent until the healer had returned and seen to Anise's wounds, allowing her and Tira to finally exit the gardens. The moment they were alone again, Kate turned to Tira and said, "Defiance it is, then."

Tira grinned, looking like a cat that had just caught sight of a mouse. "Let's go talk to Harue."

THE GODKING'S PALACE RESIDED AT the center of the city of light. From the terrace of his new quarters, high in the eastern tower, Corwin could understand why Luxana had been given such a name. With the sun rising over the horizon, the city looked afire. Most of the buildings, including the Sun Palace, were built from the red clay so common in Seva. The fiery effect came from the shale mixed with the clay to form the bricks. Mined from lake beds long since drained, the shale contained minuscule crystals that reflected the red of the clay whenever light touched them, as it did now.

Corwin drew a slow breath, finding no comfort in the beauty. He was surrounded by too many beautiful things these days to care, his rooms alone an obscene example of the Godking's wealth. A blanket made of the white fur of snow leopards from the far northern country of Ruzgar adorned the four-poster bed, whose columns boasted exquisitely carved galloping bulls circling around them from bottom to top. The satin sheets beneath were woven from the silk of Furian spiders, found only in remote islands scattered throughout the Fury Sea. More furs covered the gold-inlaid marble floor, these made from the hides of black panthers, animals native to Seva. Even Corwin's robe and the loose-fitting pants and shirt beneath were the finest he had ever worn, woven from a cotton so soft it felt like a second skin.

With a sudden restlessness, Corwin turned away from the terrace and reentered the bedchamber. He took a pace about the room, feeling as if he'd been awake for hours instead of mere minutes. The month since he'd been freed from the mines had wrought a startling change in him. Most notably in his body and how much stronger he felt, how much more like himself. He could run laps around the room and not grow tired.

And yet, he remained a slave in a golden cage. The truth galled him: as with the mines, there was no way to escape.

Coming to a stop, Corwin glanced down to see he'd arrived at the trestle table set next to the door to the terrace. His stomach clenched as he stared at the bottle on the table, the dark glass hiding the bright content within. He hadn't meant to stop here. He didn't want to drink any of the concoction inside. And yet the sight of it—and the smell leaking out from the uncorked top—set his senses afire, making his throat ache with the thirst of a man three days lost in the desert.

*Don't drink it, Corwin,* he told himself, but even as the thought slid through his mind, his hand reached for the bottle of its own accord, the glass smooth and cool beneath his fingers, a tease of what the drink would feel like as it slid down his gullet.

*Don't drink it. Don't.* He tipped the bottle over the edge of the goblet, the pale-blue liquid almost seeming to glow as it sloshed into it. Or maybe it was glowing, just a little. Corwin could never be sure, but it wouldn't surprise him. Although the drink was partly wine, made from white grapes grown in the Florri province of Seva, it was mixed with something else—*nenir.* Godtears.

Corwin hadn't realized it at first, even when they'd told him the drink was called nenath. No, it wasn't until he took that first taste that he made the connection. It was the smell, mostly, a familiar sweet, musky smell, one he'd grown to associate with good fortune after his time in the mines. And the glow, of course, that too.

What a fool he'd been to drink it so willingly when Lord Gavril offered it to him. It was the first of his so-called "conditioning sessions" with the wilder, which had started the day after his confrontation with Prince Eryx and his sister. It seemed Gavril didn't suffer from the same loss of magic the other wilders had when Corwin first came to Seva, which he could only assume had something to do with the amount of time the man spent inside the Mistfold, remembering how Kate and Bonner's magic had come back to them once they were inside it. Corwin felt nothing when he drank the nenath, other than the warmth familiar to him from drinking any normal wine. It was only later, after he'd gone through several of the sessions, that Corwin began to understand the nenath was a tool of Gavril's magic. Three times a day, every day, Gavril had visited him for a session, offered him nenath, and then used his sway on Corwin.

*You will obey my every command*, Gavril would speak right into Corwin's mind. *You will not harm any of the Fanes. You will not harm yourself. You will not try to escape.*

*You will obey my every command. You will not harm any of the Fanes. You will not harm yourself. You will not try to escape.*

*You will obey my every command . . .*

Over and over again, Gavril gave the commands, forcing Corwin to repeat them, to feel the weight of them push and tug on his mind, bending his will. At first, Corwin assumed the commands would fade when night fell. That was how it had been with Kate's sway, or with any of the wilders' magic in Rime—nighttime rendered it dormant. But not here. At least, not Gavril's magic. Perhaps this was because of the nenath, that its poison of godtears made it possible. But by the time Corwin had begun to suspect this connection, he found that he was unable to refuse the drink.

Not because Gavril forced him. On the contrary, Gavril never spoke a word any time Corwin turned it down. Instead, the man waited, patient as a priest in a holy ceremony, the full bottle on the table between them, until Corwin's need for the drink grew strong enough that he gave in, guzzling down whole glassfuls to quench some unbearable thirst.

*Don't drink*, Corwin told himself now, as he did every time. But drink he did, downing the first cup, and then the second, and more until the need subsided. With shame flooding through him, Corwin picked up the empty bottle and threw it at the wall, where it shattered into a dozen pieces, glass glistening darkly against the immaculate floor.

The door swung open, and a boy wearing a page's robe entered the room. "Are you all right, your highness?" Spying the shattered glass, Zan frowned. The troubled expression made him look older than his fourteen years.

"I'm fine." Corwin cast him a cool look. "What do you want?"

Zan grinned. "Time to get you dressed, highness. The ceremony starts today."

*The ceremony.* Bile burned the back of Corwin's throat at the thought. Clenching his fists, for a second he envisioned striking the boy and then fleeing. There would be few guards this time of day; he would meet minimal resistance between his room and the south doors of the palace. But the moment the thought came to him, a violent shudder struck his body. Sweat broke out on his skin, and his legs trembled so fiercely he nearly collapsed. He stumbled toward the bed and sat down, drawing a ragged breath.

If Zan noticed his strange behavior, the boy made no comment as he headed toward the wardrobe in the room and swung the doors open. "It's to be black for you today, I'm afraid, an unfortunate color in this heat, but the Godking's box is nicely shaded, and there will be servants with fans and misters for your comfort."

Finally recovering, Corwin stood from the bed and faced the boy. "Why are you so excited for a wedding? You sound like a besotted child."

Zan glanced over his shoulder, a flush rising in his cheeks. "It's the Spectacle, your highness. There'll be wilder matches today, and it's not often we're treated to those."

Corwin pressed his lips together, saying nothing even as disgust roiled through him. The Spectacles of Seva were known throughout the world for both their extreme violence and grandeur. Several of the mercenaries Corwin had served with in the Shieldhawks had been former Spectacle fighters, some of the rare few who lived long enough to earn their way free. The fights were commissioned by the crown, and the Godking spared no expense in the entertainment he provided, often pitting fighters against rare, exotic beasts when they weren't pitted against each other. And now, it seemed, he'd added his captured wilders to the contest. It seemed that like Gavril's, their magic must work beyond the confines of the Mist-fold, at least for a time.

Oblivious to Corwin's quiet fury, Zan turned back to the ward-robe, prattling on as he pulled out a black silk tunic trimmed in gold with breeches to match. "There's nothing like watching wilders fight. They hurl lightning and fireballs, make windstorms strong enough to knock down towers. You've got to see it to believe it."

He had seen it. Memories of battle stretched through his mind like a slowly unwinding tapestry. He remembered the horror of it, the awesome power. Zan's excitement disgusted Corwin, but he was in no mood to get into an argument with this boy so eager for the "spectacle."

Zan brought the clothes over to Corwin, who reluctantly slid out of his robe. There was no point resisting. Every attempt at defi-ance made him ill, all of it coming back to those simple commands Gavril had magically chiseled into his mind; Tenets, he called them. They were like traps waiting to be sprung.

After helping him into his riding boots, polished so bright they looked like glass, Zan insisted on placing a thin gold circlet on Corwin's head, the faint color nearly disappearing into his dusty-blond hair.

"Today will be even more exciting than you know," Zan said, adjusting the circlet. "I heard tell that the Godspear will be fight-ing today in honor of your nuptials. There's never been a fighter so fearsome. It's a great honor."

*Oh yes, because ritualistic slaughter is such a fashionable bridal present.* With a tight leash on his sarcasm, Corwin asked, "Is this

Godspear a wilder then?" If so, he must have been one of the first captured. Corwin had been in Seva long enough to understand the "god" moniker wasn't given lightly. The fighter must be the God-king's personal champion and favorite.

"To be sure," Zan replied. "He defeated an inferna in his first match. It was near on the size of a house."

Corwin knew the boy wasn't exaggerating. Inferna were the infamous red bulls native to Seva. Corwin had seen only one in his life, a monstrous beast with hide the color of raw meat, four horns on its head, a spiked tail, and hooves sharp enough to slice through rock as if it were bread. He and his shield brothers had given it a wide berth.

"Impressive." Corwin held out his arms to allow Zan to fasten gold bands around his wrists. Carved in the shape of galloping horses, the bands were necessary to hide the scars left behind from the shackles he'd worn as a prisoner in the mines. The golden horses were to remind everyone who saw him that he was Corwin Tormane of Norgard, high prince of Rime. King Magnar preferred it that way, wanting to flaunt his prize to his court. And soon to all the world, once the marriage ceremony was complete. The fact that the ceremony took four days was torture of the worst kind.

Unbidden, thoughts of Kate slipped into Corwin's mind, threatening to undo him. He should've married her first, before coming here. But there hadn't been time, and now it was too late. Even if he had a means to escape, he didn't have the will. Gavril had stolen it from him. Besides, he didn't think a marriage would've stopped Magnar.

*But at least she lives.* Gavril might be the main source of his torment, but the man was a wellspring of knowledge about Rime. With no hesitation, he'd answered nearly all of Corwin's questions about the state of his country, including the reputation of Kate Brighton, champion of the Rising, the Drake Killer, and the Wilder Queen. Yes, she lived, having survived the Wilder War, no less. And for now she was rumored to be safe behind the walls of Farhold. *Sweet goddess, may she remain so.*

After breaking his fast, Corwin was taken by litter to the Desol, the amphitheater where the Spectacles were held. The journey took nearly an hour as the litter bearers slowly navigated the crowds lining the streets. Corwin was thankful that the litter was enclosed. Everyone in the city from the lowliest servant to the highest noblemen had come out to celebrate Princess Eravis's marriage, many of them eager to catch a glimpse of the Rimish prince. Corwin was just as much a spectacle as the wilders and the other fighters soon to compete.

He watched the bustle through the narrow slit of a window in the litter's side, surprised by how normal it all seemed, how familiar. If not for the language and slight difference in clothing, he might've been on the streets of Norgard. Strangely, the familiarity only made him more aware of his isolation, how utterly alone he was in this foreign place.

At last the litter came to a halt, and Corwin climbed out onto the threshold of the Desol. Even though he'd glimpsed the amphitheater from the Sun Palace, the sheer size of it stunned him this close. Constructed entirely of gleaming white marble, it was said capable of hosting eighty thousand people at one time. Corwin believed it.

With Zan trailing behind him flanked by four Sevan guards, Corwin climbed the stone steps into the columned portico where the Godking and his entourage awaited, including his eldest son and heir, Mazen, and his youngest son, Eryx. His other five sons were all away, playing war and politics in different parts of Seva's immense kingdom. Lord Gavril was present as well, of course, lingering off to the side as if he were a mere attendant. Eravis stood on the right hand of the king, resplendent in a dark-green gown threaded with gleaming silver. Corwin's breath caught at the sight of her, as if he had been burned. He couldn't help but notice that he wasn't the only one lured by her beauty. Gavril's gaze kept returning to the princess, his eyes moving at liberty down the length of her.

Magnar Fane clapped his hands as Corwin approached. Although he was more than seventy, the Godking looked like a man in his prime, broad chested and with a narrow waist, emphasized by a golden belt fashioned to resemble dragon scales. Only the wrinkles on his face and the salt threaded through his brown hair belied his age.

Magnar swept toward Corwin and greeted him with a kiss on the lips. "My newest son has arrived at last." Magnar took a step back, gripped Corwin's hand, and raised it in his own, motioning to the assembled noblemen and dignitaries of Seva. They applauded as the king bade them. Corwin felt heat rise in his cheeks, every muscle in his body clenching with hatred for this man who dangled him about like a puppet. But he kept his thoughts carefully in check, remembering Gavril's Tenets. He didn't want to be sick now, in front of his assembled enemies.

Finished with displaying his prize, Magnar reached for his

daughter and placed her hand in Corwin's. Corwin started to let go, but saw Gavril shake his head no. At once, the tenet asserted itself in Corwin's mind, a sickening wave washing over him in warning. He had no choice but to obey.

"You look well, my lord." Eravis leaned close to him as she spoke, and the soft, flowery scent of her hair filled his nose.

Corwin coolly regarded her beauty once more—she was a fair blossom nourished beneath the sun of wealth and privilege, like many princesses he'd known. And yet she repelled him at every turn, representing as she did this gilded cage he had no hope of escaping and whatever worse trap the Godking had planned.

Fighting to keep the snarl out of his voice, Corwin replied, "Thank you, my lady. As do you."

Eravis bowed her head in acknowledgment of the compliment, her long hair spilling over her slender shoulders like a dark, silken wave. When she raised her head again, a warm smile remained on her face, her eyes glinting as if with merriment. Corwin couldn't understand it. She should hate him, as he did her. He remembered clearly her disgust at the news she was to marry him. And yet every time he'd seen her since, she treated him warmly, almost affectionately. Even now she stood beside him docile and happy, the fair blushing bride awaiting her joyous wedding.

As they entered the Desol, she smiled and waved at the people, many of whom tossed flower petals down at them to cover the ground as they walked. With a glance at Gavril walking just behind them, Corwin wondered yet again if the man and his sway were to blame for the princess's change in attitude. The idea disgusted him. It was bad enough he was being forced into this marriage, but even worse to think Eravis was being made compliant for the union through magic. He didn't dare question why Gavril didn't include a tenet to love Eravis among the others. He could only be grateful that he'd been left the choice of hating her, if only in his own mind.

Arriving in the king's box, Corwin took his place two seats to the left of Magnar, Eravis a buffer between them. For once, he was grateful for her presence. Gavril sat just behind them, like a dark shadow.

Despite his dread of the events to come, Corwin soon found himself caught up in the day's festivities, which started with a race—twelve sleek, well-bred horses running their hearts out. Corwin's eyes felt full and hot as he watched them run. Several of the horses were Norgard bred, their superior features clearly distinguishable beside the Sevan mounts. Corwin couldn't guess how they'd ended up here. Stolen, no doubt, by Rendborne's servants, same as the wilders. To the north of the box, the undulating fog of the Mistfold was visible over the edge of the Desol.

After the races, the fights began. The first few matches were between warriors from other nations—Endra, Rhoswen, even Ruzgar. There was a female fighter from the Esh Islands who reminded Corwin of Signe, and it sent an ache through his chest. What he wouldn't give to be surrounded by loved ones, instead of these vipers. To be with Kate again.

His despair only intensified when the Eshian fighter took a blow from a morning star in the second round, the weapon's spikes crushing half her face with a spray of blood and brain matter. The fights didn't have to be to the death—a fighter could yield and plead for mercy—but few of them ended that way, the prize of winning a decisive match too great. Soon the white sands filling the center of the Desol's combat area were stained as red as Sevan clay, the blood transforming it to mud. Corwin finally looked away from the fighting. Beside him, he noticed Eravis doing the same, her face wan and her applause meager at best.

At midday, the games halted to allow the attendants time to refresh. Corwin broke bread with the Godking and the rest, and when his thirst for nenath came upon him, Gavril was there to see to his need. The odious man with his elegant hands smiled at Corwin as he handed over the glass, his eyes bright with triumph. Corwin bared his teeth in response, envisioning himself cutting off the man's head with a single stroke of a stolen sword. Imagining this, at least, didn't pain him. Gavril had commanded Corwin to obey him, but left open the subject of doing him harm.

Not that it mattered. With a single word, Gavril could stop any attack Corwin attempted. *Perhaps I should cut off his tongue.* But no, it wouldn't make a difference. He needed to cut off his magic. *But how?*

With no answers to be had, Corwin sat down again as the fight resumed. The next round featured a pair of wilders, a hydrist pitched against a pyrist. Unlike the fights before, Corwin found he couldn't look away. Zan had been right. This was something to behold, and far different from the war he'd been through. In the heat of a large battle, the wilders rarely attacked one another one-on-one. But these two fought head to head, the clash of magic loud and stunning. The pyrist and the hydrist struggled to gain an upper hand with their respective magic, and Corwin realized that was the point. This was theater—they were not meant to kill each other. There could only be one reason for the difference: the Godking didn't want any of his prizes to meet the same fate as the Eshian fighter. He wanted his wilders alive and unharmed, fit for battle. Could this mean he still planned to invade Rime? But then, why this entrapment, this farce of a marriage? Deep down, Corwin knew the answer. *The uror.* In Norgard, the gods chose who would rule. And he who ruled Norgard ruled Rime. Magnar might be able to break Rime's defenses with an army of wilders, but he wouldn't be able to hold Norgard on his own, not against the power of the uror.

*But he can through me.*

It made Gavril's tenet that he not harm himself make sense. Corwin would do it, end his own life in order to save his country. But even that option had been closed to him.

Still, he refused to give up, to give in. Retreat wasn't in his nature. *There must be a way.* He just needed to find it. Corwin stole a glance at Eravis, unsettled to discover she'd been watching him. Perhaps she would be the key. If he could convince her that he truly loved her, and she fell in love with him and trusted him, he might be able to use that advantage to escape . . . No, it was a repugnant idea, and he knew he couldn't go through with it. There must be some other way.

With the final match set to begin, a hush fell over the crowd as the Godking stood from his chair and walked to the edge of the box, which extended out over the grounds below. Raising his arms, he said, "Good citizens of Seva, there is but one more match this day, which we dedicate to our beloved daughter in her marriage to Corwin Tormane, high prince of Rime. May their union bring us the peace and prosperity we have so longed for."

The crowd applauded at this, and Corwin rolled his eyes. What more prosperity did the Godking need? He was already rich beyond measure, and yet he wasn't satisfied. He wouldn't be, until he claimed Rime.

"To that end," Magnar continued, "our champion in this final match will be none other than the Godspear!"

At this, the crowd erupted into applause, one far greater than its predecessor. The fervor increased as the entry doors to the killing floor opened and a lone figure stepped out onto the sands. The Godspear was massive and well-built, chest rippling with muscles and arms and legs like tree trunks. Same as the other fighters before him, he wore a loincloth and sandals, his only armor a pair of thick iron vambraces and a helmet with a white plume rising out of it, the nose guard and cheek pieces obscuring his face. He carried no weapon—perhaps because *he* was the weapon. Corwin wondered what sort of wilder the man was.

He strode all the way to the center of the ring and bowed before the Godking, going down on one knee.

"Arise, my champion." Magnar waved him up. Then he addressed the crowd again. "As his opponent, the Godspear will face a foe never before seen in Seva. We give you . . . the scourge of Rime, the deadly nightdrake!"

The loud creak of metal gears overpowered the shouts of the crowd as a massive cage rose up out of the floor opposite the fighter's entrance. More than a dozen dragon-like beasts filled the cage. They came in different sizes, some as small as pigs, others as large as horses, all of them boasting poisoned fangs and claws like curved daggers. With their keening screeches, these creatures knew only one desire—to feast on human flesh. The sight of them made Corwin's skin prickle with memories of the pain and death they wrought.

They weren't nightdrakes as Magnar claimed, however—they were daydrakes. No nightdrake would be able to survive in this sun, and the black scales of the daydrake were unmistakable. Like the Norgard-bred horses and wilders, they must've been smuggled here. No easy task, and one Magnar could've only accomplished with help from magists of the gold order—or from the Nameless One himself, the man responsible for all of this. Questions of when these daydrakes came to be here rose in Corwin's mind. But where Rendborne was now and what he might be doing hardly seemed to matter compared with what Corwin faced in the coming days. It was one subject Gavril never had any information about either.

Eravis leaned toward him, a faint shudder sliding through her body. "They are so ferocious. Do those beasts really emerge every night in your homeland?"

"Indeed. You would never want to visit." Corwin leaned away from her as best he could in the narrow seat. Oblivious to the reaction, Eravis slid her arm under his and took his hand, fingers gripped in such a manner that warned him that pulling away from her wouldn't be wise. The ferocity of it surprised him. *Who are you really?* He cast a sidelong look at her, wondering at the girl he'd first met, the one who'd stomped on his foot to escape him, then threatened to kill him if he hurt her brother. She must still be in there, hidden beneath this pretty, compliant facade.

The fight began a few moments later, the door to the drake cage opening by an unseen force. The beasts charged out, moving as one. They were one, Corwin knew, creatures magically bound by a sort of hive mind. His heart clenched inside his chest as he once again thought of Kate. If she were here, she could stop the beasts with a single thought.

*Gavril could as well*, Corwin realized. Not that he would.

The Godspear raised his arms toward the drakes, which moved with the speed of snakes striking. The ground in front of the drakes rose up like a wave, transforming into a solid wall. The man must be an earthist, and Corwin's heart sank at the realization. An earthist's power would be fine for fending off the drakes, but he couldn't see how it would help him kill them. Even as he watched, the drakes were already finding their way around the wall, drawn straight to the Godspear by his human scent.

The wilder put up another wall and another. At the same time, the vambraces on his wrists began to elongate, transforming into crude spears that rose up to cover his hands. One of the drakes broke through the line of walls and charged the Godspear. He raised an arm toward it, muscles flexed. Heedless, the drake impaled itself on the spear with a force strong enough that the Godspear stumbled backward, nearly losing his footing. Corwin sucked in a breath, his pulse quickening both from fear and awe. It wasn't easy to impale a drake, their hides stronger than chain mail. With the drake already dying, the Godspear yanked the spear free, then spun to meet another drake coming at him.

There were so many. Too many. And yet the wilder slew them one by one, using a combination of his spear arms and his earthist magic. Corwin watched mesmerized as the man wielded the sand as a weapon, casting it at the drakes hard enough to make them stumble or turn back to escape the grains burning their eyes and clogging their throats. One of the smaller drakes got by him, soaring up over his defenses with its flightless wings stretched out behind it. It barreled into him as it landed, sending both man and beast sprawling. But the Godspear recovered quickly, rolling up onto his feet in time to stab the drake through the neck and shoulder before it could regain its balance.

The remaining drakes attacked, again in unison—still far too many for the Godspear to counter. And yet, the spears over the man's hand began to blur and separate, transforming into small oblong shapes, like bullets. The Godspear launched them all in a powerful volley. It was a bold move, the metal too dispersed to reform into his spears in time to use as defense. But the gambit paid off as all the drakes fell beneath the onslaught until only the God-spear remained standing. Covered in sweat and blood, he turned a circle, surveying the sea of felled drakes surrounding him, before coming to a stop in front of the Godking and raising his hand in a sign of victory.

The crowd went mad, their screams shaking the walls of the Desol. Even Eravis was clapping hard, the sound striking Corwin's ear like it was a drum. She turned and placed a hand on her father's arm. "What is to be his reward, Father?" she shouted over the cheers.

Magnar looked at his daughter, his face flush as if the victory below had been his. "Why, our admiration, as always."

Eravis shook her head. "It's not enough. Not today. I would like to gift him a kiss."

Magnar frowned, his gaze flicking to Corwin for a second and then to Gavril.

Gavril leaned forward and said, "Her highness is as gracious as she is beautiful. It is a splendid idea."

Eravis stiffened at the comment. Or perhaps Corwin had imagined it.

Magnar looked back at his daughter and nodded consent.

Rather than allow the Godspear to approach the king's box to claim his prize, Eravis was escorted down to the floor by six guards while Corwin remained behind. The Godspear waited, arms hanging limply by his sides. Coming to a stop before him, Eravis motioned for the man to remove his helm. When he did, the sight of his face sent a lightning bolt of shock through Corwin.

He should've guessed. Should've known when he saw the wilder's power. But he hadn't dared. The idea that this man had survived, that he had been in the city this entire time, was too much to hope for. And yet here he stood.

Bonner.

His body had changed so much, leaned and hardened with corded muscles, it was difficult to believe it was him, but there was no question of it. For the first time in nearly a year, Corwin felt the oppressive loneliness flee, his heart soaring as Bonner's gaze turned up to him, recognition in his eyes. Corwin returned the look with a single, quick nod, his heart a clenched fist in his chest. Eravis stood on her tiptoes to plant a kiss square on Bonner's mouth, the crowd cheering. Corwin wished he was down there with her. He would kiss Bonner, too, embrace him as a brother. For together, the two of them might find a way free.

Or, at the very least, they could die together trying.

"WHERE ARE MY SPECTACLES?" Harue said as she rummaged through the sacks strewn across the table of her workroom. "Has anyone seen them?"

Kate turned away from her post by the door. "Shhhh, you'll wake the whole city."

Ceasing her search, Harue looked up at Kate, a frown creasing her brow. "That's just not possible, Kate. To wake so many would require a noise far greater than one person could possibly—"

"She's only exaggerating, Harue," Signe said from where she stood leaning by the door next to Kate. "And you're already wearing them."

"What? Oh." Harue patted the top of her head, searching through the tangles of her black hair until she found the eyepieces set across her crown.

They'd been in the workroom for at least the past twenty minutes while the three of them packed the last of Harue's supplies for their journey to Norgard. Tira and Wen, Harue's young assistant, were outside, keeping an eye on the horses and doing their best to avoid suspicion. This early in the morning there were few people about, but those who were would doubtlessly wonder at their presence there with more horses than they could ride alone. News would spread quickly, Kate knew, but she could only hope they would be away from the city before anyone who mattered caught wind of it.

Then again, with Harue's slowness and general loudness, the odds were stacked against them. Harue should've been ready the evening before, but instead she'd gotten distracted in her packing and had spent half the night trying to decipher some obscure text in a moldy old book she'd found buried in the city archives weeks ago but had misplaced until her packing activities uncovered it once more. It had taken all of Kate's willpower not to lose her temper when she arrived this morning to the general—and entirely normal—state of disarray in Harue's workroom. She'd been half tempted to leave without her, but it wasn't an option. Even with Harue along, Kate wasn't confident they'd be able to keep the nightdrakes at bay for the entire journey. Harue was only one magist, after all, and conjuring the amount of wardstones they needed to form the barriers each night would be a massive undertaking. Wen would be able to help some, but she was just a child and still a long way from mastering her craft. *Too bad my powers don't work at night*, Kate thought. If they did, she could end any drake threat with a thought.

"Are you about ready?" Kate said, turning her gaze back to the door. She reached out with her magic, checking for at least the hundredth time that no one nearby was yet awake. With the sun only just cresting the horizon, her magic was sluggish at best. Still, she could tell that everyone nearby was asleep. Harue and Wen both resided in the magist quarters, a section of houses less than a block from the governor's mansion. With far too few magists in the Rising, both wilders and magists alike were actively recruiting young people with signs of magist talent, a common form of spirit gift that remained dormant without training. Like it or not, magist magic was still crucial in many tasks throughout the city, including keeping the walls fortified against nightdrakes.

"I suppose so." Harue sighed, examining the bookshelf in the far corner of the room with longing. "It's a shame I can't take the Atreyum Chronicles or the Elevia Scrolls. I might need them if—"

"There's no room." Signe crossed to the table, her limp barely noticeable for once, and started fastening one of the sacks closed. More than any of them she was impatient to leave. Although less than a week had passed since they received the doll, it seemed like an eternity. Raith's messenger had left days ago, but it was far to early for any news. Anything could've happened to Dal and they wouldn't know it. How Kate wished her magic was strong enough to span the continent, allowing her to reach Dal's thoughts even from so far away.

Turning to the table, Kate picked up one of the remaining books, examining the title. "Do you really need this, Harue? *The Diary of Melchor the Mad*?"

"Are you joking?" Harue tilted her head in genuine puzzlement.

Rolling her eyes, Kate shoved the book into one of the sacks before pulling it closed. She slung it over her shoulder and reached for the next. "Come on, then. Let's get these down to the horses."

Signe eyed the sacks with a look of disdain. "This will slow us down. Harue, can we please leave some behind? We must stay ahead of any riders the council might send after us."

Seeing the look of horror spreading across Harue's face at the suggestion, Kate quickly intervened. "Raith won't do that. He won't want it to get out that you've left the city."

Signe scowled. "You can't be sure of that."

"I am, though."

Somehow they managed to carry all the sacks between the three of them, although Kate's steps wavered as she descended the stairs with the massive weight of books across her shoulders. She felt sorry for the two packhorses they were bringing with them to be faced with such a burden.

As they walked, she kept her magic at the ready, listening for any unexpected company. Although no one would be overly concerned to see Harue or Kate, nearly everyone would be alarmed to see Signe out and about in the city unescorted. Kate was prepared to use her sway to keep them from reacting, but she would prefer not to if she could avoid it.

It seemed luck was with them this day as they made it to Tira and Wen without incident.

Tira grinned at the sight of them. "You look like a herd of pack mules."

"I feel like one," Kate replied, groaning at the effort it took to hoist one of the sacks over the packhorse's back. The little bay mare turned to pin her ears at Kate as she set it down. Kate frowned at the horse. "Don't make that face at me. It's not my fault."

Tira snorted in amusement but made no further comment as she took a bag from Signe and placed it with a little more care over the other horse's back, the effort easier for the taller woman. Wen scurried forward to help Harue, even though half of the sacks weighed more than she did. The dark-haired, willowy girl moved like a mouse, quick and quiet and always with an air of fearfulness, as if a cat waited around every corner.

Once done loading the horses, Kate double-checked Nightbringer's saddle and bridle before mounting. A nervous flutter rose in her stomach as they set out, a thousand questions and doubts skidding through her mind. Sensing her unease, Night crow-hopped and tossed his head, unhappy to only be walking. With an effort Kate forced herself to relax.

Again, good fortune remained with them as they made their way to the city gates without running into anyone who cared enough to take note of them. Once at the gates though, the watchman on guard called for them to halt, and his fellows moved across the path, blocking their way.

Kate sighed. She knew all these soldiers. Several she'd fought beside in battle, while two others were newly promoted cadets. But before she could allow herself to question her actions, she reached out with her sway and gently coaxed them to step aside. All of them went easily, except for Jessalyn, the youngest of the group and one of the cadets Kate had been particularly fond of, appreciating her feisty spirit and sharp wit, with an equally sharp mind behind it. But even Jessalyn's resistance wasn't enough against her magic. Kate could only hope they wouldn't be punished too severely if it was discovered they escaped the city on their watch.

The moment the path was clear, Kate urged Nightbringer into a trot and hurried through the gate, the others trailing close behind. She kept the pace quick but steady as they headed down the eastern road toward Marared. The cornfields along both sides of the road remained barren, no sign of sprouts yet. Still the earthists insisted the harvest would be decent, so long as the armistice remained, allowing them to spend their time coaxing the crops along instead of fighting. If they were right, there would be enough for winter, Kate hoped. She wondered if she'd be back by then. The idea that she might not didn't bother her as much as she would've thought. Not with the people she cared about most riding beside her now. She might've fought and bled for the city she was leaving behind, but it didn't feel like home. No place did. Not without Corwin. Her hand rose up to touch her tattoo, and a flutter once again went through her belly. He wasn't in Norgard, she knew, but the ghost of him waited there just the same.

They rode hard for the first four hours. Although neither Harue nor Wen were used to much riding, Kate refused to slow down until they were a fair distance from the city. Then finally, after the tenth request for a gentler pace from Harue, she conceded.

"That was remarkably easy," Tira noted as she reined her horse next to Kate's. She sounded disappointed.

Kate glanced over her shoulder, checking on the others. Harue and Wen seemed all right so far, although both bore uncomfortable grimaces. For once, she didn't have to worry about Signe. Astride a horse, she became her old self, fierce and unbroken. Unburdened. Like Tira, Signe wore dual swords on her back and a revolver on her hip, her blond hair pulled back into a severe braid.

Kate looked ahead again. "They might send someone after us yet."

Tira snorted. "Raith wouldn't be so foolish. Not when he knows you can turn them back with a single thought."

In the end it seemed Tira was right. They rode the rest of the day at varying speeds without seeing so much as a speck of dust on the road behind them. Although the fields around Farhold had been barren, this stretch of land was in the full bloom of spring, the hills swathed in glistening everweeps and the trees boasting vibrant green leaves that swayed in the gentle breezes.

With dusk approaching, they finally stopped at an abandoned campsite along the road. Before the war, the site had been kept stocked with firewood and supplies for travelers, all provided by the royal crown. This close to Farhold though, it was no longer maintained.

They made camp, Harue setting up the wardstone barrier with relative ease, albeit slowly, as she took the time to explain everything she did to Wen. The little girl listened with an intent expression, licking her lips in concentration and with her eyebrows drawn together so closely that they resembled a pair of butterfly wings perched over her nose.

Once she'd seen to the horses, Kate took up the watch, sitting atop a rocky hillock just inside the barrier's edge, her gaze fixed to the west on Farhold. Just in case she'd been wrong about what Raith would do. She knew him, yes, trusted him, but she didn't believe in relying on trust these days.

Her instinct proved true when she spotted a lone figure riding up the road toward them. The grim gray of twilight hung in the air like a bad promise, and in the distance, the nightdrakes were already howling. With her magic waning along with the light, Kate couldn't quite reach the person from so far, but even still she knew who it was and made no effort to challenge him as he approached.

Raith dismounted just inside the barrier and tethered his horse before facing her. "Hello, Kate."

She inclined her head, wary and tense. And also a little ashamed at her defiance. *Remember Dal*, she told herself. "You've come a long way for no reason," she said.

Raith shrugged and sat down beside her, drawing his knees to his chest. "What if I only wanted to say good-bye?"

Taken off guard, Kate drew a slow breath, realizing how foolish she was. Of course he wasn't angry. Raith had a remarkable capacity for empathy and understanding. That, along with his even temper, was what made him such a good leader.

On an exhale she said, "I'm sorry to defy you like this, but I had no choice."

Raith waited a few moments before answering, the silence an uncomfortable weight. "I know that's how you feel, and I understand. I only wish I could change your mind. Breaking the accords could throw our entire city into peril."

"If any harm comes to Dal in Norgard, the accords will already have been broken," Kate countered.

Raith nodded thoughtfully, but his expression remained grim. "Even if you're right, I fear there's nothing but trouble waiting for you in Norgard."

"I can take care of myself. I always have."

"Do you have a magestone diamond?"

In answer, she reached for one of the two leather cords about her neck, pulling free the one that held the diamond, its glittering surface bearing faint marks from the spell woven into it, one designed to hide the use of wilder magic from magist detector stones. She showed it to him.

"Good. Make sure you wear it at all times. King Edwin might

have halted the Inquisition, but I doubt he'll be inclined to remember that if his magists find you."

"I know." Edwin would kill her given half the chance. The last time she'd seen him he'd come close to doing just that. He'd only been high prince then, but that didn't stop Kate from putting him and all of his men to sleep with her magic in order to escape. Once, she and Edwin had been friends, of a sort, but fate had turned them enemies. He hated wilders with a passion that bordered on madness, blaming them all for the death of his mother, and it was no secret that the war ending in an armistice instead of the Rising's defeat infuriated him.

She slid the stone back beneath her tunic, adjusting it so it lay comfortably next to the other necklace, this one a crystal vial filled with blood. Like the diamond, it gave her protection, but not the kind she would need against the magists of Norgard. The magic in her father's blood trapped in the vial would protect her from someone with the gift of sway. Rendborne and Vikas both had worn such a talisman. Kate had taken this one from Vikas after she killed her. Rendborne wore his still, she assumed.

Kate turned a sidelong gaze onto Raith. "Are you really not going to try and change my mind?"

"Would there be any point?" Raith looked over his shoulder at the others in the camp. Tira and Signe had noticed him, of course, and probably Wen as well, but not Harue. She was already nose-deep in that awful diary of Melchor the Mad she'd brought.

"No. Making sure Dal is safe is too important." Raith's lips and nose twitched as if he were holding back a scathing reply, and Kate's temper sparked at the sight of it, that feeling of being a little girl defying her parents coming over her again—and getting the best of her, it seemed. "If you've something to say, out with it, then."

Again, Raith waited several moments before answering, tact his weapon of choice. "Has it occurred to you that Dal might not be the target at all, but Signe? That threatening Dal may draw her out, as it seems it has?"

Kate's stomach clenched. No, it hadn't occurred to her, but it made an awful kind of sense now that she thought about it. Signe was far more important to the Rising and to its enemies than Dal was. Kate remembered Signe's reaction to the doll, the way she'd known it was going to ignite before Kate touched it. And there was her response afterward as well, the way she'd been agitated, preoccupied, impatient. For as long as Kate had known her, she never acted this way. Even under torture she'd remained calm and controlled, certain that she would win in the end. Not so now.

Kate bit her lip, worries bubbling up in her mind. "Even if you're right, it doesn't matter. I can't make Signe turn back."

"You could," Raith said, matter-of-fact.

"But I won't." She didn't dare use her sway on Signe. She would never forgive her.

"Not even to save her life?"

Kate scowled. "Is it truly her life you're concerned with, *chancellor*? Or rather those you imprison her to protect?"

"That's not fair, Kate, and you know it." Raith rubbed his eye with a knuckle, something weary about the gesture. There was weariness in his whole manner. "All the lives I'm responsible for matter equally."

Kate kicked at the dirt with one boot, making no reply. She'd heard this axiom from him before, but couldn't embrace it. How many lives would she give to save Corwin or Kiran or Bonner? How many lives would she be willing to end to get to Rendborne? They were uncomfortable thoughts, and as Signe had pointed out, she was glad to keep them private.

"What Signe risks being out here is a threat to us all," Raith added in her silence.

"I can't use my sway on her," Kate said. "And even if I did, it would fade the first night and she would leave again, this time without me. You know Signe as well as I do."

Raith sighed, the sound a summation of this truth. "Then you must do whatever you can to protect her. You must keep a watch on her at all times. Do you promise?"

"You don't have to ask." Kate fixed her eyes on Signe, who was staring right back her, as if aware that she was the subject of their discussion. Kate couldn't make herself look away, even though she knew she ought to before she raised suspicions. Losing Signe, on top of everyone else, would be more than Kate could bear.

At last she returned her attention to Raith. He watched her intently, his neutral expression veiling his thoughts. She could've gleaned them if she'd wanted to, but she feared what she would find.

"Is that all you came to say then?" Kate gestured toward the road back to Farhold. "All this way for a good-bye and a promise you knew you didn't have to ask me to make?"

A thin smile spread across Raith's weary face. In the dim light, his birthmark looked like nothing more than a shadow peeled from the dark. "You need to be careful in your hunt for Rendborne. Dal sent word weeks ago that there's been some kind of activity near the Hellgate. It seems that Edwin is mining for something."

Kate knew she shouldn't be surprised at how much Raith had guessed about her secondary motives in wanting to journey to Norgard, and yet she still was. He knew her well enough at this point to have guessed so much. The thought made her feel uncomfortably warm, and she shook the feeling off. "Mining the Hellgate? For what?"

"We don't know. Dal's attempts to find out have proven fruitless. But it can't be anything good. No good has ever come from there."

"You have a gift for understatement." The stories claimed the Hellgates were the very portals that had unleashed the nightdrakes onto Rime. And indeed, when Rendborne had been using the Hellgate near Norgard as his secret camp, he'd somehow engineered the daydrakes as well, breeding them from nightdrakes and twisting them with his magic and that of the gold order that served him.

"If you can," Raith continued, "report back whatever you find. We might have forged a peace, but it's a brittle one at best. A blow of any kind will break it."

Kate frowned, a shiver sliding through her at the fear she sensed in him. Perhaps his pleas for her to attend the meetings had been about more than just appearances. She considered pressing him, then changed her mind as she remembered Master Janus. Since these worries over Dal had started, she hadn't found the time to bring her concerns about the master magist to Raith. She considered easing into the discussion, but when the loud howl of a nightdrake broke around them, she plunged ahead. It seemed the beasts had caught their scent and would be on the camp soon, making all conversations tense at best.

"Speaking of blows," Kate began, "we need to talk about Master Janus."

By the time she finished explaining what she'd sensed in him—or, more accurately, what she hadn't—Raith's neutral expression had turned sour. "I appreciate your insight, Kate, but I can assure you that you have nothing to fear where Janus is concerned. I have noticed that his memory is not what it was, but he is old and not entirely well."

"But—"

"I said it's nothing." He fixed a sharp look at her. The sight of it shocked her. She hadn't just touched a nerve, it seemed, but given it a good pinch. Raith rose to his feet. "Now if you don't mind sharing your fire for the night, I will be off at first light."

And with that, he walked into the camp, where the others promptly stole his attention. Even little Wen came out from the tent they'd pitched to stare at him in fearful amazement.

Kate sighed, wishing she'd made certain of Master Janus before she'd left. But she'd been too distracted by everything else. *A distraction.* Maybe distracting her from Janus had been the point? The doll had arrived with the same caravan as he had. But no, she was being paranoid. Raith might have personal feelings where Master Janus was concerned, but he would never allow his trust to put the city at risk.

And what about Signe's reaction to the doll? How had she known not to touch it?

She turned to look at Signe, vowing that she would get to the truth.

The moment dawn winked over the horizon, Raith departed as promised. Kate and the others quickly broke camp and moved out as well, heading east toward Norgard. Riding beside Signe, Kate broached the subject of the doll head on, knowing it was pointless to take the indirect route where Signe was concerned.

"Raith seems to think that the doll wasn't a warning about Dal at all," Kate said, with a quick glance at her friend to gauge her reaction.

Nothing showed on Signe's face, but Kate could sense the sudden tension spreading through her just the same. She arched an eyebrow. "Is that so?"

"He seems to think the doll was a ruse to get you out of the city."

Signe smiled, lips parting as if in genuine amusement, but still the tension lingered, expanding like a shadow at evening time. "Raith would say anything to get you to change your mind about coming. He probably hoped you would compel me back to the city."

Doubt peaked inside Kate. Raith had suggested just that, after all. And yet—"How was it you knew the doll would ignite when I touched it?"

"It was doused in lithna," Signe replied with a causal shrug. "I smelled it the moment I opened the box. It reacts to the oil in human skin. A single touch will cause it to ignite."

"Lithna? I've never heard of it."

"On the islands, we call it widow's touch."

Kate frowned. If they had a special name for this whatever-it-was in her birthplace, then that might validate Raith's claim—that the doll had more to do with Signe than Dal.

She said as much, and Signe shrugged again. "The name means nothing. Lithna is used everywhere. Every circus in Rime will have a barrel of it. Don't let your own ignorance feed into Raith's manipulations."

Kate flinched at the vehemence in Signe's tone, sensing her disproportionate anger with her magic. And something else. A memory. The face of a woman Kate had never seen before flashed inside her mind, drawn there unintentionally through her sway and the strength of Signe's reaction. She was white-haired and beautiful, her looks striking, due in no small part to the four ruby-like stones pierced around her lips, one above and below and two on each side. The piercings marked the woman as one of the Furen Mag, a sisterhood of craftswomen from the Esh Islands, a mysterious, secretive, and almost religious sect. Unable to help herself, Kate searched for the woman's name in Signe's mind, finding it at once.

"Who is Synnove?"

Signe blanched, then just as quickly red rose in her cheeks. "How dare you, Kate. Stay out of my mind."

"I'm sorry. I didn't mean to, I swear. Your thoughts were so loud just now," Kate said, feeling a sting of guilt about bending the truth.

"She is . . . no one."

This time Kate sensed the fear inside Signe, a peculiar mixture of both dread and regret. "She must be someone. Why are you so afraid of her?"

Signe raised her hand sharply. "Enough, Kate. What you're asking about is Seerah."

Kate drew a deep breath, desperate for more, but knowing full well that Signe wouldn't talk, not if she considered it Seerah. The Eshian belief in the divine silence was unbreakable. Even now, after years of friendship, Kate knew next to nothing about Signe's life before she came to Rime. It was an unfathomable mystery, not the least of which was how she came to have knowledge of black powder in the first place. Even the secret of the less-powerful variety of explosive powder used in ordinary firearms was well guarded, known only by the Furen Mag, but Signe wasn't one of them. The only marking on Signe's face was the scar that ran from her brow to her chin, left there by Rendborne in a failed attempt to pry her secrets. Still, Signe's fear must have something to do with her secret knowledge. It was a troubling possibility.

But in the end the only thing Kate could say was, "I know you're not telling me everything, Sig, but that's all right. So long as you tell me the truth when I need to know it."

Signe regarded her for several long moments before nodding. "I will. Always."

The rest of the long journey to Norgard was uneventful. They passed few travelers on the road and at night were bothered only a few times by nightdrakes. The ease of it pricked at Kate's nerves. Still, when the white walls of Norgard came into view at last, she couldn't help the swell of nostalgia that went through her.

She and Signe had both donned their magestone disguises. Kate wore the face of a much older woman, one fair-skinned with brown hair threaded with fine strands of gray. Signe was an unmemorable, plain woman, her hair a dull brown, same as her eyes. Every time Kate glanced at Signe, her heart clenched inside her chest as she remembered Corwin as he'd last looked—as unremarkable as Signe was now. Kate could only hope the memory wasn't a bad omen.

But all thoughts fled her mind the nearer they came to the city. The statues of Niran and Nelek rose up to greet them. The two rearing horses, one carved in the blackest of onyx and the other the whitest of ivory, had stood guard at the gate of Norgard for more than a thousand years. Kate's eyes filled with tears at the sight of them, her thoughts awash with both painful and bittersweet memories.

*Get it together*, she screamed at herself. She needed to be focused on the challenges that lay ahead. They wouldn't be allowed to just ride into Norgard unchecked. Harue had prepared fake papers for them to show the guard captain, and Kate was ready to use her sway if the need arose. Even if it didn't, she planned to wipe the memory of their arrival from the mind of any who saw them. They could've used the secret mage door, known as the shade door, Raith had installed at the start of the Rising to get into the city, but with the armistice, everyone needed official patents, sealed by the guard and verifying their right to be here. It was too risky not to have them on hand.

The guard captain examined their papers, which declared them to be citizens of Carden, joining their relatives in Norgard, who had come ahead to set up a new brewery in the Burnside district. It was a believable enough story. Carden was renowned throughout Rime for its wineries and breweries, but the guard captain seemed uninterested either way. In fact he seemed distracted, agitated. Before Kate could delve into his thoughts to learn why, the man had approved their entrance and was pushing them out the door.

Once inside the city, Kate sensed a similar agitation from everyone they passed. There was a fervor about the people, their movements hurried and their words hushed. It was the kind of thing Kate often felt from soldiers the night before battle, the dreadful anticipation and cloying doubt of what the morrow would bring.

As they passed onto the city streets, a woman was walking toward them, her gaze fixed on the newspaper in her hand, the *Royal Gazette* by the look of it. She was clearly unsettled, and before she knew what she was doing, Kate gleaned the woman's thoughts. But what she saw in her mind made no sense.

"Excuse me," Kate said, waylaying the woman, who nearly ran into her. "What's the news that's gotten everyone in such a state?"

The woman blinked several times, her expression dazed for a moment. Then slowly the shock slid from her face, replaced with something like astonishment. "Why, haven't you heard?" The woman paused long enough to turn the front page of the paper around and into Kate's view.

In bold, black print, the headline read simply:

## HIGH PRINCE CORWIN LIVES

CORWIN WOKE TO FIND HIMSELF alone, his new bride nowhere to be seen. Only the faint scent of her lilac perfume remained in the air. He closed his eyes and wished for leave from his senses, even as the events from the long, tumultuous day before passed through his mind unbidden.

Last night, after four days of pomp and celebrations, he'd finally been wed to Princess Eravis. The ceremony took place atop the central tower of the Sun Palace, in the final hour before sunset, the surrounding rooftops awash in a rosy glow. Eravis wore a red gown trimmed in gold, the royal colors of House Fane. Corwin wore the blue and silver of Norgard, the first time he'd been permitted them. He would've refused if he could, understanding as he did that the colors were meant to legitimize this false union, one that was anything but peaceful—or willing.

With the top echelon of the Sevan nobility in attendance, the Godking himself performed the ceremony. There were no priests or priestesses, no rituals to enact as there would've been in Rime—the cleansing of spirit and body, the laying of wreaths, and the exchange of the Goddess Kiss. Seva had no religion at all save for the king. Magnar merely gave a speech about loyalty, honor, and duty, and at the end he handed Eravis a golden chalice filled with clear, cool water. She drank from it, then offered it to Corwin, who was bidden to do the same. Once done, Magnar declared them married in his eyes—husband and wife, "forevermore," he proclaimed.

Afterward there'd been a feast so grand Corwin didn't believe his taste buds would ever be the same again. He hadn't thought he'd be able to eat at all for the knots in his stomach, and yet the food proved irresistible. Dishes from every nation had been present, including several Rimish delicacies. And the wine, as well, rare vintages bottled in Carden. Corwin abstained as best he could, wanting to keep a clear head, but even still he could not resist indulging in one cup. And the nenath, of course. There was no denying that.

Not long after the final course was served, the assembled guests began a slow clap like the steady beat of a drum. Corwin's face flushed as he realized their intent—a call for the new husband and wife to be off to their marriage bed. Corwin refused to go, sitting stonily in his chair. That was, until Lord Gavril intervened. With a single thought, he compelled Corwin to stand and take his bride's hand. Then side by side they left the great hall with more than a dozen lords and ladies following after them, still clapping as they laughed and told bawdy jokes to one another.

Corwin ignored them all, his heart small as a pebble inside his chest. He was keenly aware of Gavril walking just behind them and what his presence might mean. He and Eravis had been given new quarters in the central tower, not far from where Magnar and his current queen resided. Corwin stopped outside the door, unable to make himself go in. Eravis stepped forward and pushed it open, heading inside first. With a quick glance at Lord Gavril, Corwin hurried in after her and shut the door behind him. Cheers echoed beyond it, but at least the infuriating clapping finally ended.

But the silence inside the room was far worse. Eravis had crossed the living quarters to the table where more wine and food had been set. She grasped the decanter and poured a glass.

"Would you like some, my lord?"

Corwin shook his head, marveling at her calm. Not at all what he would've expected from a young woman alone in a bedroom with the stranger she'd just been forced to marry.

With a shrug, Eravis downed a glass herself. Then with a pointed look, she turned and entered the bedchamber beyond, which was aglow with candles. Through the open doorway he counted half a dozen at least. Feeling awkward and tense, he paced about the living quarters, stopping to examine the art on the walls and then to test the softness of the divan. The firm cushion and expansive size would more than do for sleeping. That was good. That was, if he could manage to sleep at all given the circumstances.

Reconsidering his earlier decision, he poured himself a glass of wine only to hear Eravis call for him from the other room. With gritted teeth, he approached the door to the bedchambers. The sight beyond surprised him. He'd thought he'd seen the height of opulence in the Godking's palace several times over, and yet this rose above it. The bed itself stood on a stone platform like an altar, the four posts canopied in white, shimmering lace. To the right of the bed, the room extended out onto a terrace with no doors that Corwin could see, only delicate, fluttering curtains. A cool breeze flowed in from outside, the night sky luminescent in the glow of stars that seemed close enough to touch. It was lovely, romantic, and for a second he pictured Kate here with him. The longing the image provoked in him cut like a knife, and he pushed it away, turning to take in the rest of the room.

Tucked into the far corner adjacent to the terrace was a fireplace, a single log burning in its hearth. In front of it was a small pool, sunk deep into the floor, water flowing down into it from a miniature waterfall built out of colorful rocks. The sight of that flowing water made Corwin shake his head in dismay. Everywhere else in Seva, water was a scarce resource, one carefully controlled and meted out at Magnar's whim. Yet here, in the Godking's palace, it flowed freely.

"Would you mind fetching me a robe?" The voice came as if from nowhere. Corwin blinked, belatedly realizing that Eravis was *in* the pool—nothing but her bare shoulders visible above the water and her hair piled on top of her head in an untidy crown. He jerked his eyes away the moment he spotted her and stepped back from the pool's edge.

She made a sound like a stifled laugh. "Honestly, I'm not going to bite, you know."

"Are you sure?" Corwin arched an eyebrow her direction, still not looking at her. "I seem to recall the first time we met that you threatened to kill me."

"Well, you did have a knife to my throat. But please, would you fetch me a robe?"

Corwin sighed and looked about until he spotted one. Grabbing it off the hanger on the wall, he set it beside the pool. Then he retreated back to the living quarters, closing the door behind him.

With nothing else to do, he sat down on the divan, trying to will himself to grow sleepy. Eravis strode into the room moments later, her hair still piled atop her head and the thin robe clinging to her damp body, leaving little to the imagination. The possibility of sleep scampered away, his muscles growing taut as he beheld her.

She regarded him with a cool, tense look. Then slowly, she started to lower the robe from her shoulders.

Corwin stood up, fists clenched. "Don't," he said, his voice harsh, commanding. "What you're attempting isn't going to work." He glared at her, wishing he could sear this truth to her soul with his eyes. "We may be married in the eyes of your father, but we will never be as man and wife."

She paled by a fraction, and a cord flexed in her slender throat. "You're being a fool, Corwin Tormane. I can only hope you realize it before it's too late."

Corwin frowned at the cryptic warning, but said nothing as she returned to the bedroom, closing the door behind her this time.

He'd fallen asleep on the divan sometime later, only to wake as he was now, certain he was alone in the chambers. He double-checked both rooms to be sure. The bed was rumpled, but the sheets long since cooled. Eravis had clearly left for the day. That was good. One night done—the gods knew how many to go.

With nothing else to do and still tired from the restless night, Corwin was about to avail himself of the bed when a knock on the door sounded. With a mumbled curse, he went to answer it. An elderly woman in a stately gray dress that matched her hair offered him a polite smile before bowing.

"Good morning, your highness. We've come to take the record." The stewardess motioned to the little man in a clerk's uniform standing to her right.

"Record?" Corwin cocked his head, puzzled. "Of what?"

"The consummation, of course."

"The consu—" He broke off, fire rising in his cheeks as he understood their intent. He shook his head. "I'm afraid not." He started to push the door closed, but the woman blocked him with a raised hand.

"Apologies, your highness, but it must be done. The Godking demands it."

Corwin stepped toward the intruders, meaning to shut the door on their faces if he had to, but he froze at the sound of a familiar voice beyond.

"Is there some trouble here?" Lord Gavril strode into the room, Zan following behind him carrying a tray with a dark bottle and a single empty glass balanced atop it. Even without seeing it or smelling it, Corwin sensed the nenath inside, his throat suddenly parched and aching.

"We are here for the record, Lord Gavril," the woman said, "but Prince Corwin doesn't wish to let us in."

"I see." Gavril peered at Corwin, his eyes seeming to see right through him. "Sadly, you're wasting your time checking the sheets this morning."

The woman appeared aghast at the thought, and she eyed Corwin with a sideways look, as if she'd never seen the like of his particular species before. "But my lord, the Godking will insist on seeing proof."

"Very well, then. Go in and do what needs to be done." Gavril waved at the woman and the clerk, and helpless to stop it, Corwin stepped aside, giving them entry. Eravis had been right to call him foolish—he should've known this would happen. The marriage wouldn't be considered official until it had been consummated. Which meant he still had time to escape it altogether—if he could just find a way free.

Lord Gavril and Zan stepped into the room, the page crossing the floor to the trestle table by the divan, where he set down the nenath bottle and glass. Corwin pulled his eyes away, desperate for something to distract him from the need to drink.

Patient as ever, Gavril waited, hands clasped in front of him. The seconds felt like hours as Corwin held his ground, arms fixed at his sides, a defiant glare on his face. The woman and clerk returned from the bedchamber a moment later, the former carrying the sheets balled up in her arms.

"You were right, my lord," she said, addressing Gavril. "The Godking won't be pleased." She turned a quick, scathing look on Corwin. She'd recognized his species after all and found him wanting.

"No, but he won't be surprised either." Gavril offered the woman an encouraging smile. "There is no need to worry. He will not vent his wrath on you."

The woman bowed, then she and the clerk exited the room.

Gavril turned to Zan. "Please see to his highness's clothes. The Godking requests his presence in the war council."

*War council?* Corwin opened his mouth to demand an explanation, then closed it again as the thirst for nenath intensified. Already he felt a quake in his belly. If he didn't drink it soon, he would be sick. *You must resist*, he told himself.

With excruciating effort, he followed Zan into the bedchambers and allowed the boy to assist in dressing him. By the end, he needed the help as violent trembles coursed through his body.

"Just drink the nenath already, your highness," Zan whispered, casting a worried look toward the living quarters where Gavril waited. "There's no point fighting it. There's magic in the nenath, and you can't beat that."

Corwin looked at the boy, hating him, hating everything. "You're wrong," he said through clenched teeth. He knew more about magic than this boy ever could. It could be fought. It could be stopped. Somehow, someway. Like how he'd stopped the Nameless One, a man with more magic than all the magists and wilders combined. He just needed to find a way, to find some help.

He needed to find Bonner.

But first he would need a clear head and some marginal control over his own body. He grasped Zan's shoulder. "Fetch me a glass."

With a quick nod, the boy turned and rushed off to retrieve the nenath. As always, the shame burned through Corwin when he drank it, mixed with the sweet release the poison gave him from his suffering. It had only been a scant few minutes, yet it felt like eternity. At least he no longer had to listen to Gavril's Tenets. They were embedded so deeply in his conscious there was no need to repeat them, it seemed.

All too soon though, Corwin was fit again, and returned to find Gavril wearing a smug smile.

"Don't look so gloomy, your highness. It's not every day one arises from the dead," Gavril said.

Corwin arched an eyebrow, tensing. "What do you mean?"

"Now that your marriage ceremony has taken place, the

Godking saw no reason not to announce it to the rest of the world. If I'm not mistaken, the newspapers in Rime will have the story soon. And your brother as well."

Inhaling slowly, Corwin strove to keep his temper in check. He'd known it was coming, of course, that there was no way Magnar would keep it secret, but still, he dreaded what the people of Rime would think. What Kate would think. *I love you, Kate*, he thought. *I will never betray you.* How he wished she could hear him now.

"Well, congrats to me then," Corwin replied at last, teeth gritted to hold back his tumultuous emotions.

Gavril's smile widened, then he turned and headed through the door, beckoning to Corwin like he was a dog needing to be brought to heel. Corwin followed Gavril down to an antechamber off the throne room where the so-called war council waited.

Magnar was there, of course, standing at the head of a sand table with Mazen and Eryx to his right and left. At a quick glance, Corwin recognized the map that had been constructed across the sand table's pliable surface—he'd know the cities and structures of Rime anywhere. The image on the table depicted everything from the eastern cliffs of Thornewall on the shore of the Penlaurel River to the Ash Mountains that flanked Farhold in the west. The borders of Seva were shown as well, the area currently filled with models representing warships and the troops they would carry. A chill shot through Corwin at the sight of it. He swept his gaze over the others present, recognizing many of them as various councilors to the king, although he didn't know any of their names. He was just glad to see that the woman and clerk from this morning weren't present. They must've delivered the record—or lack thereof—and been dismissed.

But then all thoughts of his unwanted marriage fled his mind as he spotted the man standing in the far corner of the room, his hands clasped behind his back and his eyes fixed straight ahead. As before, Bonner was barely recognizable, his body changed by the rigors he'd faced in the Spectacles and as a prisoner in the Mistfold. Gone was the gentle roundness of his face, replaced with hard planes and angles. Although he'd always been big, thanks in part to hours spent wielding a blacksmith's hammer, he'd never been so lean, the veins and striations of those muscles rigidly pronounced. Unlike during the Spectacle, he wore the garb of a Sevan soldier, a boiled-leather breastplate bearing the red bull across its front.

Corwin stared at his old friend, willing him to turn and look, to acknowledge him in some way. Bonner did not. He might as well have been a statue for all the attention he paid. Doubt began to beat a steady tattoo in Corwin's head. Perhaps his mind had been bent by the same magic Gavril had been working on Corwin, and the ally he'd hoped for was nothing more than a dream. Why else would Magnar have him here? At this war council?

That question was soon answered as the meeting began. One of the councilors at the table, a man wearing the uniform and insignia of a military general, continued to outline a strategy for the invasion of Rime.

"Once the warships have breached the harbor of Penlocke," the man said, "the Godspear will lead the wilders in the assault against the city itself, supported by our own infantrymen. With the wilders' powers and our army's numbers, it should be easy to take Penlocke and to hold it. Lord Gavril's magists will ensure we are safe from the nightdrakes this time and any other tricks the Mage League attempts."

*This time.* Corwin couldn't forget that Seva had invaded once before, back when Magnar had been a young man. That assault had failed quickly, with the Sevan forces having no way to defend against the nightdrakes. A problem that Gavril had resolved, it seemed.

"Once we have Penlocke," the general continued, "we will march to Norgard, High Prince Corwin riding with us, of course." He indicated Corwin with a casual wave. "But I'm afraid taking the capital won't be as simple. They will no doubt have received warning and will be prepared to meet us."

Magnar nodded, his gaze fixed on the sand table where someone had taken the care to paint the wall representing Norgard white. He raised his eyes slowly and fixed them on Corwin. "What can you tell us, my son, about how your brother will respond to our attack?"

Corwin gaped. "You don't truly expect me to answer that?"

A slow, snakelike smile spread across the Godking's face. "Why, yes, I do." He motioned to his left where Gavril stood, apart from the others, as if he were somehow less important than the rest.

Hatred boiled up in Corwin's gut as he felt Gavril invade his mind, the touch of his magic like an unwelcome caress, an assault on his very being. *Tell him,* Gavril insisted. *Tell him all.*

Corwin tried to resist. Sweat beaded his forehead, nausea cramped his belly, and his head pounded from the effort. He thought about Signe and how, once, she'd been able to lie to Kate when Kate had been forced to use her sway on her at Rendborne's bidding. He tried to do the same, to focus on Kate and Signe and everyone else he knew and loved who would be caught in the cross-fire when Seva attacked Rime.

But he failed. With a deep and shuddering breath, the truth came spilling out of him. He told them everything, and more. How large the cavalry would likely be, how many swords and guns and spears. He even made guesses based on what he'd heard about the Wilder War and its effect on Rime. He told them where Edwin would be stationed during the battle and the best way to get to him. *To kill him.* So many of the secrets the city architects had built into its defenses in case of invasion, he betrayed. By the end of it, he felt hollowed out, the very marrow in his bones drained by Gavril's sway, by his part in this betrayal. At last, Corwin fell silent, eyes downcast and burning as he held back tears.

"Is that the last of it?" Magnar asked.

"Yes, your majesty," Gavril replied.

"Very well. Is this enough to move forward with the invasion, General Ramir?" At the man's nod, the Godking returned his gaze to Gavril. "How soon until the wilders are ready?"

Gavril seemed to consider the question before answering. "Five weeks should be enough to ensure the final group is fully compli-ant. The shortage in nenir has slowed things down considerably. Six would be better."

"Very well." Magnar's gaze flicked to Corwin. "That should give us plenty of time to settle matters here."

A smug smile rose across Gavril's face. "Indeed it will."

At the sound of amusement in the man's voice—his spoken voice, so much like that which Corwin felt in his head every day—rage exploded inside of Corwin, driving out all thought and reason. With a guttural cry, he leaped toward Gavril, intent on ripping his throat out. Before Gavril could react, Corwin raked his nails down one side of the magist's face, leaving behind two bleeding gashes before his fingers closed around his throat and started to squeeze.

"I will kill you, you poisonous, evil—"

Heavy hands grabbed Corwin by the shoulders and jerked him back. He stumbled, feet catching on each other, and crashed to the floor. Blinking back the starbursts crossing his vision, Corwin saw Bonner standing over him, eyes hooded in a glare. He put a rough boot on Corwin's chest.

"Lord Gavril is not to be harmed," Bonner said in a voice Corwin recognized and yet didn't. It was so cold, so hard, like steel, as if someone else was wearing Bonner's skin.

"Bonner, what are you—"

"You may release him," Lord Gavril said from somewhere Corwin couldn't see, not with this giant of a man above of him. "He won't try that again." As Gavril spoke, Corwin felt the command in his mind, the order to do no further harm.

"Are you sure, Lord Gavril?" Bonner said, not moving his gaze off Corwin.

"Quite sure."

Bonner nodded once, then stepped back, but he kept his gaze fixed on Corwin, his muscles flexed as if braced for another attack. Corwin slowly climbed to his feet, any satisfaction he felt at seeing the wounds of Gavril's face smothered by the despair pressing down on him. Bonner was Gavril's man through and through.

*Soon I will be as well.* He'd known men like Gavril before. He was the kind never satisfied by mere obedience in a dog or horse or some other pet, but who demanded a frenzied sort of loyalty and admiration. Such men would give their dogs a bone only to yank it away and beat them with it, taking as much pleasure in the cruelty of it as in the success of utter domination.

Corwin walked back to his place at the table, and the meeting resumed, the general and other councilors digesting all the information Corwin had given them. He listened so that he might know their plans in the event he could escape, but he found it difficult to concentrate, his heart heavy in his chest. All the while, he felt Bonner's eyes on him. But he refused to look at the man, refused to torture himself with the pain of dashed hopes.

When the meeting ended, Bonner strode over to Corwin and grabbed his chin, forcibly lifting his head. "Best not forget your order to leave Lord Gavril alone," he said, his voice a low, guttural growl.

Corwin tried to pull away but couldn't. Bonner was too strong. Still, he refused to respond to the threat. Bonner was not Gavril; he couldn't command Corwin's obedience so easily. Bonner didn't care though, and a moment later, he let go of Corwin's chin. But just as he did his expression changed—it softened, eyes wide with recognition and intent. Then Bonner's lips formed two soundless words.

*Stay strong.*

A small smile crossed Bonner's face and vanished so quickly Corwin might've imagined it. But it didn't matter. The message had been received. Hope rekindled inside Corwin, a brightly glowing flame that even a monster like Gavril couldn't put out.

CORWIN IS ALIVE.

But no, he couldn't be. Kate had seen him fall, seen him buried beneath rubble so heavy no one could've survived it. And yet . . .

She pulled the paper out of the woman's hands, her gaze drawn to the sketch occupying the center of the page. It showed Corwin standing next to a young woman, one with hair hanging loose nearly to the ground, a thin crown upon her head. Corwin wore a crown too, and he was richly dressed in clothes of a foreign cut, same as the woman next to him. Kate didn't recognize her, and it took her shock-drenched brain several terrible seconds to make sense of the words typed just below the sketch.

*Prince Corwin and his new bride, Princess Eravis of Seva.*

Kate would've laughed at the absurdity of it all, if the news that Corwin may still be alive hadn't already slashed her to the heart and left her bleeding.

"Excuse me," the woman said, tapping her foot. "I paid for that paper, so you best give it back now."

"Let me see it." Signe came up next to Kate, both of them ignoring the woman.

"I said give it back."

"And I said *go away*," Kate snapped, and without thinking, she invoked her sway. A blank expression rose to the woman's face. Then she turned and walked off without a word.

Signe glared at Kate. "That wasn't necessary. We aren't thieves."

"How could anyone spread such a lie as this?" Kate pointed at the picture. "He can't be alive . . . can he?" She hated the terrible desperation she heard in her voice, childlike and weak.

Signe pulled the paper closer to her, getting a better look at the sketch. Kate didn't recognize the newspaper. It wasn't the *Royal Gazette* as she'd first thought but something called the *Rime Review*.

"It's strange," Signe said after a turn. "This looks exactly like him, and yet . . ."

"He's so *thin*," Kate said, gleaning Signe's thought and seeing the same when she examined the sketch more closely. "And older." More than a year it had been since he fell.

Was it possible?

No, she refused to believe it. Not on the basis of some sketch in a newspaper. She needed proof. She couldn't risk the devastation of learning it wasn't true. That would be like losing him all over again. Belatedly, Kate realized she was rubbing the top of her shoulder, the flame tattoo hidden beneath the long-sleeved tunic she wore. She forced her hand down to her side.

"Can we go now?" Harue said, weariness weighing down her voice. Although she wasn't wearing a disguise like Signe and Kate, she might as well have been. Deep, dark bruises rimmed her eyes, her face wan from the strain of working so much magic on the road without rest. She needed food, a good night's sleep, and several days of not using her powers.

With a deep breath, Kate resumed their trek down the street toward the Marin District, an area just to the east of Mirror Castle that boasted several respectable inns, the kind that drew new folks to the city looking to rent a room until they could secure permanent residences. The plan was for Tira and Signe to watch the comings and goings at the castle in case Dal ever emerged, while Kate searched for him inside the castle itself. To do that, she needed to secure a position as a servant, giving her easy access to Dal—and anyone else she might want to drop in on. In her experience, servants could come and go without notice.

It was a good plan, solid, and yet Kate couldn't think about any of it as she walked, her thoughts consumed by the *Rime Review*. She knew that Rimish law prohibited papers from consciously publishing falsehoods with harmful intent, but the punishment for doing so had never been severe. More than a few of the papers were known to take great liberties with the truth, often bending it in order to sell more copies. And speculating that Corwin still lived would sell hundreds, if not thousands. This truth seemed to anchor her, loosing the shock that had made her feel so light-headed.

Their path took them past the main gate to the castle, the portcullis drawn as usual during the day and with no current threat to the city. Guards in the blue and silver of Norgard marched slowly along the ramparts above, keeping watch on the street below. As they passed, Kate fought the urge to dart through the gate and into the castle. With her sway, she could reach Edwin easily. If anyone knew the truth behind the claims about Corwin, surely it would be him. But she couldn't risk it. Not with all the lives she would put in jeopardy if caught. Caution, not haste, would be her watchword.

They arrived in the Marin District a short while later, and Tira checked them into an inn called the Blue Haven. It was small, as were the two adjacent rooms they'd been given. Wen, Harue, and Harue's books were sharing one room, while Tira, Signe, and Kate were crammed into another—the distribution about equal.

Sighing as she sat down on one of the narrow beds, Kate said, "It feels like old times, doesn't it, Sig? Our room at the Crook and Cup was nearly this size." She smiled, the memory not exactly fond, but not painful at least, not like the others swirling in her head. Norgard had a different feel and energy than any other place in the world. The air was sweeter here, the colors more vibrant and true—all of it reminding her of what used to be, and what might have been.

Signe didn't reply, and Kate looked behind her to see her friend standing in front of the small window, gaze pointed down at the street below. "Sig?" Kate said. "Did you hear me?"

"What?" Signe turned around, a desperate look in her eyes again. She slowly nodded. "Yes, the Crook and Cup. It was small and smelly. This place is a paradise by comparison."

"That might be stretching things," Kate replied, taking a deep breath to shake off the nostalgia. Then she quickly set about unpacking. Once done, she changed into clean clothes and washed the grime of the road off her face. If she hoped to secure a servant's position in the castle, she needed to look the part. To that end, the dress she donned was a fine cut and quality, the sort of outfit a servant of some experience would be able to afford. The dress felt strange and unnatural after years of wearing only breeches, especially the way the moonbelt rested beneath it. In breeches, the belt was held down so close she barely noticed she was wearing it. In a skirt, it moved about, reminding her of its presence with every step. She would've preferred hiring on as a stable hand instead, but the job would hardly give her access to the parts of the castle she needed.

According to the references Harue had forged for her, Kate had recently been handmaid to Countess Irons of Carden, an elderly woman with a reputation for abusing her servants. Kate had actually met the woman once, back when her father was still alive. Her mother had been courting a friendship with the countess, trying to improve her connections at court. In addition to being difficult to check—it would take weeks to get an audience with the countess, and the palace butler would likely not bother—the reference would hopefully garner sympathy and understanding from the person in charge of hiring at Mirror Castle.

"I'll be back before nightfall," Kate said, turning to face Tira.

With a glint of amusement in her eyes, Tira said, "Be careful, and make sure you don't trip over that hem."

Kate made a face. "Don't make fun or we'll have you wear the skirt next time."

Tira's expression turned indignant. "Only way I'll be wearing a skirt is if I'm a corpse. And even then, I doubt my ghost will stand for it."

Kate turned to the door. "Oh, and make sure Harue stays out of trouble. Absolutely no explosions of any kind."

Closing the door behind her, Kate headed down the stairs and outside. Once on the street, she glanced up at their window to see Signe still standing there, her stranger's face even more unfamiliar from this distance. Kate gave her a small wave, then hurried down the street, checking with one hand that the little slip of paper she'd hidden in her pocket while unpacking remained in there.

She waited until she'd rounded the corner out of view of the Blue Haven before pulling the paper out. It was a torn section of the *Rime Review*, the top of the paper where their address was printed. Eighteen Norrell Square. Not far from here, and only a little out of the way back to the castle. With her sway at the ready to help her, it shouldn't take too long to get the information she wanted—the source for the story on Corwin.

A short time later, she rounded the corner from Childress Road onto Norrell. The square was the largest in the city and served as a center of commerce, populated by various industries as well as inns and taverns. The wealth of the area, evident in the precise angles of every rooftop and corner and the unblemished brilliance of fresh paint, told Kate that the *Rime Review* must be doing quite well for itself. *Spreading its lies.*

*Or not . . .*

Swallowing, Kate scanned the building fronts, looking for the newspaper's sign atop one of the shops. She spotted it across the way but froze as she stepped out onto the street, a commotion in the distance drawing her gaze. A great swell of people filled the cross street to Norrell, the sound of their voices a low rumble. She didn't sense violence or even trouble brewing, just a frenzied excitement, like a stifled shout waiting to be expelled.

After a moment she spotted the source of the disturbance— High King Edwin himself, riding this way. He sat atop a tall horse of impossible coloring. It was the uror sign—a horse marked by the goddess herself, one half of it inky black and the other white as salt. The sight of it brought an ache to Kate's throat, and she swallowed it back, Corwin's face swimming before her mind's eye. The horse should've been his.

The people in the street were pressing in toward the king, running their hands along the horse's sides or touching the heel of Edwin's boots, if they dared. For his part, Edwin was smiling down at them, bestowing kind words along the way. He looked notably different from the last time Kate had seen him—older and harder, the soft roundness of boyhood stripped away to reveal the man beneath. More than anything, he resembled the Corwin she'd seen in the newspaper picture, and she guessed the illustrator must've used Edwin's countenance as the inspiration for Corwin as he would look now, if indeed he still lived.

A woman with a golden circlet upon her brow rode beside Edwin, sitting sidesaddle atop a chestnut palfrey, the horse smaller than the uror sign by nearly a hand. Unlike her husband, Queen Sabine of Kilbarrow barely glanced at the people, her expression aloof, like a beautiful statue. Flanking the king and queen were a cadre of armed guards, all afoot and keeping a careful watch on the crowd.

For a moment, Kate felt the urge to hide. Then she remembered the disguise, and touching a finger to the ring in her ear, she held her ground, eyes fixed on the king and queen.

The crowd was growing bolder, shouting questions at Edwin.

"Is the news true, your majesty?"

"Is Prince Corwin alive?"

"Will you rescue him?"

Waving the questions away, Edwin rode toward the statue occupying the center of the square. It depicted Rowan, the first king of Norgard, sitting astride a warhorse with Summoner, the sword of Rimish legend, held above his head in one hand. Dismounting from the uror horse, Edwin handed the reins to one of the guards, then climbed atop the edge of the statue and raised his hands toward the crowd below, beckoning them to silence.

"Good people of Norgard, and of Rime," Edwin began in a sonorous voice, the voice of a king. "It was only days ago a rumor reached our shores that our brother is alive, living in Seva, and married to the Godking's daughter. Like you, this news took us greatly by surprise." Edwin paused, allowing the crowd a moment to react.

Sensing there was more, and unwilling to wait, Kate reached out to Edwin with her magic. She would never have a better chance to glean his thoughts. Not only could she learn everything he knew about Corwin, but she could find out about Dal as well, determine if he was currently safe, and if the threat against him came at Edwin's order or not. But the moment she tried, she felt something blocking her way, like an invisible wall. It was a sensation she'd experienced only once before, and instinctively she raised a hand to touch the vial of blood hidden beneath her tunic. When Isla Vikas had worn the necklace, the magic in the blood had blocked Kate's sway, in much the same way as it was being blocked now.

The realization sent a jolt of fear through her. She couldn't see such a necklace around Edwin's neck, but it could be hidden beneath his tunic. Where would he have gotten it? The spell could only be worked using the blood of someone born with sway, a gift so rare even Rendborne had coveted it. *Rendborne*. Was the Nameless

One here, in Norgard? No, she quickly decided. At least not as himself. Edwin and the rest of the high council had known about Rendborne's treachery and would've recognized his face. Unless he had a new one, Kate considered, again remembering the magestone earring she wore. The magic to disguise one's face was outlawed by the Mage League, but Rendborne wouldn't care about that any more than Harue did.

With frustration building inside her like steam in a lidded pot, Kate withdrew her magic. There would be no answers found here.

"Since that time," Edwin continued, "we have been working to uncover the truth. Our sources have confirmed that while there was indeed a Sevan ceremonial wedding for the daughter of the Godking and our brother, the man they claimed to be Corwin is nothing but an imposter. We don't yet know the reason for the deception, but I can assure you we will uncover it. For now, you must not give these rumors any credence. I, Edwin, am the only living heir of House Tormane and king of Norgard and of Rime, chosen by holy uror to rule." At this, Edwin raised his right hand, palm out so that his uror mark was visible, even from this distance.

Kate stared into Edwin's eyes, her heart sinking inside her chest at the truth she sensed in his words. Even without her magic, she felt it. And didn't this explanation make more sense? That the Godking would fake the alliance? The whole world knew of Rime's troubles, the war of magist against wilder. By pretending to have found Corwin and spreading word of his union to the Sevan princess, the Godking would create further unrest in a kingdom already in turmoil.

The crowd applauded, solemn but determined, at Edwin's

declaration, and once the noise died down, he said with hands clasped before him, "Now, we will take this truth to the publishers of the *Rime Review*, so that they will have an opportunity to retract this misinformation. May Noralah bestow her blessing upon you all."

With that, Edwin stepped off the statue and walked toward the newspaper office's front entrance. Kate could see figures standing behind the large glass window. Queen Sabine had also dismounted and now joined her husband outside the door, offering her hand for him to hold. He took it with a warm smile that made Kate's insides burn. There was no justice in the world when a man like Edwin possessed such happiness and prosperity while a man like Corwin had perished.

With the king no longer visible for ogling, the crowd began to disperse. Kate knew she should leave as well. She had business at the castle and Dal to worry about. But the uror horse was only a few yards away, standing with its eyes closed and head hung low, one back foot resting. Drawn to it by some invisible force, either magic or memory, Kate touched it with her sway.

Immediately, she sensed the horse's mind. Only, what she felt there was nothing like what she remembered the last time she had touched the uror horse in this way. Before, she had sensed the creature's great power and presence, hiding behind an impenetrable veil. Skittish and unknowable, it had seemed to flee from her touch. This time she felt a normal horse, no different from Nightbringer or any other.

What was going on? But even as she asked the question, the answer came to her.

This wasn't the uror horse at all.

Kate withdrew her magic, the world spinning about her as she puzzled out the implications. The horse wore a bridle bedecked with sapphires on both sides where the brow band met the cheek pieces. Either one of them could be a magestone, one designed to transform an ordinary horse into the uror sign. Even when it wasn't bridled, a halter could easily hold the same enchantment, hiding the truth from prying eyes.

But why would Edwin want to fake the uror sign? Corwin had once told her that the chosen king and the uror sign shared a special, magical bond. Indeed, Kate remembered the previous uror sign, the wolf called Murr, and how the animal had followed Corwin's father about like his very shadow. If Edwin were truly king, chosen by the uror, then his relationship with the uror horse would be undeniable, and he'd have no use for such a ruse. That was how it worked—the uror sign remained wild and untamable, until the uror completed and the bond was formed.

There was only one reason she could see why Edwin would ride about Norgard on an imposter like this: because he couldn't ride the real one.

Which meant Corwin was indeed alive, somewhere, after all.

IN THE WEEKS THAT FOLLOWED the disastrous war council meeting, Corwin's life fell into an uneventful pattern. He spent most of his days in the royal library, wandering through the stacks of books and scrolls that occupied nearly every empty space of the four-story building, one nearly large enough to be called a castle. Or a fortress, perhaps.

Despite his aversion to all things Sevan, he liked the library, the time he spent there giving him a small measure of freedom. It was the one place where his guards kept their distance. Among the books, they didn't have to worry about him talking to anyone he shouldn't or trying to fashion a weapon or steal one. In there, the only weapon was knowledge, but it wasn't one his captors feared much. And why should they? With Gavril's Tenets planted so firmly in his mind, he wouldn't be able to wield any weapons against them, words or otherwise.

His nights he spent sleeping on the divan and trying to keep as much distance between himself and Eravis as possible. It proved more difficult than he anticipated, although not because she did anything untoward. After that first night, she never again attempted to disrobe in front of him or even to bathe with the door open. But she was still there, sharing the same space, breathing the same air, and reminding him that the two of them had been forced into this unwanted marriage. Her presence also served to remind him of just how alone he was here. In the mines he'd at least had the other prisoners to talk to, their lots enough like his own to make them kinsmen of a sort. In the Sun Palace, everyone was an enemy. *Including Eravis*, he constantly reminded himself.

One evening, he entered their quarters to find her sitting at the table in the living area, her chin cupped in her hand and her eyes fixed on the playing cards spread out before her. Curiosity borne of isolation and idleness peaked inside him at the sight of the game, but he held it back, going into the bedchambers instead to bathe and change into his sleeping clothes.

When he returned, she was in much the same pose as before, only this time she glanced up at his entrance, her eyes finding his. Before he could stop himself, he asked, "What are you playing?"

"The Queen's Tower, and I've almost won." She made it sound as if this were quite the feat and returned her attention to the game, her lower lip caught between her teeth in concentration.

"Never heard of it." Corwin stepped nearer to the table, his gaze taking in the cards. They were different from those in Rime. Although there were face cards and numbered cards like he was used to, the suits were comprised of lions, wolves, eagles, and turtles. Still, he recognized a little of the pattern she'd placed them in. "But it looks a bit like a game we have in Rime called Solo."

She looked up again. "Would you like to play?"

"I wouldn't know how."

"It doesn't have to be Queen's Tower," Eravis replied, her expression suddenly shy. "I can teach you something else, or perhaps . . . perhaps you can show me a Rimish game." Bending toward the table, she retrieved a second deck of cards from the drawer.

A pleasant warmth spread through Corwin as he picked up the new deck and examined the familiar suits of candles, jars, flutes, and stones. It was a full Rimish deck, complete with the shade cards. He ran his finger over one of the shades, a figure in a black cloak wearing a horned crown, while a dozen memories of old games won and lost slid through his mind.

"It must be hard," Eravis said, drawing him out of his reverie. "To be away from your homeland. I've never even been out of Luxana before, much less Seva."

Corwin drew a breath, pushing the memories back, and looked down at Eravis. He knew he should walk away now, but the allure of an hour spent doing something familiar, something from home, was too much to resist. Sitting down across from her, he said, "Shall I teach you how to play Peril?"

The princess raised her eyebrows in surprise, then a look of delight lit up her features. "Please do. It's one of Eryx's favorite games, but he refuses to show it to me."

Corwin shuffled the deck, doing it with a flair that made the cards seem to dance in his hands. "Why not?"

She rolled her eyes. "Because betting games are not fit for high-born ladies."

Despite himself, Corwin was reminded of Kate by her annoyance, and the way she used to bemoan not being allowed to learn the fighting arts alongside the boys. Instead she had to sneak out late at night and learn what she could on her own—and from him.

Ignoring the old familiar ache in his chest, he returned his focus to the cards, explaining the rules to Eravis. She listened intently, only asking a few questions for clarification. Then they began the game. With no coins for betting, they used dried helian seeds and charis nuts, both foods native to Seva. There were always bowls of them set about the room. Corwin liked the charis nuts best and so chose them as his chips. He just had to discipline himself not to eat them all, lest he go broke.

Eravis proved a quick study, and before long they were playing the game in earnest, Corwin no longer needing to give her allowances for inexperience. He won the next two rounds, but she took the third.

With a wide grin on her lips, an expression that could only be described as radiant, Eravis leaned back in her chair and said, "I have bested you at last."

"One victory does not win the war." Corwin regretted his words at once and raised his wine glass to his lips, to hide his scowl at the reminder that every day brought them closer to war with Rime— and there was nothing he could do about it. He'd asked to visit the Mistfold only to be given an emphatic no. He didn't dare ask again for fear of arousing suspicions. He had no idea what Bonner was up to, but he trusted him implicitly and would not risk betraying him.

Glancing away from his dark expression, Eravis took her own drink. Then, wiping her mouth with the back of her hand, she said, "My brother tells me that in Rime cards are played using real magic."

Corwin smiled, grateful for neutral ground. He set aside his wine glass and picked up the queen of candles. "Cards there are imbued with magist spells, and ordinary people like you or me can invoke them with a spoken word."

"I would hardly call us ordinary."

Corwin supposed she had a point. To most people, a prince and princess would be seen as extraordinary. Only his time spent in the mines and as a Shieldhawk before that had taught him better. He was no different from any other man. He bled and wept and suffered and loved. His mistakes were as frequent as his triumphs, if not more so. The titles bestowed on a small few were mere luck and pretense, not inalienable proof of something greater inside the individual.

"But what does the magic do?" Eravis leaned forward as if eager to see it done.

"Not all that much. The candle on this card will glow as if truly lit." He traced a finger down the candlestick and around the halo over the woman's head. Then he picked up the seven of jars. "These will glisten as if wet, and all the suits will have a distinctive smell, too. And once these spells are invoked, it prevents cheating. A played card stays played, cannot be replaced or swapped out with sleight of hand."

Eravis made a face. "Is that all? Why, it's nothing more than parlor tricks."

"There are others who'd say differently, especially in a high-stakes game," Corwin said, feeling the urge to smile at her indignant tone. "Besides, those are the spells only on the most common cards. Other sets possess more powerful ones."

"Like the Death Bones?"

Corwin frowned. "You know the game?" If Peril was considered unladylike, that one would be downright scandalous.

"Only a little. Eryx has mentioned it once or twice, but he refused to go into detail. When it comes to magic, he's like my father—both secretive and covetous." She made a face again, but this time Corwin felt no urge to smile. Instead, a sudden tension spread through his body at the turn in the subject, the opening it provided.

"Is that so?" he said, trying to keep his voice neutral. "And is that why your father plans to invade Rime? For its magic?"

Eravis cut her eyes to him, her gaze suddenly sharp. Then she visibly relaxed. *She's clever*, Corwin thought, not for the first time. *Far too clever.* The vapid-princess persona she played so often in public was an act and nothing more. Despite his better judgment, she intrigued him.

"Why else?" Eravis pulled a lock of her long hair over her shoulder to idly run her fingers through it. "Seva has enough wealth on its own not to need that of Rime. My father is no fool. He doesn't conquer merely for the joy of conquering, but to get what he needs. What Seva needs."

"Does he hope to restore magic to Seva by stealing it from Rime, then?" The knowledge that there had once indeed been magic in Seva had come as a shock to Corwin when he'd stumbled across an entire section in the library devoted to the subject. He'd always been told magic only existed in Rime, but it seemed he was wrong. Once it had existed everywhere. There were just too many chronicles stating otherwise for him not to believe it. And he'd seen the Mistfold as well and the way it had restored Kate's magic the moment she set foot in the pit. Magic was here already, some of it at least.

Eravis hesitated before answering, as if afraid of saying too much, her gaze fixed on her silken strands. "I believe that is the idea, yes."

Corwin leaned back, his arms stretched toward the table. He was suddenly grateful for the isolation that had driven him to spend so much time reading of late. "It's ironic, considering it was his very ancestor who destroyed all the magic in Seva in the first place."

"What are you talking about?" Eravis pinned him with a cool stare.

"The Ascension, I believe it was called. When your ancestor, Fanen, slew the gods of Seva and started the rule of the Godking." He'd come across the story just this morning, in an old book called *The Rise and Fall of Magic*. "Surely you know the story. It's said that when Fanen killed the gods, the 'magic of Seva dried up like water and drained away as if like blood from the body.'" The last was a direct quote, one that had stuck in his mind for no particular reason he could fathom, other than the gruesomeness of it.

"Tell me, Prince Corwin, are all people from Rime affected with this strange need to read so much?"

Corwin arched an eyebrow, offended on multiple levels, not the least of which was the implication that reading lacked value. "I sincerely hope you're not likening me to Lord Gavril." He seemed the only Rimish person Eravis could've possibly been exposed to. There was no one else, save the wilders, but he doubted she made a habit of visiting the Mistfold. Even if she did, it seemed unlikely the wilders there had access to books.

"I would never," Eravis said, her voice quiet and her expression suddenly soft. While he regarded her, he caught her quick glance at the trestle table where the nenath waited, as always, for when the need came upon him.

Corwin swallowed, uncomfortable with the tension growing

between them, all the things they didn't talk about, like the stewardess coming each morning to collect the sheets for the record. Gathering his composure, he asked, "Who then, if not Gavril?"

Again, Eravis seemed to consider her response. "A man called Rendborne. He's visited several times over the years. But this last visit he spent nearly every waking hour in the library. It showed, too. The man was so pale he looked like death."

The name struck Corwin like a fist, and he sucked in a breath, struggling to keep his reaction to himself lest he frighten her into silence. Like him, Eravis too seemed aware that they were still enemies, despite this congenial interlude. "How long ago was this? When did Rendborne leave?"

"He departed some six months ago. Why, do you know him?"

Corwin considered how much to tell her. Judging by the casual way she spoke about Rendborne, he guessed she had no idea who he truly was, how important his involvement had been in laying the foundation for her father's quest to conquer Rime. He wondered how much of the truth he should tell her. Not all of it, he decided—especially not how Rendborne was Corwin's great-great-granduncle, a Tormane who had rebelled against the power of uror and been cast out. But perhaps something to open her eyes to the truth.

"A little," he said, clearing his throat. "Enough to know he is guilty of the worst treachery. That he is evil to his very core."

"Evil? Rendborne?" A disbelieving smile curled one side of Eravis's mouth. "Why, I've rarely met a more charming man."

Corwin nodded, understanding her reaction perfectly. He'd felt the same about Rendborne, trusting him, liking him, only to be rocked by the truth of what he was. "Rendborne is the reason your father has his wilder army, but he will regret trusting him in the end." Corwin had seen the hatred inside the Nameless One that day, when he'd used his uror mark to block the spell Rendborne had unleashed on him and Kate and their friends, magic designed to kill them all in a single blow. Rendborne had an uror mark as well, his faded with age, but still there, still powerful. It had linked them, however briefly, but long enough for Corwin to understand that Rendborne didn't care about Seva and the Godking's quest for magic.

All he wanted was to see Rime fall.

"Why do you say that?" Eravis asked, raising her glass for another drink.

Corwin told her how Rendborne had orchestrated the creation of the gold order, how he'd served as minister of trade to the high king for years before his machinations had been uncovered.

"That's some story," Eravis said when he finished. "One worthy of a place in the great library."

"You don't believe me?" Corwin drummed his fingers on the table, annoyed that he let himself trust her enough to share it with her, to hope that beneath the public persona she wore, the true Eravis might sympathize with the plight of the wilders imprisoned in the Mistfold. It seemed he'd imagined more behind her reaction to the death and carnage of the Spectacles than was truly there.

"Yes, I believe. He's just like my father. An ambitious man who will do whatever it takes to get what he wants. No matter who it might hurt." Her fingers had tightened around the glass, the knuckles showing white, and when she raised it to her lips, it shook slightly in her hand.

Pity swelled in Corwin's chest as he put himself in her position. He might not understand how she could play the game as well as she did—acting the part of the happy bride for all those watching eyes—but he could understand the feel of being a pawn in the Godking's game.

When she set the wineglass down once again, Corwin reached out and placed his hand atop hers. "I am not like your father or Rendborne. If I can, I will stop him from using us both."

Eravis jerked her hand away, scowling. "You understand nothing, Corwin Tormane. You are a hopeless fool if you think you can stand against Lord Gavril. Once the time has come he will—" She broke off, her gaze livid, although Corwin had a feeling her anger wasn't only directed at him.

"What time? What do you mean?"

Eravis stood abruptly, her chair rocking so hard it nearly toppled over. "It's . . . nothing. I misspoke. Thank you for your concern." She drew a deep breath, and Corwin watched as the true Eravis—one full of anger and resentment—slid away, the false princess taking her place. She smiled at him warmly, lips parted. Then coming around the table, she leaned down to him, her hands sliding over his shoulder and her long hair closing around him like curtains. The robe she wore slipped open at the movement to reveal the nightdress beneath, made from a fabric so sheer it might've been nothing. Her perfumed skin filled his nose, an assault on his senses that made his head spin.

Before he could stop her, her lips found his. She kissed him softly, the barest of caresses, more a promise than anything else. Then she pulled away from him. "I enjoyed our game. Perhaps we can play again tomorrow night. I look forward to everything else you have to teach me."

The air seemed to thicken with the innuendo in her words.

Corwin blinked, coming back to his senses, but she was already gone, retreating to the bedroom. He watched her go, worry swirling inside him. He thought he'd gotten the measure of her, but he couldn't have been more wrong. He didn't understand it. All he knew was that he needed to find a way out of here before it was too late.

But at least she had given him something to think about, to concentrate on. Rendborne had been here and now was gone. Back to Rime, Corwin guessed, which meant that the danger his loved ones faced back home was even greater than he imagined. *Loved ones.* Like his Kate. He must do whatever he could to protect her, to protect them all.

And finding out just what Rendborne had been searching for in the library was the place to start.

IT TOOK TWO DAYS FOR Kate to get hired on as a chambermaid. They were the longest two days of her life.

With the revelation that Corwin was still alive, every other matter seemed less pressing. All she wanted was to ride south to the harbor at Penlocke, board the first ship that would take her across the sea, and find Corwin. She didn't care what the *Rime Review* said about his supposed marriage. Corwin was being held against his will, forced to play whatever part the Godking was concocting for him and for Rime, with no one to help him, no one to trust.

And she'd left him there, all this time.

She tried to tell herself it wasn't her fault, but it didn't matter. Nothing assuaged the guilt, or lessened her sense of urgency. Still, in the end, Signe convinced her to remain in Norgard.

"Just until we've finished our mission," Signe said, grabbing Kate by the arm and forcing her to stop her pacing. She'd been doing it ever since she returned from Mirror Castle, where she'd spent nearly two hours waiting to talk to the housekeeper about the job, her impatience like a wild horse tethered against its will and fighting to be unleashed.

"Signe is right," Tira said from where she sat next to the door, idly eating an apple. She wiped the juice off her mouth with the back of her hand. "If we're going to Seva, we will want Dal with us."

"We can't bring him," Kate said, pulling free of Signe's grasp. "If he leaves Norgard without permission it will restart the war." She hated herself for saying it. She agreed with Tira; they would need Dal's help and more in order to rescue Corwin, but she hadn't sacrificed so much for the Rising to be the cause of their fall now. Her coming here to protect her friend had been a big enough gamble as it was, but Dal's absence couldn't be kept secret as easily as her presence in Norgard.

"We will go without him if we must—once it's certain he is safe," Signe said, arms crossed and feet planted.

Tira took another loud bite of her apple and through the crunching said, "Did you forget what happened last time we were in Seva, Kate? Your magic vanished with the very first sunrise away from these shores. How do you expect to march into the Sun Palace and whisk your true love away from under the Godking's nose without your sway?"

Kate clenched her fists at this unwelcome reminder. Even after that brief spell in the Mistfold when her magic had come back to her, it was gone again not long after they left Seva. And Tira was right—without her sway their small team stood little chance of rescuing Corwin. She shook her head. "My magic came back to me inside the Mistfold. There must be a reason why."

And she knew just the person to ask.

She arrived in Harue's shared room with Wen a few heartbeats later. To her complete lack of surprise, she found Harue with her nose buried in a book. At least she was lying down, taking her ease physically, if not mentally. A mind like hers never rested, Kate supposed. Harue didn't look up at her sudden entry.

"Mistress Harue," Wen said in her squeak of a voice. "Mistress Kate is here to see you."

Waving the girl off, Kate marched up to the bed, close enough even Harue wouldn't be able to ignore her. "Why did my magic vanish when I left Rime? And why did it start working again in the Mistfold?"

Harue blinked up at her, brow furrowed over her glasses. "I need more information if you expect a proper analysis."

Kate quickly explained the way her magic behaved during that trip over a year ago. For so long she had refused to talk about these events, but now, knowing Corwin was still alive, it was easy. And to her credit, Harue listened without distraction.

"There were everweeps in the pit, you say?" Harue asked once Kate finished her story.

"Yes," Kate said, her voice breathy with exasperation.

"Are you certain it wasn't crylilies? They're native to Seva and might be mistook for everweeps by someone in distress or—"

"They were everweeps, Harue." Kate motioned toward the window, where she could glimpse a patch of them growing at the foot of the alley across the way. The colorful plants grew everywhere in Rime—anywhere the sun fell. "I've lived here all my life. I would never mistake them. They're the reason why, aren't they?"

Harue didn't answer. Her gaze had turned inward, and her churning thoughts could almost be heard aloud. Then suddenly, her expression changed, wonder lighting up her face like a sunrise. "Do you know what this means?" Harue stood up, the book she'd been reading tumbling to the floor, forgotten.

Kate just stared, exasperated, as Harue failed to elaborate. The woman swung off the bed and toward the wardrobe, one currently so stuffed with books the doors wouldn't close, and started pulling volumes out one by one.

Sometime later, she found the book she was looking for and placed it on the bed. It looked new, the pages crisp and the binding not yet cracked. Harue opened it and began thumbing through the pages. Finally she stopped and leaned toward the book to read, her eyes sliding back and forth in a dizzying motion.

Kate waited as long as her patience would allow, before bursting out, "Well? What does it mean?"

Harue ignored her, reading the rest of the page. As she closed the book, that look of wonder crossed her face again. "Roderick's theory on the synthesis of magical energy and transference is right." She stared at Kate, her look expectant now.

"*What?*" Kate nearly screamed in frustration.

"Hiram Roderick," Wen said, stepping out of the corner where she'd been hovering. She pointed at the book. "Better known as Hiram the Heretic."

Drawing a deep breath, Kate let it out slowly, keeping her temper in check. The expression of anger or frustration, or practically every other human emotion, was wasted on Harue. "I don't know anything about this theory."

"It's simple, really." Harue opened the book once more. "Hiram believed that the magic of Rime—that is, the magic of wilders and magists—is somehow connected to the everweeps, as you said. He postulated it was a chemical process, where the everweeps release some kind of invisible substance into the air, and we in turn breathe it in, activating our magic. That's why it stops working at night.

The sun must play a part as well, since the flower blossoms close when it sets. He believed sunlight was the start of the process."

"I don't understand," Kate said, calmer now to have her suspicions confirmed. "What do you mean by a chemical process?"

Harue raked her hands through her tangle of hair, jarring her glasses askew. She righted them with an automatic gesture born of long habit. "It's a reaction, like when you set a pot of water to boiling. The everweeps—along with the sun—act like the heat. It sets the magic inside us to bubbling. Puts it into a usable state."

Kate ran her tongue along her teeth, thinking it over. "Are you saying all I need to ensure my sway will work in Seva is to bring along some everweeps?"

"Well, yes, but it won't be that simple. You'll need a fair amount of them, I would expect. And they must be kept alive and healthy. Everweeps won't grow in any soil except for Rime's."

Kate puzzled over this, remembering the vast amount of them growing inside the pit. No wonder it had felt like a homecoming when she first saw it. The idea that Magnar Fane and Rendborne had managed to transport all that soil in order to grow them in Seva was stunning. It also seemed to prove Harue's theory. Why go to all that trouble unless to ensure the wilders in the Godking's army could activate their powers? Soldiers needed to train, after all.

"But if it's a chemical process, as you say," Kate asked, "do you have to be breathing them in all the time in order to use your magic?"

Harue considered the question a moment, then gave a quick shake of her head. "Not all the time, no. But you would need some exposure daily."

"This could truly work then," Kate said, excitement building inside her and bringing her mind into sharp focus, body tense with anticipation.

"I wonder what else he was right about?" Harue picked up the book by Hiram the Heretic once more.

Kate resisted giving her a good shake, certain she would lose her to the distraction of the book if she wasn't careful. "Harue, do you think you can devise a way for me to get enough everweeps to Seva to keep my magic working?"

Harue cocked her head, mildly intrigued by the idea. "I'm hardly skilled at growing flowers, but I suppose I can read up on it." She returned her attention to the book, and Kate held back pressing her on the matter. That was the best she would get out of Harue, she knew. At least until she finished giving the book a thorough examination.

*But we've got time*, Kate told herself. Corwin was married, not dead. Even still, her chest swelled with dread, a desperate worry that it might already be too late.

The next two days passed with the slowness of a frozen lake thawing in spring, despite the activities involved in securing the maid's position. But now, at last, Kate had access to Mirror Castle, and soon to Dal.

Only she quickly realized that the wait wasn't over. She spent the first three days in training, following after one of the senior servants, Betty Shaw, who painstakingly explained every duty Kate would be required to perform. When Kate insisted she knew everything there was to know about this job already, Betty still refused to turn her loose inside the castle.

"Not until I'm certain you know your way around," Betty said, hands on hips and her expression stern. "This is a big place, and I don't want you using the excuse of getting lost to shirk your duties."

Kate chewed on the sides of her cheek to keep from replying, lest her annoyance give her away. She knew this castle better than anyone. She lived here for years and had spent hours wandering the corridors and disappearing down hidden passageways. She had half a mind to show Betty just how well she knew it, if only she could. She considered using her sway on Betty to let her go on her own, but feared what the other servants might say if they found out Kate had been given special treatment. Rumors spread too quickly for her to take that chance.

Still, it turned out not to be wasted time. Because she was in training, Betty made sure that Kate was familiar with all the rooms—both for the royals and for the guests. Which meant that Kate soon learned where Dal was staying: a small suite at the top of Nowen Tower, with Laurent in the suite across from him. She should've guessed. Nowen Tower was set apart from the rest of the living quarters, and often used to house unwanted guests, those likely to be troublesome or who were simply less important than others.

It was also a stroke of good luck. As the new maid, Kate's first assignment, when she was finally sent off on her own, was to clean the rooms in Nowen Tower. She started at the top, letting herself into Dal's room right away. She would've known it was his even if Betty hadn't told her the day before—his pet falcon, Lir, was in the room, resting on a perch inside her massive cage. Kate greeted the bird with her magic, glad to see she was alive and well. She probed her thoughts, learning what she could about Dal. There was nothing in Lir's memory to alarm her though.

Relieved, Kate set about her duties. As she finished, she slid a note beneath Dal's pillow, placing it in such a way that, according to Signe, he would be sure to find it. *Meet me here tomorrow at ten,* it read. She'd signed it with just her initials, hoping it would be enough. She would've liked to have him meet her and the others back at the Blue Haven, but she couldn't risk it. Dal was sure to be followed everywhere he went.

When she returned the next day, she stopped outside the door, using her magic to determine if Dal was alone. Then she pushed open the door, slid through, and closed it again. She spotted him next to the window, looking down at the city far below. He turned at her entry, frowning in confusion. Quickly, Kate pulled the magestone from her ear. The moment the spell broke, revealing her true face, a smile lit his features.

"Kate!" Dal rushed to greet her, wrapping his arms around her waist and hoisting her into the air. "Gods, I've missed you." He set her down again. "But what in the three hells are you doing here?"

She waved off his glare. "Shhhh, before someone hears you."

"What, up here?" Dal snorted, the old scars running down the side of his face from brow to chin turning the gesture into a grimace. "We're more likely to be overheard in the dungeons."

Kate supposed he had a point. There weren't even guards posted at his door. Instead, they were stationed at the bottom of the staircase, the only way out of the cramped tower.

"But what are you doing here?" Dal said, his voice more restrained than before.

Quickly, Kate told him everything that had happened: about the doll carved in his likeness, the fire, and their decision to leave Farhold despite Raith's orders.

"Signe is here, too?" Dal said, when Kate finished. There was a hitch in his voice, like a promise waiting to be spoken.

Kate nodded. "She's at the—a nearby inn." She corrected herself at the last moment, distrusting what Dal might attempt with the information. He could be as headstrong as Signe. "She desperately wants to see you, but we couldn't figure out a way to sneak her in." There was no way to disguise her limp, and as unfair as it was, Kate knew that Edwin's people would likely never hire someone with that kind of condition as a servant.

"Is she all right then?" Dal said, again with that hitch in his voice.

"She's fine, same as she's been, at least. But what do you make of the doll? The package had your handwriting on it, I'm certain."

Thinking it over, Dal scratched idly at his cheek, where he'd been attempting to grow a beard, it seemed—without much success. "I did send her a package a few weeks ago, but there was a wax rose inside, not a Dal doll." His confusion quickly turned to concern. "You shouldn't have let Signe come here, though, Kate. It's not safe."

"Like I could stop her. You know how she is. But what has you so worried?"

Dal glanced around the room, as if suddenly afraid someone

might be listening in. "The Hellgate. They've been *mining* it."

"I know. Raith told me before we left. He was concerned I might go there." She didn't need to add the part about searching for Rendborne. Dal would already know. "But what are they looking for?"

"Not more drakes this time, that much I know." Dal raked his hand through his hair. "It hasn't been easy getting information when I'm watched night and day."

"How have you been doing it then?"

A wry grin pranced across Dal's face. "My little rats."

"Excuse me?"

"Street kids, urchins. I pay them for information. You'd be surprised what they can find out when properly motivated."

Kate shook her head, dismayed, though not entirely surprised. "Where have you been getting the coin?"

He winked. "Gaming, of course."

"Gambling, you mean." Kate waved it off. It didn't matter to her where Dal was getting the money so long as he didn't get himself hurt or in trouble. "If not drakes, then what?"

The good humor fled his face. "I don't know. One of my rats said they're calling it Hellsteel."

"I've never heard of it." But it couldn't be good. Nothing good ever came from there.

"Me either. It sounds like some kind of special ore. But that's not even the most worrisome part." He paused, fixing a dark look on her. "The Furen Mag are here, overseeing the mining. And the Arch Mother, as they call her, well . . . I think she's Signe mother."

For a second, his words failed to make sense in Kate's mind. Although she loved Signe like a sister, her past was so shrouded in mystery that Kate had long ago decided her friend had sprung into being fully grown, rather than through any ordinary birth and childhood. "Why do you think that?"

"Well, she looks just like her, for one thing. For another, her real name is Synnove Leth."

*Synnove.* Kate remembered Signe's fear of the woman. What did it mean, her mother being here? She didn't know, but it seemed Raith's suspicions might've been correct, that the doll was a trap meant for Signe. For a second, panic threatened, but then Kate remembered that Signe was wearing a disguise, same as her. "I've got to warn her, but we need to talk about Corwin."

Dal scowled. "I've heard the ridiculous rumors."

"They're not rumors," Kate said, trying to keep her voice even. She told him about the false uror sign.

Shock lit across Dal's features, but before he could respond, a knock sounded on the door. "Dal, are you in there? We're due in the king's antechamber." It was Laurent, the other wilder ambassador. Kate didn't know him well, certainly not enough to trust him with these secrets. Quickly, she slid the magestone earring back in place while Dal let out a curse.

"Just a moment," he called, then in a lower voice said to Kate, "Meet me tonight at the Horned Crow. It's where I usually game, but not this evening. Instead I'll drink and make merry with the womenfolk." He winked again, for a moment appearing like his old mischievous self, but his voice shook as he added, "Bring Signe with you."

Kate nodded, frustrated by the short time they'd had and the lack of progress, but it would have to do for now. She would use the time in between to come up with a better way to talk, a safer way.

Once Dal left, she made the bed and finished her other chores, all the while her thoughts on the Hellgate and the Furen Mag. It was a welcome distraction from worrying over Corwin. She recalled all the sleeping quarters she'd seen with Betty. Not one of them had belonged to the sisterhood, which meant they weren't staying in the castle. She should've asked Dal if he knew where they could be, but it was too late. No matter, she would learn the truth soon enough. In the meantime, she needed to warn Signe.

But when Kate returned to the Blue Haven after the workday ended, Signe was nowhere to be found. No one had seen her go. No one knew where she went, not even Wen, who seemed to observe everything. Kate searched for her, using her magic, to no avail.

"She's probably fine," Tira said as they were forced to halt the search. With night approaching, they needed to meet Dal soon. "It's unlikely someone recognized her with the magestone disguise."

"Not unless she had a reason to take it out," Kate replied. She couldn't help but wonder if Signe had known her mother was in the city. If she had, maybe she had sought her out. *Curse this Seerah business*, Kate thought, her insides eaten up with worry for her friend.

"Signe is cunning. She can take care of herself."

"She's also reckless."

Tira laughed. "I think you two have that in common. But come on. Maybe she's with Dal even as we speak."

Kate clung to this hope as they made their way to the Horned Crow, but a quick scan of the place revealed no sign of Signe, disguised or otherwise. They found Dal, though, leaning against the far side of the bar in his usual place. He always picked a spot near the door in case he needed to make a quick escape.

Kate sidled up next to him and ordered a drink. It took all her effort to appear like an ordinary barroom patron here to relax when inside she felt like a bowstring pulled too taut. At least the place was packed, the air smelling of beer and bodies and vibrating with the roar of dozens of voices. "Has our foreign friend been here?" she said to Dal, afraid of mentioning Signe's name aloud.

He lowered his cup slowly, as nonchalant as ever. Except for the white of his knuckles. "No. I haven't seen her at all yet. What happened?"

"When I got back to the inn she was just gone."

Dal took another drink, spilling half of it down the front of his shirt. "Think, Kate," he said, wiping it off. "Has there been anyone following you? Anyone asking questions? Anyone—"

"For goddess sake, Dal, no. You know how careful I am. She probably just—" Kate broke off at the sound of a commotion by the door, one loud enough to halt the conversations. With an instinct honed by war, Kate spun around, her magic at the ready.

Norgard soldiers had burst into the room, swords drawn. Of all the bad luck. Why did they have to raid the place right now? Irritated, she reached out with her magic, determined to change their minds, but before she could, the room erupted in a blinding white light and a noise like the world breaking in half. The flash stones— ones twice as powerful as any she'd seen—knocked her back, along with everyone else in the room. Her head smacked the floor as she landed, and her vision went to black.

When she came to, she was lying on her back with shackles around her wrists and ankles. She reached for her magic only to find it wasn't there, a magestone collar encircling her throat, the stones softly glowing. With a surge of panic, Kate touched her ear to find her magestone disguise had been removed. *They were after me.* Fear of her and her magic was the only reason they would've used flash stones on their own people. Dread thudded in her chest as footsteps echoed nearby, and a figure stepped into view.

"Welcome home, Kate." Edwin Tormane leaned toward her, the gold in the thin crown he wore winking in the light of the torches in the chandelier above them. "Or should I call you the Wilder Queen?" He smiled, clearly intending the title as an insult.

Kate's mind spun. How could they have known she would be here? She couldn't make sense of it, not at first. But all too soon rough hands pulled her to her feet, and she understood. Dal was there, also in chains. So was Tira.

And Signe.

She shook her head at Kate, tears in her eyes. *I'm sorry,* Signe mouthed, and Kate's heart sank at the admission. Somehow, some-way, Signe had been found out, her magestone disguise removed. Kate looked away, gaze drawn to Edwin, who had come to stand before her now.

He reached into a pocket and withdrew a long, flat magestone. The marks on it glowed brightly, like captured sunlight. Raising the stone to his lips, Edwin spoke into it, but rather than a word of invocation, he gave a command, talking as if someone else were listening.

"We have Kate Brighton," Edwin said. "Take the city as soon as the sun sets."

"Yes, your majesty," a voice echoed from out of the stone. "The black-powder stores have already been destroyed. Farhold will be ours again by morning."

Kate's stomach clenched like a fist. It couldn't be possible. This small stone communicator, or whatever it was, couldn't reach all the way to Farhold. And yet, she could tell by the smug smile on Edwin's face that what she was hearing was real. Somehow he'd found a way to breach Farhold's defenses.

"I must express my gratitude, Kate," Edwin said. "For leaving your city so *conveniently*. Now, thanks to you, this gods-cursed war is finally at an end."

NEVER BEFORE HAD CORWIN FULLY appreciated the magic of a library, and the magicians who wielded its power—librarians. Previously, when Corwin had gone to the royal library, he'd avoided those who worked there, distrusting them same as any Sevan. But once he started on his quest to uncover Rendborne's activities, the librarians quickly became willing allies, happy to help. The pursuit of knowledge was a unifying endeavor, it seemed.

"Why yes, of course I remember Lord Rendborne," the senior librarian said. He was a small man, made even smaller by the too-large robes he wore, and bearing the unlikely name of Lutho Lazerleen. To Corwin's surprise he was not Sevan by birth but from one of the nations Seva had conquered years before. "He spent most of his time in the ancient history section."

Corwin frowned, turning to gaze at the section in question— one that occupied the entire top floor. It would take him years to go through it all. "Do you have any idea what he was looking for?"

Lutho gave him a curious look, as if one could want more from a library than the sheer joy of reading. "I'm afraid not." He paused and rubbed the bridge of his nose, giving Corwin's guards a side-long glance, but they weren't paying much attention. One yawned in obvious boredom, and Lutho turned his gaze back to Corwin. "But I can give you a list of the books he borrowed during his time here."

"These books are available for borrowing?"

"Only to those granted the trust by the Godking."

Corwin nodded. "Yes, I would like to see it, please."

A short while later, Lutho returned with the list, which contained more than two dozen texts. To his curiosity, one of them was *The Rise and Fall of Magic*. Many of the others bore similar titles, and several were histories of Seva, including one whose title had been circled in heavy black ink. Corwin showed it to Lutho. "What can you tell me about this one?"

Lutho's bushy eyebrows drew together in a scowl. "That is one Lord Rendborne failed to return."

Corwin suppressed a smile at the little man's outrage. "I'm sorry to hear that. But I don't understand the title. *Li Mevath de Sevan?*" he said, struggling with the foreign words.

"Yes, that's correct," Lutho said. "It means *The Death of Sevan*. It's written in Aeos, the language of the gods."

"I've heard of Aeos," Corwin said. "The priestesses in Rime speak it."

Lutho gave a polite cough. "I'm sure they speak some dialect of it. They're varied, you know. Many scholars believe that when the gods still roamed the world in their physical form, all the peoples spoke the same language. We only diverged after the gods ascended to the incorporeal realm."

"*The Death of Sevan*," Corwin said, staring at the title. "Do you know what it's about? Is it a prophecy?"

"Not at all. The title refers to *Sevan* the god, not *Seva* the land, although once the two were more or less one, such as how Norgard is derived from Noralah, or Farhold from Farrah. But the story is about just what it says: the death of Sevan at the hand of the first Godking, Fanen."

"That story is in *The Rise and Fall of Magic* as well." Corwin pointed to the title on the list, intrigued by the coincidence, which must not be one at all.

"Yes," Lutho said, "although the *Li Mevath* goes into much more detail. The entire book is dedicated to the story instead of one small section."

"Was there only the one copy?" Corwin asked.

"I'm afraid so, but there is a translation into the common tongue. It's not a very good one, though. The author wasn't well versed in Aeos, and so much of the nuance is lost. He also had a reputation for impatience and was said to have left out whole sections he deemed irrelevant."

Corwin found the idea of an impatient scholar both amusing and improbable. "May I see the translation? And I would like to see the rest of the books listed here as well."

Rather than look put out at what was surely a large request, Lutho appeared delighted. "I'll start fetching them now."

Corwin spent the rest of the day poring over volumes, reading until his eyes felt like shriveled grapes inside his skull and his thoughts like grain mash. There was so much here, much of it interesting, but none of it particularly useful to figuring out what Rendborne was up to, at least not that Corwin could see. A fair number of the books dealt with myths and stories about the gods as they'd been before the Ascension, when they'd lived like ordinary men in human bodies. The most compelling part of these, Corwin felt, was the way they spoke of the gods as if they had been real. Not in the sense that he knew them to be real—as enigmatic beings to be worshipped from afar, appeased with prayers and sacrifices—but real like Corwin was real, or Eravis or Zan or Lutho, hardly more than humans with extraordinary powers.

*Perhaps that's why Rendborne wanted to read of them,* Corwin thought. The Nameless One called himself a god, the Lord Ascender. Perhaps these readings were nothing more than an attempt to validate those beliefs.

An hour past nightfall, Corwin finally closed the books and returned them to Lutho, who was still in his tiny office, examining a manuscript.

"May I borrow the translation of *The Death of Sevan?*" Corwin asked. It was the only one of the group that he felt was significant enough to read from cover to cover.

Lutho reluctantly granted him permission, once Corwin pointed out that he was the Godking's son-in-law and surely worthy of the trust. "But you must promise to return it the moment you're done. We've already lost the original and can't afford to lose both, no matter how poor the translation."

"I swear by the goddess Noralah herself." Corwin put a hand over his heart, smiling as he remembered one of the stories he'd read earlier, about Noralah as a young woman and an argument she'd gotten into with her brother Rindar, patron god of Rin and ruler of the wind. The two decided to resolve the matter with a horse race. But Rindar cheated, giving his horse wings halfway through and soaring across the finish line first. In retaliation, Noralah bound all future horses to be too heavy to ever fly again. The story made her seem very human indeed.

Satisfied by Corwin's vow, Lutho handed him back the book, and Corwin took his leave, heading quickly for his quarters. He was past due for his nenath, and the need was upon him.

He arrived in the main chamber to find Eravis sitting at the table playing cards once again. A crystal decanter sat in front of her, containing some amber liquid. She looked up at his arrival, and he saw something strange in her gaze, her eyes slightly out of focus. "Have you been drinking, your highness?" It was a stupid question—clearly she had—but what he'd really meant to say was, "How much have you been drinking?" It didn't seem she could've consumed enough for her eyes to be out of focus—the decanter was nearly full.

She raised her glass and took a large swallow. "Emberic, the very best brandy in all of Seva. It was a belated wedding present from the governor of Belloss. Cheers to us."

Corwin knew of the drink. When he was a mercenary for the Shieldhawks, they used to smuggle it in by the cartload. Emberic was potent stuff, and clearly Eravis had little tolerance to be so far into her cups after so little.

Uneasy with this version of her, Corwin crossed the room to the end table where the nenath waited. He poured a glass and drank it down, wishing it were mere brandy. He considered helping himself to Eravis's bottle but decided not to. He was too tired. All he wanted was to go to sleep and give his mind a chance to recover before starting the search for answers anew in the morning.

He turned toward the door, but stopped at the sound of Eravis hiccuping. She had proved useful last night with her information about Rendborne, and he wondered what else he might learn from her, especially in an intoxicated state. Pulling out the opposite chair, he sat down. "Would you like to play another game of Peril?"

"No," she said, not looking up. She was playing with the Sevan deck again, the Rimish one nowhere in sight.

Corwin wasn't a fool. Sensing her anger was for him, he stood and headed for the bedroom, intent on a bath and sleep. She could take the divan for once.

"We're already playing a game, you know," Eravis said as he reached the door. "And we're both going to lose."

Corwin sighed, debating the wisdom of rising to her bait. Any other night, he would've ignored her, but he knew from experience that alcohol had a way of stripping off masks. He wanted to meet the real Eravis. He faced her. "And what game is that?"

"This . . . this *marriage.*" She gestured around the room. "We've been playing at it for weeks now. You sleeping out here, tiptoeing your way around me, avoiding me like I'm some repulsive creature you can't bear the sight of." She broke off abruptly, her voice thick, tears eminent.

Despite all the reasons he had to despise her, he felt a wave of pity. She was just a young royal after all, inexperienced and naive, and a pawn in her father's machinations, same as him. And enemy or not, she was still human, her emotions real and raw. It occurred to him for the first time that his rejection of her was something she felt personally and not just for the political reasons that motivated him. *And personal ones as well,* he thought, worry for Kate pricking him.

With a sigh, Corwin forced his expression to soften. "None of this has anything to do with you."

Eravis looked away, the delicate cords in her throat flexing. When she finally answered, anger had steadied her voice once more. "It has everything to do with me. I'm the one who lies in that bed by myself every night and who sneaks away every morning to avoid the shame of those untouched sheets, and the certainty of the worse shames that are coming."

"What shames? What are you talking about?" He balled his hands into fists, flustered by the uncomfortable topic. Did she think he wasn't furious as well? Mortified by the scrutiny?

Eravis picked up the glass and took another gulp, slamming it down again. She did it badly, tipping the glass on its side, but she didn't even notice as the remnants spilled out. "Could you really be so dense, Corwin? I'm talking about Lord Gavril, and his little mind tricks." She tapped her forehead with her finger hard enough he heard the thump. "Do you really think that this farce will be allowed to continue? Our marriage isn't real until it's been consummated, which means this alliance isn't real. My father won't stand for it much longer." Her sides were heaving as she righted the glass, poured another, and downed it.

Corwin stared at her, his mind on fire with a truth he'd tried to keep at bay. "Are you saying that Gavril can *compel* me to lie with you?" He'd convinced himself it wasn't possible, that it was one limitation to Gavril's power. That seemed the only explanation for why the man hadn't forced the issue on their wedding night.

He should've known better. The truth was clear in every line of Eravis's face and the rigidity in her slender body.

In answer, she poured another drink. If he'd had any doubts of her drunkenness, they were quickly dissipating. If she didn't slow down she would pass out.

Corwin drew a deep breath, grateful that he'd already taken the nenath and had his wits about him, at least as well as he could under the circumstances. "If what you say is true, then why hasn't he done it already?"

"Because I asked him not to!" she said, nearly shrieking.

"Why?" Corwin braced for more anger, knowing the moment the word escaped his mouth that it was the wrong one.

"Because I can't stand the thought of it . . . the violation." Her grip on the glass tightened until he thought it might break. "Do you know how his sway works? When he enters someone's mind he can see everything, *feel* everything, as if he were doing it himself."

Shock made Corwin stiffen. Yes, he did know how sway worked. Far better than Eravis could possibly imagine. Every time he was with Kate, they shared more than their bodies. With her sway, she made it so that they shared their minds, their thoughts and feelings intertwining until they could no longer tell whose was whose. Was that what Gavril would experience when he compelled Corwin?

No, he decided, at least it didn't have to be that way. And yet . . .

Disgust roiled in Corwin's belly as he remembered the licentious way Gavril had stared at Eravis the day of the Spectacles, and the way she had recoiled from him when he drew near to her. Gavril would not be the type of man to withdraw and allow them their privacy.

"Did Gavril hurt you?" Corwin said through gritted teeth.

Eravis laughed, the bitter sound sending a shiver down Corwin's spine. "He wouldn't dare. And why should he when all he has to do is wait until my father gives the command."

Corwin turned away from her, fists clenched with the need to hit something. It was an impossible situation. He needed to get out of it more than ever. And yet there wasn't a way out. Not yet.

Forcing his outrage to retreat, he turned back to Eravis. To his dismay, he saw the tears standing in her eyes threatening to fall. Gently, he asked, "Is there anything we can do about it?"

She shook her head, the tears slipping past her restraint. "If there was I would already have done it. But . . ." She hesitated, lips parting with an expelled breath. "You could at least make it bearable."

Corwin's chest tightened with dread. "By being with you of my own free will?" He refrained from telling her that it might not keep Gavril from listening in just the same if he chose.

She nodded once and scrubbed away the tears on her face even as more fell. Pouring herself another glass, she walked over to the divan and slumped down on it. "Is that really so bad a thing for me to want? To have one thing in this life that is completely mine to have and to give? To not have it forced upon me by duty?"

"No, it's not so bad." Corwin said, uncertain if he fully grasped what she meant, but having a feeling he did. The part about duty at least. He understood how it felt to be torn between a desire to fulfill the duty you'd been raised for and to resent it at the same time. He'd been born a prince, destined to compete against his brother in the uror trials, and maybe, if the gods willed it, to rule. Eravis, on the other hand, had been born a princess, her duty only to marry whom she was told and produce heirs who would strengthen the alliances of her kingdom. It was unfair, but there was little she could do about it.

And being forced to share such an intimate experience with a lecherous man like Gavril because she'd been saddled to an unwilling partner was the final insult.

"It's perfectly understandable," he said. And he wondered if there was even more—if she didn't also want to be loved in earnest, not matched by decree. *Isn't that what all of us want, in the end?* he wondered, thinking of Kate like always. *Simply to be with someone who loves us, and to love in return?*

"So glad you understand." Rolling her eyes, Eravis drank the rest of the brandy and set down the glass on the end table, upright this time. Then she leaned on the edge of the divan and closed her eyes. "If you truly understood then you would do something about it."

Corwin was grateful her eyes were closed so she didn't see him wince. It all made sense now. Why she had tried to seduce him that first night, and why she had seemed so uneven every night after. He could imagine the conversation she must've had with her father, begging him to give her time to . . . to . . . *try and make me fall in love with her.* Guilt welled up inside him, squeezing his chest. How naive she'd been to ever hope it could happen.

Corwin considered what he could possibly say in response to that, only to realize she was asleep. No—not just asleep, but unconscious. Passed out from too much drink. Sighing, he approached the divan and leaned down, gathering her in his arms. For such a slender thing, she was surprisingly heavy as he lifted her into the air, her head lolling over his arm. Carrying her into the bedroom, he placed her on the bed. He considered covering her but decided against it, his feelings a knotted ball in his chest.

As he turned to go, he spotted movement out of the corner of his eye, someone walking on the balcony. Alarm surged through him, and he spun toward the intruder, hands fisted. "Whoever you are, there are guards just beyond the door."

"Shhhh," a low, rough voice said. "It's me, Corwin." A large shadow seemed to melt away from the darkness, the shape of Bonner.

With a sudden burst of elation, Corwin rushed forward and embraced him. "Bonner, I was starting to think I'd never see you again."

His friend pulled back from him, his body stiff with tension. "We don't have much time." He motioned behind him, and another shadow transformed to reveal a young woman, tall and dark-skinned.

The woman glanced toward the bed. "Did you drink any of the brandy?" She spoke in the accent of someone from Kilbarrow. *Rimish, then. Another wilder.*

"No, only the princess. Who are you?"

"Not here." Bonner waved them toward the door to the sitting room. "We may not have long."

Dozens of questions swirled through Corwin's mind, but he held them back. Once inside the living quarters, Corwin shut the door and faced Bonner and the unknown woman. As before, Bonner wore the uniform of a Sevan soldier. The woman wore a plain beige robe fitted with a green belt.

Bonner motioned to his companion. "This is Nadira Walker of Kilbarrow."

"Your highness," she said, bowing.

Corwin inclined his head. "You drugged the brandy?"

"Yes," Bonner said, matter-of-fact. It was eerie to see him talk, the way his expression didn't change, no hint of humor or happiness or any of the emotions Corwin used to associate with the man. Even after his father had been brutally murdered by Rendborne, he hadn't been quite this . . . hard. "It's not a terribly powerful sleeping agent, but it's a reliable one. We were prepared to revive you if you drank it as well. Nadira is a healer, of sorts."

"How did you even get up here?" Corwin glanced between the two of them. "I thought all the wilders were under Gavril's control." The man had bragged of such to Corwin several times.

"Not anymore," Bonner said, and Corwin noted the way his fingers curled into fists. "We found a way to break his hold a few weeks ago, not long before you were discovered."

Corwin breathed in, hope filling him at this news. Here was the escape he needed. "That's wonderful."

Bonner grimaced. "Don't get too excited. We've pretended to remain under his control as we've been working to free all the wilders we can, but it's slow and dangerous. I don't think we'll have enough turned to change the outcome of the invasion. Not on the Godking's timetable."

"How many do you have? How many do you need?"

"Only a handful, and we'd need half to even consider it."

The woman beside Bonner added, "Maybe even more than half, your highness."

Corwin couldn't help but scoff. "Why so many? I saw you fight those daydrakes. With such power surely we can count you as more than double."

"You don't understand, Corwin." Bonner pursed his lips. "All of us have enhanced powers. It's this nenath Gavril forces us to drink. It makes our magic stronger than ever before."

At the mention of nenath, Corwin felt the blood drain from his face.

Bonner didn't seem to notice as he went on. "But those of us who are free will be able to escape once we reach Rime. Then once we're strong enough, we retaliate."

Corwin's hope returned, albeit in a smaller measure. Right now, all he needed was a chance—and breaking free of Gavril's control was the first step. "Even late is better than never. But for now, if you can break Gavril's hold on me, that will be enough." Once free, he might be able to escape. If he could get to Rime before the invasion, he could warn them, and maybe that would be sufficient to turn the tide. At the very least, he could escape this marriage before Gavril forced his hand.

"We can break it." A grim smile appeared on Bonner's face, and the sight of it made Corwin shiver. He'd never seen anything colder or more frightening.

"All you have to do to get free," Bonner said, "is die."

KATE HAD NEVER BEFORE BEEN inside the dungeon of Mirror Castle. The closest she had ever come was the barred door at its entrance. When her father had been arrested for attempting to assassinate King Orwin, she'd pounded on this door, begging and pleading to be allowed to see him. She'd been denied—first by the guard captain, and then by Corwin.

The inside of it was worse than she could have imagined back then, and she didn't want to think of her father inside such a place. Dark and damp, the thick stone walls seemed to veer inward, making every inch of it feel cramped and ominous, like a mouth closing around you, swallowing you whole. Kate found it hard to believe such a place could exist beneath a structure as grand and beautiful as Mirror Castle. It was like biting into a ripe red apple to discover the inside rotted and worm-ridden. Even the Hellgate hadn't been like this. That place had been large and open and heated by the ever-present exhale of the Hellgate itself, the vast, fathomless hole in the middle of it. Here, the chill seeped into her bones.

The prisoners had been placed in individual cells, tall enough to stand in but barely long enough to lie down. Tira was in the cell next to her while Signe, Dal, and Laurent were opposite them. At least the hallway was narrow enough that they could talk easily.

And they had plenty to talk about.

"What happened?" Kate asked Signe, focusing all her attention on her, anything to keep her mind off what was happening in Farhold this very minute.

She shook her head, lips pressed together.

The gesture pricked Kate's anger, giving her tumultuous feelings an avenue to vent. "Where did they find you? *How* did they find you? You were wearing your disguise, right?" Signe hadn't been wearing the magestone earring when they brought her to the Horned Crow, but given that Kate's had been removed after she'd been captured, that didn't mean anything.

Again, Signe shook her head.

Kate smacked the bars of the cell with the heels of her hands. "Damn it, Sig. You can't use the excuse of Seerah this time. We're all involved now."

Signe's stare pierced her, sharp enough to cut, her mouth a razor-thin line. Kate braced for another denial, or worse, one of her tall tales, but then Dal reached through the bars toward Signe and touched her hand.

"Were you looking for your mother?" He spoke so softly Kate barely heard him.

Signe turned to look at him through the bars separating them, her gaze sharper than ever. Then, abruptly, it softened, and she nodded. "I knew she was here the moment I saw the doll. That she'd found me at last."

"How?" Dal gently prodded.

Kate pressed her lips together, afraid he would scare her away with his questions, like startling a skittish cat.

Signe exhaled, her gaze sliding off Dal and onto the stone floor.

"She left her mark on it, a signature she knew I would recognize." Her expression turned wry, dark and cynical. "Her message was clear. Either I come to Norgard, to her, or she would kill Dal."

"Why didn't you tell me?" Kate said, wounded by the deception. *How can you not trust me, after all we've been through?*

Signe raised her gaze, meeting Kate's without flinching. "Because you never would've let me go. Not if you knew."

"That's not true."

"Isn't it?" Signe shook her head. "There's no reasoning with you these days. Ever since the Mistfold. When it comes to the welfare of someone you love you believe you know best and that's the end of it. You think keeping us safe justifies any actions you choose, no matter how wrong."

Kate opened her mouth to protest, then closed it again, Signe's words cutting to the quick. Was she really that way? Signe made her sound like a tyrant, a ruthless dictator. And maybe it was true—she was willing to do whatever it took to protect her loved ones—but was that really so bad? Unbidden, the face of Jonathan Bailey rose in her mind, the way he had looked in those few seconds before she'd executed him, the fear rising off him like heat from a fever. She'd pulled the trigger with no hesitation. It had been easy.

*I did it to save them, to save us all.*

But it hardly seemed to matter now.

Scooting back the scant few feet to the rear of the cell, Kate folded one arm around her waist, the other resting on her shoulder where the hidden tattoos seemed to burn beneath her fingers. How many more would she have to add if Farhold fell?

"I'm sorry, Kate," Signe said with a loud sigh. "I've wanted to tell you, but things with my mother aren't . . . easy."

Kate cocked her head. "You mean like things weren't easy with my father?"

Signe had the grace to flinch, even as she nodded. "And you're not wrong about the Seerah either, so I will tell you what I may." She straightened up, as if braced for battle. "My mother is Synnove Leth, the Arch Mother of the Wrensfell Furen Mag. Only the queen of Wrensfell holds more power in our island. As her only daughter, there was no question that I would follow in her footsteps."

This revelation shocked Kate to her core. Signe had always seemed too free of spirit and independent to have been born into such a rigid lifestyle where her very destiny had been determined at birth.

"The moment I was old enough, I became an initiate," Signe continued. "The idea of me ever being anything but one of the Furen Mag was unthinkable. That was, until I betrayed our greatest secret." She swallowed, the tendons in her throat flexing like some unwilling instrument.

"Black powder," Kate said, and Signe tilted her chin in acknowledgment. It wasn't a surprise. Kate, and anyone else familiar with both the Furen Mag and Signe, knew what their most valuable knowledge must be. "But what did you do?"

Signe shook her head, gaze dropping to the floor again. "It's too shameful to tell."

Dal reached through the bars to touch her once more. "You don't have to. Not until you're ready."

Kate's frustration slid away from her at the sight of her friend's misery. Whatever this secret, it was a heavy weight upon her shoulders. Besides, Kate didn't have much room to talk. In the search for the truth about her father, she'd done several questionable things. And in her heart she knew her anger was nothing more than fear over what was happening in Farhold.

"Dal's right, Sig," Kate said at last. "Whatever you might've done . . . it doesn't matter to us."

Signe started to reply but broke off at the sound of a door opening. They all turned to look at the small room adjacent to the cells, one fitted with shackles on the walls next to instruments of torture. Two guards appeared, followed by King Edwin; Grand Master Storr, head of the Mage League; and a woman wearing the black cape of one of the Furen Mag. Kate understood immediately how Dal had known she was Signe's mother. They were alike enough to be versions of the same person, one old and one young.

Kate recognized Synnove from Signe's thoughts as well, but just barely. It seemed Signe's feelings for her mother had clouded the truth of her appearance, recognizing only the differences between them and none of the similarities.

Beneath the cape, the Arch Mother wore all black, except for the crimson sash at her waist. Reedy muscles lined her arms, bare in a fitted sleeveless jerkin, and her white-blond hair was pulled back from her face in an elaborate braid that allowed not a single strand to escape. The four red jewels around her lips, one on each corner above and below, winked dully in the torchlight.

"Bring the Eshian out," Edwin said to one of the soldiers, who came forward, key in hand. He undid the lock to Signe's door and motioned her out into the hallway. She went without protest, her shackled wrists held in front of her. They hadn't bothered shackling her feet, likely because of her limp.

"Hello again, Miss Signe," Edwin said, patronizingly cheerful. "How glad I am to see you, and even more to place you in your mother's care." He faced Synnove. "That is, once the Arch Mother has fulfilled her end of the bargain."

Signe's mother fixed a cold stare on the king, her back as rigid as a spear. Whatever relationship there was between the two, it wasn't an easy one. Synnove turned her gaze onto Signe, her expression unchanging. "Signe Malina Leth, daughter of my body, I command you to tell me the secret to your black powder, the one that makes the revolvers possible."

Kate felt a wild urge to laugh. This woman must not be Signe's mother after all, not if she thought she could get an answer so easily. Then the meaning of Synnove's words struck her. It wasn't just that Signe possessed the knowledge of black powder. It was that she had concocted her own version of it, one so special it seemed even the Furen Mag weren't able to recognize it. How was that possible?

Then to Kate's shock, Signe bowed her head. "The secret . . . is kaiolah," she said.

The Arch Mother's gaze sharpened, and she went utterly still, not even drawing a breath.

"What is this kaiolah?" Grand Master Storr said, stepping toward the woman. It was the first time Kate had seen the head of the Mage League in more than a year, and his ragged appearance surprised her, as if he'd aged ten years in that time. His skin seemed to hang from his face, revealing the prominent shape of his skull and nose. In stark contrast, though, his eyes seemed to blaze as if lit by some fire from within, his expression eager for the knowledge.

The Arch Mother didn't look at the man, but kept her gaze fixed on her daughter, as if Signe were a snake—venomous and ready to strike at any moment. Only to Kate's eyes, she'd never seen Signe look so subdued. Not even after Rendborne had tortured her, leaving her face scarred and the bones in her foot shattered.

"Your Eminence," Edwin said, "what does she mean?"

Synnove shook her head. "Apologies, your majesty, but I can't explain it. There are no words that a garro would understand, and even if I had them, the laws of Seerah would forbid speaking of it. But it's no matter—what she is saying is not the truth behind the black powder, I'm certain."

Edwin's brows drew together in a scowl. "That is a shame. But I'm afraid until you are certain, your daughter must remain here under my protection." He motioned to the guard, who stepped toward Signe.

"Wait." Synnove raised her hand, and at once the guard fell still, obeying the command without hesitation. Synnove inclined her head toward Edwin. "If you give me time alone with my daughter, I'm sure to learn the truth, and I will share it with you the moment after."

Edwin ran his hand over his chin, stroking the fine wisps of blond hair there, not quite enough to be called a beard. He glanced just once at Storr, who nodded. "Very well. I will have a chair brought in for you."

"Not here, your majesty. There is room for her at the Hellgate, and I shall speak with her there."

"Is that really necessary?" Edwin scrunched up his nose.

Synnove glowered at him, nostrils flaring as if affronted. "She was raised to be Furen Mag and knows well the arts of deception. Questioning her will take time."

Again, Edwin glanced at Storr, who nodded a second time. Ever his lap dog, Kate thought, watching the exchange.

"I suppose now that Farhold has fallen, the need for the black powder is less urgent," Edwin said. "Very well. Take her to the Hellgate then, and do what you must."

Synnove bowed, and a few moments later, she left with Signe trailing behind her, escorted by the soldiers. The Grand Master came after them.

When Edwin made to follow, Kate called out, "I know the truth, Edwin." He stopped but didn't turn around, not until she added, "about the uror sign."

Slowly Edwin pivoted toward her. "I would be careful about telling lies, Kate. By law you cannot be executed until after you have been given a fair trial, but further acts of treason will do you no favors."

"It's not a lie. I saw the imposter steed you've been parading about on. But tell me, where is the real uror sign?"

Edwin's teeth clicked together as he shut his mouth, a flush rising up his neck. Then his jaw relaxed. "I know what you're hoping, my dear Kate, but it's foolishness. Corwin is dead, and never coming back." He smiled, his manner smug once again. "Don't worry. You'll soon be joining him."

Kate watched him go, a chill inching down her spine. Edwin was deceiving everyone with the fake uror horse, and yet just now he'd seemed so certain about Corwin's fate, cocksure and arrogant. Could there be some other reason he was so convinced Corwin was dead? Desperately, she longed for her sway, for some way to learn what he knew. But it was no use with the collar around her neck.

"What will they do to her?" Dal said, once they were alone again.

Kate's mind leaped to this new worry. "I don't know." She wished that Signe had shared more of her life with them before now. As it was, she had no idea what to expect. Hardly anything was known about the Furen Mag, other than their fierce reputation for secrecy. They might execute Signe the moment they learned the truth, or they might simply ship her back to the Esh Islands to spend the rest of her life in chains.

"Surely nothing too awful," Tira said. "That's her mother."

Dal shook his head. "That doesn't count for anything."

He would know, Kate thought, remembering his family's sordid history. His father hadn't wept or cared at all when Dal's brother was killed by daydrakes. And Kate's own mother had been equally as cold, abandoning her for a life of comfort and ease. Love was not a universal parental trait.

"Well, at least Harue and Wen are still out there," Tira said. "Between Harue's knowledge and Wen's cleverness, maybe they'll conjure some way to get us out of here."

"Maybe," Kate said with no real conviction. The truth was, without Signe, everything felt hopeless. She'd been Kate's rock to stand on for so long that it now seemed as if the ground had given way beneath her feet and she was in free fall. *There's no reasoning with you these days*, she heard Signe saying once again. *Ever since the Mistfold.*

"Do you think it's true?" Dal said. "About Farhold."

"There's no telling," Tira replied. "But I have a feeling we're going to find out sooner rather than later."

Tira was right—except for the part about it being soon. More than three weeks went by with no word from the outside. They saw hardly anyone except each other and the guards who came in to check on them, escorting the poor maids sent to bring them their food and change out the chamber pots.

Kate lost track of herself in all that time, retreating into her mind to escape the torture of idleness. The worries cycled over and over in her thoughts. Where was Signe now? What happened at Farhold? Who was still alive and who dead? What about Corwin and the uror and Edwin and Rendborne and every other thing wrong with this world?

The others seemed to do the same, talking little at first. But slowly, boredom started to overtake them, the worries growing dull like an overused knife blade. They began passing the time with stories and songs, anything to keep themselves engaged and feeling like human beings instead of rats trapped in a cage.

Then finally, something strange happened one morning when they broke their fast. The servants came in twice a day to feed them—porridge in the morning and broth at night. With the light unchanging in the dungeon, Kate had used the meals to count the days and to let her body know when to sleep and when to rise. This morning, she dug into the porridge with something close to enthusiasm, the act of eating making her feel alive for however briefly it lasted.

She swallowed the first bite, then the second and third. The fourth bite, she felt something wriggling in her mouth. With a yelp, she spit the food back into her bowl.

Dal froze, spoon midway to his mouth. "What is it?"

"Poison?" Tira said, straining to look at Kate through the bars.

Kate didn't answer, her gaze transfixed on the writhing object in her bowl. It resembled a worm, long and slender and the color of vomit. For a second, Kate thought *she* might vomit, but then the worm started to unfold.

Blinking, she realized it was a piece of parchment and plucked it out of the bowl just as words began to appear on its surface.

*We're working on getting you out. Leave some of your hair in the bowl. Everyone else should do the same just in case. Eat this once you've read it.*

"Kate?" Dal said, annoyed now. "What's going on over there?"

"It's a note, from Harue." She read it aloud.

Laurent made a face, indignant. "Why in the three hells does she need some hair?"

"For a spell, of course." Tira grinned. "I knew she'd come through."

"Don't get too excited," Dal warned. "Harue's wild ideas don't always go off as planned. Remember the time she wanted to make giant attack spiders?"

Kate winced at the memory. Harue had wanted Kate to be present to control the spider with her sway once it was big enough to eat a person. But the poor creature had collapsed under its own weight the moment the spell was completed, spraying Kate and Harue both with the gore of its innards, which exploded like a popped soap bubble.

Shaking the memory off, Kate dangled the sodden note before her. "Do I really have to eat this thing?" She couldn't forget the way it had a resembled a live worm just moments ago. And felt like one too inside her mouth. She shuddered.

"Yes, you must. We can't let anyone find it," Tira said.

"You do it then." Kate held the note toward her through the bars.

Tira looked affronted. "It was already in your mouth! Besides, Harue sent it to you. There must be a reason."

"Coward," Kate groused, only she had to include herself in that statement. She began to tear the parchment into small strips and drop them back in the bowl, where thankfully they blended in with the porridge. Once done, she forced herself to take huge bites, swallowing it all down quickly. She felt that wriggling again several times more, but decided it was just her imagination. Still, it took her a long time to eat it all.

When the servants came back that evening with their broth and to take the morning's bowls, Kate examined their faces, wondering if maybe one of them was Harue in disguise, as both were too tall to be Wen. It was impossible to tell. Each of the maids wore earrings and were unremarkable in appearance. In the end, Kate could only hope that the hairs they'd each placed inside their bowls would be enough for Harue to work her magic—and hopefully not get them all killed in the process.

*Perhaps we will be free by morning*, Kate thought as she curled up on the floor, legs tucked and her head resting on her arms. She didn't think she would be able to sleep, but before long she drifted off—only to be awakened a short time later by the loud creak of the door in the outer room opening, far too early for breakfast. Kate sat up at once, heart hammering against her chest. Her days had fallen into such a steady rhythm that this disturbance felt like the entire world tipping sideways.

Four guards entered the room, carrying a prisoner between them. The man was slumped over, unconscious. His head lolled from side to side as the guards dragged him toward the cells.

Kate's pounding heart slowed and seemed to stop altogether as she recognized the man's face beneath the heavy swelling and myriad of bruises. She would know that birthmark anywhere, like spilled wine across his nose and cheeks.

*Raith.*

Kate's heart sank into her stomach, and tears welled up in her eyes. It seemed Edwin had been telling the truth all along—Farhold had indeed fallen. The Rising was defeated. All they'd fought for was gone.

CORWIN LAY AWAKE CONTEMPLATING his death.

Bonner and Nadira had left hours before with a promise to return in a few days, as soon as they were able to slip away. They didn't tell Corwin any details of how they were able to move about the palace unseen, and he supposed that was wise. Gavril might see it in Corwin's mind and learn the truth. Even now, he would have to try to hide the memory of their visit if Gavril entered his mind again.

*All you have to do is die*, Bonner had said. It would be easy, he had explained. With her magic, Nadira would stop Corwin's heart. Once he was well and truly dead, she would reach in and start it up again.

"How many times have you done this?" Corwin asked, casting her a wary glance.

"Enough," she answered cryptically.

"And how many times have you been unable to revive the person?"

"Enough," Bonner replied for her. "But the risk is worth it. It's the only way to be free of him." Bonner had then gone on to explain how they had discovered the solution.

"I died during a training session. I was sparring with another earthist, and she hit me square in the chest with a rock the size of my fist." Bonner thumped his left breast with his palm. "It stopped my heart on impact. For four minutes it didn't beat. Not until Nadira restarted it. Afterward I realized that even though Gavril still spoke into my mind, he could no longer compel me. And for those of us who have risen, all the nenath does is enhance our power. It's no longer addictive."

Hearing this, Corwin knew Bonner was right—it was a risk worth taking. Corwin would've done it right then if they'd been able. But like that of all wilders, Nadira's magic didn't work at night. Corwin could barely hide his disappointment. At least not then.

But now, as he stared up at the shadow-strewn ceiling, his neck aching from the harsh angle of the divan, he realized that Bonner's solution wouldn't work. He raised his right palm and traced the uror brand with his left index finger, feeling each swell and divot, the memory of how much it had hurt still fresh. He couldn't risk it, not with the uror unresolved. It wasn't that he was afraid of dying. Instead he feared that if he did die, no matter for how short a time, the uror trial might end and Edwin would have a rightful claim to the throne. The magic was released at death—that much he knew.

And he couldn't let that happen. He couldn't give up his birthright and abandon his people to Edwin permanently, not when so many of those people were wilders—targets of Edwin's hate and prejudice. He would have to endure. For Kate. For Bonner. For all of them, and the future that might still be possible once the threat of Seva was ended.

The night wore on, and sleep eventually overtook him, but he woke up early, pale light seeping through the door into the bedroom.

He dressed quickly and slipped out while Eravis still slept, heading back to the library. He spent the entire day there, attempting to read *The Death of Sevan*. Zan brought him his meals and his nenath dose. The drink was bitterer than ever before now that Corwin knew what Gavril could do, would do, sometime soon. He wanted to resist, but it was pointless. *Only death will free me.*

*Mine . . . or perhaps his?*

He wondered why Bonner hadn't just killed Gavril already, for surely his death would free them all in one blow, like slicing through an impossible knot with one quick swing of the knife. Then again, he supposed Bonner surely had considered the idea, remembering his palpable hatred of the man. The fact that Gavril remained alive must mean killing him would be no easy feat, free will or not. It made sense. Gavril was well insulated, surrounded by hundreds of wilders still bound to his will, ready to die for him at a moment's thought. Bonner needed to break Gavril's hold over the wilders—only then would they have any hope of killing him.

It wasn't a great plan, but it was better than nothing. The chance that it might work brought Corwin some small amount of comfort throughout the rest of the day, allowing him to focus on his readings. His good mood waned only as he returned to his chambers that night, well past dark.

The soft sounds of music lured him out onto the balcony, where he found Eravis seated near the ledge, a harp set on her lap while her slender fingers caressed the strings. She had her eyes closed in concentration, a blissful expression on her face, unlike any he'd ever seen there before. For a moment he worried this was another attempt to seduce him, for indeed the music was beautiful and soothing, but then she struck a bad note, and her eyes flashed open in a glare.

"Dammit," she said, the curse completely without guile. "That was terrible."

Corwin cleared his throat. "Oh, I don't know. It was quite pretty up until that last bit."

"Oh." Eravis stood abruptly, fingers grazing the strings to produce more unpleasant sounds. "I didn't know you were here." She paused, her nervous manner making Corwin wonder just how much she remembered about their conversation last night. "I mean, it was so late, I guessed you were sleeping somewhere else tonight."

*Where else could I go?* Corwin's emotions churned inside him as he stared at her. He didn't know what to do. There seemed no right answer in this predicament, no option he could live with. Yet after hearing what she feared about Gavril, he could no longer view her simply as his enemy.

"The time got away from me," Corwin replied.

With a stilted nod, she turned toward a nearby table and set the harp back in its case.

"Please, you don't have to stop playing on my account," Corwin said. "It truly was pretty."

Eravis looked up, her expression courteous but distant. "Thank you, but no. I play only for myself."

"Very well." He considered leaving it at that, but her vulnerable expression now, combined with the memory of what she'd confessed the night before, refused to let him. "Would you care for another game of Peril then? If I recall, you almost won last time. Your luck might be better tonight."

Doubt crossed like a shadow over her face, then faded. "Perhaps it will." She offered him a small smile, a sign she was willing to accept this truce he was offering.

They played on the balcony, beneath the glistening, star-kissed sky. The pleasant breeze restlessly toyed with Eravis's long hair, forcing her to spend half her time brushing it off her cheeks. She barely seemed to notice.

Corwin won the first hand but Eravis beat him on the next two, her glee in the victory almost childlike in its sheer delight. For the first time since his emergence from the Sevan prison, Corwin found he was enjoying himself, feeling almost comfortable for once. It helped that he no longer felt the urge to glean useful information from Eravis. Instead he asked her normal things, about her life and interests. She was standoffish at first but slowly began to relax, revealing her love of both music and art, as well as climbing trees, of all things.

"You see this scar?" She pointed to the tip of her elbow, marred by a jagged white line. "I was climbing a tree in the west garden not realizing it had been infested by beetles and was starting to rot. I almost made it to the top when the bough broke. I managed to grab onto the trunk and slide down, but not before gouging myself on a limb."

Corwin winced. "That must've hurt."

Eravis grinned. "You'd think, but what was worse was all the splinters in my legs. My nurse had to sit on me to get them out."

Picturing a young Eravis fighting her nurse with the same ferocity she'd used to fight him the day they first met made Corwin laugh. Then he started to tell her one of his own childhood tales of woe but stopped himself as he realized he couldn't relay the story without talking about Kate. She'd been a part of all his favorite childhood adventures. And he couldn't talk about Kate to Eravis, no matter how congenial the atmosphere between them this night. Thinking about her was hard enough, let alone speaking her name aloud.

Eravis seemed to sense the sudden tension in him, for she quickly gathered the cards, then rose from her chair. "Thank you for a pleasant evening, but it's late." With that, she turned toward the bedroom.

Corwin watched her retreat, but called her name as she reached the door. "You look lovely tonight," he said, meaning it. He might not be able to give her what she wanted from him, but he could at least offer her some reassurance about her part in it. "And I think under better circumstance we might've been friends."

"Yes, I suppose you're right." She turned, then stopped halfway, glancing back at him with a solemn expression. "For what it's worth, I'm sorry for what my father has done to you and your people."

*And to us*, he thought, as if hearing her silent words.

"Good night, Eravis," Corwin replied, his tumultuous emotions putting a rasp into his voice. "May you rest easy."


The next few days passed in the same manner—Corwin leaving early to spend his time in the library and then returning late to find Eravis waiting for him with some sort of game at hand, sometimes cards and sometimes on a playing board. The time passed easily between them, the tense, awkward moments occurring less frequently as they established the boundaries of their new relationship, determining through trial and error which subjects were safe and which were not. That was until they went to say good night. There was no helping the awkwardness then as Eravis disappeared into the bedroom and Corwin lay down on the divan. Even still, Corwin's evenings quickly become the best part of his days, a few hours of peace where he could be himself for a little while.

Then one night, a week later, Bonner and Nadira came again.

They didn't drug Eravis this time. Corwin had suggested there was no need so long as they waited until it was late and met him in the main room. When Corwin told Bonner why he couldn't go through with breaking Gavril's hold on him, he watched the man's expression darken.

"Who's to say there will even be a Rime left to save if we don't free you, Corwin?" he said.

"There might not be," Corwin admitted. "But if we give up Rime to Edwin's wilder-hating regime, everyone here will still be without a home. I can't take that risk, not when there's another option. We should focus on killing Gavril."

Nadira scowled in a way that made him think of a wildcat hissing. "You think we haven't tried? He's impossible to get to. It's not just the other wilders and the soldiers. He's protected by charms and spells as well. Even with my magic, I can't get near him."

"She's right." A muscle ticked in Bonner's jaw. "Gavril is nearly as powerful as Rendborne."

"We have to try," Corwin insisted, refusing to give up hope. He had to be free of Gavril. Getting to know Eravis these last few days had only made it more imperative. "I was thinking he might be vulnerable on the journey across the sea. Or when we get to Rime."

Their departure was just a few days away now, but they had decided earlier that they couldn't send someone to give warning. If even one wilder was discovered to be free of Gavril's control, the whole plan would collapse. To make matters worse, Corwin had no hope of escaping Eravis on the journey either. Magnar had already decided that she would sail with them, her presence an undeniable symbol of the union between Rime and Seva. But her presence was also a complication he didn't need. He'd come to care for her. Enough that he didn't want her thrust into the danger that surely awaited them, especially if Bonner succeeded.

"If we don't either stop Gavril or free you from his control before we reach Rime," Bonner said, sounding grimmer than ever, "the kingdom will fall."

Corwin looked at his uror brand then, weighing his decision, but in the end he held to it. He would rather have Rime fall than allow it to rot from within.

The next day, Corwin once again went to the library. He was nearly through reading the translation of *The Death of Sevan*, and it was as Lutho had said—lacking. Not only were there clearly sections missing, the author was inconsistent about the translation, sometimes leaving in words in Aeos. Whenever he did this, the footnote was always the same: *There is no appropriate corresponding word in our language, and any substitute might risk distorting the meaning.*

Corwin couldn't decide if the man was lazy or excessively paranoid about inaccuracies. He did at least occasionally add clarifying notes, although they were sometimes less than helpful. Such as the one concerning how Fanen was finally able to kill the god Sevan.

It was no easy thing to kill a god—impossible, most would say. Indeed, even this book chronicled how "no iron could pierce the god, no fire burn, no magical poison affect." But Fanen had found the answer in something called "daleth." It was a weaponized substance of some sort, but Corwin couldn't discern anything about it beyond that. The footnote simply added that it was a "godslayer."

"That's useful," Corwin muttered under his breath. If he had some of this daleth, he could use it on Gavril. A mere wilder would be no match for such a power, no matter how insulated he might be. But it didn't matter. Daleth was as unknowable as the rest of the story—while some elements were likely real, the idea of the Fanes' ancestor having killed a god was nothing more than vanity, and he didn't know what parts of the tale to believe.

Then Corwin remembered where he was—a place filled with people devoted to knowledge and learning. Surely, if daleth did exist, one of the librarians could offer insight on it.

Leaving the book opened on the table, he got up in search of Lutho, but he wasn't in his office. There were other librarians about, but Corwin didn't want to ask them in the event Lutho might take offense. He'd gotten to know the man well enough to sense his pride when it came to his position. He wasn't just a librarian, but a *senior* librarian. Making a mental note to ask him about it later, Corwin returned to the desk where he'd been working only to find someone sitting in his chair, leaned over the book.

Corwin froze, debating whether he could retreat unnoticed, but before he could, Eryx Fane spoke. "Strange choice of casual reading material, your highness. All this talk about godslaying." Sitting up, the prince leveled a cool gaze at Corwin over his shoulder. "One might wonder if you're up to something."

Undaunted, Corwin folded his arms across his chest. "It passes the time."

Eryx stood from the table, putting himself on eye level with Corwin. Looking at the man, Corwin was struck by his resemblance to Eravis. They were closest in age of the Godking's children, and it showed in more ways than one.

"Did you know I used to admire you?" Eryx said, examining his fingernails now. They were longish, immaculately clean and manicured. He wore an emerald ring on his right index finger, the jewel identical to the one embedded on the hilt of the dagger belted at his side. "All those tales about the Errant Prince. How you just disappeared so mysteriously for three years, only to return home and become a contender for the throne." He smiled. "I'm sure you can understand the reason for my envy."

Corwin could. Seventh-born of Magnar's sons, Eryx would never be king of anything. There was no uror here. "If you feel that way, why not head off on an adventure yourself? There's nothing keeping you here that I can see. Unlike me."

"You're right. There is nothing. Other than my sister's welfare."

The malice in his tone was a tangible thing, a slap across Corwin's face. He should've seen this coming, and he wondered what shape Eryx's threat would take. That dagger might be ornamental, but the blade was still sharp enough to cut.

The Sevan prince glanced down at the table, idly flipping the pages. "I found her in the west garden this morning, crying among the rosebushes. She didn't want to tell me at first, but eventually . . . she did." Eryx closed the book, the restraint of his actions more

effective than if he had slammed it. "Her confession made me realize that maybe I'd been mistaken to admire you all along. A true
man, a true prince, faces his duty. He doesn't run from it."

Heat rose up Corwin's neck. "What does a seventh-born son
like you know about duties?"

Eryx's expression remained cool, unaffected by Corwin's taunt.
"I know that my sister hasn't told you that tonight is the last day
of grace my father has given her to do *her* duty. The last day he's
giving *you* to do right by her. To choose to be a man instead of a
mindless beast."

*Mindless beast.* That was indeed how Gavril's power worked—
turning him into something less than a person. Corwin scowled,
his anger breaking through the tight leash he'd been trying to keep
on it. "As if you have a right to talk about what it's like. How many
times has Gavril compelled you against your will, *your highness?*"

"Never, not once," Eryx said, his voice and expression suddenly
hard. "Magic doesn't work on my family."

Corwin laughed, the sound a humorless bark. "You don't really
expect me to believe that."

"It's true. Why do you think my sister fears it so? She can't be
made willing. She can only be forced, or not, by you—or, more spe-
cifically, by the strength of the power Gavril will wield over you."

As the meaning of Eryx's words struck him, Corwin felt a wave
of nausea rise in his stomach. Was it true? All along he'd believed
Eravis would be made to be as compliant in the act as he would be.
But if Corwin had to force her physically . . .

Sucking in a breath, he fixed a hard stare at Eryx, hoping to
discover he was lying. "How is that possible?"

Eryx motioned to the book on the table. "Hasn't your reading told you? We Fanes are protected from any magic that would do us harm by the blood of the gods that flows in our veins. Fanen didn't just kill a god, you see. He killed his own father." At Corwin's look of surprise, Eryx nodded. "Yes, that's right. Fanen was Sevan's son—half human, half god. And that is why Gavril can't touch us."

Corwin didn't want to believe it, but the likelihood was too strong to ignore. Why would an ambitious man like Gavril not just use his sway to have the Godking marry him to Eravis instead of Corwin? It was clear he desired the princess, and by doing so he would not only gain her but the title as well, prince instead of a mere lord. Why, with a little of his magic, Gavril could position himself to be the next Godking. It must be true then. *Godsblood.* It was Corwin's turn to be envious—if only he had such protection as well.

He gritted his teeth, the sick feeling in his stomach turning to anger at his helplessness. "So is that it? Are you here to threaten me on behalf of your sister?" He eyed the dagger in such easy reach. "I don't see how that will make it any different for Eravis to have someone else force me instead of Gavril." That was, aside from stopping Gavril from having a front-row seat, as it were.

Eryx shook his head, his expression solemn. "I would never do that to her. It would only add to her shame. And she's had enough of that to last a lifetime."

Corwin frowned, taken off guard—not by his words, but by the emotion he sensed behind them, the tenderness when he spoke about Eravis. No matter his motivations, there was no denying Eryx's love for her.

Eryx drew a deep breath, then went on, resigned. "When we were children, my father gave her a kitten. She had never loved something so much. She would play with it, pet it, let it sleep in her lap or beside her head on her pillow at night. For six months, Blossom was her whole world. Then one day, our father demanded she give it back to him. When she refused, hysterical at the thought, he had her whipped. Ten strikes on the back of her legs. Once done, he took Blossom in his very own hands and snapped its neck in front of her." Eryx mimed the gesture. Then he cocked his head at Corwin. "Do you know what my father told her afterward?"

"No," Corwin said, nausea burning stronger than ever in his stomach.

"That there was nothing she would ever have that wasn't his to take as he wished," Eryx replied, letting his hands fall to his sides. "It's a lesson she's been learning all her life. So no, I would never threaten you. I would simply ask that you consider doing what she wants. Come to her by choice. Let her have this one thing that only you can give, and that my father cannot take. That will make a difference to her. I know my sister, Corwin, well enough to see that she has developed true feelings for you. If you come to her of your own free will, she will give herself freely in return, and she will love you for it."

Corwin felt his anger slipping away, shame rising up in its place as, for once, he started to truly see things from Eravis's point of view, to understand just how powerless she really was in her own life, all because she'd been born a princess instead of a prince. And yet, even still she was trying to make the most of her situation, to bend it into a shape she could live with. That took a certain kind of strength indeed.

"I'll . . . I'll think about it," Corwin said at last.

Eryx sighed, dissatisfied with such a response, but wise enough not to press the matter. He bowed his head toward Corwin. "I will leave you to your thoughts then." He turned to go, then paused. "Oh, one more thing. This arrived for my father yesterday. I thought you might want to know." He withdrew a folded newspaper from his back pocket and set it on the table opened to the front page.

At once, Corwin's eyes scanned the headline, printed in bold letters across the top:

## FARHOLD HAS FALLEN.

His lips parted on a gasp, his shock so great he barely noticed Eryx departing. The newspaper was one Corwin knew well, the *Royal Gazette*, a reliable source of information about Rime and Norgard in particular. As much as he wanted to, he had no reason to believe this news wasn't true.

With his heart thudding loudly in his ears, Corwin read the rest. Farhold had been sacked in a single night by a contingent of Rimish soldiers and League magists. They'd taken the city unawares, the article said, successfully rousting the wilder government in place and bringing Farhold under the control of Rime and High King Edwin once again.

Corwin read faster, desperate for news of Kate. Surely she had escaped. She was so clever and brave and strong. She'd survived worse before.

*As for the infamous Wilder Queen, Kate Brighton, she wasn't in Farhold at the time of the battle. Our sources have since learned that she was apprehended in Norgard during a failed assassination attempt of the king, which took place not long before the assault on Farhold began. Like her traitor father before her, Kate is scheduled to be executed within the week.*

Corwin stopped reading, his heart in his throat as he searched for the date of the paper. It was already nearly two weeks old. Of course it was. Norgard was miles away, an impossible distance of space and time.

Was it true? Was she gone? He didn't want to believe it, and yet he remembered with vivid clarity how much his brother hated wilders, a feeling that bordered on madness. But even if he didn't hate them so much, Kate's crimes against the throne were well known and numerous. *Like her traitor father before her . . .* The memory of Hale Brighton kneeling before the executioner appeared in Corwin's mind, his imagination easily twisting the image into one of Kate.

Rising from his chair, Corwin stumbled toward the door, the tears already blurring his vision. He gasped for air, struggling to breathe through his grief. Desperately, he searched for some private place where he could be alone, but there weren't any. The moment he left the library, his guards followed, their footsteps loud and intrusive behind him. In a daze, he made his way to the nearest garden, finding some small refuge by a fountain tucked in a far corner. Ignoring the guards as they settled into their watch, he knelt on the edge of the pool and buried his face in his arms. Then as the tears came in earnest, he silently poured his heart out to Noralah, begging the goddess to make the news untrue. But the goddess remained silent, far less real than the words he'd read on that newspaper page, far harder to believe in.

Corwin remained there for hours, his knees and back aching, his throat raw and his heart a stone inside his chest. He would've stayed there all night, but as always the need for his nenath dose came upon him. He resisted as long as he could, his despair giving way to his hatred of Gavril and Rendborne, and all the others who had come between him and Kate. But in the end, the thirst forced him to his feet and back to his quarters.

He drank the nenath first, then helped himself to wine, downing an entire glass in nearly a gulp. It didn't help. He doubted anything would, but that didn't stop him from reaching for another.

Feeling the heat of the wine in his cheeks almost at once, he headed onto the balcony for some fresh air only to find Eravis there, staring out at the night-dark sky already speckled with stars. With her hair undone, as always, she was a lovely sight, the shapely curves of her body outlined by the thin silken robe she wore.

At the sight of her, Corwin almost turned around again, but changed his mind. She wasn't his enemy, even now. He came up next to her, resting his hands on the balcony's edge as he leaned against it. Eravis stayed in place beside him, her gaze fixed on the expanse of sky. The pale moonlight lit up her features, quiet and sad. Resigned to her fate.

Corwin waited for her to speak, to tell him that this was her last chance to escape Gavril's machinations, but she remained silent. He felt a swell of tenderness for her, and respect for her strength in choosing not to tell him, as if she meant to spare him. He supposed he could've loved her, under other circumstances. If not for Kate.

*But Kate is gone.*

The pain struck him anew, and he drew a raspy breath.

Eravis turned to him, concern creasing her brow. "Are you all right?"

He shook his head.

"What is it?" She took a step toward him, laying her palm against his forearm.

"I . . . I can't tell you. I can't talk about it. Not yet."

Eravis bit her lip, clearly wanting to know more, but she held back, again showing him a strength he had no trouble admiring. "Well, if you change your mind, I'm happy to listen. Or if there is anything else I can do."

He nodded, covering her hand where it lay on her arm. "Thank you."

*Would it really be so bad?* a voice whispered in his head. *To love this woman? To give her what she wants?* The question sent a wave of dizziness over him. Or perhaps that was just the wine.

Even so, Corwin found himself examining his heart, searching through the pain for an answer. *No,* it came to him. *It wouldn't be so bad.* What was more, it was going to happen regardless. He was as powerless to stop Gavril's magic as he was incapable of holding back the tide or keeping the sun from setting.

With a soft exhale, Eravis took a step toward him, encouraged by his touch. Corwin stiffened for a moment, then forced himself to relax. She looked up at him, gaze hopeful, lips parted. Then she stood on her tiptoes and kissed him. On instinct, Corwin raised his hands to her waist, his fingers grazing the silken strands of her hair. Eravis slid her arms around his shoulders, pulling him closer. Corwin accepted, deepening the kiss. She tasted like she smelled—sweet and sensual, arousing an ache in him, both physical and something more—the need for connection with another. To love and be loved. He'd been alone for so long, the isolation adding to his grief.

He moaned, his thoughts shutting down in the onslaught of sensations. She pulled back from the kiss at the sound, a coy smile cresting her lips as she took his hand and drew him away from the ledge toward the bed just inside. Letting the robe slip off her shoulder, revealing her nakedness beneath, she lay back on the bed and pulled him down for another kiss. He went, easing toward her like something that might break if he pressed too hard, that might burn him if he got too close.

Boldly, Eravis ran her hands down his chest, toward his belt, which she unfastened with trembling fingers. Once done, she leaned up to reclaim his mouth again. He leaned into the kiss, eyes sliding closed as she pushed up against his body with hers.

Closing his eyes was a mistake. If he hadn't, he might've been able to go on pretending. But the moment he did, the memories rushed in. Memories of this very act, this closeness . . . with someone else.

With Kate.

Her face appeared in his mind's eye, and for a moment, his desire intensified, becoming an inferno inside him.

"Corwin," Eravis whispered against his ear. "My Corwin."

At the sound of her voice—the wrong voice—the flame inside

him went out. He pulled back from her, wiping his mouth with his hand.

"What is it?" Eravis peered up at him, startled, lips red and swollen.

Shaking his head, Corwin climbed off the bed and retreated a few steps from her. "I can't do this."

With a blush flooding her cheeks, she scrambled upward and pulled her robe back over her shoulders once more. "Why?" The word sounded more plea than question.

There were a hundred different reasons he could give her.

But only one that truly mattered right now, in this moment.

"Because I love someone else." He couldn't bring himself to use the past tense. In his heart, Kate still lived. She would live there forever.

Still on the bed, Eravis drew her knees to her chest, wrapping her arms around her legs. Corwin braced for her anger or her tears, but she surprised him by asking gently, "Who is she?"

He swallowed, afraid he would start crying if he dared speak her name. Yet he needed to talk about her. "Kate. Her name is Kate." Several tears escaped his eyes, sliding down his cheeks.

At the sight of them, concern creased Eravis's brow. "What happened?"

Again, Corwin tried to resist, but the need to speak was too great. He told her about the newspaper. And then he told her about Kate. Who she'd been to him, of their childhood and tumultuous teen years, and of the way they'd eventually reunited. Eravis listened, never once interrupting, but only encouraging him with questions whenever he hesitated, doubting the wisdom in confessing these truths to her.

But finally, the well of memories ran dry, and Corwin at last felt the ache in his chest ease, his grief spent for the moment. Guilt quickly took its place. "I'm sorry, Eravis. I truly am. I know this is our last night of grace from your father, but there's nothing I can do. Not willingly."

Blanching, she looked away from him. Several moments passed before she found the will to respond. Then, with a sigh, she turned back to him. "I wish I could hate you for it, but how can I? You love her, and that's not easily set aside."

Corwin nodded, noting the hint of jealousy in her voice. And yet that was far from the worst of it. Gavril was still coming for them.

Eravis seemed to be thinking the same thing. "I just wish we had more time. Things could be different, better, if . . ." She trailed off into her own thoughts. Then she abruptly stood. "Maybe we can make more time." She turned and hurried over to the dressing table.

"What do you mean?" he said, trailing after her.

"It'll be difficult and risky," she said, mumbling to herself as she pulled open a drawer and began rummaging through the contents. "If my father finds out . . . but it's better than—" Finding what she wanted, she broke off and faced him once more. In her hand she held a ruby-encrusted golden brooch nearly as large as her palm and with a long sharp pin on the back of it.

Corwin arched an eyebrow at her. "What are you thinking?"

She closed her fingers over the brooch. "That we convince my father that the deed is done. All we need is some theater."

Although Corwin understood her plan at once, he couldn't keep from gaping. "You would help me deceive your father?"

"Yes," she said, a hint of steel in her voice. "But we must be absolutely convincing. He must believe that the act has happened. And so must Gavril."

It wouldn't be easy, and remembering the story about her murdered kitten, Corwin had a feeling the risk would be far greater for Eravis than him, but if she was willing, so was he. More than willing.

"Whatever it takes," Corwin said, his lungs expanding with gratitude. He eyed the brooch once more. "But what exactly do you have in mind?"

HE WOKE THE NEXT MORNING in a languid haze, his body wrapped in a pleasant warmth. He'd slept long and deep—and late, he realized as he slowly opened his eyes to see the sun already high over the horizon beyond the window.

At the sight of Eravis nestled beside him, all of the previous night's events came rushing into his mind. He tensed, uncomfortable with their intimacy, she in nothing but her shift and him in only his underclothes. They'd spent the entire night lying side by side. Then he remembered the blood she left on the sheets from a cut she'd made high on her thigh with the brooch's pin, and he reached out to wake her, wanting to make sure she was okay.

The sound of a door opening stopped him, and he craned his neck to peer through the doorway into the living room. It was the same elderly woman who came every morning to check the record. Marching into the bedroom, she froze at the sight of Corwin and Eravis.

Heat rose up Corwin's neck, but before he could admonish the woman for her intrusion, Eravis came awake. With a loud yawn, she sat up, her hair a rumpled mess around her face.

"Good morning, Malva," she said. "Give us just a moment to get out of your way. I'm afraid we were both overcome by tiredness this morning." Eravis cast a shy, albeit mischievous, smile at

Corwin, playing the part perfectly.

The heat rose farther up his neck, but with relative ease, he smiled back at her. It helped that she seemed so genuinely happy. He supposed maybe she was, that actively defying her father brought her a dark satisfaction. But he couldn't help but be nervous. Fooling Mistress Malva was far easier done than the Godking. *And Gavril.*

Malva bowed. "Pardon the intrusion, your highness."

"No need." Eravis slid from the bed, giving a slight wince as she stood. There was no question that it was genuine. Probably from the cut she'd given herself last night, but easily misinterpreted by an unsuspecting Malva.

Corwin followed her lead, climbing out of the bed as well. Reaching for the robe he'd left tousled on the floor, the sudden need for the nenath struck him, making his knees almost buckle. With a stifled groan, he managed to straighten up and avoid falling. It must be even later than he thought, and he wondered if Zan had come and gone while he and Eravis slept. But as he walked into the living room he found all the tables empty save for the wine from the night before. For a second the panic started to rise in him, but the next moment Zan appeared in the door, tray in hand.

"Apologies, your highness," Zan said, walking in. "But you must drink this quickly, Lord Gavril—" He broke off at the sight of Eravis sauntering through the doorway in nothing but her robe.

"Good morning, Zan." Eravis approached the stunned page, reaching toward the tray, which she had to nearly pry from his fingers. "I will serve my husband this morning." Setting the tray on the nearest table, she poured a glass of the nenath and offered it to Corwin.

Unable to fully hide a smile at Zan's continued shock, Corwin raised the glass to his lips and downed the nenath, sweet relief rushing through him at once. "Thank you," he said to Eravis.

In answer, she reached up and kissed him, her body boldly pressed to his. Corwin stiffened for a second, then, remembering the act, he kissed her back.

As they pulled apart a moment later, Malva entered the room, the bedsheets clutched in her arms like a treasured prize. "Thank you. The Godking will be most pleased." She bowed and left.

Zan at last came out of his stupor. Blinking several times, he cleared his throat. "Please, your highness," he said, addressing Eravis. "But Lord Gavril has need of Prince Corwin this morning."

Eravis frowned, and Corwin sensed the tension spreading through her body. It was spreading through his as well, dread like a roll of thunder. "Very well, but see that he doesn't keep him too long. My love and I have plans for the day." She smiled at Corwin, reaching over to squeeze his hand affectionately.

"Certainly, your highness." Zan bowed, then, rising, he ushered Corwin back into the bedroom to help him dress.

Eravis lingered in the bedroom as well, watching from the balcony, but any hope they might've had to discuss Gavril's sudden need to summon Corwin was ruined by Zan's presence. In the end, Corwin could only whisper a word of encouragement in Eravis's ear as he kissed her good-bye.

Corwin's guards fell into place behind him the moment he and Zan stepped outside, but when they reached the bottom floor, Zan turned and waved them away. "I will escort Prince Corwin from here. Lord Gavril insists he come alone."

The guards looked dismayed for a moment, but the feeling didn't last, not with the prospect of a morning off. Once alone, Zan continued on the way, soon heading toward the bailey where a litter waited.

"Where are we going?" Corwin eyed the litter askance. He had only ever seen Gavril inside the palace. In fact, this would be the first time he'd left the palace since the wedding ceremony.

"The Mistfold," Zan replied, a note of excitement in his voice.

Worry clawed at Corwin's thoughts. Bonner and Nadira were most likely in the Mistfold, and the possibility that they'd been discovered made him shudder.

The journey through the city to the Mistfold took an eternity, and yet all too soon Corwin found himself stepping out onto the broad field beyond that towering red wall with the pit waiting just ahead. It looked the same as he remembered, the long squat buildings, the severed head of the ancient statue, and everweeps everywhere. Their sweet smell washed over him, making him sway with the sudden onrush of homesickness.

Zan led him down into the pit and then to the arena in the center, a low wall surrounding the statue. To Corwin's surprise, he recognized the statue's face. It was a depiction of Sevan, same as he'd seen in several books in the library. *The dead god.* Somehow the realization only made the situation more ominous.

That, and the multitude of Sevan soldiers assembled inside the arena before the raised dais at one end. For a moment, Corwin wondered where all the wilders were, but when he finally spotted Bonner standing in the front row, closest to the dais, he realized this must be them. Their conversion into the Godking's weapons was nearly complete.

Reaching the dais, Zan mounted the steps and dropped into a bow before Gavril, who'd been watching their approach. "I've brought the prince, my lord."

With a scowl stretching across his face, Gavril folded his hands primly in front of him. "What was the delay?"

Zan hesitated, color rising in his cheeks. "His highness and Princess Eravis slept late, my lord."

Gavril's scowl gave way to a look of surprise. "That can't be." Doubt rang clear in his voice, and Corwin braced for the assault of his magic. Concentrating hard, he forced memories of the night before to the front of his mind, of kissing Eravis, embracing her, lying beside her, everything he wanted Gavril to see and nothing he did not.

The man's sway slid inside him like a spider disappearing into a crack in a wall. He made no effort to hide the intrusion. Corwin gritted his teeth, trying in vain to fight him back, all the while his thoughts on Eravis. *This isn't going to work.* But no sooner had the thought started to rise in his mind than he felt Gavril withdraw.

"I see," Gavril said, his jaw clenched in disgust.

Observing the man's reaction, Corwin allowed himself a moment to feel the sweet rush of victory. Gavril believed him, and what was more, Corwin suspected he was unlikely to go prying again. A man of his pride couldn't handle confronting the failure, the missed opportunity. Better to pretend he never cared to begin with. Or perhaps it had never been about the sex at all, but the chance to wield the power itself.

"Have a seat, your highness." Gavril motioned to the single chair set on the dais. Resting on a small platform, it had a distinctive throne-like appearance that quickly drove away Corwin's sense of victory as he sat down upon it, helpless to resist Gavril's direct command.

Turning toward the silently waiting army of conscripted wilders, Gavril addressed them in a raised voice. "It seems that one of you has rejected my Tenets." He motioned below him to the nearest wilders. "Bonner, bring the defiler here."

With no sign of hesitation, Bonner grabbed the arm of the man standing next to him, who Corwin could now see was bound at the wrists and wearing a magestone collar. The man was old enough to be Corwin's father, but slight of build, with a craggy face offset by a perfectly straight nose. He walked stiffly beneath Bonner's grip, his spine rigid and head high even as fear shone in his eyes.

Once atop the dais, Gavril held out his hand to the man. "Yesterday, this man, Alton Dailey, disobeyed my direct order. An act which, by now, should've been impossible." Gavril paused, running his gaze over the still, silent assembly. "And yet it undeniably happened. This raises the question of whether there are any other defilers of my Tenets among you."

Corwin drew a deep breath, trying to stop his heart from racing for fear that Gavril would notice. The hope he'd built up these last few days began crumbling inside him.

"Which means," Gavril continued, "that I have no choice but to test each and every one of you for your loyalty to me."

A ripple of movement went through the crowd, but it was so

slight Corwin wasn't sure he didn't imagine it.

Gavril turned toward Bonner. "We will start with you, God-spear." Gavril pointed to Alton. "I order you to kill this traitor. But you must do it slowly, punishing him as his disobedience deserves."

Corwin couldn't guess what Gavril planned, but he knew Bonner did, the command sent right to his mind with Gavril's sway. Bonner shifted to the right, raising his arms toward something in the distance. There was a groan of metal, and a rectangular object rose up in the air above the heads of the wilders and soared over them toward the dais. It came to rest at Bonner's feet, a metal cage of a size that might hold a nightdrake.

Or a person.

Corwin's rib cage seemed to close in around his heart as Bonner swung toward Alton, grabbed him by the shoulders, and forced him into the cage.

"Please," Alton said, struggling, but Bonner didn't relent. He couldn't. They weren't ready to fight Gavril, the numbers of those freed far too small to fight back the rest of the group still bound by Gavril's Tenets. No, Bonner had to prove himself now or they would lose all.

A moment later, Alton was closed inside the box. With a wave of his hand, Bonner warped the bars with his magic, flattening the metal outward so that the cage became a solid box. Then he slowly began to draw his hands closed. As he did the box grew smaller and smaller. Even so it was a long time before the screams started, but when they did the sound was like a force in Corwin's skull, stabbing his ears, his mind, his heart, with horror.

It must've been worse for Bonner, who had surely known this

man, and who didn't have the luxury of Gavril's compulsion this time. What he did now, he had to do with his own force of will, driven by a loyalty to the other wilders he still had a chance to save.

When the screams finally ended, and the cage was less than half the size it had been, shortened and flattened both, Bonner turned toward Gavril and bowed.

The man smiled back in satisfaction. "Very good. Let's see if the rest will comply as easily."

Knowing there'd been nothing easy about it, Corwin's heart ached for his friend, for the guilt that he would now be forced to carry. And it might not even prove worth it. Not unless the other freed wilders were strong enough to do the same.

One by one, Gavril called the soldiers onto the dais and put them to the test. Some he made do harm to themselves, and some harm to others. But Alton was the only wilder victim, the rest condemned prisoners of Seva.

Nadira was tested not long after Bonner. Gavril ordered her to stop the heart of a young man, hardly more than a boy. His right hand was missing, a consequence of thieving in Luxana, yet a crime far undeserving of death. Nadira faced the boy, placing her palm against his chest, her expression a mask of indifference. All except for her eyes, which sparkled darkly with emotion. Corwin held his breath, certain she would relent, but a moment later, the boy lay dead at her feet.

On and on it went, taking hours. And yet none of the wilders disobeyed. Sometimes Corwin thought he could tell which of them had been freed and which hadn't, but mostly not. As the last one came and went, Corwin finally let himself take a full breath.

That was until Gavril motioned to him. "Your turn, Prince Corwin." *Stand and come here.* Gavril's silent command echoed inside Corwin's head, his body reacting at once.

"Bring up the last prisoner," Gavril said when Corwin reached him.

Bonner, who'd spent the day escorting the often struggling victims onto the dais, forced a final one up the stairs. It wasn't difficult, the man so thin and frail his struggles were hardly more than those of a child. As Bonner positioned the prisoner into place before Corwin, recognition tore through him.

"Henry." The name slipped involuntarily out of Corwin's mouth as all the memories of the long year he'd spent as Clash came crashing over him.

Henry looked up in confusion. "My lord?"

With his hands clenching into fists, Corwin turned to Gavril. "Let him go. I've given you no reason to doubt my loyalty, and this man has suffered enough to last a lifetime already."

"Indeed he has," Gavril said, pleasure in his voice, and a smile hidden beneath his solemn expression. He would have his victory now, it seemed. "That is why it is up to you to give him mercy, your highness. Secure him to the platform, Godspear."

Bonner obeyed, flicking his hands to raise up the iron shackles he'd earlier fixed to the floor with his magic, the restraints needed for many of the victims who'd come before.

Once Henry was secured, wrists and hands bound to the floor, Gavril turned and bowed toward Corwin. "Kill him, your highness."

An image appeared in Corwin's mind of exactly how Gavril

wanted it done. Corwin opened his mouth to protest, but at once felt his lips pressing closed, as Gavril's sway forced him into silence. Mutely, he turned to Bonner, who handed him a jar of oil, which Corwin upended over Henry's head, dousing him.

"Please, my lord," Henry said, lips smacking from the slickness. "What are you doing, my lord?"

For a moment, Corwin let himself hope Gavril would silence Henry as well, but he should've known better. Gavril wouldn't give him any mercy.

With the jar now empty, Corwin handed it back to Bonner. In return Bonner gave him a torch, one already brightly burning and hungry for more.

At the sight of those flames, Henry began to scream. With the sound of the man's terror driving him, Corwin reached deep inside himself for strength, desperate for a way to resist, to get free. *Let me go. Please, sweet goddess, give me the strength.*

But Gavril only tightened his grip. *Go on, your highness. Be the man your father raised you to be. Deliver justice and punishment on the deserving.* Gavril's words rang with irony, both of them knowing this wasn't justice at all.

*No!* Corwin silently screamed, fighting harder, but Gavril only pressed near in response. With a sudden flash of inspiration, Corwin changed tactic, embracing Gavril's presence in his mind as he'd learned to do with Kate before. Maybe he could squeeze Gavril out, make him so uncomfortable he would have no choice but to withdraw.

Corwin felt the man's mind opening up to him, thoughts and feelings and memories rushing in. He saw Gavril as a young boy living on the streets of Rin, thieving to stay alive, without a home or family. His parents had rejected him when he first showed the signs of his sway. They feared him, hated him—and his magic. Gavril had fled from them only to return later, once he'd come to understand that magic made him more than they could ever hope to be, made him better, superior to such fools. He killed them to prove it. He would kill any who dared treat him as less.

*Get out.* The thought pierced Corwin's skull, and he stumbled backward, losing his focus. At once Gavril's control strengthened inside him, closing around his will with a viselike grip, compelling him forward, torch raised.

"Please, my lord. Please, have mercy!" Tears streamed down Henry's haggard face as he pulled on the chains.

"I'm sorry," Corwin said, somehow managing to push the words past Gavril's control. But they didn't matter. They couldn't stop the agony of the death Corwin would give this man, one who had been a friend, a brother in the darkness.

The oil covering Henry's skin and hair caught fire at once, the strength of the ignition forcing Corwin to retreat. Henry's screams became mangled shrieks. Gavril's grip on Corwin released, allowing him to experience the man's suffering without interference or distraction. Corwin was alone with his misery and horror of what he'd done, what he could never undo. This mockery of a king dispensing justice.

When it was over, the fire extinguished by a pyrist, and Henry's screams silenced at last, Gavril turned and clasped Corwin on the back. "Well done, your highness. I'm satisfied that my Tenets hold true."

Corwin didn't reply. He could only stare as his hatred for this man burned inside him, the flames made hotter by his certainly that nothing, no amount of cruelty or display of power or victory, would ever satisfy such a monster as Lord Gavril.

No, in the end, only death would satisfy. *And I will give it to you,* Corwin silently vowed.

FARHOLD HAS FALLEN.

No matter how many times the thought charged through Kate's mind, the shock of it, the pain of it, refused to lessen. She never should've left. Never should've let them draw her out of the city. But Edwin and his advisers had learned all too well what a threat she was, how her sway was capable of turning the tide of battle. The guilt burned like acid inside her, and she was almost glad that Raith had been unconscious since arriving. For surely, when he did wake, he would look at her with condemnation. For choosing her friends over her duty.

The day passed without a single sound or movement from Raith's cell. He simply lay there curled in a ball on the damp, hard floor. None of them could tell how extensive his injuries were, although Kate reasoned if he'd survived the trip from Farhold they couldn't be life-threatening.

Raith at last stirred around the time the guards arrived with the evening meal. He remained lying down until the maids retreated, and they were alone once more. Then he slowly sat up, arms trembling from the effort.

"Raith," Kate said, drawing his gaze to hers. "What happened?"

He shook his head, and to Kate's dread she saw tears in his eyes. She couldn't bear to see him like this, so . . . so *broken*.

"Why don't you eat," Dal said. "The broth is about as flavorful as soggy socks, but you'll feel better."

Raith didn't seem to hear him, not at first. Then, slowly, he reached for the bowl and started eating. Kate ate too, hoping with each bite to find another message from Harue, but there was nothing but the thin, colorless soup.

When Raith finished eating, he set down the bowl, eyes still fixed on the ground before him. It occurred to Kate that he hadn't looked at any of them, not directly, and the realization unnerved her.

"Please, Raith," Kate said, "tell us what happened. We have a right to know."

"I suppose you do," he finally replied. "Even more than you realize." He raised his gaze to her at last, and she felt something hollow expand in her chest. There was no anger in him, she could see, not even at her. There was only guilt. "You were right, Kate," he said. "I never should've trusted Master Janus."

She drew a breath, eyes widening with horror. "What did he do?"

"What did I do to enable him, you mean." Raith shook his head. "I didn't know he was a spy, and like the worst fool, I gave him a room in my house, giving him easy access to all the information he needed. The guard rotations, the location of the black-powder stores. He had everything right at his fingertips, even the keys to the city. I never saw it coming." Raith broke off, choked by emotion.

"I'm sorry," Kate said, "so very sorry." Never in her life had she wished more to have been wrong. Despite their differences, she loved Raith like a father, a mentor, a person so admirable she could only aspire to walk in his shadow. And yet here he was, brought low, exposed to be as fallible as everyone else she had ever known. And yet somehow that made her love him more. She wished her arms were long enough to bridge the space between them.

"Don't be, Kate." A tired smile stretched across his bruised lips. "I should've listened to you. I usually do, you know, even when it seems like I don't. But this one time, I let my feelings cloud my judgments. I will regret it for the rest of my life."

Kate shook her head. "You've always let your feelings determine your judgments, and they've never failed you until now. Just the opposite. Without your feelings the Rising would never have happened."

Raith refused to be consoled though. "Yes, but now it's gone, thanks to me."

"I don't accept that," Dal said, his expression stern. "It seems to me that you were tricked by a cunning and formidable opponent. Anyone would've been taken in."

"Dal's right," Kate said, desperate to spare Raith some of his pain. "Master Janus is an old man. Magist or no, how did he manage to do so much without help?"

"I wish I knew," Raith replied, and Kate was relieved to hear that his voice sounded closer to normal. "None of us ever saw him do anything suspicious. Not once. It was as if he could make himself invisible. I've never known him to possess such powers before. By the time we realized what was happening it was too late to stop it. We were overrun in just a few minutes, helpless with the sun down and all the black-powder stores destroyed. The Mage League must've spent months preparing all the spells they used. Their barrage was devastating."

Dal's knuckles were bloodless as he gripped the bars. "But how did they get so many troops near the city without being seen?"

Raith sighed in defeat. "Who would've reported their movements to us? A city full of traitors? No, I'm sure getting close to Farhold was relatively easy. Our guards can only see so far, and there are plenty of areas near the city where they could've hidden."

Kate nodded. "And the League has been busy creating new spells as well." She described for them the device she'd seen Edwin use to communicate with his commanders all the way in Farhold. "This was well planned, and in motion for a long time."

Raith leaned back against the wall of his cell, knees raised to his chest, arms resting atop them. He dropped his head into his hands, overcome by grief once more. "I should've suspected something. Should've been more careful." He coughed, the gesture a sad attempt to disguise his tears. "So many died. Most of the council are gone. Talleen was killed in the first wave, and Jiro was taken prisoner along with me. Genet and Deacon might have survived, but I can't be sure. Francis surely perished as well—the soldiers set fire to the governor's house, and he went in to save Anise. Neither of them came back out."

*At least they died together*—or so Kate hoped, trying to draw comfort from the idea. But there was little of it to be had.

"Did any manage to flee?" Tira asked.

"A few, perhaps." Raith sighed. "We sounded the retreat not long after the attack began, once we knew what we were up against. Genet and Deacon were overseeing it, along with most of the magists. If any did make it out, they should have protection against the drakes, but there's no telling how long they'll last with nowhere to go."

Kate heard the truth in his voice. Even if they had survived, there wouldn't be enough to mount a resistance. Her stomach twisted at the thought. With the Rising destroyed, the Inquisition would surely resume. Wilders would be hunted down one by one—their kind purged from the earth.

"I never should've left," she said, the admission a self-inflicted wound to her heart.

"Perhaps that's true, Kate," Raith said, "but they attacked at night. Even if you'd been there you could've done little to help." With that, he retreated to the back of his cell and fell silent once again, leaving the rest to their private griefs and fears, not just at what had happened but at what tomorrow would bring.

Kate woke to the sound of a storm outside, loud peals of thunder that were soon followed by rain trickling down the walls of their cell from the runoff on the ground above.

The guards and maids arrived shortly after with the morning porridge. The food no longer held any appeal for Kate, not now when so much was lost. Even if Harue could get them out of here, what then? Where would they go? What would they do? There were other countries they could flee to in an attempt to find a new life, but Kate couldn't forget the way she had felt in Seva with her magic gone, as if a part of her had been carved out. She didn't know if she could live like that for the rest of her life. If she could give up her sway. Even these last few weeks with the collar on had left her feeling like a mere shadow instead of flesh and bone.

"Are you not going to eat, Kate?" Dal said around a mouthful.

She shrugged and picked up her bowl, not interested in a lecture.

And at least it passed the time. There was nothing worse than a long wait for something dreadful.

As she took the first bite, though, she felt something hard and heavy form inside her mouth, clanking against her teeth. Spitting it out, she heard Dal gasping across the way. She looked up to see his face turning purple.

"He's choking!" Laurent tried in vain to reach Dal through the bars.

Next to Kate, Tira was also spitting out her porridge. Kate looked down into her bowl. A key lay there, looking as out of place as a beetle in a drinking glass. Realization was instant, and she plucked it out, rammed her finger through the bars, and started to frantically work the lock. Next to her Tira had caught on and was doing the same. Kate got through first, and she dashed to Dal's cell, using the key once more and wrenching the door open a moment later. His face had gone from purple to puce.

"Bang him hard on the back," Raith said, demonstrating uselessly.

Kate slammed her open palm against Dal's back as hard as she could. Tira appeared next to her a moment later, and they took turns beating him, until finally the thing lodged in his throat shot across the cell and clanged against the bars. Another key.

"Damn that Harue," Dal croaked, hands rubbing his throat. "She could've warned us."

Tira put a hand on one hip. "Or you could try not eating like a hungry goat all the time."

Dal made a face. "What's the sense in sending us so many keys? One would've done the trick."

"Harue likes to be thorough," Kate said, brushing past them both to unlock Raith's cell.

"Good thing, too, if you'd managed to swallow yours," Tira added, as she unlocked Laurent's cell.

Despite her earlier feelings about just giving in, Kate felt electrified now, hope pulsing through her veins. She was a survivor, and she would survive this, same as all the other hardships she'd endured. There were still wilders out there who needed help, and this was their home. She would rather die fighting than surrender and live.

"Will this work on the magestone collar?" Kate said, shoving the key into Raith's hand. He shook his head. "We'll have to make do without then." It would be hard, but Tira and Dal were two of the best fighters Kate knew, and Laurent had received some training as well. Besides, they might get lucky and be able to sneak out undetected.

The corridor beyond the door was deserted when Kate went to check it, although she could hear the sounds of a disturbance far away, muffled but audible enough to set her nerves on edge. It wasn't the storm. That had stopped abruptly sometime before. Something was wrong here.

Kate eased down the corridor toward the exit, Tira, Dal, Raith, and Laurent following just behind her. She kept her hands fisted, ready to strike at any enemy that appeared and hoping she came across some sort of weapon. Even a broomstick would do.

Ahead, the doorway creaked open, and Kate hissed between her teeth, motioning at the others to get ready. But the figure that appeared was tiny, hardly more than a child.

"Wen! What are you doing here?" Kate rushed toward the girl, panicked at the sight of her. She had no business taking such a risk, sneaking into Mirror Castle. If she'd had access to her sway, Kate would've ordered the girl to flee right this moment.

Wen pressed a finger to her lips. "This way." She didn't wait for confirmation, but spun soundlessly on her heels and headed back through the door.

Teeth gritted, Kate followed after her. She would throttle Harue for this. Once she thanked her for getting them free, that was. Wen led the way with the ease of someone familiar with the place. They took the stairway up and made a left down another corridor. The sounds of disturbance grew louder, the discordant clang of steel, the shrieks of people fighting, dying. Kate knew the symphony well.

"Wen," Kate said. "What's happening?"

She glanced over her shoulder. "The city is under attack."

"What? Who's attacking?" For a moment she pictured Genet, leading the remnants of Farhold against Norgard. It was absurd, but the object of hope so often was.

"Seva," Wen said, not looking around this time.

*Seva.* Every hair on Kate's body stood up at once. *The Godking's wilder army.* They were here, at last. She couldn't fathom it. All this time, she'd allowed herself to put other worries first, to forget about what she'd seen in the Mistfold, and the danger that would surely be coming one day, one that the Rising had never been in a position to do anything about. *Damn Edwin and his prejudice. If he'd only listened . . .*

"The Godking's army arrived with the storm," Wen continued. "They've already breached the city walls and will be here soon. We must hurry."

Questions crowded into Kate's mind, but she held them back, trusting Wen and whatever plan Harue had devised to get them out. They made their way up several more flights of stairs, at last arriving in the corridor outside the throne room.

"Through here." Wen opened the door to the throne room itself. It was deserted, the Mirror Throne dull in the murky light, the sky ashen beyond the windows lining the edge of the vaulted ceiling. Wen raced across the chamber, heading to the far door in the opposite corner. She waited, checking for noise outside, then pushed the door open.

They continued on, and soon realized that they needn't worry about finding cover as servants came running past on some unknown mission, and a gaggle of courtiers rounded a corner in search of a safe hiding place. No one noticed them, and the air felt charged with panic, the sounds of battle growing ever louder. Kate hoped the chaos would give them cover to escape unnoticed, while the castle guards were focused on the invaders.

Sometime later, Wen came to a stop by a window facing the west side of the bailey. Heavy drapes hung from each side of it, the navy-blue velvet tied by a silver sash. Wen undid the sashes on both sides, letting the drapes fall closed and obscuring the window behind them. Then she uttered a word beneath her breath.

"What are you—" Kate began, but broke off as a bright light flashed around the edges of the drapes, the telltale sign of a magist spell activating. When Wen pulled the drapes back once more, the window had been transformed into a doorway, a secret mage entrance.

"Wen, I owe you a puppy." Dal patted her on the head. A rare smile scampered across the girl's face as she motioned them through. Kate went first, hands balled into fists once more, wishing she had her sway or any kind of weapon at all.

The space between the buildings she emerged into was as deserted as the corridor before. Once all of them were through, Wen again took up the lead. There was a turn ahead, and just before they reached it, someone stepped around the corner toward them.

Kate skidded to a halt, her mouth falling open as she recognized Master Janus. He looked the same as he had in Farhold—impossibly old and spent, back bowed with age and head bald and liver-spotted. At the sight of him, Wen plucked a magestone out of her pocket and threw it at him, shouting the spell of invocation as she did so. Momentary light burst around them, but when it cleared, Janus was still standing there. Kate gaped at the sight of the magestone cupped in his hand and him unaffected by the spell's power. Janus examined the stone, as if curious, then closed his fingers around it, turning it to dust. He shook the remnants away then stared back at them.

"Janus, please." Raith moved in front of Wen and Kate, holding his arms out to shield them with his body. "Let us go."

Kate watched from around Raith's shoulder, unnerved by Janus's eerie calm. It was true that without access to their magic, neither Raith nor Kate were much of a threat to him on that front, but there were six of them against one old man. Magic or no, he would be hard-pressed to stop them if they attacked en masse.

Janus shook his head, lips parting into a black, toothless smile. "I'm afraid letting you go is out of the question."

Raith sighed, the sound a desperate plea. "I don't want to hurt you. I owe you my life, but you've betrayed my loyalty, everything I stand for. Things you once stood for too—goodness and love, not oppression and hate. But it's not too late to right that wrong. Just let us go."

Janus only smiled in response, a look of madness in his eyes.

Kate balled her hands into fists, pity squeezing her chest at Raith's desire to redeem his old mentor, even now. "It's too late for that, Raith." She glanced at the others. "We take him down together."

With a grim nod, Raith stepped aside. Kate lunged at the old man first, Dal right beside her, along with Tira and Laurent just behind them. Wen, too, reached into her pocket for another magestone. But before any of them could get to him, Janus raised a hand and a fierce gust of wind shot out from it, knocking them all back. Kate stumbled and fell hard on her rump, teeth clanging together. Cursing, she scrambled to get up, only to feel an invisible force holding her down.

It was a sensation she'd experienced only once before, inside the Hellgate a year ago when she'd foolishly attacked Rendborne, the Nameless One. This was impossible. Janus shouldn't have such power. Control over the air was a wilder gift—no magestone could conjure it, and no person alive possessed both.

*None save for Rendborne.*

The truth dawned in her mind slowly, bringing unspeakable darkness with it.

Janus approached Raith, the latter pinioned to the ground by the same invisible force that held the rest of them. Squatting down next to him, Janus shook his head with an exaggerated sigh.

"Consider it a mercy that the real Janus didn't live long enough to see you beg like this. He surely didn't beg. Not even when I peeled the skin off his face."

Raith stared up at the man, mouth falling open and brow furrowed. "Who are you?"

In answer, Janus raised his hands to his neck and slowly began to pull away the skin on his face. No, a mask, one hiding his real face beneath—Rendborne. He looked unchanged from the last time Kate had seen him, his golden eyes ablaze and his features refined and handsome—the regal features of House Tormane, to which he once belonged.

"You," Raith said in a faint whisper, the quiet, trembling sound belying his horror.

"Me." Rendborne stepped even closer to him, the mask wriggling in his hand. A wrench went through Kate's stomach as she realized the mask wasn't some illusion like that wrought by the magestones Harue fashioned for them; it was made from actual skin, the underside of it veined with red striations.

Struggling, Kate tried to throw off the magic holding her. She had to get free, to escape. The sound of footsteps echoed nearby, and Rendborne glanced over his shoulder as a squad of soldiers rounded the corner toward them. All wore the red and gold of Seva, the Godking's bull emblazoned across their breastplates.

"Lord Rendborne," the leader said, bowing. "We heard a disturbance."

"Yes, these prisoners were attempting to escape. Why don't you round them all back into their cages." He paused, gaze fixed on

Raith. "Except this one, he's outlived his usefulness. Well, almost, that is."

Helplessly, Kate watched as Rendborne reached into his pockets, withdrawing a silver knife from the right one and a crystal vial from the left. A moment later, he slashed the knife across Raith's throat. Raith's eyes went wide, and a sound like a wet exhale escaped him, and then he slumped over, blood pooling from the wound in his neck.

Kate screamed, only to have Rendborne wave a hand at her, silencing the sound with his magic. Rendborne knelt beside Raith, positioning the vial beneath the wound, letting the flow of blood spill into it. Tears slid silently down Kate's cheeks as she watched it fill up, the life of her mentor, her friend, draining away.

Once it was full, Rendborne stood and stoppered the vial. Then he turned to Kate, smiling down at her. This close, she could see that his right hand—the one that still bore the uror mark—was black and twisted as if from a wasting disease. She knew the truth—he'd been damaged when the magic in his uror mark had reverberated against Corwin's own. That sight gave her hope, helping her keep her head above the despair threatening to drown her. Despite his godlike powers, Rendborne could be harmed, could be killed, defeated. *Somehow.*

"Don't worry, Kate," Rendborne said, his voice a chilly caress. "You won't be joining Master Raith just yet. I still have a use for you, too."

# PART TWO

## The Paragon and the King

CORWIN HAD EXPERIENCED TWO HOMECOMINGS in his life before. The first when he returned to Norgard after having disappeared for three years to parts and adventures unknown to the kingdom. His arrival then had been heralded by bright sunshine, followed by an almost frenetic energy from the people who longed to know where he'd been, what he'd been doing. His second homecoming had followed his presumed death at the jaws of daydrakes. It had been heralded by a terrible storm the night before, and his appearance in the city was a cause for celebration among the people, eager for the start of the uror trial and the competition of the princes who might become king.

His third homecoming was heralded by blood.

Seva's armies of mind-controlled wilders attacked Norgard at dawn, not long after the city gates were opened. Before they came in view of the city, the wilders conjured a storm at Magnar's command—the rain and thunder and heat producing a thick mist that hid the army's approach from the city watchmen atop the wall. It worked all too well, and Corwin could only observe it all from afar, in awe at the wilders' power. He'd seen their magic in action before, but never this many. Now, watching them all working in conjunction, he understood their awesome power, and he had to give credit to Magnar for recognizing the potential—and exploiting it to its fullest.

But he also saw the irony—that by trying to eradicate such power through the Inquisition, Rime had only left itself vulnerable to it.

Still, the awe didn't lessen the horror he felt once the killing started. He was kept a safe distance from the fighting, under a protection of guards, but it wasn't far enough to stop him from feeling the ground tremble with the terrible might of the earthists as they rained down rocks on Norgard's soldiers, riding out to fight them. It didn't insulate him from the screams of dying men and beasts, the splintering of wood and shattering of stone, the crack of gunfire, and the screech of steel meeting steel.

*These are my people.* Corwin felt their suffering, hands fisted around his horse's reins, his body rigid with the war raging inside him. He desperately longed to help, to fight back in defense of his city, but Gavril's Tenets held him firmly in place, as strongly as ever. He couldn't even utter a word of protest. All he could do was sit there, a toy prince and nothing more.

*I should've let Bonner kill me.* The thought reverberated inside his brain, regret bubbling up like acid inside him. Corwin hadn't been the same since the day of Gavril's loyalty testing. Henry's death, as well as the others', haunted him. Nightmares plagued his sleep, the memory of Henry's screams playing over and over in his dreams, his head, everywhere. Corwin had killed before, but never like that. The lives he'd taken had been in battle, his opponents given the chance to kill him first if they could. But Henry's death had been murder, and his part in it had left Corwin feeling soiled inside, damaged in a way that could never be made right.

Surprisingly, his sole comfort had been Eravis, his nights with her beside him easier than if he'd been alone. When he couldn't sleep, she stayed awake with him, telling him stories and asking him questions to help keep his mind off the terrors plaguing him. Although they remained as before, only pretending to be husband and wife, their relationship had become intimate in other ways, an undeniable emotional bond forming between them. He almost wished she were here now with him on the battlefield instead of back at camp.

And bad as it was for him though, it was far worse for Bonner and Nadira and the other freed wilders. Corwin had been compelled in that act of evil, a weapon in Gavril's hands. They'd had to pretend, to see the thing through despite having the option to act otherwise. Watching the battle now, Corwin wasn't sure they'd been right not to rebel then. The situation seemed even more hopeless than before. At least it certainly was for him.

When Bonner and Corwin met one last time, the night before their departure to Rime, they'd agreed that Bonner would wait until they reached Norgard before making his escape, taking as many Rimish citizens with him as he could. But it was clear to Corwin now that he wouldn't be escaping with them. Magnar had kept Corwin by his side the entire time with Gavril hovering nearby as well, ensuring the Godking's prize was kept on his leash.

*But the rest of Rime might stand a chance*, Corwin thought, trying to comfort himself. Magnar's army had taken Norgard by surprise, but the other cities would have warning, and there were many of them in this vast land. Yet as the battle wore on, he had no choice but to accept that they would all fall eventually—the power of the wilders and magists combined with the sheer number of Sevan soldiers was a force too powerful for any one city to be able to stop.

With the truth weighing him down, Corwin closed his eyes, retreating into himself as far as he could go, only to be drawn out again by the sound of a horse approaching.

"Your majesty!" The page rode up to the Godking, who sat astride his own horse.

Magnar's brow furrowed beneath the ornate helmet he wore, one bearing the horns of a bull. "What is it?"

The page's eyes flicked to Gavril, whose horse stood as still as if it had been carved from stone, not so much as turning an ear or flicking its tail to shoo a fly—the beast a prisoner beneath his sway the same as the rest of them.

The page glanced back at Magnar. "Some of the wilders have . . . disappeared inside the city. The Godspear was leading them."

Corwin tensed, his heart fluttering inside his rib cage. *Sweet Noralah, guard their steps, allow them to flee.*

"What do you mean?" Magnar addressed the page, but his gaze shifted to Gavril.

"Just that, your worship. General Ramir saw it himself. The Godspear was supposed to secure the east garrison, but instead he and some of the other wilders turned on our soldiers and killed them where they stood. Then they fled into the city."

"That's impossible." Although Gavril spoke calmly, the color leached from his cheeks. He had kept the knowledge of the disobedient wilder in Seva a secret from the Godking. Corwin resisted a smile at the man's squirming.

"Explain this, Lord Gavril," Magnar commanded, but Gavril only shook his head in dismay and claimed ignorance. As he did,

Corwin felt something like hope.

A small, useless hope. But hope nonetheless. It seemed no matter the circumstances he faced, his capacity for the feeling would never die.

By dawn the next day, the city had fallen to the Sevan scourge, and there had been no further sign of Bonner, not in help nor hindrance. Magnar and his men moved into Mirror Castle at once. Corwin and Eravis were given Corwin's old quarters, which he supposed was another form of torture. An effective one. Every moment he was surrounded by the familiar turned painful. Eravis's presence only made it worse, plaguing him with guilt. Corwin endured though, his hopes on Bonner and the others now. At least here in Norgard, he might find allies among the Rimish survivors. Magnar wasn't a fool. He would leave as many Rimish alive as he could, showing mercy alongside his might.

For the first week, Corwin was confined to his quarters, more of a prisoner than ever. The isolation drove him half mad, especially with the need to know what was happening. Where was Edwin? What of the high council? How many were dead? Although Eravis was allowed to come and go, she couldn't ask the questions for him, not without arousing suspicions about her loyalty, and she wasn't permitted near any of the important meetings taking place. In the end, the only news she brought was that the Godking had dispatched half his forces to take the port city of Penlocke, a strategic move that would allow him to more easily move his troops in and out of the country. Corwin didn't doubt the city would fall quickly.

But finally, just as Corwin thought he could bear it no more, the

Godking summoned him and Eravis together. With an escort of guards, they were taken to the barbican situated over the main gate of Mirror Castle. The structure had been transformed, no doubt by wilder magic. The roof and walls of the barbican had been removed, leaving an open platform with a low safety wall surrounding it, one that gave the people assembled on the platform a clear view into the city outside, allowing them to both see—and be seen. A crowd packed the streets below, Norgard citizens among throngs of Sevan soldiers in their red armor.

Magnar stood center of the platform, pressed against the wall and looking down at the people below. Just behind him on the left stood Gavril, his small, prim hands folded in front of him, a hint of a smug smile on his lips. Corwin looked away, hatred heating his blood. Then he half stumbled as his gaze alighted on another familiar face to the right of the Godking.

Rendborne. The Nameless One was here, parading about for all to see, this man who had once been a Tormane, Corwin's great-great-granduncle, alive despite the years that should've claimed him long ago. Rendborne stared at Corwin with his sharp eyes, golden-hued like the eagle uror sign he'd once slain, claiming the magical being's powers for his own.

Resisting a shudder, Corwin turned away from Rendborne, aware of Gavril watching them both, eyes bright with interest. Corwin wondered how much the magist knew. Rendborne was protected from the power of sway by the vial around his neck, the blood inside it that fueled the spell drained from Kate's father before he died.

*You will not harm Lord Rendborne,* Gavril spoke into Corwin's mind.

Recoiling in disgust at the intrusion, Corwin surveyed the rest of the people on the platform. They all appeared to be Sevan, but then he spotted his brother standing near the back, flanked on each side by heavily armed guards. He looked thin, pale, but unharmed. He wore Norgard colors, the ornate cut of his clothes fit for a king. A hand seemed to squeeze Corwin's heart at the sight of him, gripping even harder when Edwin saw him, too. His brother's expression darkened, jaw clenched tight enough that rigid muscles stood out on his neck. Corwin flinched at the hate he sensed in his brother. Shame prickled over his skin. He could practically read Edwin's thoughts—he believed Corwin was complicit in the ransacking of their city, a traitor to his very core. He longed to tell him the truth of what happened, but there was no point with Gavril nearby. And with Eravis clinging demurely to his arm.

Magnar began to speak, drawing Corwin's attention. "Good people of Norgard and of Rime. Although it may seem that we are a foreign invader come to rule over you, I swear on the name of your goddess that it is not so. I am here to save Rime, and to deliver her to her rightful heir. Your very own Prince Corwin, who, as you've no doubt heard by now, was recently wed to my daughter Eravis." Magnar motioned behind him toward Corwin and Eravis.

*Go to him now,* Gavril said inside Corwin's mind. Powerless to resist, Corwin trailed beside Eravis as they approached the God-king, who first embraced him like a beloved son, then nudged him toward the ledge so that all below could see his face. Murmurs echoed through the crowd—though no one dared to shout insults, he could feel their sense of betrayal, just as he could Edwin's.

Magnar continued. "To that end, our only aim is to permit our beloved son-in-law a chance to claim his birthright through the completion of the uror trials, which his brother has, to this point, denied him." Magnar nodded solemnly at the doubtful murmurs. "Oh yes, it is true. The corruption in Rime has been widespread. Your high priestess was part of the deception as well. She allowed Edwin to be named king even as she knew Corwin to still be alive."

Magnar motioned to his left, and Gavril stepped aside as two guards dragged forward a woman bound in chains. Corwin barely recognized the high priestess, her face bruised and swollen, ceremonial robes ripped to shreds. The guards pushed her toward the wall, holding her bent over the edge so that everyone could see.

Magnar allowed her to stay there a moment, then said, "Place her in the dungeons to await her trial." Once she was gone from view, he pressed his hands together before him and addressed the crowd once more. "The order of Noralah priestesses have replaced their old leader with her first acolyte, who vows to root out the corruption." Magnar motioned toward Gavril a second time. Another woman came forward, her face unfamiliar to Corwin. Her outfit, though, he recognized at once—the diaphanous robes worn only by the high priestess.

The new high priestess approached the edge, where her predecessor had previously stood. She raised her hands toward the crowd and said in an emphatic voice, "The final uror trial will be administered following all the solemn and holy rituals of the generations of trials before. I will bear witness to the event, and its outcome, and we will at last crown the true goddess-chosen regent of Norgard, king of Rime."

Although the voice was hers, the words were Gavril's—and Magnar's. Corwin didn't need magic to know that the woman was under Gavril's sway. Even still, the crowd below applauded, convinced by this ruse, that a true Rimish king might still be crowned—not an empty husk enslaved by magic to this Sevan usurper.

With the speech at an end, Magnar turned away from the wall and left the platform, an entourage of guards preceding him. The rest followed, heading back inside Mirror Castle. Once there, the new high priestess led the way to the throne room, where the passage to the Vault of Souls waited a few feet behind the Mirror Throne itself. Dozens of servants were in the throne room to give witness to their procession as the high priestess unlocked the door to the vault and swung it wide open before heading down first.

Magnar stopped long enough to order Eravis to remain behind, then stepped in after the high priestess. Dread thudded in Corwin's ears at the command, wondering what the Godking planned that he didn't want his daughter to see. The rest followed after Magnar. Corwin walked just behind Edwin, with Gavril behind him. Cold air filled the passage, dry as a cellar, but it warmed the farther down they went—hundreds of feet below the surface to the vault itself. Like the wide mouth of some primordial beast, the massive cave was filled with the stone teeth of stalactites. In the center of the floor rested the hole of the Well of the World. Fathomless and black as pitch, it felt to Corwin like a giant eye watching him, judging him—and finding him wanting.

His skin prickled, and the palm of his right hand began to

ache, like it had in the days after he'd received the uror brand. This wasn't supposed to be how this happened. He wasn't ready for the third and final trial. Often he'd thought about this very moment, standing on the edge of the Well of the World. The trial was simple—he was to step willingly off the edge into the abyss to face whatever judgments the gods might give him. To emerge either as victor—and king—or not.

Corwin felt the weight of his unworthiness pressing down on him as memories of all his betrayals flashed through his mind. Unwilling though he might've been in some of those actions, he was still guilty of them. Once again, he regretted not taking the way out Bonner had offered him. For standing here, facing his fate, he knew that Edwin would be chosen over him, that any thought he had of saving Rime from itself was nothing more than pride. He glanced at his brother and was surprised to see his fear reflected in Edwin's face.

Magnar cleared his throat, the sound echoing against the stone ceiling until it became a dull roar. Ignoring it, he motioned to one of the soldiers. "Prince Edwin is no longer needed. Kill him."

*Kill him, kill him, kill him.* The words reverberated in a chorus, their meaning first distorted, then amplified. The soldier drew his sword as two others grabbed Edwin by the arms, holding him in place.

"No!" Corwin lunged toward the first soldier, only to freeze as Gavril's command ripped through his mind. With his arms pinned to his sides, Corwin could only watch as the soldier approached Edwin—and thrust the tip of the blade against his chest.

There was a loud crack, and the sword broke as if the soldier had rammed it against solid stone instead of human flesh.

"What is this?" Magnar demanded, nostrils flared. "Kill him, I say."

Another soldier came forward to try again with a fresh sword, only to fail in the same way, another broken blade clattering to the floor.

Corwin watched, openmouthed in disbelief. The uror brand on his palm burned as if lit from within, pulsing with magic.

"If I may, your majesty," Rendborne said, stepping into view. "I feared this could be the case. It is the uror, you see. Both princes are under the protection of the gods until after the uror trial has completed. They can only die as part of the trial itself."

Corwin blinked, trying to make sense of his words. Was it possible? He remembered Kate once telling him that Rendborne had tried to kill both him and Edwin before the uror trials even began, only to fail. But one of his great uncles had died during the second trial, his heart giving out from the strain of it. Both seemed to support Rendborne's claim.

With the truth dawning in his mind, Corwin realized that Bonner's plan had never been a possibility for him. Even if they'd tried, they wouldn't have succeeded in killing him. The truth only compounded his feelings of guilt.

"This is intolerable," Magnar said. "I can't leave him alive."

"I agree, you cannot." Rendborne grimaced. "You have two choices. Either let the princes actually finish the uror"—he motioned to Edwin and Corwin in turn—"or . . . let me take Edwin back with me to the Hellgate."

Magnar's eyes narrowed on Rendborne. "To what purpose?"

"The Hellsteel. We've almost found it."

The Godking shifted his weight from one foot to the other, his expression grim. "Our only purpose in procuring the Hellsteel is to revive the magic of Seva. Not to kill with it."

Rendborne bowed his head. "Indeed, that has been our purpose and will continue to be so. But I think it would be foolish to dismiss the daleth's other properties. If there is any weapon capable of slaying a god—or those protected by them—it is that."

*Daleth. Hellsteel.* This was the reason Rendborne had stolen that book from the great library. Only, Corwin hadn't seen mention of the substance having any other purpose beyond delivering death. And yet Rendborne claimed he would use it to revive Sevan magic. Was it true? He didn't know. The only thing he could be certain of was that Rendborne couldn't be trusted. Even now he had the sense that Rendborne was merely acting in deference to the Godking, pretending to be less than what he was—same as he had when he'd been just the minister of trade before revealing himself as the Nameless One—the Lord Ascender, as his followers called him.

Magnar stroked a hand over his beard, his gaze shifting from Corwin to Edwin, then back to Rendborne. "What is the risk of letting them finish the uror?"

Rendborne shrugged. "Who can say? With the gods meddling, anything is possible. But know this: no Tormane who has won the uror has ever known defeat afterward."

"Do you mean to say the protection will continue even once they're made king?"

"Perhaps." Now Rendborne turned his gaze on Corwin, malice in his eyes. "And there is no guarantee that Corwin will come out the winner, and thus no one to ensure your claim to Rime through your daughter."

"That's too great a risk." Magnar drew a deep breath, then let it out slowly. "Very well. Take Edwin to the Hellgate, but make sure no one sees. As far as the rest of Rime is concerned, Corwin was chosen by the uror and Edwin died in the trial." Magnar raised a hand toward Rendborne. "But the moment you've found the Hellsteel, bring it to me. I will use it to kill Prince Edwin myself. No one else may wield it."

Rendborne bowed, the very picture of subservience. Every muscle in Corwin's body tensed at the sight of it. *What is your game?* He remembered clearly the man's hatred, how he wanted nothing less than to see Rime destroyed forever. Rendborne didn't give a damn about the magic of Seva.

"And what of Edwin's wife, Sabine?" Gavril asked.

Magnar considered the question a moment, then waved his hand in a dismissive gesture. "Keep her here for the next month to see if her courses come upon her. If they do, send her back to her family. If they don't, arrange for her to meet an end, same as her husband."

He was eliminating any chance of an offspring to challenge for the throne. Corwin shook his head, pitying his brother, fearing for him. Edwin didn't react to this news. He'd made no sound at all since the first sword had struck him. Corwin didn't know if it was shock or merely Gavril exerting his control.

Magnar turned to Corwin, clapping his hands once. "I know it's not the uror trial you hoped for, but, well . . . congratulations on being crowned High King of Rime. We must conduct the coronation as soon as possible. But first"—Magnar glanced at Gavril—"we must be certain that Corwin remains under your control. We can't have him running off, like the Godspear."

With pursed lips, Gavril bowed his head in acknowledgment, giving Rendborne a quick glance that told Corwin all he needed to know about who was truly in charge here. "Yes, your majesty."

Then he turned to Corwin, a smile broadening his face. "I have a test in mind to prove his loyalty beyond any doubt. I'm told his former love, the traitor Kate Brighton, is still a prisoner here. I say it's high time she be executed—at his hands."

THERE WAS NO ESCAPE FROM the haze of pain. Even asleep she felt it. It was a dull pain, but deep, seeping into her bones, making them heavy. For days it had gone on. How many, she didn't know. Couldn't know, not with her head in constant spin, the world tilting around her whenever she opened her eyes. Only the spin didn't stop with them closed, not truly. She was caught in a vortex of agony.

*My blood*, she would think in brief moments of clarity. That was the cause of her suffering. Rendborne was stealing it, harvesting it. Not long after her recapture, Rendborne had her brought to a secret room in the dungeon, the entrance hidden behind a mage door. The moment Kate saw it she knew it had been Isla Vikas's workroom within the castle. She'd seen it in the Maestra's memories in the moments before Kate killed her. The fact that Rendborne had brought her here, a room so important to his dead lover, only increased Kate's fear of what was coming.

He'd forced her to lie on a stone table in the middle of the room, her legs and arms spread to the sides and secured by leather straps so that her extremities hung over the edges. Rendborne stood over her then, staring down at her with a hateful glint in his eyes.

"I would kill you now if not for the treasure that flows through your body," he said, raising the knife in his hands. Then he cut her, slicing into her wrist so deeply she felt the blade scrape against bone. "For Isla," he whispered as Kate held back a scream, the blood pouring hot and sticky over her hand.

Three more times he cut her that day. On the other wrist and at both ankles. The pain was excruciating at first, but then slowly faded into a dull throb, one that spread through her whole body. Until at last she was certain the Nameless One had taken too much and that she would die on this stone table, her life and magic drained from her. But just before she slipped into that final sleep, Rendborne healed her, mending her skin back together with his magic to stop the precious flow.

Then he sent her back to her cell, only to bring her back the next day and start all over again. And again. And again.

*Sweet goddess, let me die*, Kate thought as she lay on the stone table now. That she could form a rational thought in the midst of this dull pain, constant dizziness, and confusion should've brought her comfort, but it didn't. She was too tired for any emotion, exhausted to her very soul.

"Are you sure it's not too much, my lord ascender?" someone said nearby, the voice seeming to slide over Kate like a wave in the sea. "She seems to be fading." She didn't recognize the speaker, but she knew the address. All of Rendborne's servants called him that.

"She will be fine," Rendborne replied. "Kate has proven herself resilient many times already."

"Yes, I'm certain that is true," the man replied. "Only, may I ask why you need so much of her blood? There's a great deal already."

Through the dim haze of her vision, Kate saw Rendborne shift toward the other man. "I would harvest a thousand times more if I could. There is no telling how much protection we will need against the Hellsteel's power. That is, unless you want to volunteer your own blood in her place, Gavril."

Clearing his throat, the man bowed his head. "Whatever my lord ascender needs of me." But even in her addled state, Kate detected the reluctance in his voice.

Rendborne made an amused sound, as if he disbelieved the man's claim. "Have you secured the uror horse yet?"

This question, the man called Gavril answered at once. "Yes, I just came from doing it. I swapped out the magestone Edwin had been using to disguise it with a new one and moved the real uror horse to a different area of the stable, one not under rigid guard like where it had been before. Magnar will never expect to find it there, out in the open."

"Good. He must not get his hands on it." Rendborne shifted toward Kate, pressing his fingers into her forearm not far above the cut, as if he meant to help the blood flow more quickly.

"My lord ascender . . . ," Gavril began again, hesitant, "if she does die before tomorrow, it might make it difficult for me to convince Magnar of Prince Corwin's loyalty quite as effectively."

Shock jolted through Kate's mind at Corwin's name, and for a second the haze seemed to part. *Corwin is here?* If only she could access her sway, she could find him, make sure he was alive, that he was safe. But the infernal collar remained in place around her neck. Even if it wasn't there, she was too drained for her magic. *Magic is in the blood*, Vikas had told Kate once. And hers was nearly gone.

With a shrug, Rendborne turned away from the other man. "So be it. If she dies, there is still his best friend. Having Corwin execute Lord Dallin will be enough to convince a man as arrogant of his own superiority as Magnar."

*Dal*, Kate thought, making sense of the conversation. Only Corwin was to kill her first. *But how?* Corwin would never hurt her willingly. Then, with sick realization, she understood. *Sway*. This man must be a wilder, one gifted with the same power as her. She shuddered, and the gesture tugged at her wounds, sending a stab of sharp pain through her skull. She sucked in a breath, the world spiraling around her. Shutting her eyes, the haze closed over her once more.

Desperately, she fought it back, forcing her thoughts on Corwin. She knew full well what a wilder gifted with sway could do. *He will kill me.* He wouldn't be able to stop it. Even worse, he would know it was happening, fully aware of his actions even though they weren't his own. It was the worst thing she could imagine. Not for herself, but for him. Despair spread through her, the weight of it so heavy she thought it would crush her.

For the first time in a long time, since she could even remember, Kate turned her thoughts to the goddess. *Sweet Noralah, save me. Save us both.*

For a second, she sensed a warm glow behind her eyelids, but just as quickly it disappeared. And her blood continued to flow. A never-ending ebb, while the goddess remained silent.

THE EXECUTIONS BEGAN A FEW days later. The Godking held them on Goddess Tor, a towering hill to the south of the city with a massive stone altar, the Asterion, residing on its peak. The Sevan armies had spent the night camped at the foot of the hill when they first invaded, its size providing them cover from Norgard's watchtowers.

Terror thrummed through Corwin as he ascended the stairs, his legs soon screaming from the effort. The steep climb was known as the Steps of Sorrows. Thousands of people had climbed it before, each heading to their deaths. But never like this. Goddess Tor and its altar was a holy place, revered and reserved only for those whose lives were being given over willingly to the goddess in sacrifice. But Magnar sought to pervert its purpose, executing unwilling criminals. *And he will demand Kate's death at my hand.*

The thought sliced through him, severing any of the happiness he'd been able to feel at learning that she was indeed still alive. He wasn't delusional. This would end the same way it had with Henry.

And Kate would just be the beginning.

At least Edwin was safe for now. There was that comfort at least. He'd been taken to the Hellgate, in the middle of the Wandering Woods. For how long, Corwin didn't know. But the moment Rendborne discovered this Hellsteel, it would be over. Corwin raised his eyes to the sky, entreating Noralah. He saw no way out of this situation without divine intervention.

Behind him, Corwin heard Gavril's wheezing breaths as he labored with the climb. He fantasized giving the magist a push—one single, hard shove that would send him sprawling to his death on the craggy rocks at the foot of the hill. As ever, though, the Tenets held him tight as a noose.

When they reached the top, Corwin saw a vast assembly of people already present. The last time he'd been up here had been for the second uror trial. At that time, a large pavilion had taken up most of the area before the altar. Now it was filled with Sevan soldiers. There were no wilders among them, and Corwin guessed the Godking was taking no chances, not until they'd all demonstrated their loyalty to Gavril's sway. Those tests would be conducted in private. Eravis was absent as well, her father wishing to spare her from the carnage.

Gavril motioned for Corwin to continue up the far shorter flight of stairs to the Asterion, the raised stone platform resting atop more than a dozen pillars, each engraved with holy symbols that spoke of the birth of Norgard: how Noralah herself marked this land as her own, becoming both its mother and its guardian. Another crowd waited here, highborn Rimish citizens among more throngs of Sevan soldiers. Magnar and his usual entourage stood near the center of the platform where a narrow scaffold had been erected, an executioner standing atop it, a red mask covering his face and a gleaming ax in his hands. Two more soldiers hovered near each end of the platform, both helmeted with nose guards that obscured their features.

Corwin scanned the crowd, recognizing many of the Rimish citizens. Most were courtiers, the sycophantic sort who would bend the knee to Magnar the moment they were asked to do so, if they hadn't already. Anyone of consequence—Minister Knox, the master of arms; Alaistar Cade, master of horse; or even Captain Jaol, head of the royal guard—wouldn't be permitted to roam freely up here. They were either in chains somewhere, or already dead.

When Magnar's gaze alighted on Corwin, he raised his hands, and the entire crowd fell silent, the air thick with tension. "Let the trials begin," the Godking said.

One by one, Norgard soldiers were brought onto the platform and given the choice to either swear fealty or die. In the beginning, with hope and defiance still beating inside them, many chose the latter, and soon the gray expanse of the Asterion turned red with blood. Although Corwin wanted to look away, he forced himself to watch each death. These men who died for Rime, for Norgard, deserved his witness. It was all he could give them.

After the soldiers came their leaders, along with Norgard elite. When Master Knox stepped onto the platform, the old man held his head high, expression like stone. "I choose death," Knox said before the judge even had the chance to present the question. As he knelt in front of the executioner, he turned his gaze onto Corwin. Corwin braced, prepared for his scorn, his condemnation. Instead his old arms instructor nodded once.

And then it was over, only to start again. On and on it went. Not all chose death. There were just as many and more who swore fealty. These, too, Corwin watched, without judgment. He understood. This wasn't about loyalty or treason. This was survival. Even without the wilders and magists, the Sevan force was massive, far too many for what was left of the Norgard force to defeat, not without their own army of wilders. Watching his people stand up there, Corwin couldn't say for certain what he would have chosen in their place.

When the sun reached its zenith, a new set of prisoners was led toward the platform. At first, Corwin couldn't see them, the light too bright in his eyes. But when he raised a hand to his forehead, his heart gave a leap at the familiar face of the first person in line. Dark-haired and tall, the left side of his face a cavernous ruin, Dal looked thin and weary, his skin pallid and gaze dull. That was, until his eyes alighted on Corwin. Hope brightened his expression, the sight of it tearing Corwin apart from the inside. *Goddess, please, no.*

After Dal came Tira, she thin and diminished as well, as if she'd been starved for weeks in a dank hole somewhere, far from the sun. Even still she cast him a lazy smile, as if bored. Corwin saw the truth underneath, though, fear threading her body, sinewy muscles taut. Corwin stared at her, wishing she could see his thoughts. *Goddess, please, just swear fealty.* Live now to fight later.

But then Corwin's gaze lifted, and he spotted the figure just behind Tira.

The world seemed to stand still, the sudden stop shifting him off-balance, making his head spin. He barely recognized her. She looked so small, so . . . diminished. Her skin was like ash, with dark smears beneath her eyes and cheeks like sunken pits. She could barely walk, her gaze downcast and hair falling in a tangled mass around her face. A magestone collar encircled her throat. She was like a stranger, and still he would've known her anywhere.

"Kate."

Her name came out as nothing more than an exhale, and yet she lifted her head, hearing him.

"Be quiet and stay still," Gavril whispered, and Corwin felt the insidious pressure of the man's sway in his mind. His lips closed at once, but Gavril couldn't stop him from seeing, from feeling. His heart beat wildly in his chest, and he clenched every muscle in his body as he fought to get free, to go to her.

And to stop what was coming.

*Oh goddess, save me from this.*

A moment later, Kate and the others were past him and climbing up to the platform. They lined up, facing the Godking and his entourage. But the judge didn't pose his question this time. Instead Magnar addressed the crowd, motioning to the platform. "These prisoners—Dallin Thorne, Tira Salomon, and Kate Brighton— have been found guilty of sedition against Rime itself, crimes that by both Rimish and Sevan law are punishable by death and only death." Now he turned to Corwin. "As a show of his devotion to Rime as—we are certain—its future king, Prince Corwin will perform the executions with his own hand."

Magnar drew a gold-hilted dagger from his waist, twirled it around, and held it out to Corwin.

*Take it,* Gavril spoke inside his mind. *Take it and do as he bids, starting with Kate Brighton.*

*No, I won't. I can't.* But already Corwin felt the sway seizing hold. His hand tightened around the hilt, and his feet turned him around, carrying him forward to the platform's ladder. *Don't do this, Corwin. Don't do it. You can't do this.*

That was the worst part, the consciousness he maintained in the midst of these vile acts. He was himself, but not. Someone else was in control, as if he were a passenger in his own body.

Too soon he reached the top of the platform. The wind buffeted his body, cooling the sweat on his neck, the rest of him still drenched in it, a physical manifestation of his internal struggle. Reaching the top, he tripped and stumbled forward. The soldier guarding the entrance reached out to steady him. Corwin blinked at the guard, head muddled by the terror gripping him. The soldier touched Corwin's hand, the one not holding the dagger, and Corwin felt the press of metal against his palm.

"Don't look down at it," the soldier said. Corwin stared, trying to get a look at her face, but he could see nothing through the helmet.

His fingers closed round the object in his hand, the unique shape of it easy to recognize. A key. Stepping forward, Corwin's gaze moved to his friends, the four of them standing in a line, wrists bound with rope. Chains were too tiresome to remove from the dead. There was only one purpose for the key—the mage collar around Kate's neck.

*Get on with it,* Gavril's voice hissed in Corwin's mind, and with it came a vision of Corwin stabbing Kate through the heart. Although the sight made Corwin recoil, he was grateful for it, aware that while Gavril was busy enforcing his will, he wasn't paying attention to Corwin's thoughts and the knowledge of the key he carried.

But all too soon, he reached Kate. She looked even worse this close, veins visible in her forehead like sinewy shadows. Yet she remained the most beautiful thing he had ever seen. His heart ached.

"Corwin," Kate said, and the sound of his name on her lips sent an electric shock through him. "Don't do this. Fight him. It's me. It's Kate."

*Kill her.* Gavril's magic swelled like a gale-force wind inside Corwin's mind, driving everything else out. He raised the dagger.

"I love you, Corwin. I always have," Kate said. "Please . . ."

A war raged inside him as he fought against the sway. Fought to be himself and in control. And most of all, not to harm this woman he loved.

*Do it. Kill her.*

Corwin drew back his arm. *Do it now. Kill her. Pierce her through the heart.*

*KILL HER.*

"NO!" Corwin screamed, even as his arm thrust forward, straight for Kate. She flinched backward, terror on her face. Time seemed to slow, the world halting until nothing existed but the silent war in Corwin's head—Gavril's will against his own.

"*No!*" Corwin shouted again, drawing all the strength there was inside him. His uror mark burned red-hot against the hilt; his whole body was on fire, and at the last moment, the last fraction of an inch, he tilted the blade down, twisting it backward—until it pierced his own side.

Pain shattered through him, and with it sudden clarity and

control. Corwin thrust his other hand toward Kate, slipping the key into her palm. "Run."

Kate seemed to come alive, the fatigue retreating from her face as she raised the key to the back of her collar. There was a loud bang, and Corwin saw thick white smoke spreading across the platform—a magist spell designed to give cover. Shouts came from below the platform, along with the sounds of struggles—the crack of pistols, the bangs and shrieks of wilder magic and magist spells, and the shriek of swords being drawn. For a second, Corwin was back in the second uror trial, when the entire area had been covered in mist, his worse nightmares appearing from out of nowhere.

*Kill her!* Gavril screamed. *Kill them all!* The sway's power tore through Corwin's pain, and he found himself gripping the dagger once more, pulling it free of his body, ready to do Gavril's bidding.

The collar fell away from Kate's throat. "Stop!" She reached for the dagger, trying to pull it out of his grip. *Stop it, Corwin.* He felt her inside his mind, her sway so much like Gavril's he was instinctively terrified by it. Corwin's mind became a battlefield, the two wilders fighting for control. Corwin sensed Kate's weariness, her magic as weak as her body. He could see her memories—how she'd been captured by Rendborne, and how he'd spent the last few days draining her body of all the blood he could while still leaving her alive for this demonstration. She should've collapsed by now.

Instead she clung to him fiercely.

Around them, the fighting had grown louder. The soldier who had given Corwin the key appeared beside them now.

"It's me, your highness, Harue. We've got to go. Hurry." Dal and Tira were grappling with the other soldier at the end of the platform, Harue having given them each a dagger.

"Help me with him," Kate pleaded as she took Corwin by one hand. "Someone is controlling him with sway. It's just like Anise."

Frowning, Harue reached for Corwin's other hand and together they pulled him up. Pain lanced down his side at the movement, his tunic drenched in blood, and yet Gavril's will blazed inside his mind as strong as ever. *Kill them, kill the Godking's enemies. Kill—*

Abruptly, Gavril's hold on his mind vanished. Glancing down at the area beneath the platform, Corwin saw Gavril lying on the ground, blood flowing from his forehead where a rock had struck him. Struck—but not killed. Corwin knew that to be the case, as the man's prior orders remained a strong as ever in Corwin's mind. *You will not try to escape.*

He pulled back, trying to free himself from Harue and Kate. "Let me go. I can't go with you."

Face pinched with fear, Kate plunged into his mind once more. Again, he recoiled from the feel of her there, hating the sensation, his revulsion even greater than the pain.

*You will come with me now*, Kate said, and he felt all the strength of her sway behind it. Somehow it was enough to hold Gavril's Tenets at bay, even as they remained there, like a taut bowstring waiting to be released.

Now that he was no longer fighting them, Kate and Harue were able to help him stand and drag him off the platform down into the chaos below. The pain of his wound throbbed with each step, and the loss of blood made him dizzy. They headed across the Asterion as a group, Dal and Tira leading the way and fighting off any who challenged them. There weren't many, the smoke making it too difficult for open fighting.

Soon they reached the Steps of Sorrows and were making their way down. Corwin sensed Kate's power weakening in his mind, and the Tenets growing stronger by the second. Any moment now, and she would no longer be able to hold him. Yet they made it to the ground as they were. The smoke was still thick down here, but Harue continued guiding them on as if she could see through it. Soon they reached a group of horses and riders, Bonner and Nadira leading them. Corwin's heart lightened for half a moment.

But then he felt Kate's hold on his mind slipping away. "Help," she said, falling to her knees. "I can't hold him any longer." Bonner rushed toward Kate, grabbing her just as she started to fall forward, unconscious.

At once, Gavril's Tenets sprung into place, seizing control of him. *You will not try to escape.* Corwin spun on one heel, ready to flee back to Gavril and the Godking. Hands seized him from behind.

"Where are you going?" Dal said.

"Let me go." Corwin spun toward him, fist swinging. It connected with Dal's jaw, his head slamming backward as he lost his grip.

"Stop him," Bonner shouted. "He's not in control of himself."

Dal tried again, but Corwin was already out of reach. *I don't want to do this. I want to stay, to be with Kate and my friends.*

But he couldn't. The magic wouldn't let him.

"Nadira, put him under!" Bonner screamed.

A moment later, Corwin felt something grip his chest. Then it was inside him somehow, making him feel light, his breath growing short. A gray fog swirled across his vision, quickly turning to black. He felt himself falling down, legs giving out as his mind went blank. Then a black sleep dragged him under, freeing him from Gavril's hold.

At least for now.

WHEN KATE FINALLY WOKE SHE thought she was back in the dungeon of Norgard. Her sleep had been so deep, it had felt like death. Had it all been a dream? The Asterion covered with Sevan soldiers, Corwin alive and standing there in front of her, knife in hand and pain etched across his face, their frantic escape?

No, it hadn't been a dream. Bonner had been there, too. Alive but changed too much for it to have been mere imagination. And this wasn't Norgard at all, but a cave. The walls were sloped in places, jagged in others, none of it uniform or carved by human hands. So where was she? Slowly Kate tried to sit up, vaguely aware that she was lying in some sort of makeshift bed consisting mainly of horse blankets piled one atop the other.

"Aw, you're awake at last." The voice was unfamiliar and so was the face that peered down at her, dark-eyed and angular, with skin the color of tree bark. She spoke with the accent of someone from Kilbarrow.

"Where am I? What happened?" Kate tried again to rise, but couldn't quite manage it. Her body felt as if the bones had been turned to noodles and the muscles to lead.

"Take it slowly, Kate. You're a long way from recovered." The woman placed a firm hand on her arm. "My name is Nadira Walker. I am one of the freed wilders from Seva, and we are in the old dragon caves of Cobalt Mountains."

"Dragon caves?" Kate squeezed her eyes shut, her body starting to ache now and her head to swim. She might be free of Rendborne, but the damage he'd wrought with those repeated bloodlettings would take time to undo. And what of her blood? What horrible use would Rendborne put it to?

"That is the story behind these formations," Nadira said, motioning to the walls of the cave around them. "That they were carved by dragons in ancient times. But either way, we are deep inside the Cobalt Mountains."

Cobalt? The base of these mountains was several days' journey north from Norgard. Kate couldn't imagine how they'd managed to get her here, unconscious, what with the whole of the Sevan army surely pursuing them.

"Where is everyone?" Kate said. She'd almost asked about Corwin, but she couldn't bring herself to say his name, the very thought of him making her already pinched stomach twist even harder. She'd felt the torment in his mind. It had taken all her strength to force him to flee with them. It had been so much like Kiran and Vianne that day. And Anise, too. Would he turn out like her in the end? Driven to madness?

No, she couldn't think about that.

"They're here, but you must eat something first and then rest again."

"But I need to—"

Nadira raised a hand toward Kate as if she were an unruly child, and Kate decided it wasn't worth the effort arguing with her—she had no effort to spare at the moment. With Nadira's help, she sat up, ate and drank, and quickly fell asleep again, only to wake some short time later and repeat the process.

Now, though, Bonner was there.

Kate stared at him, her eyes aching at the sight of him, same as her heart. "I thought you were dead."

Bonner craned his head to the right, and the shadow of a smile passed over his face. "I was. For a while."

Kate reached for him, and after a moment's hesitation he came toward her and wrapped his massive arms around her. But he didn't squeeze her tight like he might once have done, and all too soon he pulled away.

Kate ached to let him go, sensing the deep chasm of time and hardships that seemed to separate them now. He was so changed, in more ways than she could count. Although he'd always been big, he was now enormous, wrapped in muscles nearly as hard as these limestone walls. He bore scars she didn't recognize as well, up and down his arms, across his knuckles and the backs of his hands, and even some on his face.

"Tell me your story," she gently urged, hoping for a way to bridge the gap between them. "How did you get here?"

Nadira cleared her throat and stood from where she'd been sitting on the cave floor. "I've others to attend to, but I will be back shortly, to ensure you rest again." She cast Bonner a stern look before leaving.

Once Nadira was gone, Bonner began without preamble. He didn't start at the beginning, as Kate had hoped he would, but instead talked about his escape from the Godking's army during the attack on Norgard. "It was mere chance when we came across

Harue at the shade door. She was waiting there for Wen and the rest of you that day."

The timing might have been chance, Kate thought, but not the location. Most members of the Rising knew about it—and more importantly how to open it. It hadn't been used since the cease-fire, but thankfully Raith hadn't removed it in that time. Tears pricked Kate's eyes at the thought. She couldn't believe Raith was dead. She kept forgetting. It was so easy to believe he was still back at Farhold, waiting for her to return.

"It was Harue's idea to come here." Bonner gestured to the room. "She'd been certain there was a cave system hidden in the mountains, one supposedly made by dragons long ago. Claimed she read about it in a book."

"And you believed her?"

Bonner shrugged. "She's a bit batty, but she's read every book there is." Kate supposed he had a point. "One of the earthists with us has an affinity for the limestone in these mountains. He found the entrance easily enough. We should be safe here for now. Every way in and out has been warded against intruders and drakes both. We managed to free quite a few magists when we rescued you and the other Rising prisoners."

"There were magists imprisoned in Norgard?"

Something like amusement appeared on Bonner's face, although it was too cold to be mistaken for humor. "Apparently when Norgard fell, Grand Master Storr was quick to swear allegiance of the Mage League to the Godking. But not all his magists were so willing to roll over alongside him."

Kate scowled. "Storr always was a coward."

"Yes, but not a fool. He saw what they were up against and knew it was in his best interest to fold. But at least his selfishness paid off for us this time. Without those magists we might never have escaped, and we'd surely have been overrun by drakes."

"I'm surprised they were willing to join us at all."

Bonner grimaced. "It hasn't been an easy alliance so far, but they seem to regard wilders as a better choice to cast their lot in with than invaders from Seva, no matter what the Godking claims his intentions are."

Kate rolled her eyes in disgust. "I guess we should feel glad to be counted so high."

"They're proving helpful, at least," Bonner said. "Several of them volunteered for the search party to find Genet and the rest of the Farhold survivors. Laurent is leading it. They left two days ago."

"That's good. I hope they find them. But what about the rest of it? What happened in Seva?"

Bonner glanced away from her, a muscle ticking in his jaw. Then he drew a deep breath, his massive chest expanding like bellows before he let it out again. "What I said before was true, I did die in Seva," he began, and then he told her the full breadth of his story.

Kate listened with her heart in her throat, marveling at each turn that he'd survived the ordeal at all. So much of it was painful to hear, like the way Bonner had been conditioned by Lord Gavril, the same man she'd heard that day with Rendborne, to serve the Godking—and Rendborne of course. She learned about nenath, the powerful drug Gavril used to enhance his magic and to ensure his sway held without fail, through each day and each night, forever—until death.

Then, finally, Bonner came to the worst part of all—when he'd finally made contact with Corwin, the day of his wedding to Princess Eravis.

It was all true. Corwin was married. Kate went numb from the shock of it, unable to cry or scream or react at all. She only wanted to lie down again and return to that deathlike sleep once more.

"You must forgive him, Kate," Bonner said, coming to the end of his tale. "He had no choice but to marry Eravis. Gavril forced his will at every turn."

Kate heard the truth in his words. She'd even experienced it herself, the terrible influence Gavril wielded over Corwin, and yet she still felt the sting of betrayal. All the reasons in the world didn't make the act hurt any less. "Why not stop his heart and let him come back again, freed like you?"

Bonner sighed, his scarred hands fisted in his lap. "We wanted him to do just that, but he refused. He was afraid it would end the uror trial and that Edwin would become king. He didn't want to abandon the wilders to that fate. Didn't want to abandon us."

A surge of warmth cut through the pain, but it wasn't enough to abate it. An image of Corwin in Eravis's arms kept appearing in her mind, the vision easy to conjure thanks to the illustration in the *Rime Review*.

"Besides, it wouldn't have worked," Bonner went on. "Corwin can't be killed, not while the uror trial is happening." Then he told her about how the Godking had tried to have Edwin killed in order to declare Corwin winner of the uror and the new king of Rime, but he was protected from all harm by the power of the uror.

Kate cocked her head, puzzled by this news. "How do you know that? I thought you escaped the day of the attack."

"Corwin told me."

"How . . . how is he?" she asked, not daring to hope that he was in his right mind once more.

"We've had to restrain him to keep him from escaping and returning to Norgard—apparently Gavril's sway has instilled certain behaviors in him, including an addiction to nenath—but he's in full possession of his wits . . . for now." Bonner looked uncomfortable with the subject.

It had been the same for Anise, Kate remembered. She would often have periods of lucidity, where she seemed almost completely herself, only to have the madness strike again.

"I need to see him," Kate said.

"He—"

Nadira appeared in the doorway. "That is out of the question. You are not yet recovered enough to move about, let alone try to use your magic."

Kate flushed, ashamed at how clearly the woman had read her intention. She did plan to use her sway, despite how depleted she felt, like a well run dry. She might've failed to find a way to free Anise, but she wouldn't with Corwin. She couldn't bear the thought of it.

And yet, even as she was determined about what she needed to do, she dreaded it. What memories might she see in his mind? Might she experience? When she invaded someone's thoughts, she wasn't some passive observer. She felt what they felt. There was no hiding the emotions connected to a memory or thought, no faking it. The reality made her sick to her stomach.

In the end she was grateful for the delay, another three days of eating and resting before she was recovered enough to move about.

Once there, she didn't immediately go to Corwin as she'd planned. Faced with the reality of seeing him, she found it easier to deal with everyone else first. She wanted to check on Tira and Dal, Harue and Wen and the rest. Her thoughts inevitably turned to Signe, but she forced them away, the pain of her absence almost too much to bear. Far as anyone knew, she was still a prisoner in the Hellgate.

Bonner had told Kate there'd been much debate about what they should do next among their strange band of refugees, and that debate was exactly what she walked in on as she followed Nadira out of her small cave and into what had become the main hall of the camp. More than fifty people loitered about inside and still the vast cavern was far from overcrowded. Kate moved next to the wall, sticking to the shadows so as to go unnoticed for as long as possible.

Most of the people were congregated near the center of the cave where one of the earthists among them had fashioned a stone table and chairs out of pieces of the cave itself. Jiro was standing at the head of the table, the pyrist having resumed his role as council member since their escape from Norgard.

"There is no question," Jiro was saying, a nervous humming in his voice with every word, "we must flee Rime. Even if Laurent is successful in finding Genet and the others, it won't be enough to mount a resistance. The Godking has thousands of men and hundreds of wilders and magists under his control. No force on earth could stand against such a conglomeration."

Kate rolled her eyes. Jiro always did have an annoying habit of using big words when simpler ones would do. She suspected he did it on purpose.

"But where can we go?" asked a woman on the far side of the room, an aerist Kate recognized from Farhold, although she couldn't remember her name. "Our magic doesn't work beyond Rime." She placed a hand on her belly. Seeing it, Kate reached out with her sway and sensed the child growing within her.

"It doesn't have to be that way," Harue replied, and Kate was surprised to see her here and not off somewhere with her nose in a book. She didn't doubt for a second that Harue had brought all of them with her when she escaped Norgard. They would've been her first priority. "If we take enough everweep seeds and the soil in which to grow them, we can maintain our magic anywhere in the world."

"It's true," Nadira said, coming to stand next to Bonner in the middle of the room. "That is how we were able to use our magic in the Mistfold."

"But how many would we need?"

"How would we transport that much?"

"Where could we go where we wouldn't be feared for what we can do?"

The questions came quickly, most of them directed at Bonner, who seemed to have become their de facto leader. He nodded his head at each one, seeming more like the general of some army than the blacksmith she used to know. He didn't address any of the questions, though, allowing the argument to continue on its course.

"Getting out of Rime won't be easy," Jiro replied. "But neither was winning Farhold. We can do it, if we work together and plan carefully."

Dal, who'd been sitting leaned on the stone table, chin cupped in his hand, stood abruptly and cleared his throat, the sound both loud and rude. All eyes turned to him at once. "You wish to flee? I understand it. But what about the people of Norgard? And the rest of Rime? Do we just leave them defenseless to the Godking's rule?"

"Yes," Jiro said, eyes narrowed. "Have you forgotten already? They never wanted us here anyway. We have no duty to help them now."

There was a chorus of agreement from many of the people, although not everyone. There were magists among them after all, easy to recognize in their gray robes. They were sitting together near the edge of the crowd. Among them was an older woman Kate recognized but couldn't place. She wasn't wearing a gray robe but was clothed in a plain brown dress, clearly one not made for her. For some reason, she envisioned this woman in ceremonial robes instead—and then the answer came to her.

Kate gasped. It was the high priestess of Noralah.

"What about the land?" Dal gestured with both hands, palms up toward the ceiling. "This is Rime. It's who we are. All of us— wilder, magist, and nonmagic alike."

Jiro tapped his foot as the room murmured. "It's a lovely sentiment, Lord Dallin, but it doesn't change the fact that we are hopelessly outnumbered. Better to live as refugees in a foreign land than to die at home."

Silence answered him this time, stretching out into several long moments before someone worked up the nerve to break it.

"What does Saint Kate think we should do?"

To Kate's surprise it was Jessalyn speaking, the very guard she'd had to subdue with her magic in order to leave Farhold with Signe. Kate hadn't known she'd been captured and brought back to Norgard. Despite Kate's treachery toward her, Jessalyn was looking straight at her now, gaze trusting and hopeful.

*Saint Kate*—the moniker sent shame burning through her. *Don't look at me that way,* she wanted to say. *I betrayed you. I was a fool who did exactly what Edwin—that is, what Rendborne wanted.* Rendborne had orchestrated it from the start, assuming Janus's identity and leading Edwin by the nose as easily as he would a dog with a bone.

The eyes of everyone in the room settled on her now, many looking at her as Jessalyn did, while others—most of the magists— were openly wary.

Kate shook her head. "I'm no saint. Not now, not ever."

Jessalyn swallowed, looking chastised. But then her expression turned defiant. "You're the Wilder Queen. You led us through the Wilder War. You helped secure Farhold. We followed you then, and we'll follow you again now."

*Follow you.* The words hung in the air. Kate felt the eyes on her again, the silence in the room as oppressive as the straps Rendborne had used to tie her down for the bloodletting.

She gritted her teeth, hardening her gaze. "I don't know what to do. Not this time. But Jiro is right. The Sevan force is larger and more powerful than anything we've ever faced." She turned to Bonner. "Would you take me to Corwin, please?"

Relief passed over his features as he nodded, both of them eager at the excuse to escape the argument, it seemed. Kate followed him to a side passage off the main hall, but before they'd gone far, Dal called after them.

"Kate!"

With a sigh, she stopped and faced him. Fatigue and irritation tugged at her in tandem. "What is it?"

Dal's eyes narrowed. "We can't run away. You know that. They still have Signe."

Drawing a deep breath, Kate willed her voice to remain even. "We can't be sure she's there. Her mother might've taken her back to the islands already." *Or Rendborne might've killed her like he'd nearly done before.*

A scowl stormed across Dal's face. "So that's it, then? You've given up on her?"

"Of course not." Kate's nostrils flared, her sudden anger making her feel more alive than she had in weeks. "Signe was my friend first. No one cares more for her than me."

"Prove it." Dal folded his arms across his chest, his chin stuck out defiantly.

Refusing to let him draw her into a fight, Kate carefully replied, "We will decide what to do later. Once I've spoken to Corwin." Then, without waiting for a response, she turned around and motioned for Bonner to continue. To Kate's relief, Dal didn't follow.

They moved down the broad passageway past several more caverns, all of them vast though not so big as the main hall. Although Kate still didn't believe the supposed origin of these caves—drakes were one thing, but dragons large enough to cut through a mountain were something else entirely—she understood why some would. Every room she'd seen in this place was large enough to hold a dragon like the kind described in old tales. Including the cave where they were keeping Corwin.

Kate froze at the sight of him, sitting atop a stone chair padded with blankets. They'd lashed him to the chair with a rope, and although he wasn't struggling at the moment, the skin on his wrists and arms bore the signs of it, fresh scabs and even fresher wounds. He looked asleep, or passed out, head tilted to the side and eyes closed. Deep, dark circles rimmed his eyes and the tops of his sunken cheeks. He seemed to have aged ten years since she'd last been by his side, barely a year before. He looked far too much like his father in the final years of his life—a specter of death.

"Should we come back later?" Kate said as Bonner entered the room.

At the sound of her voice, Corwin's eyes flashed open, and he became fully alert in an instant. His gaze locked at once on hers. Kate wanted to go to him, to wrap her arms around his shoulders and pull him close. But his wary expression, like that of a cornered animal, held her in place.

"Kate," he said, and the sound of her name on his lips sent an electric shock through her. He was truly alive. Truly here, in reach of her arms. And yet the distance between them was a continent. "What are you doing here?"

"What do you mean, Corwin?" Her voice came out as tremulous as a newborn foal first trying to stand. "I'm here to see you."

He turned away from her. "I don't want you here."

His words sliced into her, and automatically she reached out to him with her sway, wanting to know if he was being truthful or not—he was, and wasn't. As before, his mind was a battlefield, evidence of Gavril's terrible work threaded through every turn inside him.

*Corwin*, she whispered into his mind.

"Get out of my head." Corwin jerked against the ropes, teeth gritted. "Get out!"

Kate withdrew, her insides liquefying at the rejection, which she had felt in all its visceral sincerity. For a second, she almost fled from him, but then rage rose up inside her as the faces of the dead flashed through her mind. *Raith, Anise, Francis, Vianne, Kiran.* She'd been unable to save any of them.

*You will not take him*, she thought, shouting it to the air, the gods, anyone who might be listening.

She strode toward Corwin, who leaned away from her, trying in vain to avoid her.

"What are you doing? Leave me alone, Kate. Leave me—"

She gripped the sides of his face with her hands, fingers sliding into his hair as she pressed her palms to his temples—this sort of physical contact strengthened her sway. Then she plunged into his mind, ignoring his protests, his mental resistance like a hail of bullets. His panic and fear tasted like bile in her mouth. Even worse was the ache of need inside him, his desperate desire for nenath. *What is it?* Kate thought into his mind.

He refused to answer. Or maybe he couldn't. *Get out, get out, please, please, please. Get out!*

*No—I'm here to free you.*

*You're just like him!*

Ignoring the claim, Kate dug in deeper, searching for the root of the magic that held him captive. His memories came to life for her as if they were her own. She saw faces she didn't know, places she'd never been—a dark, damp cave, deposits of glowing, bluish crystals, prisoners dressed in rags. This was the mine, where Corwin had lived as Clash in the long months after his fall at the Mistfold. Then he was discovered and brought to the Sun Palace, with its gleaming red spires. She saw the towering walls of the Desol where Corwin had first learned Bonner was still alive. Then he was in a vast library filled with enough books to render even Harue satisfied.

Kate saw Gavril, and felt Corwin's hatred of the man. It ran deep inside him. Memories of the torture he'd put him through blazed inside her, stoking her own hate for him. Gavril had forced Corwin to kill a man he'd cared about, condemning him to a brutal death. In response, outrage ignited like a fire inside her.

"Get out!" Corwin jerked his head hard, nearly freeing himself, but Kate tightened her grip, fingers slick with his sweat—and hers. She almost had it. She could feel the root of Gavril's magic just out of reach, like writhing snakes made of shadows, insubstantial but deeply entrenched inside him. She just had to hold on.

The feel of the memories suddenly changed, becoming less random and more pointed. Gavril faded, and a woman took his place, tall and slender, with long silken hair that slid like water down her back. Hate gave way to affection, a sense of comfort and peace, a haven in the midst of the storm. Kate's head spun from the emotional shift, knocking her off-balance. She shook it off as understanding blazed inside her. This was Eravis. Princess of Seva.

Corwin's wife.

*No.*

Senseless with hurt, Kate called on every ounce of magic there was inside her, feeling the drag of it in her veins, her blood.

*Forget,* she thought.

If she couldn't undo the damage Gavril had wrought, she would obliterate these memories, make it like they had never been. Distantly, she heard Corwin's agonized scream, but it couldn't reach her this deep into his mind. Nothing could.

But then hands closed around her shoulders, and she felt herself jerked backward, her grip on Corwin breaking, along with her sway.

"That's enough, Kate." Bonner spun her around hard.

Kate blinked up at him, slowly coming back to her senses. She looked over her shoulder at Corwin, confused by the tears running down his wan, bruised face. His eyes were opened and staring at her, brimming with fear—and something else she couldn't name at first.

And then she could. She felt it herself. Shame. For what she'd seen. What she'd done. *What he'd done.*

Fighting back tears herself, Kate faced Bonner once more, but words failed her. She couldn't give voice to what she'd seen, what she was feeling.

Yet somehow, Bonner understood exactly. He pulled her close, hugging her like he might once have done. "It's not him," Bonner whispered. "It's Gavril. He did this. He's responsible for everything."

Kate inhaled, choking on tears. But they weren't just of sorrow, but rage as well. It was Gavril's fault. He'd orchestrated all of this.

*Are you sure?* a voice of dissent whispered in her head. *You felt his affection for her . . .*

Kate shut the voice out, letting hatred replace the doubt.

She pulled back from Bonner. "You're right. Gavril is responsible."

And there was only one way to free Corwin—*Gavril must die.*

Kate scrubbed the tears off her face and drew a steadying breath. "I need to talk to Dal and the others. We aren't going to run. We're going to fight."

WHETHER AWAKE OR ASLEEP, CORWIN'S heart raced. It wouldn't stop, as if he were running a footrace, one without end.

It couldn't end. Not until he made it back to Gavril.

He strained against the ropes, barely feeling the pain of the shredded skin around his wrists. His tongue lay in his mouth like a dead thing, swollen and rough as tree bark. They brought him water, and even forced it down his throat, but it was as if his body had forgotten how to process it. It rejected everything that didn't contain the nenath it so desperately craved. Anything that didn't bring him closer to satisfying the edicts laid into his soul. *You will not try to escape.*

He knew that if he didn't get out of this chair soon he would die. A part of him longed for death. But he couldn't even ask his captors for that mercy. Death would only be an escape. The final one. *They couldn't kill me even if they tried*, he remembered, feeling the burn in his uror mark. He couldn't die. Not without a weapon designed to slay the gods themselves. It was hopeless. He couldn't even mention the Hellsteel aloud. The Tenets wouldn't allow it, sensing as they did that Corwin might use it to free himself from their control.

And so he sat and waited and suffered. But at least he was allowed to do it in private. After that first meeting with Kate, he'd asked to be left alone, his only visitor Nadira, who came in twice daily to see to his well-being as best she could.

She came into the cave now, appearing in front of him as if from nowhere, his senses so dulled by misery he failed to notice her arrival until she spoke.

"Good evening, Prince Corwin."

He didn't reply, as it would take too much effort. Besides, they'd run out of things to talk about days ago. Or maybe it was weeks, or months. He couldn't be certain. There was no sense of time in this place or in his head, just the relentless, pounding need to return to Gavril.

"I know you asked for no visitors," Nadira said as she leaned down to set the night's meal on the makeshift table beside his chair, "but we must make an exception." She stepped aside, revealing a figure standing just behind her.

At first, Corwin's addled mind couldn't make out the person's face, but then the features slowly resolved into Kate. His first instinct was to reach for her and call her name, but a second later Gavril's Tenets tightened their control—they understood the threat she posed, this other wilder with sway.

"Hello, Corwin." Her tone was painfully civil, as if she were addressing him as prince, instead of what he'd once been to her. She stood rigid as a sword, arms at her sides and hands clenched into fists. Tattoos he didn't recognize ran down her arms, bare in the leather jerkin she wore, so many flames she looked as if she were on fire. He wanted to ask her what they meant, but he could only stare.

"I will be back shortly to help you eat," Nadira announced. Then she turned and strode from the room, leaving him alone with

Kate. Silence hung thick between them as the memories of their last encounter played in Corwin's head. The things she'd seen. The things she'd learned. The horrible violation of it, and the burning shame he couldn't escape.

Finally Kate drew a breath and, again in that emotionless voice, said, "Harue believes she might have found a way to ease your suffering. It won't undo Gavril's magic, but it will . . . might . . . block it." She raised her hand toward him, turning her palm upward to reveal the object she'd been holding, a crystal vial filled with blood.

Corwin recognized it. "Is that your father's? The one you took from Vikas?"

Kate shook her head, not meeting his eyes. "No, the blood is mine." Corwin inhaled sharply at the knowledge. Ignoring his reaction, she added, "At the very least it will prevent anyone with sway—including me—from entering your mind."

He looked away from her then, feeling as if his insides had become his outsides, raw nerves exposed. "You never should've done it," he said, managing to speak at last. "You should've stayed out." He couldn't bear this thing inside her that was so much like Gavril. Not yet, not with the pain still so close.

Kate's face was stony. "I know. I never will again."

He'd heard her make such claims before, but they always came with exceptions—*unless I have to, unless you want me to.* Not this time, though. And he knew why: she feared what she might see. He wanted to tell her the truth—that he still loved her more than anything, anyone—but the words didn't come.

Kate held out her hand holding the vial once more. "I will give this to you now, but I can't release you from these bonds. Not until you're able to convince me that you won't try to run. Do you understand?"

He nodded, unable to speak for the Tenets raging inside him. *No, no, no. You mustn't. You must return to Gavril. Obey, obey, obey.*

Kate approached him slowly, being careful not to touch him as she leaned forward and dropped the cord around his neck. Then she stepped back.

The vial settled next to Corwin's chest, and he felt the heat of it at once, warming him from the inside. It spread over him like a vapor, enveloping him. As it settled into his mind, he felt it slowly quieting the Tenets that had twisted his will, subverting it. His racing heart at last began to settle. The knotted threads of Gavril's control didn't undo themselves; they merely loosened enough to allow him to move, to think and act on his own. It took effort, but it was a manageable effort, no longer like trying to swim in quicksand. Tears stung his eyes at the sweet release of it. For the first time in weeks, in months, he was himself. Or as close to it as it was possible to be with Gavril still in his head, lingering in the shadows. And with the need for nenath still burning inside him.

Blinking the moisture from his eyes, Corwin let his gaze fall on Kate once more. "Thank you," he said, stammering. He drew a shaky breath. "Thank you. I am myself." He started to smile, only to falter at the look on Kate's face.

She regarded him darkly, her spine still stiff and expression guarded. They'd never been further apart than they were now. Not even after he'd condemned her father to death. It was the closeness they'd shared before that made it that way. The gap greater because of the sum of its parts.

"How can I be sure?" she said at last.

"You can't, not without coming in here again." Corwin inclined his head, unable to indicate it in any other way. Only she couldn't come in anymore, so long as he wore the vial.

"You sound more like you." Kate bit her lip.

"It's me, I swear it. There's so much I need to tell you, to explain." He hesitated, grasping for words that didn't exist. "I'm sorry, Kate. What you saw wasn't what—"

"It's all right," she said, cutting him off. "I will untie you, but if you try to run, know that I will stop you."

Eyeing the sword strapped across her back, he didn't doubt her words. He was a threat to every remaining wilder if he were to run back to Gavril. For a second he felt an urge to do just that, but this time he was able to squash it before it could take control. "I won't run. Besides, Nadira isn't far. She can still reach me with her magic if necessary."

Kate frowned. "Might it be necessary?"

Corwin debated his answer, drawing a small sense of comfort in knowing that he could lie to her, if he wanted to. He didn't. "I still feel Gavril's will inside me. It's easier to ignore it now, to subvert it, but I can't be certain it won't take hold if I let my guard down."

"Fair enough," Kate said. "We will make sure someone is watching you at all times."

*Someone.* Not her. Corwin sighed, his heart heavy in his chest.

Kate approached him again, drawing the dagger sheathed at

her waist. Once more, she was careful not to touch him as she cut through his bonds. The moment he was free, she stepped back again, quickly.

Corwin stretched his arms over his head, savoring the tingly pain of moving limbs too long kept in the same position. For a moment, he felt lighter than air. But all too quickly the euphoria left him, as he looked at Kate again. She hadn't moved, her muscles tensed as if she expected him to bolt at any moment. When he didn't, she slowly relaxed, not at her ease but no longer ready to fight.

"What now?" he said, not knowing what else to say.

"First you must eat and drink. Regain your strength. Then you must decide if you wish to go or to fight."

"What do you mean?"

Kate gestured to the door behind her. "There's been an ongoing debate among what is left of the Rising about what we do next. Many think it best to leave Rime, forever."

Corwin wasn't surprised; he'd seen what the Sevan forces could do. Yet the idea of fleeing, of letting go of his homeland, repelled him. "What have you decided?"

"I'm going to fight. Our first step is to get to the Hellgate. That's where Signe was taken last we saw her. Her mother is one of the Furen Mag. They were helping Edwin mine for something called Hellsteel. Far as we can tell, they're still there."

*Daleth, Hellsteel*, Corwin remembered, and this time he could think about it without restriction. He could even talk about it, although the Tenets shuddered in the back of his mind, fearing this weapon that was strong enough to destroy them.

"Rendborne is mining it now," Corwin said. "He was probably behind it from the beginning."

"Yes, I believe you're right. He's been behind everything from the start." Kate paused, pursing her lips hard enough a muscle ticked in her jaw. Then she explained what had happened at Farhold, how she had been lured away and how the Rimish forces had managed to take down the city. He'd heard some of the story already, but not about Rendborne disguising himself as Master Janus.

Disgust rose up in him. There seemed no limit to the man's evil or cleverness, a deadly combination. Rendborne had known the Rising might be the only true threat against the Godking's army, and he'd gone to great lengths to take them down before the invasion. Only . . . "Why is Rendborne doing this? What does he hope to gain?" Corwin had never understood it. He'd witnessed Rendborne's true desires—all he wanted was to destroy Rime, not to rule it himself and certainly not to hand it over to someone else to rule.

Kate raised one shoulder and let it fall. "Who can say? And it doesn't matter. All that does is that we stop him."

Corwin couldn't argue with that logic, and yet his unease remained. There had to be something more behind Rendborne's actions, and there weren't any answers to be found here.

But there might be solutions. Corwin took a step nearer to Kate, who held her ground, although he sensed the effort it took her not to retreat. "I need to speak with the others, anyone with any influence over the people. I may have a way to convince everyone to stay and fight with us."

Kate's mouth turned up at the side. "How?"

Corwin allowed himself a small smile, the defeat he'd felt

retreating and making Gavril's magic shrink even further away. "I know how to defeat Rendborne. I know how we can defeat them all."

They met in Corwin's room. The moment Nadira returned, she insisted that he eat and rest—no walking about and tiring himself out. He'd gone too long without proper nourishment. Corwin submitted to her care, but only because Kate promised to bring the others to him. She was eager to finalize plans to infiltrate the Hellgate and rescue Signe.

Jiro arrived first, followed by Bonner, Nadira, Tira, and Dal. Next came Harue, with Wen trailing behind her as her ever-present shadow. After them was a magist called Yaron, who was elected to speak for the Norgard magists. Lastly, to Corwin's surprise, came the high priestess, the one that Magnar had replaced and the same woman who had once burned the uror brand onto his palm. She gave her name as Valora and addressed him with a meekness so unlike the woman he'd known, a pale reflection of her former self.

"I asked her to come," Bonner said quietly, pulling Corwin aside for a moment. "She is a holy woman still, no matter what Magnar says. She might be helpful in unifying this group to fight."

Corwin glanced at the priestess then, doubting she could convince so much as a flea to bite a dog's back. She was barefoot and dressed in a too-large, shabby dress, looking more like a beggar on the streets than a holy woman. And despite Bonner's claim of her usefulness, there was no denying that she'd played a part in deceiving the people of Rime into believing that Corwin was dead and his brother the chosen king. Then again, he could see Bonner's point about belief in the gods and goddesses of Rime being a common thread between these disparate people. He just didn't know if it would be strong enough.

"Thank you all for coming," Corwin said as they settled in, each taking one of the chairs Bonner had hastily forged with his magic. They were crudely made of stone, but they would do for this. Corwin's father always told him that people were more apt to be reasonable when they were comfortable.

"Kate says you have a plan to defeat the Sevan force," Jiro said at once, circumventing any preparatory speeches Corwin might've made.

Corwin stared at the man, trying to get the measure of him. He didn't know him well, having met Jiro only briefly in the time before he'd left for the Mistfold with Kate and the others, more than a year ago now. He couldn't believe it had been that long.

He addressed the rest of the group, refusing to let Jiro rile him. "Yes, it's true. The key lies in killing Lord Gavril."

Several of the others murmured at this, and Corwin wondered if they all knew what he'd been through. He supposed they must. Heat rose up his neck, and he drew a breath, willing it not to rise any further.

"As Bonner can attest, all of the wilders in the Godking's army are acting against their will. Gavril is controlling them through his wilder magic and with the help of a drug called nenath, which increases the effects of his sway tenfold. It's made from nenir—or as we called it in the Sevan mines, godtears."

Valora drew a sharp breath. "That's impossible. Godtears don't exist. Not anymore."

Corwin frowned at her, surprised by her reaction. "Yes, they do. I've seen them. I've mined them." *I even drank them.* The very thought of the nenath made his stomach cramp with need, strengthening Gavril's Tenets until he had to grip his hands around his chair to fight off the urge to flee. Sweat broke out on the back of his neck at the effort.

"What Corwin says is true," Bonner said. "All the wilders in Seva were given this nenath, always before Lord Gavril used his sway on us. It also enhanced our powers, same as it did his. Gavril drank it, too."

Valora's gaze dropped to the floor. "I meant no disrespect. But godtears are one of the divine elements, once gifted to the lands of Seva by the gods themselves, the source of all the magic in Seva."

"A divine element?" Harue asked, her expression perked with curiosity. "But they sound no different from our everweeps. They're the source of all magic in Rime."

Valora eyed Harue askance. "Well, yes . . . ," she said, hesitant. "You're right. Everweeps are another of the divine elements, the only one still in existence."

Harue's gaze widened. "You mean to say that the priesthood knew the function of everweeps all this time, and you never told the magists?"

"This is secret knowledge," Valora said, a flush rising up her neck. "And we were charged with protecting it. But how did you know?"

With giddy excitement, Harue explained how she'd come to the knowledge after learning about the everweeps in the Mistfold, the way they made the wilders' magic accessible once more. Hearing it, Corwin felt no true surprise at all, only a sense of awe at the truth—the realization that the gods themselves had bound magic into specific elements for humankind's use.

Valora gave a solemn nod as Harue finished. "Rime alone remains favored by the gods with our magic. The other divine elements—starfall in the lands of Ruzgar and ashcrystal in the Eshian islands—disappeared from the world generations ago, not long after the loss of godtears."

"But why are they gone?" Harue asked, sounding offended by the notion.

"Punishment. The gods purged all magic from the world, save Rime's, after the death of the god Sevan at a human's hand." Valora turned to Corwin. "The priesthood has ancient manuscripts that document these events. They are secret and holy. I've never spoken of them before."

"Manuscripts?" Harue said.

Kate rolled her eyes. "Not now, Harue."

Corwin nodded. "Then why have the godtears returned now?"

Valora shrugged. "The gods' will. The gods' way."

It was an easy answer, a phrase that these days was hardly more than a quip. If Corwin had to guess, he suspected it had something to do with Rendborne. Perhaps the presence of everweeps in the Mistfold had done it. He couldn't be sure. But it did seem to him that the mining for godtears' in Seva now was relatively new. That explained the conditions of the mines, how all the structures were in such a good working state, as if recently built.

"Either way, though," Valora continued, "if this Gavril has been consuming a divine element to enhance his magic, that makes him a powerful threat indeed."

"All the more reason to kill him quickly," Corwin said, glad to bring the conversation back to the main point. "If Gavril dies, the magic releases, and the wilders under his control will be free—and surely will turn to fight with us."

"How can you be certain they will fight, and not instead flee?" Yaron asked, head cocked to the side. He was a slight man, unassuming with his black hair tinged with gray and age-lined face, but there was a quiet strength about him when he spoke.

"Any wilder harmed by Gavril's sway will want justice," Bonner said, his tone absolute. He pinned Yaron with his gaze. "We remember everything he did to us, ever made us do. Vile, disgusting things you can't even imagine. They will fight, no question." Bonner craned his head toward Corwin. "But as I told you before, Gavril is nearly impossible to kill. He's as untouchable as Rendborne. Both are protected by a magic more powerful than any of us possess."

"Yes, I remember," Corwin said, "which is why we need to get our hands on a substance known as Hellsteel."

Dal sat up. "That's what they're looking for in the Hellgate. But what is it?"

Before Corwin could respond Valora said, "It's the weapon that Fanen used to kill the god Sevan—the only thing that can kill a god."

Corwin regarded her more carefully, wondering what other secrets she possessed. Although she spoke the truth as he knew it, there was something in her voice he didn't trust. But he nodded at her, appreciating the help just the same. "That's right. And if this Hellsteel can do that, then neither Gavril nor Rendborne can stand against it."

Jiro scoffed. "You're talking about ancient myths. How can we be certain any of it is real and not just a story?"

"We would have thought the same about the godtears," Bonner said. He gestured to Valora, who confirmed the statement with a bow of her head.

Corwin swept his gaze over the room. "Rendborne is looking for the Hellsteel as we speak. He intends to use it to kill my brother." Corwin relayed the story of what happened in the Vault of Souls for those who hadn't yet heard it.

Silence greeted him when he finished, and he let it stretch on for nearly a minute. "I know the odds are against us, but I will not leave Rime to Sevan hands, and I will not leave my brother to be killed by a foreign invader, no matter his crimes. I will fight."

A moment passed, and then Valora stood from her chair. She turned to Corwin and bowed. "I must beg your forgiveness, my prince, for the part I played in deceiving the people of Rime about the truth of the uror. I know nothing I say can excuse or undo those actions. But we were at war, wilder against magist, the entire kingdom threatened. With you gone, I believed that any king was better than none at all. I know now I was wrong."

Corwin returned her bow. "I understand. The history of Norgard, of Rime, has made one thing clear. We are always better united than we are apart."

"You will make a wise king, Prince Corwin." Valora laid her

palm against her heart. "I will stand and fight with you. For Rime."

Dal, Tira, Nadira, Harue, Wen, and Kate echoed the sentiment. Then they waited for Jiro and Yaron to cast their lots. Corwin held his breath, knowing in his gut that he would need them both. Even with the Hellsteel, the odds remained against them.

Yaron drummed his fingers on the side of his chair, gaze fixed on Corwin. "What happens afterward, your highness, if Rime is indeed ours again? You are married to the Godking's daughter, after all."

Corwin's eyes automatically went to Kate, dreading her reaction. She sat rigid in her chair, carefully not looking at him, not looking at anyone. He opened his mouth to respond, but again Valora beat him to it.

"By Rimish law, the union is not legal or binding," she said, matter-of-fact.

"How can you be certain?" Jiro said, eyes narrowed.

Valora drew a deep breath, puffing out her chest. For a moment she looked like the high priestess Corwin remembered. "Magnar Fane calls himself a god, and as such, he doesn't recognize any god save himself." She turned her eyes to Corwin. "Is that not true, your highness? Were there any priests or priestesses present for your union?"

"No, Magnar performed the ceremony himself."

A tight, quick smile passed over Valora's face. "Then in the eyes of the true gods, you remain unwed. The Sevan princess will have no claim on Rime's throne."

Corwin exhaled, unaware that he'd been holding his breath. He nodded, and with a glance at Kate, said, "Even if that weren't the case, the marriage was never consummated." He hoped to see relief pass over her expression at this revelation, but it remained unchanged.

"It is undeniable then," Valora said, "on all fronts."

Corwin forced his gaze to Yaron. "Does that answer satisfy?"

The man slowly rose to his feet and bowed toward Corwin. "The magists will stand with you as well." He motioned toward the others. "We will stand side by side with wilders and reclaim what is ours from Sevan hands."

Jiro openly scoffed at this proclamation. "And how long will this unity last? What will happen once Seva is gone? Will wilders be hunted once more? Condemned to either die or flee?"

Corwin weighed his answer carefully. "No, not so long as it is up to me. Wilders and magists will be treated equally. Both equally free and all of us Rimish."

"And what if Edwin is made king, once the uror is finally complete?"

"That question isn't fair, Jiro, and you know it," Kate said. "Prince Corwin can't predict the future, but if he is made king, he will do as he's said. He risked his life to free the wilders taken by the Inquisition."

Her support stunned Corwin, and made something hot burn behind his eyes. He watched Jiro carefully, wondering what he would do.

The pyrist rolled his eyes, then grudgingly got to his feet. "Very well then. What remains of the Rising will stand with you as well. May the gods help us all."

Despite Jiro's doubt, hope filled Corwin's lungs, expanding his chest until he thought it would burst. They were united now, magist and wilder and nonmagic together for the very first time. *We are Rime*, he thought, and the uror mark on his palm tingled in response. That was what it meant to be king—uniting disparate people together, not breaking them apart as his brother had done.

"Thank you all," Corwin said, wishing he had a cup of wine to raise to them. "Let us celebrate our unity today, for tomorrow we fight."

KATE PEERED THROUGH THE THIN, white-barked trees at the battlements that surrounded the Hellgate, memories swirling through her head. It seemed a lifetime ago since she'd first seen this place, the day she'd been taken prisoner by Vikas at the behest of Rendborne. The events of that day were seared into her brain as if by a brand. The way Rendborne had forced her to assault Signe's mind for the secret to the black powder by killing Bonner's father and threatening to do the same to him. How during the fighting, after Corwin's arrival with the Rising to rescue them, she'd killed Vikas, and Corwin had faced Rendborne, driving him off long enough for them to escape.

Yet despite the vividness of the memories, the place before her seemed altogether new. Back then the structures had appeared ancient, the stone crumbling and broken through in places. Now the battlements were in perfect order, the walls smooth and solid, as if they'd only just been built.

*Wilder magic.* It seemed Rendborne had been putting Gavril's slave army to good use. Or not so good, Kate mused, wishing there was an easier way in. They'd been in the Wandering Woods the last three days, watching the comings and goings around the Hellgate from the trees, where Xia, an earthist with a strong affinity for plant life, had constructed elevated platforms and intricate walkways by drawing the branches and boughs together. It had taken her nearly a day to do it and an entire satchel full of magestones enchanted with a dampening spell to hide the magic. They couldn't be certain how many magists were working with Rendborne now, or if Rendborne himself would able to detect the magic. It was a lot of magestones to lose, but they couldn't risk discovery.

*We're already risking too much as it is.* Kate cast a furtive glance at Corwin. He stood crouched in the brush next to her, gaze fixed on the wall ahead and his face hidden behind a magestone mask. They were all wearing them for this mission, disguises to make them appear like Sevan soldiers. Kate had tried to convince Corwin to stay behind, afraid that Gavril would ensnare him again the moment he drew near, but he insisted on coming, and she didn't press the issue. After what had happened between them, she no longer knew where she stood, if Corwin cared what she thought anymore or if his heart longed for another.

During the journey here they'd barely spoken, avoiding one another at every turn, it seemed. Even now, in such close proximity, there might as well have been an ocean between them. She longed to touch him, to grasp hold of what once had been and make it so again. She just didn't know how.

As if sensing her gaze, Corwin turned toward her. "What do you think?"

Kate focused her attention on the wall once more, reaching out with her sway to see who was waiting behind it. She sensed several minds beyond there, but they remained distant enough not to be of concern. "The path is clear."

He nodded, then gestured to Bonner, who stood on the other

side of him. Kate clenched her teeth, willing her nerves to settle as Bonner stepped out from the brush into the open area just beyond the wall. He was not the man he'd been before the Mistfold. She wasn't even sure she could call him a friend anymore. Something had changed him in Seva, even worse than the death of his father. She remembered the hours he'd spent making his revolvers long ago, dozens of designs before he'd finally come upon one that worked. He'd done it for her, he claimed, to keep her safe from the nightdrakes. Now she seemed barely a passing concern to him. She missed his care more than she dared admit, especially now.

She missed her revolver, too. She felt the absence of its weight at her hip. Without Signe and her black powder, the weapon had been rendered useless.

*Maybe she's in there still*, Kate thought, her gaze tracking Bonner's movements as he approached the wall. But she didn't put much hope in it. Over and over again she'd swept her magic as far as it would go, searching for Signe, but felt nothing. Kate couldn't say for sure she wasn't there; for some reason, her magic faltered whenever she turned her mind to the center of the fortress, where the Hellgate itself cut deep into the earth. It would be working fine and strong one moment and then fade the next, as if she'd suddenly stepped into a ream of fog. The blind spot made her uneasy, but it wasn't enough to stop her from venturing inside, searching for Signe and the Hellsteel both.

Bonner placed his right hand against the wall. The other he raised to his lips, and he spoke the word of invocation on the magestone in his palm, activating the dampening spell. A faint shimmer spread over his hand, then swept outward, the only sign of the spell working. No wilder or magist would be able to sense the magic he was about to do next, but they could still hear it as Bonner pulled pieces of the wall apart to form a makeshift ladder.

Kate concentrated her sway, on the alert for anyone approaching. If they came, she would send them away with a thought. Or kill them, if she had to. Whatever it took to accomplish what they were set to do today. Now more than ever, she must be decisive.

Despite the mechanics of the magic Bonner worked, the process was surprisingly quiet, just a few cracks and splinters, like the sound of ice sliding off a roof. Still, Kate braced, expecting an alarm to be raised. A flock of birds took flight above them, and she started. But nothing else happened, and she sensed no minds drawing nearer.

"Let's go," she whispered to Corwin. He gestured behind him, where Dal and Yarin waited. The magist had volunteered for the mission, a boon Kate had not expected. He'd been elected leader of the Norgard magists because he was the most powerful among them, and his skill would be invaluable to the mission. Harue had come as well, but she was back at the base camp with Wen, Xia, and Valora, trying to replenish as much of their stock of magestones as they could. It seemed the former high priestess had a great many ideas for new spells as well, ones she claimed had existed hundreds of years ago and were remembered now only in the priesthood's secret archives. Harue had insisted on keeping the priestess by her side ever since.

Kate went up the ladder first, ready to use her sway if anyone spotted her. She climbed quickly, trying to move without noise, a difficult task in the purloined Sevan armor she wore. Once at the top, she slid over the edge of the wall and dropped down. To her relief, there was no one in sight. Kate motioned for the others to follow, and moments later, they made their way toward the gatehouse at the front of the battlements. As they drew near, one of the Sevan guards stepped out to question them.

Kate plunged into his mind. *You know us. We belong here. Let us go about our business.* For half a second, she felt his mind resist, and panic clutched at her thoughts. Rendborne had told Gavril that day that he'd stolen her blood to protect them from the Hellsteel, but it occurred to her now maybe she'd heard it wrong and that he was using it to protect his followers from her sway instead. But a second later, the man's expression went blank, and he waved them through.

Bonner took the lead now, heading down the steps and out of the gatehouse onto the bailey. Of all of them, he was the most believable as a Sevan soldier. His armor fit perfectly, each dip and crevice molded to his body. It was the same armor he'd been wearing when he escaped, but with the spear emblem removed from the breastplate. He also spoke perfect Sevan, thanks to his time in the Mistfold.

The others fell into step behind him, each doing their best to mimic his movements. Rows and rows of white canvas tents had been erected all across the bailey. The sight alarmed Kate. There must be far more soldiers here than they thought. But then she realized it was so much worse than that. A woman clad in Sevan armor sat in front of one of the tents. That was a bad sign since the Godking did not permit women to fight in his army—unless they were a wilder or magist. The woman raised a pipe to her mouth and lit it with a wave of her hand. *A pyrist.* Kate's nerves prickled. Their entire mission just became all the more dangerous. A fight against

Sevan soldiers they might win—wilders would be a different story entirely.

Disguising her fear, Kate followed after Bonner, trying to look like she belonged here. Twice more they were questioned by other soldiers, and twice more Kate turned them away with her sway. Once inside the fortress, there were far fewer soldiers about, making it harder to blend in but with fewer eyes around to notice. The building was simply constructed, a single outer hallway with several small rooms connected to it, surrounding the main chamber that housed the Hellgate itself. Kate did another survey with her sway, sensing no one in the immediate vicinity of the hallway. But as before, the rest of the area remained clouded to her.

"Why would Magnar keep the wilders here?" Kate said once they were inside.

A muscle tensed in Bonner's jaw as he shook his head. "I don't know, but we need to be careful."

"Hooray for understatement." Dal made a face. "So what now?"

"We split up." Bonner motioned down both sides of the hallway. "Corwin and Yaron come with me. Dal, you go with Kate. This passage should connect on the other side. Check every room and meet up in the back."

It was a good pairing. Kate could keep Dal safe with her sway—assuming she could still use it the farther in they went—and Bonner could help the others avoid notice with his knowledge. Still, the idea of separating made her uneasy, despite the fact that they would draw less attention apart and cover more ground quickly. The objective was simple: find and capture one of the Furen Mag for questioning. There must be a reason Rendborne needed their help in mining the Hellsteel. All the better if that person was Synnove Leth—they could question her and find Signe in one fell swoop.

"We'll head that way." Kate pointed to the right where, from here, she could see a door to the room Rendborne had used as a private chamber the last time she'd been here. It was the same room where he'd killed Bonner's father—best that she take this direction. "See you soon." Turning to go, Kate felt someone touch her hand. She glanced back to find Corwin standing close to her.

"Be careful," he said, his gaze fierce as he locked eyes with her—for the first time in days.

Her throat tightened, and she could only nod in answer. Then they were walking away. Kate went first, with Dal trailing a few steps behind. She passed by the first chamber, after a quick glance to see it was indeed as empty as it felt, the only residents cobwebs and spiders. They reached Rendborne's old chamber next, but it too was empty.

They moved on. With each step, Kate sensed the strange fog growing stronger. The feeling unsettled her. It wasn't that she was cut off from her magic, more that some force was smothering it, a sensation like trying to walk in deep mud or run with a scarf tied around her nose and mouth.

"Are you okay?" Dal whispered from behind her.

Kate shushed him with an upraised hand, spotting a pair of soldiers ahead, standing guard in front of a locked door.

"What goes here?" the one nearest said as they came into view.

Kate knew that thanks to the magestone disguise she appeared to be a Sevan male, and yet the soldier looked at her with suspicion in his gaze, as if he could see right through it. She hurried toward the soldiers, trying to get close enough for her sway to be effective.

Both guards raised their spears. "Answer me now. Who are you? What are you doing here?"

Kate stretched out with her sway, just barely reaching them. "We've been sent to relieve you," she said, concentrating with all her might. Feeling their resistance, she pressed harder. "Go outside, into the forest, and take your ease until nightfall."

After a moment, the men's eyes glazed over. Lowering their weapons, they turned and departed without another word.

"That was close," Dal said. "I'm all about a good thrill, Kate, but now might not be the best time to mess with me."

"There's some kind of magic at work here. It's limiting my powers."

Dal blinked. "You're just telling me now?"

"I didn't know what would happen. Besides, we're fine. Now shut up while I figure out who's behind this door." It had to be someone important. Kate pressed her hand to the wood and invoked her sway. She sensed the person inside, but it was like seeing a shadow move in the darkness, too indistinct to identify.

"Well," Dal said. "Who is it?"

"I can't tell." Kate drew the sword from the sheath at her side, the gesture awkward after carrying it on her back for so long. "Open the door."

With a bemused huff, Dal reached into the satchel tied at his waist for a magestone, one designed to undo locks. He spoke the word of invocation and the lock fell away a moment later. Kate pushed open the door with one hand and stepped inside, braced for anything. Even still, shock struck her as her gaze fell on the person in the room.

"Signe!" Dal pushed Kate aside as he rushed in.

She was sitting at a workbench in the back of the large space, and shot up as they entered, knocking her chair over. Dal reached her before she could take another step, then she was in his arms, legs dangling as he kissed her. She wrapped her arms around his head and kissed him back. Watching them, a flush spread up Kate's neck, jealousy and bitterness and want mingling inside her like combustible elements. This was how it should've been for her and Corwin. Instead, they'd been pushed even further apart.

Dal set Signe down at last, and she turned to embrace Kate. "I knew you'd come."

"I'm glad you're all right." Breaking away, Kate glanced around the room at the bowls of ingredients spread across the table and the barrel full of black powder on the floor beside it. She turned back to Signe in alarm. "How much have you made already?"

Signe swallowed, guilt shining in her eyes. "Too much. I had no choice."

"Was it Gavril?" Kate asked, anger constricting her chest.

"Yes." Signe's voice hitched, and she visibly trembled.

Dal touched her arm. "Have they found the Hellsteel?"

Signe nodded, and sudden tears arose in her eyes. "Yesterday."

"Sig!" Dal drew her back into his arms, alarm in his voice. Kate felt it, too. Signe did not cry. Not for anything. But now, she let out a deep, tremulous sob against Dal's chest. "He killed her. Rendborne killed my mother the moment she handed him that wretched metal."

"I'm so sorry," Dal said, stroking her back now.

"It's my fault. Rendborne promised to let us go once she found it. When Mother confronted him, though, he said she could leave, but not me. She refused, and that's when he killed her."

*You are too valuable to let go,* Kate thought, wishing for a different truth for her friend. But revolvers powered by Signe's black powder turned ordinary soldiers into a force as formidable as wilders and magists. Rendborne would never give up such power. Neither would Magnar, if he knew; there was no telling what Rendborne might or might not share with the Godking. Corwin's suspicions about his motives were well founded.

Kate touched Signe's shoulder. "I'm sorry as well, but we will make Rendborne pay. We just need the Hellsteel to do it. It's the only thing that can kill him."

Stepping out of Dal's embrace, Signe wiped away her tears. "There's a forge next to the Hellgate. Rendborne has had a blacksmith on hand for the moment some was found. If it's there it'll be easy to spot. It's unlike any metal you've ever seen—deep red, like raw meat."

"Why not use an earthist to fashion the weapon?" Kate asked. "They could do it in half the time."

"Rendborne doesn't fully trust the wilders," replied Signe. "And my mother speculated the Hellsteel might be resistant to magical manipulation, though there was no earthist to test it while we had it in our possession."

Kate frowned, supposing it made sense. Rendborne's distrust certainly explained why he would keep the wilder forces here and not in Norgard. "What's the best way to the forge?"

"There's an entrance down the hallway to the left. It leads right to it." Signe took a step toward the door, but Dal reached out a hand.

"You can't go out there looking like that. Put this on first." He handed her a magestone that would disguise her face, but they didn't have one to disguise her soiled tunic and breeches to look like Sevan armor.

"Do you have some rope or twine, anything to bind your hands?" Kate said. "We can make you appear as a prisoner."

Signe turned to the narrow bed on the far side of the room. A moment later, she ripped a strip of fabric off the sheet and wrapped it around her wrists, holding it to give the appearance that she was bound.

"Good." Kate turned to Dal. "Get Signe back to camp."

"Now just you hold on." Signe jammed her hands onto her hips, dropping the disguise. "I'm coming with you."

Kate pinned her with a glower. "No you're not. It's too dangerous."

"Kate's right, Signe," Dal said, and she shot him a murderous look.

Keenly aware of how much time they'd lost already, Kate summoned her magic and entered Signe's head. *You will go now.*

Signe went stiff, eyes widened in shock. "Get out of my head. How dare you! You're just as bad as he is!"

Kate took an involuntary step backward, guilt lancing through her at the revulsion she sensed in Signe. Corwin had reacted the same the day she tried to free him of Gavril's control. *It's not the same!* She wanted to scream. What she did was for the good of her friends, to protect them. Anger rose up in her, driving back the guilt. "I'm nothing like Gavril. *Now get out of here.*" Kate invoked her sway again, turning its full strength on Signe. Her friend went rigid, and then a dazed look came over her face.

Dal reached for her as if he feared she would faint. "Kate, what did you do?"

She wheeled on him. "What I had to. Now get her to safety."

"Or what, you'll use your sway on me too?" Dal's reproachful look sent a fresh surge of outrage through her. He shook his head, and before she could answer he turned and steered Signe toward the door.

Kate followed after, locking the door again in case anyone came looking. Dal and Signe moved to the right, back toward the entrance, and Kate to the left. Listening to her friends' quick retreat, she pushed aside the doubt gaining strength inside her.

She'd done what she had to. No hesitation.

Moving on, she wondered where Corwin and the others were by now, but as before, the fog on her magic kept her from reaching out.

She arrived at the entrance into the Hellgate a few moments later, the doorway aglow with a reddish light and voices echoing from within. With her magic braced and ready as best it could be, Kate stepped through the doorway into a narrow passage between the raised platforms that surrounded the chamber like seats in an amphitheater. Last time she'd been here, those platforms had been full of cages housing drakes inside. Now they stood empty save for a handful of soldiers keeping watch.

Kate eased her way closer, spying the forge just ahead to the right. The fire was lit but no one stood nearby. The few people there were at ground level, gathered in an area not far from the Hellgate's opening. The last time she'd seen that massive hole in the ground, thick iron bars covered it end to end, darkness lurking within. This time, it stood open, and orange flickering light emanated out of it, from torches and mage lights burning inside. For a second, Kate sensed the depth of the Hellgate, and the sensation made her dizzy.

Pulling her gaze away, she focused on the group ahead. They stood semicircled around a raised area that hadn't been there last she was here. It looked like wilder work, the floor itself coaxed upward same as Bonner had done with the ladder on the wall. A man knelt in the middle of the platform, held in the position by chains attached to the floor.

*Edwin Tormane.* Kate's stomach clenched at the sight of him bound like a sacrificial animal.

Realizing how suspicious she must look, Kate straightened up, assuming the posture of a Sevan soldier as she took another few steps forward, close enough to glance about the rest of the area. To her dismay, she spotted Rendborne standing a few feet away from the raised platform with Magnar Fane beside him. Gavril hovered a few yards behind them both—a perpetual shadow, and a powerful one.

"As promised, your majesty," Rendborne said, bowing his head toward Magnar, "the Hellsteel weapon is ready."

Rendborne raised a wicked-looking trident in his right hand, the blades at its top fashioned unmistakably out of Hellsteel. As Signe had said, the metal was a raw red color, like meat on a butcher's block. The head was circular with the three prongs spaced evenly along its circumference, so that when viewed head on, they formed a triangle.

Magnar held out his hand, accepting the trident. Kate watched the exchange in disbelief. Rendborne would never give up possession of such a weapon of power. She could feel its magic from across the room, tingles running down her arms and legs.

"I assumed you would like to be the first to use it." A smile curved Rendborne's lips.

Magnar nodded, his gaze fixed on the trident, eyes wide with lust for its power, its magic. The very reason for the years of preparation he'd made to invade Rime.

"Go on, your majesty," Rendborne said. "Kill the young prince and initiate the rebirth of Sevan magic."

An alarm sounded in Kate's head. This was all wrong. A trap, a ruse, a manipulation.

Frozen in place, she watched as Magnar stepped onto the platform. Only then did she see the glass bowls set in intervals around the circular platform, their depths filled with bright-red blood. *My blood.* She knew it instinctively, and a shiver crawled down her back. Faint lines were etched into the sides of the bowls, magist magic. This was some sort of spell, but what?

She had no answer, and helplessly she stood by as Magnar approached Edwin. There were too many people for her to fight. Perhaps if she had full use of her magic, but the smothering sensation was worse in here. She had a terrible feeling it might be connected to the blood spell.

Edwin looked up at the Godking, his head tilted back and his expression proud and unflinching, no trace of the fear he must be feeling.

Magnar peered down at Edwin. "I will listen and accept your prayers now, princeling."

"May the three hells take you," Edwin said through gritted teeth.

Smiling, Magnar raised the trident, angling it toward Edwin's heart. Kate held her breath, ready to close her eyes and look away. The entire Hellgate seemed to hold its breath with her, all eyes fixed on Magnar and the would-be king of Rime.

"There are no hells," the Godking said, eyes wide and wild, "for a god."

Just as Magnar pulled back his arm to strike, a scream rent the silence. The sound of it sent Kate's heart lurching into her throat. *No, no, no, don't do this.* She stepped forward, desperate to stop what was happening, but there was no chance of it.

Corwin rushed headlong toward the platform, sword drawn and heedless of the death that surely waited him there.

CORWIN DIDN'T THINK. HE ACTED, driven by instinct and need, heedless of the danger.

He'd only just glimpsed his brother, bound in chains and staring up at the Godking with defiance on his face, but that was all it took. They hadn't meant to come into the Hellgate at all, but to move on, searching the outer chambers. But Corwin had felt the burn in his palm, the uror brand calling out to him in warning. The moment he saw Magnar threatening his brother with that strange trident, he understood.

Now, he ran with all the strength his body possessed—if he could just get there in time, he could stop this somehow. As he leaped onto the platform his foot knocked against one of the glass bowls, blood spraying outward. Someone shouted in outrage, but he barely heard it. Just as he barely felt the ground quake behind him—Bonner supporting him in this mad attempt to save his brother.

Magnar turned toward Corwin, eyes widening as he realized the threat, but he didn't move to defend himself. Instead a malicious grin crossed his face as his arm swung down, jamming the three-pronged blade into Edwin's heart.

The metal didn't break this time; it sank in deep.

"No!" Corwin skidded to a halt, the sound of his shout drowned out by the explosions from Yaron joining Bonner in the attack.

Magnar jerked the trident free of Edwin's chest, then turned to face Corwin. He raised his hand, ready to meet Corwin's assault, but froze at the red raw light emanating from the tips of the trident. The light thickened into something almost tangible, and the color transformed from red to black until it resembled a living shadow. The shadow thing rose over Magnar's hands like black smoke, and he dropped the trident as if it burned, but the shadow didn't stop. It swept over him, pouring into his nose and mouth and ears. Choking, he turned and fled just before Corwin reached him.

With an agonized cry, Corwin stopped when he reached his brother and knelt beside him, praying he yet lived, but the light had gone from Edwin's eyes even as the blood still spilled from the wound in his chest. Rage and horror and despair filled Corwin, leaving no room for thoughts or reason. With his soul still screaming, he stood and sheathed his sword, then stooped to pick up the Hellsteel weapon. If Magnar claimed himself a god, then he would die like one. Corwin spun around, dimly aware of the soldiers rising to meet the attack. But none of them were wilder or magist, and they were thus ill equipped to defeat Bonner and Yaron.

Spying the Godking, Corwin leaped off the platform after him. But Magnar was too far, and a swarm of soldiers converged around him, guarding his hasty retreat. Corwin turned, hoping to head them off, but then his focus abruptly changed as he caught sight of Gavril fleeing just ahead. Hatred spurred Corwin after him. If he could not have Magnar, he would settle for Gavril—and he finally had a weapon that could harm him.

Gripping the trident tightly, Corwin raced after the wilder.

Gavril had a head start, but he was slow and soft, his only strength his magic. *But you can't reach me now.* Not with the vial around his neck. Gavril stumbled and fell, and it was all Corwin needed to close the gap. Not waiting for the man to turn around, Corwin aimed the trident at his back. Gavril didn't deserve an honorable death.

"Corwin, don't!" Kate screamed from behind him.

Her words didn't register in his mind, which was racing with all the memories of pain and suffering Gavril had inflicted upon him. With a powerful thrust he plunged the trident into Gavril's back. Gavril cried out, but before Corwin could relish the victory, savor in the sudden freedom from the Tenets, something struck him from behind, knocking the weapon out of his grip. Gavril was plunged forward, and he fell on his face with the trident sticking out from him like a spear through a felled boar.

Corwin turned to see that it was Kate who had struck him, barreling into him so hard she had fallen over. Too bewildered to understand her actions, he turned to retrieve the trident, only to have Kate scramble to her feet and push him back away from it.

"Don't touch it." Kate pointed to the weapon, where, as before, a sickening red light was pouring out from it, quickly turning into that living black shadow. "Back away. Don't let the smoke touch you."

Corwin gaped at her, confusion muddling his thoughts. What was happening? The shadow was spreading across the ground like fog. He shook his head. "We can't leave it." He reached for the trident again.

"Don't." Kate grabbed him once more, and before he could

shake her off, Bonner appeared beside them. He reached through the smoke for the trident in Gavril's back, ignoring Kate's shout. Hands gripped around the weapon, he pulled it free.

"Now we go," Bonner said with a sharp look at Kate. She didn't argue, but turned and hurried for the door. Corwin followed after her, casting a glance at Bonner running beside him. There was no black smoke around the weapon anymore, but when he looked over his shoulder, he saw it still spreading throughout the room, emanating from where both Edwin and Gavril lay dead. The sight of it made the hairs on his neck stand on end. It showed no sign of stopping and would soon cover everything.

They raced along the outer hallway toward the exit. Several Sevan soldiers tried to stop them, but Kate reached out her hand and a moment later the men dropped to the ground. She may have just knocked them unconscious . . . but Corwin didn't think so. His stomach clenched. She'd killed them so easily, without a second's hesitation. In that moment she hardly seemed the person he'd known and loved before.

"The wilders in the camp," Bonner said over his shoulder at Kate. "Can you reach them with your sway? Tell them where to flee?"

She shook her head. "Not yet. We need to get outside."

They reached the bailey a few moments later to find the encampment in chaos. The wilders had sensed Gavril's death the moment it happened, the release of the cursed Tenets, and the reaction was as expected—they too were freed from his control, and fighting back. Triumph swelled in Corwin's heart as he took a moment to explore his own mind, savoring the realization that it was indeed his own again. Gavril's magic was gone.

"I'll get as many as I can," Kate said, a look of concentration spreading over her face. "I'll send them to the dragon caves." She stumbled, and Corwin caught her, pulling her upright.

They raced into the fray, wilders unleashing their spells left and right while the Sevan soldiers fought back. But Bonner and the others didn't engage. They only ran, their purpose escape for now, not victory. Corwin guessed Kate must be reaching at least some of the wilders, for several of them began to retreat.

"Bonner, can you make a hole for us?" Corwin pointed at the battlements, but Bonner must not have heard him, for he didn't respond. It didn't matter. A moment later another earthist did it for them, and Corwin suspected Kate might've had something to do with it. Corwin plunged through the hole in the wall after the woman, leading the way.

Once in the woods, they hurried over the familiar ground to their encampment, dodging around trees and jumping limbs and brambles. In moments they arrived at the camp, the spot so well hidden that for a moment Corwin doubted it was the right place.

"Dal! Signe! Everyone!" Kate shouted up at the trees. "We need to flee, now!"

Dal appeared from around a tree, with Signe looming just behind him. "No one else is here but us."

"What do you mean?" Bonner strode toward Dal, his stoic expression showing signs of splintering into panic.

"Just what I said. When we got here there was no sign of any of them. Harue, Xia, Wen, Valora, they're all gone. So are their horses."

"It makes no sense." Kate turned a quick circle, eyes scanning the trees surrounding them as if she could spot their path.

Corwin fisted his hands in frustration, fingernails digging into his palms. "We can't wait for them. Let's go."

They all turned at once and headed down the path where they'd been keeping their horses penned inside a makeshift corral that Xia had built using the trees and bushes themselves to form the walls. A few moments later they were on their way, racing through the woods as fast as the steeds could manage.

Once out on the road, Corwin glanced behind him to see a squad of Sevan soldiers giving chase. He drew the bow off his saddle.

"I've got this, Corwin," Kate said. Casting her gaze over her shoulder, the Sevan horses suddenly bolted sideways, dumping their riders with stunning ease. Kate slowed her own horse long enough to stretch out her hand to the fallen soldiers. None of them tried to rise, either asleep or dead by her magic. Corwin didn't care to speculate which.

They rode on at a grueling pace. Soon all the horses were panting and coated in lather, steam rising off their necks, but they couldn't slow down, not until they reached a safe distance from the Hellgate. By then, it would be nightfall. Corwin glanced at Yaron, hoping the man had strength left to set the wardstone barriers, or they would be drake food by morning.

"We must stop soon," Kate said as they breasted another hill. "Or risk killing the horses."

Yaron pointed to the west. "There are ruins nearby. It'll be easier for me to set the barrier there."

The ruins he spoke of turned out to be nothing more than a pile of stones with a few pillars still standing. It looked like it might once have been a cottage, an ancient remnant from a time before nightdrakes. Still it would be enough to give them cover until dawn. Even with magists, the Sevans wouldn't be foolish enough to pursue them at night, not with the drakes around.

They made camp quickly, Yaron seeing to the wardstone barrier and Kate to the horses, while the rest gathered wood for the fire. The nights were still too cold to go without it. As they did, they'd each given an accounting of the events at the Hellgate. Dal was shocked to learn of what had happened during the failed ritual—most notably Corwin's recklessness.

Once the barrier was set, they gathered around the fire, each taking turns keeping watch. The barrier would repel drakes only. *We could use a few of them now*, Corwin thought, in case anyone was still chasing them. Then he reconsidered, remembering the wilders in the encampment—their magic would be dormant at this point, and if the barrier failed for even a moment, they were all done for. Worry pricked at him, and he wished them goddess protection.

Corwin shifted his gaze to Kate, who sat across from him, the flames from the fire dancing between them. She seemed strangely far away and isolated, not just from him but from everyone. With Bonner and Yaron keeping watch, Dal and Signe sat at the fire as well, Signe tucked inside Dal's arms.

"Did you reach many of the wilders?" Corwin asked her after a time. He couldn't stand the silence any longer, or the thoughts it was allowing to seep into his mind, of his brother lying dead on the floor of the Hellgate.

Kate glanced at him before dropping her gaze once more. She wrapped the cloak she was wearing tighter around her shoulders. "Some of them, yes. But I don't know how many will come. They didn't want to listen to me."

Corwin sighed, understanding their reaction all too well. After being free of Gavril, the last thing they would want was another invader in their minds. "You did the best you could, under the circumstances."

Dal snorted. "By circumstances, do you mean abandoning all sense and running in like a fool with a death wish?"

Corwin flushed, his temper igniting in an instant. "You weren't there. I saw an opportunity and took it. I refuse to regret killing such a man as that."

Rolling his eyes, Dal snorted again. "Yes, because killing him when we weren't prepared to rescue the army of enslaved wilders he's been controlling doesn't matter at all."

"To the three hells with you." Anger burned inside Corwin. So did guilt, but it was almost imperceptible beneath his fury. He pointed at Dal, eyes narrowed. "You don't get to judge. Not until you've endured what I've endured, what those wilders have endured at that monster's hands. You would've killed him first chance you had too."

Dal sat up, the movement forcing Signe to pull away from him, though he didn't seem to notice. "That's it, though, Corwin, you're not just anyone. You are the king now. You need to be smarter than that. You can't just think about your own vengeance."

*King?* The notion brought Corwin up short. With Edwin gone, the crown did fall to him without contest, but the magnitude of what that meant was too much for him to think about now.

"Leave him be, Dal." Signe placed a hand on Dal's arm. "Corwin is right. You can't understand." For some reason, she cast Kate a sidelong glance as she spoke.

Feeling his emotions slipping out of control, Corwin stood as calmly as he could and walked away from the fire, his skin cooling as well as his anger with each step he took. Reaching the wardstone barrier, he came to a halt and wrapped his arms around his chest, as if he could hold his emotions in by physical force. It wasn't just anger anymore—Dal was right. Killing Gavril like that was foolish. It should've been a planned assassination, accomplished once they'd determined the best way to reach the most wilders, to ensure they would be able to escape—and join them. Instead, he'd killed Gavril on impulse rather than pursue Magnar as he'd originally intended, all of it done to save Edwin. Now the wilders he'd freed could be anywhere, fighting for their lives against Sevan soldiers or magists or drakes. He'd let them down.

And there was despair too, like drowning in black water. Edwin was dead. Corwin had been there, mere feet away, but he hadn't been able to stop it. He recalled his last few encounters with his brother, the anger and resentment between them. Even hatred. Now that Edwin was gone, there was no chance of healing the rift between them. Corwin hadn't even realized he'd wanted to until now, when it was too late. The irony of it struck him that such clarity of sight came only at the end. How cruel this life could be. *No, not life itself,* he thought, *but our own actions, those taken and not.*

But at least he was free of Gavril, forever.

Corwin closed his eyes. How could he feel such guilt and anguish and relief at the same time?

A hand touched his back, and he tensed. He hadn't heard Kate approach, but he could tell it was her. He always seemed to know when she was near.

"Are you all right?" she said, letting her hand fall away.

"No, but I will be."

She stepped up beside him, not touching him again, but close enough she could have, if she wanted to. "Edwin's death isn't your fault, Corwin. There was nothing you could've done."

He drew an unsteady breath, the realization of how well she knew him adding to his misery. He tried to answer, but couldn't for fear that he would cry. There was no time for tears now.

"And killing Gavril was the right decision as well," Kate went on. "If there's one thing I've learned, it's that you must seize the chance when it arrives and never hesitate. You might not get a second one." She stared out at the darkness beyond the barrier, a brittle sort of sadness on her face. One he guessed had little to do with Edwin or any of these recent events.

"I never had the chance to tell you how sorry I am . . . about Kiran."

Kate's spine went rigid. Not looking at him, she managed a quick nod.

Feeling her pain as sharply as his own, Corwin drew a deep breath and let it out again. He longed to reach for her, but he didn't know how. He didn't know if she would allow it, or if she would turn away from him in disgust like she had the day she'd entered his mind and seen Eravis. Then he considered what she'd just said, about seizing chances. He turned, meaning to reach for her, then changed his mind as he saw how rigidly she stood, how guarded her stance was, with her arms wrapped around her sides.

If she noticed his indecision, she didn't comment, asking instead, "Is the uror now over, with Edwin's death?"

He hated even considering the question. Was it over? *Am I truly king now?* He examined the uror mark on his palm, remembering the way his grandfather had described winning the uror, how the brand had warmed until it almost burned. How it had glowed like the sun. *Then all of Norgard knew as I did,* his grandfather had written, *that I was to be the next king.* Nothing like that was happening for Corwin. The mark felt like scarred, dead flesh, nothing more. "I don't—" he began, then broke off at the sound of pounding hooves in the distance.

"Someone's coming." Kate reached for the sword at her side.

Corwin drew his as well, and shouted for the others to arm themselves. Signe and Dal joined them a moment later, both with bows in their hands, arrows nocked.

They waited, tensed and ready, as the sound of hooves grew louder. A moment later, several horses burst into the clearing, Valora riding at the front with Harue, Wen, and Xia just behind her. Corwin gaped in surprise, lowering his weapon as they charged into the barrier.

"Harue," Kate said, sheathing her sword with a violent thrust. "We feared you were all dead or captured. Where have you been?"

"And how did you find us?" Yaron eyed Harue askance.

With a childlike grin on her face, Harue dismounted. "I didn't.

Valora did. She knew a way to track Corwin's uror mark with a spell."

Corwin frowned, uncertain what to make of this revelation. When Valora had confessed the priesthood's possession of secret magical knowledge, he hadn't known it would have such practical applications. He pressed his fingers against the uror brand on his palm, again sensing nothing but dead flesh. Still, there had to be something there if what Harue said was true.

Kate's expression hardened into anger. "Where did you go?"

Harue's grin faltered as, for once, she had enough social aware-ness to sense the menace in Kate's tone. Before she could answer, Valora stepped forward, holding out the object in her hand wrapped in a blue velvet cloth. "To get this from the temple of Noralah."

Corwin arched a brow. "You made it into Norgard and out again without being caught?" The city wasn't far from the Wander-ing Woods, but the road was open—and surely guarded.

"We used a deflection spell I know to hide us from onlookers," Harue said, handing her reins to Wen. "And Raith's mage door still hasn't been discovered. It seemed easier to get what we needed now without waiting for permission."

"Because you knew we never would've allowed it," Kate said, nostrils flaring.

"Yes, that too," Harue replied.

Valora shook her head, and in a placating tone said, "That is not how it happened. We didn't plan to go. I hadn't even realized how important it was until . . ." She trailed off, as if afraid of saying anything more.

"Until what?" Corwin pressed.

For some reason, the priestess turned her gaze onto Kate. "When we were in the Wandering Woods, I experienced a vision. From the goddess."

The words seemed to hang in the air, drawing the others into shocked silence. Their meaning stirred strange feelings inside Corwin. Was it possible? Valora was the high priestess no longer, cast out by her order, but did that mean the goddess had forsaken her in return? *Perhaps Noralah does what she chooses.* Corwin couldn't presume to know.

Yaron broke the silence first, nudging his chin toward the object in Valora's hands. "What was so valuable to be worth taking that risk?"

Harue grinned again. "A book."

Corwin shook his head in dismay. That explained Harue's involvement then, if not the others'.

"Not just any book," Valora said, her solemn attitude in stark contrast to Harue's excitement. "This is the *Invocarium: The Goddess Codex*." She pulled back the cloth to reveal a portion of the cover, soft black leather engraved in strange silver markings. A language, Corwin realized, but one he didn't know.

"It's the most sacred of all the books in the priesthood's archives," Valora continued. "I alone knew where it was kept. When Rendborne replaced me, I never had the chance to tell the new high priestess where it was. Not that I would have. Rendborne can't be allowed to get his hands on it."

"Why, what secrets does it contain?" Corwin said.

Valora pulled the book close to her chest. "No one living has ever read it. Few would even dare. But it's said to hold the knowledge of how to summon the power of the goddess herself, known as the Paragon spell."

*The power of a god*, Corwin thought. Just what Magnar and Rendborne both wanted. "You were right to get it then. But it was sheer luck that you didn't all die in the attempt." Unless maybe it wasn't. Not if the vision was true.

"Luck?" Harue said with a perplexed look. "But there's no such thing, your highness."

"Prince Corwin," Xia said, stepping forward. "When Valora told us what the book could do, we thought it best to retrieve it in case we failed to get the Hellsteel. Did we find it?"

"We did," Corwin said.

Kate folded her arms over her chest. "Yes, but I'm not sure we should use it."

"What do you mean?" Valora cocked her head.

"Magnar used it to kill my brother," Corwin said. "When he did, this smoke and shadow thing came out of the Hellsteel. Same as it did when I killed Gavril. Magnar was afraid of it, though. It did something to him." He looked at Kate, remembering her fear of it. "What was it?"

She hugged her arms tighter around her body, suppressing a shudder. "I don't know. It just felt *wrong*. Like death itself. I sensed it with my magic."

At Valora's urging, Corwin recounted the events in the Hellgate, the other listening raptly.

When Corwin finished, Dal said, "It seems that Rendborne exposed Magnar to it on purpose. I bet he'd been planning it all along."

Corwin nodded. "I agree. All this time he'd been promising Magnar he would restore magic to Seva using the Hellsteel, but given what we know about Rendborne, that doesn't fit his motivations at all."

Kate turned a grim expression toward the others. "That explains the bowls set around the platform. Some sort of spell. It must've been meant to contain the smoke. That would explain why Rendborne fled the moment Corwin disturbed the spell."

"But what did the smoke do?" Corwin said. "Does anyone have a guess?"

"Sounds like a chemical reaction to me," Harue said, seeming more like she was talking to herself than answering a question. "Something about its unique characteristics must react to the blood. Or maybe it's the release of energy at the time of impalement. Or—"

"I know what it does," Bonner said, cutting Harue off before she could really get going.

Corwin stared at him, aware for the first time how diminished he appeared, like a man suffering from a long illness. "You touched the shadow when you picked up the Hellsteel."

It wasn't a question, but Bonner nodded as if it were, his gaze fixed on the ground.

"What happened?"

After several long moments, Bonner raised his head, meeting their gazes at last. "My magic . . . it's gone. That smoke thing took it."

THE LOSS OF BONNER'S MAGIC was only the beginning.

In the days that followed their escape from the Hellgate, many of the wilders freed by Gavril's death made their way to the dragon caves—far more than Corwin would've guessed given their odds of survival, but it seemed none of them had run into nightdrakes. That should've been impossible given the creatures' ferocity, but it was true. Another sign from the goddess? Corwin wondered, hearing report after report. Or perhaps it was due to the Ruin, as they'd come to call the smoke and shadow thing, that had kept the nightdrakes away.

The name grew out of the stories the escaped wilders told upon their arrival. A few of them had been touched by it, the smoke having swelled and spread through the Hellgate like ground fog on a chill night. Same as Bonner, their powers were gone, taken by whatever magic was released from the Hellsteel when it was used to kill.

But that wasn't even the worst of it. Some of the freed wilders had seen the Ruin reach a cluster of everweeps. It had spread over them, seeping into them—and the flowers had withered and died moments later, as if struck by a blight. And it didn't stop there. The damage had traveled far beyond the boundaries of the Wandering Woods, or so the wilders had claimed. Given the quickly growing knowledge of the everweeps as the source of Rime's magic, an air of panic was steadily rising, magist and wilder alike afraid of what would happen if the Ruin didn't stop.

Despite the risks, Corwin rode out to witness the breadth of the destruction for himself. Tira and Kate went with him. The ever-weeps scattered throughout the base of the mountains remained in bloom, but the moment they reached the valley leading toward Norgard, the path of the Ruin became clear. Ahead, the fields of everweeps had turned to black, transforming the color and brilliance of Rime into a shadow scrawled over the land itself. The blight followed a clear line—on one side the everweeps had wilted and turned to black, on the other the flowers remained untouched. The sight reminded Corwin of the uror sign, half black, half white.

"My gods." Tira covered her mouth with a hand. Hardly anything seemed to daunt her.

"It's like the end of all things," Kate said, gaze fixed on the Ruin ahead.

"And the waters turned to dust, and the earth to rust," Tira murmured.

"Is that poetry?" Corwin asked.

Tira shook her head. "A nursery rhyme. It's called 'Here in the End That Was the Beginning.' It always made me sad as a kid, even though I'd never imagined anything that could compare to it. But this . . ."

They were simple words, but they said everything. Corwin swallowed the grief rising up his throat. It was as if Rime itself was dying, the heart and soul of it succumbing to a plague.

Desperate to break the swell of emotion, he smiled grimly. "I must say, Tira, it's no wonder you grew up to be a mercenary."

Tira snorted, although the sound seemed more obligatory than truly amused. "The poem isn't supposed to be sad, actually. It's about the Ascension of the Godking and Seva's rebirth."

"Well, that's a cheerful way for your people to—" Corwin broke off, suddenly remembering what Valora had said about the god-tears of Seva, and how its disappearance was the gods' punishment against humankind for killing one of their own.

"What are you thinking, Corwin?" Kate asked, eyes steely.

Corwin half-consciously raised a hand to the crystal vial around his neck, running his fingers against the smooth edge. "Valora said the gods punished the people of Seva when Fanen killed Sevan. But what if it wasn't the gods that caused the magic to vanish but the use of the Hellsteel itself?"

Heavy silence greeted him.

Then Kate shook her head. "I hope you're wrong. The Ruin seems to have stopped for now, but if Rime were to lose all its magic . . ." She trailed off, afraid to speak the words.

Corwin's fear was lit anew as well. Without magic they wouldn't be able to defend themselves against nightdrakes for long. The walls would fail, the people overrun by the nightmarish beasts.

Tira dismounted and walked toward the line of blackened ever-weeps. Kneeling down at the border, she pulled one of the healthy plants from the ground. "If what's happening here now is the same as what happened in Seva, why does the Ruin stop here? All of Seva was affected by the death of Sevan. The stories say our magic once ran from sea to sea, across the entire continent." She walked back to Corwin and handed him the flower. "But there's no sign of the Ruin on this plant, and it was right next to the blighted ones."

Corwin frowned, too cautious to be optimistic, although he was as concerned as Tira was.

"Perhaps it's the death itself," Kate said, her gaze unfocused, as if her mind were drifting far afield.

"What?" Corwin and Tira asked in unison.

"Magic releases at death." She nodded, her gaze coming into focus once more. "Remember what happened with the trident? Perhaps the Hellsteel does something to the victim's magic, changes it somehow. A chemical process, Harue would call it. A reaction."

"You mean Gavril's power is somehow responsible for this?" Corwin waved toward the blackened swaths of everweeps.

"In part, yes," Kate replied. "But also Edwin's death, and the magic of the uror that had resided in him."

*Goddess power, goddess magic.* Corwin rubbed at the old scar on his chin, the pain of his brother's death still fresh. He pushed the grief aside to focus on the why of it. "That would explain the containment spell. Rendborne must've known that Hellsteel would destroy any magic that came in contact with it." The Hellsteel by itself seemed benign. Many people had held the weapon, including Harue and Yaron, and both retained their magic.

"But what about Magnar?" Tira said, sliding a foot in the stirrup to mount. "He doesn't have magic, and yet the smoke reacted to him, too."

Corwin considered it a moment, then sucked in a breath as the truth dawned inside him. "Godsblood," he murmured, remembering the conversation he'd had with Eryx about how they were descended from Fanen and so were protected by any magic that would do them harm. That itself must have been a sort of magic—one the Hellsteel reacted to, it seemed.

Kate cast him a wary glance. "What is it?"

A flush rose up Corwin's neck, and once again he touched the crystal lying against his breastbone. This time, he caught himself doing it and dropped his hand. "Magnar and the rest of the Fanes are descended from Sevan himself. Something in their blood protects them from certain types of magic. Gavril wasn't able to use his sway on any of them."

"How do you know—" Kate began, then stopped abruptly. She looked away, gaze fixed on the horizon.

Shifting his weight in the saddle, Corwin went on. "Maybe that's why Rendborne wanted Magnar to kill my brother—to destroy the magic protecting him. Once done, Gavril could've controlled the Godking easily, making him Rendborne's puppet outright."

"And it may well have worked, if you hadn't killed Gavril first," Tira said.

Corwin nodded, feeling a grim satisfaction in the knowledge. As it was, the balance of power seemed to have remained the same between Magnar and Rendborne. Before they'd gone to the Hellgate, Corwin had dispatched spies to the cities, and the reports they'd received most recently indicated Magnar was still in control. Corwin could only guess that the Godking didn't realize what had been done to him, or Rendborne had successfully lied his way out of it. The man was certainly capable of such manipulation. *But why? What's your game?* Corwin thought, knowing beyond all doubt that Rendborne was still the driving force behind everything.

Kate turned back to them, her expression schooled into a careful mask. "The question is, what does Rendborne plan to do next?"

"And, how do we stop it," Tira added.

Aware that the questions were posed to him, Corwin raised his gaze from the scarred and ruined field to the trees in the distance, the edge of the Wandering Woods. Norgard waited beyond. He felt the press of the uror brand against the rein in his hand. It remained dead, no hint of the magic that Valora claimed was still there. "*The uror is not done,*" she'd told him on their journey back to the caves after their escape from the Hellgate. "*The goddess has not accepted you yet. She won't until you complete the last trial. Only then will you truly be king.*"

"*What happens if the goddess doesn't accept me even then?*" he'd asked her, but she'd given no answer. He had a feeling she didn't know.

*Uror.* Once Corwin had wanted to win it so badly, to be the goddess-chosen king of Rime. He'd even had dreams of riding the uror horse into battle. With his gaze still fixed toward Norgard, he wondered where the horse was now. Edwin had been parading about on a false one, but the real horse must be out there still, hidden in the city somewhere. *Unless Rendborne has found it already.* The thought made his heart plunge into his stomach as images of the Nameless One killing his own uror sign flashed through his mind. All the magic stored inside that black and white eagle had gone into Rendborne at its death, the power ripping him apart and putting him back together broken. Killing the uror sign was what made him into the monster he was today. It was the source of all his power and corruption. Rendborne had tried to kill the uror horse when it appeared too, but he hadn't been able to. The goddess magic of the uror protected it. Just at it protected Edwin and Corwin.

*Had* protected them. Before the Hellsteel.

"What is it, Corwin?" Kate said, her mount sidestepping impatiently.

"The uror horse. Rendborne tried to kill it once before, and now with the Hellsteel, he doubtless can finish the task." The terrible reality in his words seemed to vibrate in the air around them.

Reasonably, Tira said, "He'll have to find more Hellsteel first."

"It won't take him long." Corwin's gaze dropped. Rendborne was dogged in his pursuits, endowed with both tenacity and patience, a powerful combination.

A stricken look crossed Kate's face. "Killing it might not be the worst part."

Corwin eyed her. "How could there be anything worse?"

"I said it before. Magic releases at death—all of it."

"I don't understand," Tira said, although Corwin had a feeling he did, and he hoped he was wrong about what Kate would say next.

"All the magic in the land was affected when Fanen killed Sevan. What if that was because of the amount of magic unleashed? Sevan was a god. Gavril was only one wilder."

The fear doubled inside of Corwin. "The greater the death, the greater the devastation."

"Yes," Kate said, and the simple word seemed to hold the sound of doom.

Corwin pictured it now—the death of the uror sign, all the everweeps in Rime destroyed, all the magic gone from the world. Rime couldn't survive without it. Without the wardstones, the drakes would overtake every city and village. He wanted to believe that Rendborne, born a Tormane himself, would never allow it to happen, but he knew better. He'd felt firsthand the madness inside him, the unbridled hatred for Rime and desire to see it fall. Destroying its magic would surely do that. It would take Rendborne's magic as well, but Corwin doubted that would matter to the madman in the end. Or perhaps he had some way to make himself immune to the Ruin; maybe all those hours spent combing the Sevan library had taught him more than just how to find and use the Hellsteel.

Corwin turned to Kate, his own mount now impatient with their loitering here. "If we go into the city, and the uror horse is still there, could you locate it with your sway?"

"Yes," she said, and this time the word held promise. Despite the rift separating them, he trusted her, believed in her fully. "It won't be hard. I heard Rendborne and Gavril discussing it before, when they were draining my blood. Rendborne is keeping it in the stables. He's been hiding it from Magnar the same way Edwin hid it. With a magestone."

"Then let's get back to camp. I want to be ready to leave for Norgard by morning." If they couldn't save the world, at least they could prevent it from being destroyed, if only for a while.

They hurried toward the caves. It was already past noon and the magists might require all the daylight that remained to work the spells they would need to infiltrate Norgard. Corwin's mind raced with plans on how they would enter the city, where they'd look first. By the time they reached the last foothill before the dense wood that hid the cave entrance, he was so lost in thought, Kate had to shout his name to get his attention.

"Corwin!"

"What?"

Kate pointed to the rise ahead of them. "Someone's there."

He could see nothing out of place but didn't doubt her magic. "Can you tell who it is?"

She started to shake her head, then an incredulous look crossed her face. "My gods, it's Genet. Laurent found them!"

As they crested the hill and looked down, Corwin's heart soared at the sight of hundreds of people traveling the path toward the cave entrance, a procession stretching out of sight through the trees.

"Kate!" Genet called when she spotted them. She'd been waiting on the side of the path, watching her charges' progress.

Kate rode toward her and the two women dismounted to embrace. Corwin joined them on the ground along with Tira, but he waited to be introduced, listening to Genet's story of how they'd arrived here. He'd never met the former Rising councilor, but he liked her at once. She had a calming way about her.

"Laurent tracked us down in Eetmark," she was saying. After fleeing Farhold, the refugees—wilders, magists, and common folk—had spent two weeks in the wilderness, fending off drakes and avoiding Rimish soldiers. They'd learned quickly it was better to travel in small groups and, splitting up, they made their way to Eetmark and had been living there in hiding ever since. Once Laurent had found them, though, Genet and Deacon mustered the survivors once more, and they'd left the city in small caravans before joining up again here.

"I'm so glad you made it safely." The smile that crossed Kate's face caused Corwin's breath to hitch. She smiled so rarely anymore that seeing this one, bright and genuine, was like clouds suddenly parting to reveal the sun after days of gray skies. For a second he longed to see her sideways smile, as he called it, that special one he sometimes believed she reserved only for him.

Genet returned the smile. "Safely, but not uneventfully." She turned to Corwin, and to his surprise she bowed to him as formally as a noblewoman at court. "Good evening, your majesty."

Corwin's throat tightened. *I'm not king*, he wanted to say. It didn't matter if he was king in title and by the usual rights of succession. He hadn't earned her fealty, and he didn't deserve it. Not without the uror. He returned her bow. "It's nice to meet you as well."

She waved at him, her manner turning casual once more. "Two days ago we passed a Rimish army amassing in the city of Rin. Lord Jedrek of Kilbarrow seems to be leading it, or at least attempting to."

Corwin wasn't surprised. Edwin's wife, Sabine, was Jedrek's daughter. He supposed the man didn't know Sabine was dead. Pravat, one of the wilders freed at the Hellgate, had been forced to execute Sabine to prove his loyalty to Gavril. Corwin hadn't needed sway to feel the depths of the man's guilt, no matter that all of them knew it wasn't his fault. Pravat was merely the arrow and Gavril—Rendborne—the archer.

"There are soldiers and nobles from Penlocke, Carden, Thace, even Marared," Genet continued. "It's a formidable force, all ready to resist the Sevan invasion." She paused, her gaze probing him, measuring him. "But there seemed a good deal of disagreements among them about who should lead the attack on the city and how it would be done. I had the impression they'd been debating it for more than a week already."

Corwin grimaced. That sounded like every high council meeting he'd ever attended. Never had he seen all of Rime united in agreement, on any decision. "That's unfortunate to hear, madam. But perhaps they'll come to a consensus soon."

She gave him a shriveling look. "Is that really all you have to say? And here I mistook you for Corwin Tormane, the man who vowed that he would unite all of Rime so that wilder, magist, royalty, common folk, and everyone in between could live in peace as they are without shame or fear."

Corwin clenched his jaw. They were his words almost exactly, ones given not long after he'd escaped Rendborne the first time, when he'd come to accept that the persecution of wilders was wrong. He'd vowed to end it. Now, what he'd suspected had come to pass—the threat to one group of people had put the entire kingdom at risk. All of Rime stood on the brink of destruction. He cleared his throat and stood up straighter, as if to brace against this burden that fell to him and him alone. "You're correct, madam. I did indeed say that."

A knowing smile crossed Genet's face, and she winked at him. "Thought so. If you ask me, your majesty, it's about time for Rime to claim her king."

THE ARRIVAL OF THE SURVIVORS from Farhold stirred the dim and morose atmosphere in the caves into one of hopeful frenzy. None of the wilders and magists with them had been affected by the Ruin, and their number was great enough that many believed they stood a chance of defeating the Sevan forces, especially once Corwin announced his intention to journey to Rin and unite the wilder resistance with that of Rime.

He'd carefully considered the wisest course of action, consulting with Yaron, Kate, Bonner, Dal, Tira, Genet, Jiro, and Signe. In the end he'd decided to wait on rescuing the uror horse. Dal and Signe both seemed certain it would take Rendborne some time to uncover more Hellsteel. They'd used all the first deposit to make the trident, and it had taken nearly a year to find that.

"And it will be harder without the Furen Mag," Signe had said, her jaw set. "He should never have killed my mother."

Corwin had asked her what skills the Furen Mag brought to the search, but Signe refused to say. Another case of Seerah, it seemed.

In the end, Corwin decided that it was better to head to Rin before Lord Jedrek finally convinced the Rimish forces to attack. Without his enslaved wilders, Magnar's force was considerably weakened, but still large enough to be formidable. But if Corwin could succeed in uniting them all, they stood a strong chance of defeating Seva.

Kate didn't doubt Corwin's ability to unite them. In fact, she'd never felt more certain of him. Although killing Gavril in the Hellgate might not have been the most strategic move, at least he had acted and dealt a significant blow to the enemy. And despite their reactions to Kate, nearly all the wilders who'd escaped the Hellgate with their lives had joined them at the caves. It was a victory, even if it was dearly bought.

No, it wasn't defeating the Sevan forces she doubted. It was their chances of defeating Rendborne. This would never be over until he was dead. Thanks to his stolen uror magic, Rendborne had already lived hundreds of years. There was no telling how much longer he would continue on. If they defeated Magnar but Rendborne got away, he would just come after them again in some other fashion. Giving up was not in his nature. Kate had witnessed Rendborne's madness and hatred through Corwin's memories, had felt the strength of his desire to see all of Rime brought to its knees. But that was back when she'd been welcome inside his head, and the center of her churned at the thought of it.

Often, in those weeks before they'd left for Seva, Corwin and Kate would lie awake most of the night, sharing the intimacy of their bodies—and minds—together. That sharing had gone both ways, she seeing his thoughts and feelings while he'd shared hers. It had been a closeness she'd never experienced before with anyone else—and it was one she would never experience again. Corwin could barely look at her, let alone ever love her that way anymore.

The truth of it, the pain of it, expanded inside her with every breath she took until she thought she might burst. She was weary of it. If only she could shut off her own emotions, or erase her memories as she'd done to so many others. But the mere thought of doing so only brought her more pain.

*I am a monster, same as Gavril.*

Thanks to Signe, she saw the truth of what her power made her, and it felt like an iron spike driven through her chest. The first day they'd returned to the caves after escaping the Hellgate, Kate had sought Signe out, meaning to apologize for using her sway on her, and to try to help Signe understand why she'd done it. The attempt had been a miserable failure.

She'd found Signe in the small cave Dal had claimed as his own. She was sitting on a pile of blankets, her good leg tucked beneath her and the other stretched out in front of her.

"What do you want?" Dal said when Kate appeared in the doorway.

She stared at him, trying to keep her manner civil. She knew he was only angry on Signe's behalf. She understood too well how love could make one act irrationally. "I need to talk to Signe, please. Alone."

Dal rolled his eyes. "Unless you plan on forcing me out by sword point, I'm staying."

"Don't do this," Kate said, her patience already wearing thin.

"Or what? You'll use your sway?" A cold smile passed over his lips.

"That's enough, Dal." Signe turned a sharp gaze on him. "Kate is still our friend. No matter what she's done."

Kate flushed, outrage surging through her so fiercely she almost left, apologies be damned. With an effort she swallowed her angry retort.

"I suppose I'll go for a walk." Casting Kate another glare, Dal stooped and pulled on his boots, taking his time about it. Kate waited, her patience expanding to the breaking point. She tried to rehearse her apology once more in her head, but her mind went blank, her emotions making a jumble of her thoughts.

Even after Dal had left and she was alone with Signe, Kate still couldn't summon the words. She knew sorry would never be enough. She sat down on the floor across from her friend, legs bent to give her arms something to rest on. The cold from the stone floor seeped into her backside, and she resisted a shiver.

Signe merely watched her impassively. Kate wished she would do something. Juggle her knife maybe, like she used to. The stillness and quiet only emphasized the animosity between them. The fact that such existed at all made Kate want to cry, which in turn only sparked her temper. She didn't have time for tears. None of them did.

For one terrible moment, Kate considered influencing Signe's feelings. If she was careful, she could slip into Signe's mind and use her sway without her knowing. Then Kate realized what she was doing, and a blush of shame rose up her neck. *How did I get here?* she wondered. To so casually consider using her sway for such a selfish end. She didn't know. Or perhaps she was afraid to admit what she did know—that she was enthralled to the control it gave her, the power.

She pushed the unpleasant thought and all its implications

aside. "Do you remember that time Cort cut my stirrup leathers right before my Relay trial?" Kate hadn't thought about Cort All-good in years, but she had no trouble recalling the boy who had relentlessly tormented her when she and Signe had both worked for the Relay in Farhold.

Signe's lip twitched as she fought back a smile. "Of course. You fell off around the first turn and broke the arena fence."

Kate grimaced. She'd done a lot more than fall. Cort had only cut the stirrup partway, but as she'd leaned into the turn toward the second lane, the leather had ripped completely. Without the support to brace against, the thrust of the horse's turn had launched Kate off its side like a pebble in a slingshot. She'd crashed through the fence, breaking two of the three boards. Afterward, Signe had overheard Cort bragging about what he'd done.

"Cort was such a fool," Kate said. "I won't ever forget his face when you got him back for me." Somehow, Signe had managed to make his practice sword and all the arrows in his quiver so dull that none were capable of taking down a target when Cort ran his own trial the next day.

A grin broke out across Signe's face. "It was one of my more brilliant moments, I'll admit. The fit he pitched would have been unbecoming for even the most spoiled child in Rime."

Kate snorted a laugh, remembering the way Cort had stomped his feet, shouting obscenities, before finally hurling his sword toward the grandstands as if someone had broken his favorite toy. That vengeance, small as it had been, was a sweet victory she relished even to this day, and only one of a thousand reasons why she loved Signe. "You never did tell me how you managed to make all his arrows dull like that."

Signe shrugged. "Magic."

For a second, the response brought Kate up short as she recalled the strange exchange between Signe and her mother, something about kaiolah, but then Kate remembered that this was Signe, who had never told a true story about herself in her life. Kate smiled. "Well, I'm glad you did. You've always guarded my back. I never would've gotten through half of the crazy things we've gotten ourselves into without you." Kate hesitated, once again searching for the right words, but not finding any. "And I'm sorry about what happened at the Hellgate. I hope you can forgive me."

Signe's expression, warm a moment before, turned cold once again. "It's not a matter of forgiveness, Kate. It's about understanding that what you did was *wrong*." She sighed and folded her arms over her waist. "Even now, it's not your actions you're sorry for, but my response to those actions. You still believe that what you did was right."

"If you mean making sure you were safe, then yes, I do believe it was right. How can I not? You matter more to me than anyone."

Signe's eyes narrowed. "If I truly mattered to you, you would never have forced me against my will. Never."

Kate's anger rushed up inside her, and she clambered to her feet, unable to stay sitting any longer. "That's not fair. If I'd let you come, you'd probably be dead now. You'd never have been able to keep up during the escape."

"So that's it, huh? Signe's nostrils flared. "You believe because I have a limp, I deserve to have my choices taken away from me?"

Kate inwardly cursed. She knew she'd made a mistake, but she had no idea how to get out of the mire now that she'd stepped in it. "That's not what I meant."

"It doesn't matter." Signe climbed to her feet and stood before Kate as straight and unbending as a spear. "No one deserves to have their will taken away like that. It's a violation, no matter what good you think you might be doing."

Kate huffed. "That's ridiculous. Am I supposed to just stand by and let bad things happen when I can stop it? If you walked in front of a runaway carriage should I merely hope you'll save yourself?"

"I'm not talking about accidents, Kate. I'm talking about *choice*. You're not a god, and you don't get to make decisions for someone else. To do so makes you the worst sort of—."

She stopped abruptly, but Kate could finish the sentence on her own. "Monster? That's what you were going to say, wasn't it?" Signe didn't deny it, and Kate's hurt mixed with anger, turning it toxic. "And what are you then, but a liar. The runaway daughter of the Furen Mag pretending to be less than you actually are and—"

"How dare you." Signe raised a hand, finger pointed like a knife. "Get out. You don't get to talk about my mother. By all the gods in all the lands, what's happened to you? It's no wonder even Corwin can't stand the sight of you anymore."

All the air evacuated from Kate's lungs, as if Signe's words had been a physical blow against her chest. Without a sound, she had turned and fled the cave, Signe's accusations chasing her all the way back to her room. Afterward, she'd tried to forget them, tried to tell herself that Signe was just upset over her mother's death. Goddess knew she understood how the loss of a parent was like having a hole punched through your chest, one that throbbed with every beat, the pain making you want to lash out anytime someone so much as brushed it.

But in the days that followed, Kate hadn't been able to forget Signe's words. They set in so deeply that she soon realized there was no denying this truth. Kate remembered with absolute clarity the hatred she'd felt in Corwin's mind that day when she'd tried to force Gavril's magic out of his head. She'd thought it had been hatred of Gavril, but Signe's accusation shifted it into a brand-new light, painful and clear. If Corwin's hatred had been for Gavril alone, then why hadn't he come to her afterward, once he'd set himself free? Why had he avoided touching her, looking at her, even speaking to her ever since?

There were only two explanations. Either Signe was right, and he did despise her for what she was and what she had done. Or he was in love with his Sevan princess. Or perhaps both were right.

The possibilities ate away at her like acid poured on her heart. She didn't know how much longer she could take it. For a short while, the new arrivals had provided some distraction from her misery, but it was quickly waning. Instead the constant roar of human interactions only emphasized her isolation. She was a wrecked ship, adrift in a sea of strangers and former friends.

Having stood all she could of being in the main hall, Kate slipped away from the bustle, looking for a quiet refuge farther in the caves. She considered retreating to her own room, then decided against it. She'd been sharing the space with Tira, and there was no telling when she might come in. Kate wandered aimlessly at first, then paused when she heard a familiar voice. For a moment Bonner sounded like his old self, his voice a low rumble like the playful growl of a bear.

Without thinking about it, Kate turned toward the sound, and a moment later arrived at the entrance to the small cave where Bonner had been sleeping. A blush bloomed on her cheeks as she realized he wasn't alone. Of course he wasn't—it was foolish of her not to have guessed it. He'd obviously been speaking to someone. She started to turn away, but stopped as Nadira called after her.

"You may come in, Kate, if you'd like."

With lips pursed, Kate stepped inside. Her blush deepened when she saw Bonner sitting on the makeshift bed wearing only breeches. Nadira was fully dressed, yet there was something intimate in the way she moved about the space, straightening the belongings set in haphazard piles across the floor. Bonner nodded his head at Kate in acknowledgment, but his gaze followed Nadira across the room, lovingly, Kate thought.

A smile as painful as it was pleased lifted the edges of Kate's lips. She was happy for him. He'd finally found someone who stirred the deeper parts of his heart. But it did surprise her to find him content so soon after losing his magic. She had expected him to finally shatter as he'd seemed be on the verge of doing since his father's death, like steel hardened to the point that it becomes brittle.

At last, Bonner pulled his gaze away from Nadira and let it settle on Kate. He motioned to the spread of blankets in front of him. "What's on your mind?"

Kate took him up on the offer, settling down across from him as he reached for his sword lying next to his saddlebags on the floor nearby. With practiced ease, he pulled it from its scabbard and set it across his lap, while Nadira handed him a whetstone. Again, there was an intimacy to their interaction that made warmth blossom over Kate's skin. But it left her cold beneath it.

She hadn't meant to come here at all, much less to talk about anything, but watching as he sharpened his sword, she found herself saying, "Whether or not Corwin is successful in uniting the Rimish forces, we still have no solution for killing Rendborne that doesn't involve unleashing more of the Ruin."

Bonner nodded grimly. "He'll never give up until Rime has fallen. And it's only a matter of time before he finds himself another wilder like Gavril to do his bidding."

A shiver slid down Kate's back at his certainty. She supposed it was true. Rare as sway was, there was surely another out there with the ability, perhaps hiding in one of the cities. She wished she didn't understand the appeal of serving Rendborne, but she did. The Nameless One could offer power to the powerless and freedom to the persecuted, as the wilders of Rime had been for too long.

"There is a solution, though," Bonner said, his eyes following the motion of his hand as he ran the whetstone down the blade in a steady rhythm. He paused and looked up. "We use the Hellsteel anyway."

Kate frowned, certain he must be joking. "How can you say that? It destroys magic, and if we use it to kill someone as powerful as Rendborne, it might destroy all magic throughout all of Rime."

She quickly summarized the conclusion she'd drawn with Corwin and Tira the day the Farhold wilders had arrived. Bonner listened without comment, remaining silent long after she'd finished. Nadira continued her slow meander through the room, but Kate could tell she was paying careful attention to every word.

"So, no, using the Hellsteel isn't an option," Kate finally said. "Even if Rendborne's magic isn't strong enough to affect all of Rime, it would still be devastating."

Bonner pinned her with a look. "If we don't use it, Rendborne will."

Kate gaped at him. "How can you be so . . . so indifferent? Don't you miss your magic?"

"I did at first." Bonner set down the sword and dropped his hands, giving her his full attention. "I was devastated, yes. But now, it's mostly a relief."

His admission stung Kate. Their magic had been a bond, the shared secret of it what had brought them together as friends in the first place.

"I know you might find that hard to believe, but it's true," Bonner continued, oblivious to her churning emotions. "It's only ever brought me trouble. All my life I've had to live in fear and hiding. Once I believed I could do good with my magic and prove to the world that wilders weren't dangerous. And what did I do instead? Created a weapon capable of killing easy, fast, and indiscriminately."

Kate glared at him, despising such narrow thinking. "The revolvers you created were made to kill drakes, not people."

"You think that makes a difference?" His brows drew together in a scowl. "Because intentions don't matter, only results. But it's not just the revolvers. When Gavril captured me, he twisted my magic to his will. He made me use it to kill and torture, to do things no person should ever have to do."

With guilt burning in her gut, Kate tore her gaze off him. Signe's accusations rang in her head, made worse as she realized she'd been forced to use her magic once, too. It wasn't in the same way as Gavril had done to Bonner, but it didn't matter. She'd been forced just the same. And yet she'd turned around and done the same to others. How many times?

*Monster, monster, monster.*

Kate shook her head, trying to dislodge these thoughts but failing. Then she caught sight of Nadira out of the corner of her eye and turned to her. "What about Nadira's magic? It's used to heal people."

"Not always," Nadira said, her voice sharp and her gaze even sharper.

Kate swallowed, not wanting to imagine what the healer had been forced to do. She shook her head again, refusing to condemn all magic. "The magists, then? Without their magic, we'd have no way to keep the drakes from overrunning us at night." Neither of them could argue the danger of that. It was too high a price to pay even for defeating Rendborne.

Nadira crossed the room until she stood just behind Bonner. She placed a hand on his shoulder, gaze fixed on Kate. "The Ruin will kill the drakes same as it kills our magic."

"What?"

"It's true," Bonner said. "In the blighted everweep fields, Nadira found several dead drakes as well."

"I went out to restock the plants and herbs I use in some of my healings the day after we returned to the caves." Nadira gestured to the table, where such lay scattered across the stone surface. "There was nearly half a pack lying dead among the everweeps with no wounds on their bodies."

Kate couldn't fathom it. A world without drakes? She pictured the ruins they'd stayed in the night they'd fled the Hellgate. That structure had been a stone cottage once. People had lived there, right on the edge of the woods, surrounded by flowers and trees and wildlife and beneath a clear night sky full of stars and the silvery moon with its glittering ring. A world without walls.

And no magic.

Including her own. Panic, like a flock of hummingbirds, fluttered in her chest at the thought. Who was she without her magic? *Just Kate.* She was who she'd always been, wasn't she?

*Yes. No. I don't know.*

She rubbed her temple with her fingers, trying to ease the growing ache there. "Have you told anyone about the drakes?"

"No, not yet," Bonner said carefully.

"Good. Leave it to me. I'll discuss it with Corwin once—" Kate broke off at the sound of pounding steps drawing near.

Harue appeared in the doorway a moment later, her wild hair matching the look on her face, an expression of panic and something else Kate couldn't name.

"Nadira," Harue said, "you've got to come."

Brow furrowing, Nadira hurried to the door. "What is it?"

"It's Valora. She's . . . been set aflame."

AS KATE, HARUE, NADIRA, and Bonner rushed toward Valora's room, Harue's declaration was only more confusing. Kate didn't sense any reason to believe that there had been a fire at all. There was no stench, no smoke. In fact, the air was fragrant with a sweet smell like everweeps in high summer or dew-drenched leaves in the spring.

And yet, as they entered her chamber, one look at Valora told Kate something terrible had happened. The woman was lying on her back in the middle of the floor, unmoving. Her eyes were neither opened nor closed. They were gone—burned away. At least, the marks on her face looked appeared to be burns. But they looked like old scars, a spiderweb of raised white lines that radiated out from the empty pits of her eye sockets.

"Sweet Noralah, what did this?" Nadira put her fingers to her mouth. Such astonishment from the seemingly unflappable woman would've surprised Kate if she weren't so astonished herself.

"Magic," Harue said, hand lingering over her mouth as if she too were still reeling from shock. "At least I think it was. She was reading the *Invocarium*."

*The Goddess Codex.* Kate pulled her gaze off the former high priestess and examined the rest of the room. She couldn't tell if any of the disarray was the result of whatever had happened to her. This was Harue's room, after all. When they'd first arrived Bonner had transformed one entire wall of the cave into a table to hold all her books. Kate didn't see the *Invocarium* anywhere.

Nadira knelt beside Valora, taking hold of her wrist. That's when Kate noticed the shallow rise and fall of the woman's chest. Alive, then.

"Tell me what happened," Nadira said.

"Just what I said. She decided to read the *Invocarium*." Harue tapped a foot, arms folded over her middle. "We've been debating for days whether or not we ought to. I told her it was too dangerous, but she refused to listen."

Kate arched one eyebrow as far as it would go. "*You* argued against reading a book?"

Harue looked pained, the admission no doubt sacrilege. "It was necessary. There were warnings all over the cover, about the sacrifices involved in reading, restrictions about who, when, how. I hadn't even begun analyzing it all when Valora just snatched it and opened it."

"Harue," Nadira said with palpable impatience, "what happened after she started reading it?"

Harue bit her lip. "I don't know how well I can describe it. Maybe if I had a quill and parchment and a day or two to list it out and then check it and—"

Kate snapped her fingers. "Focus, please. Just tell us what you saw. Keep it simple."

Movement at the door caught Kate's eye, and she turned to see Corwin step into the room along with Genet and Yaron. Signe and Dal appeared just behind them, making the large space suddenly feel small. It seemed Harue's frantic call for help had drawn attention.

"What happened?" Corwin said, surveying the room. Kate tensed at his presence, Signe's words echoing through her mind as they'd done for days now.

Ignoring him, Harue walked over to Valora and stooped to retrieve a book lying facedown beside the woman. Kate frowned. It couldn't be the *Invocarium*. The cover was plain black, with no trace of the silver markings, and yet Harue held the book away from her, as if afraid it might do her harm.

"When she first started reading it nothing happened," Harue said. "But then the inscriptions on the cover began to glow like white fire. I tried to stop her, but she went into some kind of trance. No matter how much I shouted, she wouldn't stop reading. Before long the words on the page started to vanish, and the pages themselves began to glow like the cover had done."

Harue turned the book in her hand and held it open toward the others. All the pages were blank. But they hadn't been before; Kate had briefly flipped through the book that night at the ruins, but she hadn't been able to read a word of it, or even recognize a single character. Valora said she believed the language was some dialect of Aeos, the language of the gods, though she'd claimed it was one she'd never seen before.

Harue closed the book once more. "The light kept getting brighter and finally it erupted into something like a pillar of light. But it had physical force. When I tried to shut the book, it knocked me down, and I must've been unconscious for a moment." She touched the back of her head as if feeling for a wound. "When I came to, Valora's whole body was aflame with that white light. I went to get Nadira then, and don't know what happened next."

"Apparently," Dal said, "the light vanished, taking her eyes with it." Signe elbowed him in the side hard enough he grunted.

Casting them both a reproving look, Corwin knelt beside Nadira. "Will she be all right?"

"Only the goddess can say."

A moment later, Valora's mouth slid open and her chest rose as she drew a deep breath. With her eyes gone, it was impossible to tell if she was conscious or not. That was, until she slowly sat up.

"Be easy." Nadira gripped Valora's arm and helped her into a sitting position. "You've had a . . ." She trailed off. There was no word that fit what had happened here. This was more than mere accident, magical or otherwise. The air seemed to hum with power, but rather than heighten Kate's senses as normal magic might have done, this made her feel languid, as if she were lying on a riverbank beneath warm sunshine, listening to the steady song of the flowing water.

Harue leaned toward the priestess. "Can you speak, Valora?"

"Give her a minute," Kate said.

Everyone assembled held silent for a few moments, waiting to see what Valora would do. Kate felt like anything might be possible. The woman could sprout wings and fly. It was the strange magic responsible for the feeling, she decided. She felt like a child again after waking from one of her frequent dreams about flying, the sensation of it so vivid it certainly must've been real, as if she could do it while waking if she only concentrated hard enough.

After a while, Valora drew an audible breath and let it out again. "I'm . . . fine." She climbed to her feet, Nadira helping her once more. She led her over to an empty chair, and Valora sank onto it with a sigh.

"Now can you tell us what happened?" Harue said with open impatience. She was looking at Valora like she was a book she desperately longed to read.

Valora slowly shook her head. "I'm not sure. The book, it . . . it changed me. I feel as if I've been gone from the world for a thousand years only to return the moment I left."

It made no sense. It was impossible, and yet she wasn't lying. Kate could tell that even without her magic. But she also knew that truth was often subject to perception, and wanting to see what really happened, she reached toward Valora with her sway, ready to probe her memories. Suddenly aware of what she was doing, she stopped. With a guilty swallow, she pulled back. No, she must accept what Valora said at face value. It was only then Kate noticed how intently Signe was watching her.

"The goddess spoke to me," Valora went on. "I heard her voice. I saw her face." She motioned to her ears and then her missing eyes. If the injury pained her, it didn't show in her expression. "But Noralah was in her true form, and this frail body couldn't handle the magnificence of it. It was like staring into the sun, and yet I couldn't look away. I didn't want to."

"Was that the white light?" Harue said.

Valora turned her head right toward Harue, as if she could still see. "No. That was just a drop of her power bound into the book itself. I released it, and her essence went into me."

No one spoke, and Kate wondered if the others were questioning the woman's sanity. It was one thing to say she'd released a magical spell; it was quite another to claim the goddess's power itself had come into her. Kate shifted her weight from one foot to the other, uncomfortable with the idea. More than ever she'd begun to suspect that the gods were nothing more than a myth, and the wonders and practices of the priesthood just a different strain of the magic used by magists and wilders alike. The magic attributed to these "gods" was looking more and more like a random, uncontrollable version of the power she and others held, magic embedded in the earth itself—not the work of any sort of conscious being.

After a moment, Corwin stepped toward Valora. He did it reverently, like approaching a shrine or altar. Bending down, he took her hand in his. Valora turned her head toward him. "Did the goddess tell you anything that will help us now?"

Valora didn't respond at first, but seemed to regard him thoughtfully. Then she raised a hand to his face, touching the side of his cheek. "Yes, Corwin Tormane, she did." The high priestess cast her eyeless gaze around the room, and Kate could swear that Valora could see her. "The *Invocarium* detailed a ritual that will bestow the power of the goddess onto a person of our choosing, transforming them into the Paragon, champion of the goddess."

Kate's skin prickled. *Paragon.*

"But the book's empty." Harue said, even more oblivious than usual. "How can we know exactly what it said?"

Lowering her hand from Corwin's face, Valora turned to Harue. "All that it contained is now contained within me." She gestured to her forehead and then her heart. Harue looked perplexed but didn't respond.

"Very well," Corwin said, and there was an edge to his

voice—hope, sharp as a knife. "What do you need for the ritual?" His certainty took Kate by surprise, his willingness to believe without proof. Again, Kate felt the temptation to probe Valora's mind, and again refrained. Perhaps for Corwin the proof was the woman herself, the way her body had been transformed by a magic no one had experienced before. Or maybe it was because of his experiences with the uror trial. She couldn't say.

"Many things," Valora replied, "but mostly time to prepare. The ritual can only be performed at dawn."

"But that's just a few hours away," Nadira said.

"There will not be enough time to do it this dawn," Valora replied. "It will have to wait until the following."

Corwin ran a hand through his hair. "But I need to leave for Rin in the morning."

Genet cleared her throat, drawing Corwin's gaze. "If I may, your majesty, perhaps it would be best to send a messenger ahead, to give the lords a chance to prepare for your arrival. That will allow time to complete the spell."

With a resigned expression, Corwin nodded. "I suppose that would be wise."

"You could send Laurent," Kate said. When Corwin turned his gaze on her, she quickly added, "your majesty. Some of them will know his name and face from his time as the Rising's ambassador in Norgard. That might make them more trusting." She knew better than to suggest Dal. Signe wouldn't stand for it.

Corwin stared at her for a long moment, and her pulse quickened in response. Then he turned back to Genet. "Sending Laurent would also make it clear that I stand with the wilders." Genet offered him a quick, reassuring smile. "Laurent it is then, but Dal, I think you should go as well."

"No," Valora said, her voice ringing out like a gong.

Corwin tilted his head at her. "Why not?"

"Lord Dallin Thorne will be needed for the ritual."

"Me?" Dal pointed his thumb to his chest in obvious discomfort at the notion.

"Yes," Valora said. "The ritual requires the blood of the four lands. I will need Signe to represent Esh. Tira for Seva, and Yaron for Rime." She pointed at Signe and Yaron as she said their names.

"If Yaron is Rime, then what exactly am I to represent?" Dal said, a half smile on his lips, as if they were all merely humoring her.

"You will represent Ruzgar, of course."

Dal's smile widened, then faltered. "Excuse me?"

"Your father was of Ruzgar," Valora replied matter-of-factly, as if she had no idea of the magnitude of this revelation. No one knew the true identity of Dal's father, including Dal himself. Officially, Dal was the son of the baron and baroness of Thornewall; unofficially, his closest friends knew he'd been born a bastard, son of the baroness and another man, but that man's identity was a mystery from everyone.

*Not anymore*, Kate realized as she saw the truth dawning in Dal's expression, bringing with it a mixture of utter shock and wonderment.

"Dal?" Corwin asked. "Do you think it's true?"

Dal didn't respond for several moments. Then finally he exhaled. "I . . . don't know. How could I? But I do remember a man from Ruzgar, a privateer called Captain Brack. He used to visit

Thornewall every summer when I was a child. I only remember because he would give me the best sweets I've ever tasted, and once, after discovering I had a black eye, he taught me how to fight with just my fists." Dal paused, as if only now becoming aware that he was speaking these memories aloud. Red blotches spread over his neck as he turned back to Valora. "How can you be sure my father was from Ruzgar?"

"The goddess knows all, and I have been given her sight."

Dal shook his head. "Well, then, how can I be sure this is true and not some . . . elaborate hoax?"

Valora stared at him, and even though she was eyeless, there was no denying it was a penetrating stare. "Belief is a choice you must make on your own." Valora turned her head toward Kate now. "And so must you, Kate Brighton. I need you for the ritual as well. You are to become the Paragon."

Kate's blood seemed to freeze in her veins, and the tranquil feeling she'd been experiencing vanished. But before she could respond, Corwin spoke.

"Why her? Shouldn't I be the one who becomes this Paragon?"

"The vessel must be a woman. The goddess wills it so."

Kate wrapped her arms around her body, desperate to stave off a sudden chill—and fear. *A vessel must first be emptied if it is to be filled.*

Corwin glanced at her, then back at Valora. "We have many other women here."

At his doubt, anger crept into Kate's fear. No matter his feelings for her, she was still loyal to Rime. She wanted Rendborne and Seva defeated more than anyone. There was no reason for him to object to her taking part. She would not betray this power.

"The Paragon must be wilder born," Valora said, her expression stern. "And of those here, Kate's particular magic makes her the best suited for it. Her mind is strong. She stands the greatest chance of surviving."

"Surviving?" Corwin's eyebrows climbed his forehead. "Do you mean the spell might kill her?"

Valora nodded. "Any vessel may break if filled to bursting. But by the goddess's sight, I'm certain she is the right choice."

With hands fisted at his side, Corwin shook his head. "We must find some other way. I'll not risk Kate's life to win this war." After a beat he added, "Or anyone's. So long as I succeed in uniting the Rimish forces, we can defeat Seva with our own might."

*Seva yes*, Kate thought. *But not Rendborne.* She drew a deep breath, tasting the magic in the air, still feeling its sweet, soothing power, a balm to her fear. She might be risking her life, but becoming the Paragon was a better option than wielding the Hellsteel. Better for her to risk death than for all the magic of Rime to perish.

"I'll do it," Kate said, and Corwin wheeled on her, mouth opened to argue. She raised a hand to silence him. "We will need all the help we can get, Cor—your majesty. It's worth the risk. And it's my decision to make."

Corwin held her gaze for a long time, emotions she couldn't name churning in his eyes. Then, finally, he bowed his head. "So it is." For a second he looked like he might say more, but as always of late, silence reigned between them.

AT VALORA'S COMMAND, KATE SPENT the next day and night in seclusion. Although she was supposed to use the time for prayer and quiet contemplation, she spent most of it pacing. She hated waiting more than anything, and idleness was like a slow poison, killing her by the minute. She wanted to be out doing something, anything, but she was stuck staring at the walls of her small cave. Tira had moved out to give Kate peace, and no one was allowed in to see her.

At least the time dulled the edges of her fear. *The Paragon ritual is only magic*, Kate reminded herself over and over again. No matter what Valora called it, it was magic, same as any a magist might work. Only the labels were different—one called a ritual the other a spell. And she wasn't afraid of magic. Magic was an elemental force like wind or rain. It had no agenda, no will of its own beyond the parameters of the spell. Once she was in possession of this power, it would be her will that mattered. She would use the power to kill Rendborne and to end his threat to Rime forever. All this talk about vessels and filling up was the pretty language of a primitive era, nothing more.

*Are you sure?* A voice of dissent whispered in her head. *The uror sign's magic changed Rendborne. You saw it yourself. It gave Corwin some ability too, allowing him to defeat Rendborne that day.*

It was true, but she chose to ignore this point. It was either that or succumb to the fear.

As the night grew late, she finally forced herself to stop pacing and lie down on the pile of blankets she'd been using for a bed. No sooner had she closed her eyes, though, than she sensed someone come in.

"Signe?" Kate said, surprised at her appearance. "What are you doing here?"

Signe crossed her arms in front of her, looking uncertain. "I needed to talk to you."

Kate braced for the worst, the wounds from their last conversation still fresh. She definitely didn't need Signe to dig at them deeper right now. "What about?" she said, carefully.

"This . . . Paragon ritual," Signe began, still uncertain. "Why are you going through with it? How do you know Valora can be trusted?"

"I . . ." Kate shook her head, overcome by surprise. Not that the question hadn't occurred to her already. For her, the decision had nothing to do with trust and everything to do with necessity. That and choosing between the lesser of two fears. Rendborne must be defeated, and she would rather risk undergoing the Paragon ritual than using the Hellsteel. But she didn't want to admit it to Signe, worried she wouldn't be sympathetic to Kate's concern about losing her sway. "It's our only chance at stopping Rendborne."

Signe pursed her lips. "You didn't use your sway to check Valora's story?"

At first, Kate thought it was an accusation, but then she heard the genuine question. With her fingers clenching into fists, she shook her head. "I considered it, but no. As you said, a person's thoughts are private." She dropped her eyes, hoping that the admission would heal the rift between them, that Signe would decide to forgive her.

"Yes, they are. I'm glad you didn't. But . . . I'm still not certain you should go through with this ritual."

Kate sighed, disappointment stinging inside her. "Like I said. I have to."

"It might kill you, Kate. Valora admitted as much."

"So she did. But it's not the first time I've risked my life. It won't be the last."

Signe nodded, as if satisfied. "May the luck of Aslar be with you then."

And with that, she left, leaving Kate alone with nothing but regret for company.

Lying down once more, she closed her eyes and waited for sleep to come. When it finally arrived, it brought painful, terrifying dreams. She saw a spear plunged through the uror horse's side and her friends lying dead in a field of blood and blackened everweeps. She saw Eravis in Corwin's arms, the princess beautiful and cold and smiling triumphantly at Kate. Beside her, Corwin didn't even notice Kate, and his indifference was the worst part of all. No matter how much she screamed or cried or begged, he didn't care. She was a ghost to him, dead already.

Kate woke with her body covered in sweat, hair matted to the back of her neck. The room was dim, only a single candle burning in the far corner, casting long shadows over the walls. Seeing one of them move, Kate sat bolt upright, hand reaching at once for her sword while her mind searched for an intruder's.

But before she could use either, she heard Corwin say, "It's just me."

She relaxed, but only by a degree. Aware of how thin and flimsy the shift she wore was, she moved to cover herself with the blanket despite her sweat. "What are you doing here?"

"Valora sent me to get you. Dawn is breaking. It's time to start the ritual."

Fear rushed up anew inside Kate, and she trembled. *It's only magic*, she told herself yet again, but it didn't feel that way. It felt like the end of the world—or its beginning.

"Let me get dressed," Kate said, "and I'll meet you outside."

Corwin shook his head. "Valora wants you to wear this for now." He held out the robe that he'd been carrying slung over one arm.

"Very well." Kate climbed to her feet, letting the blanket fall to the ground as she took the robe from Corwin.

He stared at her intently as she slipped it on. "Are you sure you want to do this?"

She nodded, her throat too constricted with nerves for speaking.

Some of the intensity left his gaze, a resigned sadness taking its place. "I wish things had gone differently between us, Kate. I wish—" He broke off, drawing a deep breath. "I never meant to hurt you. I hope you know that."

Kate stared at him, searching her brain for some response that wouldn't come off as a deflection. But how could she put into words her own sorrow, her regret like a wound that wouldn't stop bleeding? In the end all she could do was parrot his words back to him. "I'm sorry as well."

It wasn't enough, and yet Corwin nodded and turned toward the door. She followed after him, arms wrapped around her sides like armor. They made their way down the uneven corridors and through the main hall to the cave mouth. The people they passed watched with open interest. Kate kept her gaze fixed on the ground and the steady back-and-forth of her feet.

Once outside, she looked up to see early-morning light filtering through the trees, the air redolent with the scents of spring. Birds chirped in the treetops and insects buzzed in the underbrush. Reaching out with her sway, Kate sensed all the wildlife nearby—deer, rabbit, squirrels. She relished in the feel of their simple minds and simple thoughts, wishing she could be one of them.

All too soon they crested a rise in the trail and arrived at a small clearing with a narrow brook cutting across its middle. To the left of the brook, Valora waited, standing next to a solid stone altar, one no doubt conjured by an earthist. A fire burned across its top, the flames gyrating chaotically in the breeze that couldn't seem to make up its mind which way it wanted to blow. Tira, Signe, Dal, and Yaron formed a circle around Valora, each standing at a cardinal direction: Yaron to the north, Signe to the south, Dal to the east, Tira to the west.

Standing outside the circle were Bonner and Nadira, come to watch, she supposed. Or perhaps Nadira believed her skills might be needed. Kate swallowed at the thought, glancing furtively at Valora's missing eyes, the sacrifice she had paid for the goddess's sight. What price would Kate pay?

Corwin came to a stop a few feet away from the circle and faced Kate. "You are to disrobe here."

Feeling the blood drain from her face, she gave a careful nod. Being naked in front of the others was bad enough, but somehow worse with Corwin, even though he'd seen her thus dozens of times. Doubt swirled inside her as she wondered how he would see her now, what comparisons he might make to the Sevan princess. But the moment she let the robe and shift drop to the dew-slicked grass, Corwin turned his back to her, facing Valora and the others in their circle. After a pause, Kate removed her moonbelt as well, and the loss of its weight left her feeling untethered.

Valora raised both hands toward Kate, beckoning her forward. "Come, Kate Brighton, chosen to be the Paragon."

Kate hesitated half a moment, then forced her feet to carry her forward. She kept her sway stretched out, feeling the animals all around. They were her only source of comfort—and distraction.

Kate's skin tingled as she stepped into the circle, evidence of the magic already swelling. As she reached the center, Valora motioned for her to kneel. Kate dropped to her knees onto the soft, cool pillow of the everweeps in bloom here. At once, Valora began to speak, but it was in a language Kate didn't recognize. At turns it sounded like music, then the wind, then the babble of the brook, the call of birds and the cries of animals, and finally the sound of the earth itself. Kate listened, sensing the meaning veiled in those alien words. They spoke of the goddess, her power, her care for humankind and for Rime. They spoke of sacrifice and courage, humility and victory.

More and more Kate felt her skepticism growing inside her, leaving her cold and empty.

Finally, Valora raised a hand to the hilt of the dagger belted at her side and pulled it free of the sheath. She turned to Yaron first, and he held out his arm, the sleeve of his tunic rolled up. With a quick motion, Valora ran the blade over the underside of his forearm, drawing blood. With her other hand, she withdrew a small wooden bowl from the folds of her robe and held it to Yaron's wound, gathering a few droplets of blood. Once done, she turned right and repeated the process on Dal before moving on to Signe and finally Tira.

Sheathing the knife, Valora turned to the stone altar and carefully tipped the bowl's contents onto the tip of a branding iron lying in the fire. The flames hissed as the liquid touched them, and the sound made Kate flinch and sent her heartbeat to galloping. She understood what was coming next, and panic expanded inside her chest until she thought she might burst from the effort of holding it in.

Closing her eyes, she reached out to the animals once more, drawing strength from them. She could even sense the horses penned nearby. They had always been a source of comfort even in the darkest times, and she leaned into them, letting their thoughts flow into her.

But all too soon she opened her eyes again at the sound of Valora chanting. She looked at the altar to see a white light glowing inside the orange and red of the fire. It was painful to look at, but also beautiful, so mesmerizing she didn't want to look away even though she was certain it would burn her. The others too were all staring, transfixed by what was happening. The ground beneath Kate's knees seemed to tremble and the trees surrounding them to shake as if they longed to pull up their roots and move toward the light as well.

Rather than grow quiet at the disturbance, the animals grew louder, the sound almost frenzied. Shadows moved overhead, and Kate glanced up to see a flock of ravens burst across the sky. Valora's voice rose, becoming urgent, and so did the intensity of the white light, until finally it seemed to crescendo, and Valora grasped the end of the rod and pulled it free from the fire.

The tip glowed so brightly it hid the shape of the brand. Even as Valora drew near Kate with it, she couldn't make it out, her eyes aching from its intense light and color. Valora continued speaking in that strange language, and in her heart Kate understood it was Aeos, the language of the gods.

*But I don't believe*, she thought, managing to force her eyes closed again. *This is only magic. There are no gods, no goddess, nothing beyond this life. Only—*

Kate screamed as the brand touched her skin. Pain exploded over her chest, the white-hot iron pressed against it, right over her heart, which pounded frantically. Agony tore through her body like a tidal wave, and she felt herself falling. Not just her body, but her whole self, mind and spirit swept away. Blackness filled her vision, and a moment later she became nothing. All sense of herself gone, like a candle snuffed out by the wind.

Time stopped, Kate's life suspended in this black void. She had no beginning and no end, just this ever-present now, a formless being in a formless space. But then slowly, the black began to brighten, and she felt herself being drawn back together, until she was whole and in her own body again.

Only she was no longer in the clearing outside the dragon caves of Rime, but in a dark place full of a mist that swirled about her in shadowy eddies. As before, she was naked, but she barely noticed or cared. Even the black mark on the left side of her chest hardly drew her attention. The brand was the shape of a star shining in the night sky, indistinct but instantly recognizable. She touched a finger to it absentmindedly, feeling only cool, scarred skin beneath, the pain a distant echo.

In front of her, the gray mist seemed lighter than before, and she walked toward it, feeling the strange give and flex of the ground beneath her feet. The light grew brighter with each step and the mist less thick until eventually she saw she was walking on a narrow path with nothing but utter, empty blackness to either side. It wasn't ground beneath her feet, but wood the color of white marble. Not the sanded planks of a floor but the limb of a tree, one so large she was merely an insect traversing its length.

On and on she walked, soon reaching places where leaves grew like giant white fans and where more limbs began to intersect with the first, turning the place into a jungle of white and black and gray. She walked around and over and through the leaves, continuing on toward that growing brightness ahead. As she walked, she sensed movement to her right and left. Turning her head, she spotted bright eyes staring at her through the darkness between the leaves. They weren't human eyes or animal, and yet she recognized their shape, the dark slit of them like a snake, the outer black orbs surrounded by gray scales. There were nightdrakes here, all around, but they didn't attack. They remained in those dark places, waiting and watching as Kate passed by them.

Eventually the limb she traversed began to widen, and ahead it intersected with two other limbs equally as wide, a hole forming in the center of their convergence. Where there should have been more of that formless blackness was a pool of white light glistening like crystal in the sun. Small, curling strands of lightning danced across its surface. The light beckoned her forward, and unable to resist, she walked toward it.

Reaching its edge, she heard a voice call out to her. It seemed to come from everywhere at once—the rustle of the white leaves, the dark spaces between them, the creak of the limbs, the whisper of the wind, and even the beat of Kate's heart in her chest. *Come, Kate Brighton*, the light said. *Paragon chosen. Come and lose yourself. Rise as something more.*

She stared down at the substance that was water and not water, light and not light, something else altogether, nameless and powerful and great and terrible as well.

"What do I do?" Kate said, and her voice sounded out of place, a clashing note in a harmonious symphony.

*Come*, the light answered, growing infinitely brighter. She understood what she was meant to do, but as she raised one foot to step into the pool, fear gripped her heart and doubts flooded her mind. "What are you? What is this? What will happen?" Clang, clang, clang, the clash of her voice grew more pronounced. And as the dissonance spread, the light seemed to dim.

When it finally answered her questions it wasn't in words, but in a vision. Its surface grew clear, like glass, and Kate saw her own reflection staring back at her. She looked exactly the same as herself, save for the mark on her breast. In the pool, the starlight brand was no longer black, but glowing like the pool had glowed. It was alive somehow, alive and inside of her, a part of her. And she understood that, to be the Paragon, she would have to let this power inside her.

*But will there still be room for me?* Kate gazed at the reflection and she could no longer recognize herself. Not the self that she knew when she looked in the mirror. This Kate was serene. This Kate was mighty and certain, a person who has never known doubt or hesitation or failure. Cold and apart, a vessel and tool, nothing more.

*That is not me.*

*Come,* the light called again as the mirror faded back into the glowing pool. *Come. Surrender. Let go and be more.*

"No," Kate said. "I can't, I—"

The light grew bright again, and she stepped back as the glowing, water-not-water substance rose up from the hole between the limbs like a dense, heavy fog. It swept over her, and for a moment she felt the light surge inside her, power like she'd never known. Joy, love, elation, every good feeling she had ever experienced in her life seemed to burst anew inside her now.

And then just as abruptly as it had come over her, it was gone. She cried out at the emptiness it left behind, like her insides had been carved out. As she fell to her knees, the limb beneath her snapped in two and fell away, taking her with it.

She was falling . . .

Falling . . .

Into darkness . . .

Into death . . .

Into nothing . . .

She woke inside the caves once more, dressed in her shift and moon-belt and lying atop a pile of blankets. Her chest ached, and she raised a hand to it, trying to ease it. It wasn't the brand, although she could feel the tender flesh there. This pain was beneath it, deeper, a place no hand could reach.

"You're awake."

Kate blinked, not recognizing the voice at first, but as she slowly pushed up into a sitting position she saw Valora sitting across from her, sightless gazed fixed on her unerringly. "What happened?"

"The ritual failed." She didn't sound angry or sad, just disappointed, like a parent who's watched a child fall, helpless to stop it.

With her eyes suddenly burning, Kate looked away. "*I* failed."

Valora took a long time answering. "You made a choice."

Kate nodded. *Come,* the voice had said, *let go and be more.* She had refused, and yet it hadn't felt like a choice, more like instinct, a thoughtless reaction. But that was ignorant, she knew, and childish. Even a choice made in the midst of fear was still a choice. She could've decided to step into that pool, but she hadn't. Briefly, it had seemed as if the magic was making the choice for her when it had swept over her, but she saw now it was merely to show her what she'd refused, to give her a taste of something that would forever leave her thirsty.

Kate pressed the heel of her hand to her forehead. "What happens now?"

Valora sighed. "As soon as you've recovered, you can head to Rin with Corwin."

"Wait, how long have I been asleep?" Kate said, alarmed. Surely days had passed since the ritual, if not weeks. She touched a hand to the brand on her chest again, where the skin had completely scarred over. Surely Corwin would've left without her. The threat was too great to delay so long.

"Three days," replied Valora.

Kate pushed herself up into a standing position, wobbling on legs gone too long without use. "Why did he wait?" She didn't bother asking how the brand could be so healed already. The answer there was simple enough—magic. She touched a finger to it again, remembering the way it had shone like a star when the power in that pool of light had come over her.

"He's been waiting for you, of course." Valora slid off the chair she'd been resting on, standing up to her full height. She seemed taller than she had before, more present. And as Kate stared at her it almost seemed as if her face were glowing. "Even if he hadn't wanted to, the Rising wilders wouldn't have allowed him to leave without you."

Kate blinked in confusion. "What do you mean?"

Valora shrugged a slender shoulder. "You are still the Wilder Queen to many of them. They didn't like the idea of the king trying to pull off his plan without you there to ensure he protects their interests."

A wrench slid through her chest at the weight of such a responsibility. "That's absurd."

"Is it?" Valora cocked her head. "Despite Corwin's many redeeming qualities, he is still a Tormane, part of the blood that condoned the Inquisition. They have reason to be distrusting of Corwin by himself. But the Wilder Queen with him is something they can believe in."

But she was not with him, and never would be again. At least not in the way she had been and wanted still—if she were being honest with herself. But perhaps she could stand beside him as his wilder general instead of the companion she once hoped to be. She thought back on the past year, all the battles she'd fought. She'd been good at it. She could be good at it again.

If she was willing to use her sway, to be the monster.

The knot in her stomach tightened. "I understand." Kate straightened, her legs growing stronger by the moment. "Then I best get ready."

Valora nodded. "So you should. But there is one thing more we need to discuss." She bent toward a pile of blankets lying on the ground near her feet and retrieved a long, slender object wrapped in cloth. She held it out to Kate.

Frowning, Kate stepped forward and took it, caught off guard by its weight that tugged her arms downward. "What's this?" she said, even as she pulled back the cloth to reveal the weapon beneath, red steel the color of an open wound. Hellsteel.

"You've one more choice to make," Valora said. "Rendborne must be stopped. If you will not be the Paragon, then you must decide to be the Purge—or not."

A tremble slid through Kate's body so hard she nearly dropped the weapon in her hands. "If I use this, all magic in Rime will die."

"So it shall." A grimace slid over Valora's lips. "But Rime can survive without magic. The nightdrakes will die, and we will dismantle our walls and live as the rest of the world does."

So Bonner and Nadira had been right—the Ruin would be the end of the drakes. She remembered them watching her in that other place as she walked along the limbs. Had it been real? Was that where they lived when they weren't stalking the night? So many questions she didn't have answers to. What was worse was knowing she could've had them, if she'd stepped into that pool. That ache expanded in her chest, and she took a breath, trying to ease it back.

Kate fixed her gaze on the three prongs of the trident's head. She tried to imagine it—a world without magic. *Including my own.*

"I've already discussed using the Hellsteel with Corwin," Valora said. "He wanted to do it himself, but I insisted it be you. The Paragon ritual might've been unsuccessful, but the brand will still offer you greater protection than anyone else. You are the only one who stands a chance of getting close enough to Rendborne to use it."

Shaking her head in dismay, Kate looked up. "You said I've still a choice to make, but it seems that this is the only choice left." She turned the weapon in her hand, feeling it grow lighter as she grew accustomed to it.

"No, Kate," Valora said. "There is always more than one choice. And I can only hope that you will make the right one in the end."

THEY RODE HARD FOR RIN, pushing the horses to the limit of their endurance. What should've taken two days they managed in a day and a half, reaching the outskirts by nightfall. They could've made it into the city before the gates closed, but Corwin decided to wait until morning. He didn't trust the reception the wilders would receive. Although he'd been absent for much of the Wilder War, he understood the wounds it had made, on both sides—ones that were a long way from healing.

They made camp atop a barrow overlooking the city, another ancient relic like the cottage. As Corwin walked across the soft grass covering the top of the hill, in between the standing stones of its abandoned altar, he tried to imagine a world where the dead had been buried instead of burned, where there was no threat of nightdrakes feasting on the corpses. It was a world that might come again, if their plans came to fruition. He disliked the idea of Kate taking on Rendborne, but he'd long since given up trying to protect or control her—her choices were hers alone. Besides, the stories the Rising wilders told about her made her sound like the daughter of the god of war himself. She could hold her own in battle.

But he was getting ahead of himself. He had to win over the Rimish lords first. No easy task, and one he feared even attempting. Riding into Rin tomorrow, he might be arrested and thrown in a prison cell to live out the rest of his life as a condemned traitor, supporter of wilders. He'd spent days thinking about what he would say, what he would do to convince them to join his side. He discussed strategy with Dal, Tira, Bonner, Genet, Yaron, anyone who would listen and whose opinion he trusted.

Except for Kate. She'd been unconscious for so long after the Paragon ritual failed, and even more, he feared how the conversation would go. But he couldn't put it off any longer. He needed her help tomorrow and could see no other way around it. Even so, he didn't approach her until past nightfall, waiting until he spotted her standing by herself on the far side of the camp, looking out past the magestone barrier at the stretch of scrubland leading up to Rin. The city wall was aglow with wardstone lights, each one like a star fallen from the night sky.

Kate glanced over her shoulder at his approach, and her spine went rigid. Corwin sucked in a breath, hating the reaction and wishing there was some way to undo it. If anything, he was sure to make it worse before he was through here.

"Do you have a moment to talk?" he asked, coming to stand next to her. It was a silly question, strangely formal. He tried to remember how their conversations used to go but couldn't. They never seemed to start or end, but were just one long moment around short pauses. Gods, how he missed it. Missed her.

"Yes . . . I mean, I've nothing else to do at the moment."

Corwin frowned at the hitch in her voice, but quickly banished the concern. At least she hadn't used his title for once, thank the goddess. "Tomorrow, I'd like you with me when I speak to the Rimish lords." The messenger had found them late yesterday, bringing word that Corwin had been granted an audience with Rin's ruler, Lord Felton, along with the other Rimish leaders in the city. The message had been terse and less than welcoming, but all Corwin needed was for the door to be unlocked. He would find a way to push it open and get through.

"If you think it's wise," Kate replied, "then yes, I'll be there."

"I do." He smiled and raked a hand through his hair. "Yaron tells me that the rest of Rime called you the Wilder Queen as well, not just the Rising. Having you there will show the lords that I have the wilders' support, and it will make it clear that in all things I stand with the wilders first."

A small smile crossed her lips. "It gives me hope to hear you say that."

"Me too." Corwin returned the smile, but all too quickly it slid from his face. "But there's more to it than that, I'm afraid." He drew a breath. "It's possible I might need to convince them of my loyalty to Rime."

Kate's brows drew together. "How could they doubt? Word has surely spread about your escape and the attack on the Hellgate."

"Perhaps." He hesitated. "But it is certain that they've heard of my marriage to Eravis Fane."

At the sound of the Sevan princess's name, Kate dropped her chin to her chest and turned one shoulder to him. "You heard what Valora said. The marriage was invalid according to Rimish law."

Corwin drew a breath and let it out carefully. "Unfortunately, the legitimacy of it matters less than the perception. If they are to follow me, I need them to trust me completely. Once the fighting starts, there can't be divisions among us. They must know the truth."

"What does any of that have to do with me?" She stared at him intently, as tense as a bowstring close to snapping.

He braced, dreading her response. "I was thinking . . . that you might demonstrate for them the nature of Gavril's power."

Shock spread like storm clouds over Kate's face. "What?"

He reached out and touched her arm, that one small act requiring more bravery than he'd ever needed before, it seemed. "I know it's a lot to ask of you, and I hope I'm wrong about the need for it, but if I'm not, it might be the only way to convince them that my coming isn't a trap set by the Godking. That I was forced into saying those vows with Eravis. Everything I did was forced."

She stepped back out of his reach and narrowed her eyes at him. "Are you sure that's true?"

Corwin paled at her words, and the memory of her in his mind rushed into him, the things she'd seen and felt. "That's not fair, Kate. You weren't with me in Seva. You can't know how it was."

"Can't I?" She arched an eyebrow. "I saw it, Corwin. I saw how she made you feel. I *felt* it."

Anger surged into him, and he clenched his hands into fists. "I asked you not to do that. Those memories were private. They should've been left to me."

For a second, fury blazed across her face, then all at once it vanished, and she seemed to sag in defeat. "I know, and I'm sorry. I wish I'd never done it." She turned away from him, gaze raised toward the city once more. "I wish I weren't a monster."

"Monster?" His anger fled him, and he reached for her, gently placing one hand on her shoulder. She tensed at his touch, but didn't pull away. "That's . . . you're not."

"Signe thinks I am."

"Well, she's wrong." Corwin squeezed, wishing she would turn around. "Gavril was a monster. Rendborne is a monster. Not you."

She swung back to face him. "Aren't I? Isn't that what you would ask me to do tomorrow? Show the Rimish lords that my power is equally as monstrous as Gavril's?"

He flinched, seeing her point all too well. He had, in fact, done exactly that. And in truth, there was a monstrous part of her, the way she'd killed with just her mind. The way she'd wielded that power with impunity.

But so had he. He might not have used magic, but he'd killed men, more than he could count in his time with the Shieldhawks. He'd stabbed Gavril in the back, without hesitation. And in the past he'd surely given orders and made decisions that affected the lives of people he'd never even met face-to-face. Could he claim that every decision made and order given was benevolent? No. But what he could say was that his intentions had always been in the right place.

Meeting Kate's gaze head-on, Corwin stared into her eyes, unblinkingly, so she could know his sincerity. "You might have his power, but you've never used it for evil like he did. Even when you've killed with it, it was always in the name of what is good and right. Saving your friends, saving your country. But even so, someone who is a monster doesn't struggle with the choice to kill, or to steal someone's will. They revel in it."

He could tell she wasn't convinced, and for a moment he considered removing the vial from around his neck and letting her in to experience what he felt. But, no, he couldn't do that. His memories had already hurt her too much.

After a moment, Kate exhaled and glanced away from him. "Very well. If it comes to it, I will make the demonstration for you."

Doubt fluttered in his chest, whether or not he was right in asking her to do this. But with an effort he pushed it away. In this dire situation they faced, there was no room left for doubt. "Thank you, and let's hope it doesn't come to it."

Kate nodded. Corwin still sensed the pain in her rigid stance. The knowledge of it squeezed his heart like a fist, and he started to retreat.

Something stopped him halfway, the truth inside him demanding to be heard. He faced her again, aware of the distance between them, both physical and not. He'd been wrong earlier—this was surely the bravest thing he'd ever had to do.

"I never stopped loving you, Kate," he said. "Not then and not now." He paused, summoning his strength, wary of deepening her wounds. "What you saw in my memories about Eravis was respect and affection, nothing more. She helped me deceive her father at great risk to her own life. She was my only friend during that time. We pretended to be man and wife to keep Gavril from forcing us to be together with his sway. But I never loved her. Not with my heart and not with my body. My heart and soul belong to you." He waited a moment to see what she might say or do, but she only stood there staring at him, as cold and unmoving as a statue. Feeling his own pain threatening to overwhelm him, he turned and walked away.

As they approached the city gates, Rin soldiers rode out to meet them. They didn't raise arms, but their weapons were a handbreadth away. Not that Corwin's forces would've dared try anything. The last thing they were here to do was fight.

Corwin ran his gaze over the party, taking in their worried expressions. Besides Kate, Genet, Bonner, Nadira, Yaron, Jiro, Valora, Dal, and Signe had come with him, the best representation of their forces waiting in the dragon caves. Wanting to reassure them, Corwin said, "The missive Lord Felton sent promised we would be welcomed."

Dal smirked. "How does that old saying go? Bait the trap with honey to lure the bear."

"That doesn't look much like honey," Signe said, grimacing.

Corwin was inclined to agree, but he squelched the doubt. "It will be fine."

And indeed it was fine, although certainly not warm or even welcoming. They were escorted through the streets under careful guard, the people giving them a wide berth. Corwin felt the eyes following him and heard the shocked murmurs. He rode with his head up, and every time he made eye contact with someone on the side of the road he inclined his head or offered a quick smile. *I am not the enemy. I am the man who would be your king—if I can earn the right.*

It was high time he got started.

Once they arrived at the castle, they were taken to an antechamber outside the great hall, where they waited more than an hour for admittance. Corwin sat still and resolute on one of the dozen chairs in the room, bare wood hard as stone and as uncomfortable as lying on the ground. He suspected that was the point, as was the wait, a way for Lord Felton to establish that he was in control of this situation. Corwin refused to be taken in by it. While the others milled around restless and impatient, he remained calm and focused, mulling over the argument he would make and trying not to think about what failure here would mean. The imagined voices of his doubters back in the caves kept creeping into his mind, but he silenced them over and over again.

Finally, the door to the antechamber opened and a guard beckoned them to enter. Corwin went first, stepping through the threshold into the great hall. Columns lined both sides of the room, reaching up to the vaulted ceiling and stretching all the way to the front, where the high table perched atop a dais. A crowd of people filled the wings of the room, high-ranking soldiers and nobles alike.

Several people sat at the high table, Lord Felton at the center with Lord Jedrek of Kilbarrow to his right and Lord Brogan of Carden to his left. As Corwin approached, he glanced at the others, recognizing Lord Luca of Thace, Lord Ormand of Marared, and, to his surprise, Lady Myrrh of Penlocke. He hadn't known she survived the Sevan attack on her city. He knew for certain her husband, Lord Timon, had perished. His spies had brought him word that the Godking had ordered Penlocke's ruler impaled on the spire of the temple of Penlin in the middle of the town square. *For all to see and know the consequences of standing against the Godking*, the proclamation posted beneath him had read.

Reaching the front of the room, Corwin bowed. "My lords and lady of Rime, thank you for this audience."

Lord Felton returned the bow with a slighter one. "You are welcome here, Prince Corwin."

"I don't come alone." Corwin turned to his companions. "This is Master Yaron, former member of the red order; Valora, High Priestess of Noralah; Lord Dallin of Thornewall; Signe Leth of the Esh Islands and bearer of the secret of black powder. . . ." He paused as the crowd reacted to Signe's name. She was as infamous as Kate. When it died down, he went on. "These are Councilors Genet and Jiro of the Wilder City; this is Tom Bonner of Farhold; Nadira Walker of Kilbarrow; and lastly, this is Kate Brighton." He did not give her a title. He didn't need to. Murmurs echoed all around him, the crowd restless at the presence of such guests. Kate stood straight as a sword. If the whispers about her bothered her, no evidence appeared on her face.

"You are all . . . welcome." Lord Felton inclined his head toward the group. "And now, young prince, we will listen to your entreaty."

Corwin cleared his throat, letting his gaze pass slowly over the assembled lords and lady. "As you know, Penlocke and Norgard have fallen to Sevan forces, and my brother Edwin is dead, slain by the Godking himself. These cities fell because Magnar, along with the help of Lord Rendborne, the former councilmember of Norgard turned traitor, had under his control an army of wilders—men and women of Rime enslaved for the Godking's use." Corwin waited a few beats, letting his words sink in. Then he went on to explain how the wilders came to be in Seva, the front that was the Inquisition, and how Gavril—another citizen of Rime—had also turned traitor, using his power to control their minds and wills.

"But I killed Gavril," Corwin said, "and the moment I did,

those wilders were free of his control. Most of them fled Norgard and have joined forces with mine." He gestured to his companions once more. "There are nearly a thousand of us—wilders, magists, and Rimish warriors—and we are ready to reclaim Norgard and drive the Sevan scourge back across the sea."

Applause broke out from several places around the room, some of the audience members lining the wings moved to it by Corwin's speech, but it died quickly when none of the people sitting at the high table joined in. Corwin waited for them to respond, hands clasped in front of him.

Lord Jedrek spoke first. "We are intent on reclaiming Norgard and Penlocke as well, but I for one am not certain that joining our strength with that of wilders is in Rime's best interest."

Corwin resisted the urge to respond with scorn, even though Jedrek and the others deserved it for their ignorance. "I understand your concern. The Wilder War has left wounds on the cities of Rime." Corwin turned and ran his gaze over the rest of the crowd. "Some of your loved ones died at the hand of wilders. Your husbands and brothers and uncles." He faced front again. "But I ask you this—how many wilders have been lost? How many innocent mothers and sons, fathers and daughters, were taken from their homes and condemned by the Inquisition? Do not those wounds run even deeper? We can't blame the wilders when all they were fighting for was the right to exist. To simply be allowed to live."

Jedrek shifted in his chair. "But who is to say that creatures with such powers even deserve to live? They are dangerous. When we come across a nightdrake, we kill it. We don't debate whether it might deserve it."

Anger pulsed in Corwin's temple, and it took all his might not to lash out. What was worse was that several of the other lords gave a nod in agreement with Jedrek, and the sentiment was echoed throughout the crowd. *But not everyone*, Corwin told himself. It was true. He could see the regret among some of the faces. Lady Myrrh's eyes glistened with sympathy.

"They are not creatures, Lord Jedrek, but human beings. No different from you or me. Jiro is from Andreas and Genet spent nearly all her life in Aldervale. And Kate, as you know, was born and raised in Norgard."

"Yes, I do know," replied Jedrek, eyes narrowed on Kate with open hostility. "She's the daughter of the very man who tried to kill your father."

Corwin drew a breath and let it out slowly. "Hale Brighton was innocent of those charges. Lord Rendborne was behind it all." He explained how Rendborne had orchestrated the whole thing from the beginning, manipulating Grand Master Storr into starting the Inquisition, the very act that enabled the wilders to be taken in the first place. "And that is not all. Rendborne was once a Tormane, my great-great-granduncle, the man called the Nameless One. He killed his uror sign and claimed the creature's magic as his own. He possesses the power of both wilder and magist. He is the true threat here, and he must be stopped. And that cannot be done without us united, one army of all who would see a free Rime."

Lady Myrrh inclined her head. "If he and the Sevans are as powerful as you claim, then who's to say even wilder strength will make a difference?"

"Rendborne and Magnar, along with their men, fight to

conquer," Corwin said, addressing Lady Myrrh at first but quickly shifting his gaze to include the others. "We will fight for this land we call home and for our very lives—wilder and common folk alike. That makes us much stronger. With Gavril dead and the captured wilders freed, the Sevan force is weakened. The time to strike is now."

Lord Felton sat back in his chair and rubbed a hand down his beard. "Perhaps you're right, Prince Corwin, but assuming we do decide to join forces, I hope you don't expect to lead us."

Corwin stared the man down, letting every ounce of surety he possessed swell inside him now. *I am a Tormane, born to rule Norgard and Rime, Goddess-chosen.* For the first time in days, the uror brand on his palm tingled with promised magic. "Yes, I do," he replied firmly. "I am still the high prince, and once this war is over, I plan to complete the uror trial. If the people of Rime will have me, I will be king. If they won't, then another may rule. But for now it must be me who leads. I know Magnar and Rendborne both. I've seen their plans. I also know the ins and outs of Norgard better than anyone. It is my city, and I will lead the charge to reclaim it."

"Yes, that sentiment is understandable." Jedrek gave a magnanimous nod of his head. "But how can we be certain of your loyalty to Rime? We know of your marriage to Eravis Fane. This could be a trap."

Corwin sighed, frustrated the subject had come up already. But before he could speak, Valora stepped forward and dropped into a bow. She had wrapped a black cloth around her forehead to cover her missing eyes, though the effect was hardly less unsettling. "My lords and lady, I have declared that marriage to be illegitimate. The

Godking alone presided over it, with no honor paid to the gods, only to himself, and it was never consummated. Furthermore, I've spent time with Prince Corwin, and I will attest to his undying loyalty to Rime."

Although some of them looked convinced, Corwin still sensed the overwhelming doubt. He stepped forward. "I swear on the name of all the gods, I remain true to Rime. Everything I did while in Seva and during the conquest of Penlocke and Norgard was done against my will, the result of Gavril's mind-control powers. But I sympathize with your doubt. You cannot understand the power of sway until you have experienced it for yourself." He motioned to Kate, a wrench passing through his chest at the stormy look on her face.

She came forward and everyone on the dais went still, like deer caught in the wolf's gaze. "Prince Corwin has asked me to demonstrate the power of sway, the very magic Lord Gavril used to enslave my wilder sisters and brothers and to force our prince into betraying Rime. To that, I say this." She reached into the fold of her cloak and withdrew a magestone collar, which she quickly fastened around her neck, rendering her magic inaccessible.

Alarm surged through Corwin. If he didn't convince them now, he never would. But he clamped his mouth shut, resisting the urge to argue with her. *I trust you*, he thought. *I always have.*

Kate turned in a slow circle, making it clear that she spoke to everyone present, and even those beyond. "It is true that sway is a most awesome and terrible magic. Lord Gavril used his sway to force my friends to do unspeakable things." She gestured to Bonner. "Tom Bonner is an earthist, enslaved by Gavril nearly a year.

During that time, Gavril forced him to fight to the death in Sevan Spectacles, to take life against his will."

She paused to motion to Nadira, standing next to Bonner. "Nadira has a spirit gift. She can make a heart start beating again and force a person to breathe even when their lungs have given up. She is a healer, and yet Gavril forced her to steal the life away from an innocent boy. He used his magic for evil and perversion at every turn."

Nadira nodded as Kate spoke, her expression hard as stone but her eyes glistening with tears.

"I could do the same with my own magic," Kate went on. She gestured to the collar. "If it weren't for this, I could make you bow down before me. I could make you scream or dance or cry. I could steal from you every trace of free will—if I wanted to. But it's not the power we possess that determines good or evil, but how we use that power. Long ago I vowed only to use my abilities for good, even if that good meant using it on my enemies, as I did during the Wilder War. But you are no longer my enemy. Rendborne and Magnar are my enemy, the Sevan threat. I will save my magic for them, and I will follow Corwin Tormane into battle. For he is my prince and my king." She turned and bowed toward Corwin then, all eyes watching the movement.

Warmth filled Corwin's chest and spread through his body. He longed to reach for her, but remained where he was. The symbolism of her act must remain unsullied.

The sound of a chair scraping against stone pulled Corwin's gaze toward the dais. Lady Myrrh had stood, and now she slowly made her way around the edge of the table and descended the dais.

Kate stood and stepped aside as the woman approached Corwin.

Myrrh stopped before him and ran her gaze over the crowd. "I, for one, choose to stand with Prince Corwin. I have seen firsthand the threat we face, and I also see that Corwin and the wilders who stand with him are our only way to defeat the Sevan army. And so I pledge my loyalty and that of Penlocke to you, my prince, and I hope to soon call you my king."

Lady Myrrh bowed low to Corwin, and as she did applause broke out, quiet at first but soon growing louder. Corwin examined the crowd, watching as one by one the people bowed to him. The lords on the dais were the last, but they too soon took the knee.

Corwin reached for Kate's hand and squeezed, knowing in his heart she had been the force that turned the tide. And he swore then that somehow, once this was over, he would prove his love to her once more. She was the Wilder Queen, and he was determined to be her king.

THE DAY OF THE BATTLE dawned dim and gray, the cloud-crowded sky like dull steel. Although it was nearly summer, this morning felt like winter, ominous with the threat of coming violence.

Corwin sat astride his warhorse feeling the weight of his armor and weapons, as well as the heavier burden of command. A force of more than four thousand waited on the hill below him, most of them foot soldiers, with less than a quarter mounted. He'd wished for greater cavalry numbers, but it wasn't to be. The lords of Rime had brought all they could, but it was Norgard that had always held the strength of cavalry. Corwin could easily guess what Magnar would do with that force, and the idea of Sevan soldiers mounted on Norgard warhorses turned his stomach.

For now though, no living thing stood between them and the white walls of Norgard. The Rimish forces had approached under the cover of night, the journey easier than it should've been with so few nightdrakes in the area thanks to the Ruin.

"They're surely ready for us by now," Bonner said from Corwin's right. Although he was wearing different armor, he was the God-spear through and through, his gaze fierce beneath his helmet and his manner calm but poised for battle.

Corwin was glad to have him, but at the same time, he regretted

Bonner's lack of magic. There were only twenty earthists among the wilder forces, and less than half of them with an affinity for stone. The walls of Norgard weren't mere mortar and rock, but were fortified with magist magic. They weren't impervious, but Yaron had told him it would take considerable strength to break through them. Bonner seemed certain the earthists could do it, but they would be spent afterward. The idea of ripping holes in the wall of Norgard made Corwin feel light-headed each time he thought of it. But it had to be done. They didn't have the time or resources for a siege, which could take weeks, maybe months.

No, it was best to go straight through. And Corwin was certain Magnar would ride out to meet them the moment they pressed.

Corwin shot Bonner a hard gaze. "I certainly hope so. We'll be ready for them." He reined his horse away from the soldiers waiting below to face the row of tents set atop the hill, where Lady Myrrh and the other nonfighting nobles would remain for the duration of the battle. Signe, Dal, and Kate were standing near the tent, the latter two dressed in armor and with their horses in hand waiting to be mounted. Signe would remain here, working to resupply their black-powder stores. Although there were few revolvers left, she had spent the last week working with the earthists to create other weapons with her black powder, including some capable of tremendous explosions.

Dal pulled Signe into a long embrace, then reluctantly let go and mounted. He turned and rode toward Corwin. Kate remained a few moments longer to talk to Signe. Corwin could only hope it was a reconciliation between the two. He and Kate had had little time to talk this past week, both of them overwhelmed with the effort involved in mustering a force this large. True to what Corwin had experienced earlier, the wilders insisted on Kate's presence or at least her approval in every decision made that affected them. Although they had declared allegiance to him, certain now that he'd succeeded in uniting the Rimish lords, that allegiance came with qualifications. He had found time to corner Signe though, and admonish her for being so hard on Kate for her use of sway. It hadn't gone well. Stubbornness was a trait Signe and Kate both possessed in abundance, but watching them now Corwin thought maybe the talk had done some good. He certainly hoped so.

"Are we ready?" Dal said, pulling up next to Corwin.

"As soon as Kate is," Corwin replied, not taking his eyes off her.

Dal snickered. "If you look at her any harder, your head might explode, my friend."

Turning, Corwin smirked at him. "Like you've room to talk. I saw that embrace. You love Signe just as much as I love Kate. Don't try to deny it anymore." Even as he said it, though, Corwin expected Dal to argue. It was a long disagreement between them, the question of whether true love, the kind that endures forever, was just a sentimental and unrealistic ideal or a real thing. Dal had always insisted on the former. Now, though, he made no reply, merely steered his horse toward Bonner to wait.

Once Kate finally joined them, a few moments later, Corwin led the way down the hill to the front of the army. Raising his hand, he called for the march forward. The sound of so many booted feet and shod hooves was like the pounding of some deep bass drum, one punctuated by the clang of armor and bits. They marched steadily, no need to hurry and weary the soldiers.

Kate rode at Corwin's left, and he caught his gaze drifting toward her. There were things he wanted to say to her, but he couldn't with so many people around, all of them waiting for his command.

As if she sensed his gaze, Kate turned to look at him, for once not avoiding his eyes.

"I doubt Rendborne will join the fray," Corwin said. He gestured to Kate's side, where she wore the Hellsteel trident strapped to one hip, its distinctive shape disguised by a magestone to look like a dagger. Corwin didn't think Harue knew what the spell was meant to disguise when she'd created it. Despite Valora's assurance that Rime would survive, Corwin was certain most of the wilders and magists with them would try to stop Kate if they knew what she planned to do.

"He is a coward at heart," Kate replied, shifting her gaze back to the city. "But once the way in is clear, I will find him."

Corwin nodded. They'd discussed as much in passing, but he hadn't allowed himself to think about it. Now, with the city looming ahead, he couldn't keep his mind off it, worry clouding his thoughts. It would be dangerous for her out here, among the fighting, but inside the city, she would be alone and surrounded by enemies.

"Kate," he said, drawing her gaze back to him. "Promise me you'll do everything in your power to keep yourself safe." He paused, fixing a fierce stare on her. "Everything, including using the full strength of your sway. Do what you must. Signe is wrong. I don't fear your sway, and I don't fear you. I trust you to always make the right choice."

Something strange flitted through her expression too fast for him to name it. "I will do whatever I have to," she said. "I've no plans on dying this day."

Sensing her sincerity, he offered a smile. "That makes two of us."

Then he forced his attention ahead, able to focus on the coming battle now that he was reassured that Kate would be able to handle herself should anything keep him from following her into the city on her hunt for Rendborne.

Before they'd come in range of the archers already filling up the parapets, the right side gate slid open far enough to allow a rider carrying a white flag to come charging through. Murmurs echoed down the line, and Corwin raised a hand to calm them. This was expected.

When the rider reached them, he handed Corwin a piece of rolled parchment sealed with the Sevan crest, the wax still warm to the touch.

"Be careful, your highness," Yaron said, stepping out of line to ride over to him. "Even an apprentice magist can enchant parchment with any number of dangerous curses. Let me examine it first."

"There is no need." For the moment, Corwin was still protected by the uror magic. Besides, he doubted Rendborne or Magnar would try such an ignoble attack. Magnar, at least, intended to rule Rime once the fighting was over, and he was too wise about the power of reputation to rely on such an underhanded tactic.

Corwin broke open the letter and quickly read it. To his surprise it wasn't signed by Magnar, but by Rendborne. He'd given his title as lord regent of Rime. Corwin frowned, wondering at the implications. A regent was appointed to rule in proxy of a monarch.

The Godking had many such regents throughout his kingdom, but Corwin had been there when Magnar discussed who his regent for Rime would be—his eldest son, Mazen, not Rendborne. Had Magnar changed his mind or had Rendborne somehow forced him to do it? Was the Godking even still in the city?

"What does it say?" Dal asked, leaning toward Corwin for a peek.

Shaking off his speculations, Corwin crumpled the parchment and tossed it on the ground. "Terms of our surrender." He turned to the messenger. "You may tell your lord that we do not accept his terms, but if he is wise, he will accept ours. Surrender now, and I will allow him and his men to retreat to Seva. He can return to his own country with some of his dignity. If he does not, he will die this day."

The messenger nodded, a look of fright on the boy's face, and he spun his mount about, fleeing back to the city.

"What now?" Dal said, a yawn stretching over his face as if he found the events boring.

Corwin motioned toward the city. "Let the earthists make the way for us."

With the order given, four squadrons broke off from the main group, all the soldiers carrying large wooden shields nearly as tall as a man and twice as wide. Moving as separate units, they each approached the city from a different angle. Walking in the middle of the soldiers were five of the earthists each. Their purpose was simple—make as many breaches in the city walls as they could.

The moment the squadrons were in reach, the archers atop the parapets let loose a volley of arrows, but the Rimish soldiers raised their shields over their heads, forming a cocoon of protection around themselves and the wilders. The group farthest to the east was slowest to react to the attack, but Corwin watched as one of the wilders among them raised his hands to the arrows and knocked them off course. The woman must've had an affinity for wood, her magic able to compel the arrow shafts to fly wide.

As the squadrons drew near, Corwin called the order to march. Like a massive beast the Rimish force advanced, moving faster now. The horses, feeding off their riders' tension, tossed their heads and tugged on the reins, some sidestepping in anticipation. Corwin's own horse began to jig, the slow up and down as the gelding lifted each foot high and then dropped it jostling him. He tried to bring it back to a normal walk, but it was no use. The horse wasn't Norgard bred, but a mount gifted to him by Lord Brogan. Corwin had no notion of its training, but expected it would pale to what a Norgard warhorse was capable of. He resisted giving the horse a name, knowing as he did that its chances of survival were slim. He gritted his teeth at the thought, hating the violence even as the anticipation of it sent a thrill through him.

Ahead, the squadrons had come in reach of the walls, and although Corwin couldn't see it, he pictured the earthists with their arms stretched out to the white stone as they attempted to break it apart. For a while nothing happened, but then slowly the sound of splintering stone began to rumble through the air. The Sevan soldiers atop the parapets grew frantic, unleashing more arrows on the figures below, with most landing uselessly against the shields.

But then a new threat appeared atop the wall: magists in the gray robes of the Mage League. A moment later, they began to unleash spells, the magic exploding across the shields. The squadron under attack managed to take several of the volleys—the shields having been enchanted to resist magical damage—but soon they broke apart. Seeing an opening, the archers renewed the attack and the Rimish soldiers began to fall in the hail of arrows.

The other archers nearby had watched and learned, reaching for the enchanted arrows they kept for nightdrakes. At first the arrows glanced off, but as the spell on the shields weakened, they began to penetrate. One of the Rimish soldiers beneath fell, but the others quickly patched the hole.

*Hurry*, Corwin thought, worry building in his mind. The sound of splintering stone renewed, but above it he heard the creak of the gate opening.

Corwin finally raised his sword and screamed, "Riders, charge!" He heeled his warhorse forward.

The rest of the Rimish cavalry followed, leaving the foot soldiers under the command of General Thakur of Marared, Corwin's second-in-command. Kate rode beside Corwin, her horse keeping pace with his. Dal, Tira, and Bonner followed just behind. Corwin tried to push thoughts of them out of his mind as a swarm of Sevan cavalry charged through the gates to stop the earthists. But the Rimish horses reached them first, deflecting the danger off the wilders.

Corwin held his sword in front of him, the steel aglow with the magic the magists had placed on it. His armor gleamed as well, the spells offering him extra protection against both magical and physical blows. He met the first assault—a vicious swipe from a Sevan blade—and pushed the attacker back, knocking the rider off-balance. Corwin didn't hesitate, but swiped at the split in the knee joint of the man's armor, slicing through skin and muscle. The man screamed, and Corwin slammed his blade against the man's breastplate, unhorsing him.

Corwin turned to meet the next attack, slashing to the left with his sword, crossways over his body. He caught the oncoming soldier on the shoulder, his sword glancing off the man's pauldron. The Sevan wore light armor, but it was still more cumbersome than the brigandine Corwin wore, which gave him an edge. Before the rider even had time to raise his arm again, Corwin had spun and slashed at him through the narrow opening in between the man's pauldron and breastplate. The sword sank into flesh, soft and yielding, and when Corwin pulled the blade back it came out red. Not waiting to watch the man fall, Corwin spun his horse and launched into the next attack.

All around him shrieks filled the air, some shouts of battle rage and some screams of agony. At first the Rimish forces were handling the onrush of Sevan troops with relative ease, but within moments the enemies' numbers swelled. Corwin was about to call the retreat—they needed to get clear before the Rimish archers could respond—but then he heard an earth-shattering crack. All motion on the battlefield seemed to halt as every head turned to the noise. A massive chunk of the western wall had collapsed, pulled down by one of the earthists. Distantly, the Rimish forces not yet engaged cheered in victory.

The Sevans turned their attention to the earthists, and as Corwin and the others moved to intervene, another loud sound reached them—a breach forming on the wall to the east. There were two now, both easily large enough to let the Rimish armies into the city.

The Sevan forces responded to the threat, more of them pouring out of the gate. But General Thakur was advancing the Rimish forces, and in moments the two met. What had been chaos before suddenly felt like the end of the world. For the majority of the wilders had been with the foot soldiers, and now they unleashed the power of the three hells.

Fires erupted in long, hot blasts, incinerating whatever stepped in their path. Jets of water flew, swallowing enemies whole and drowning them on dry land. Gusts of wind knocked rows of soldiers over like toys. The earthists who were left rained down stones from the sky. Although the wilders did their best to focus their attacks on the enemy, many of the Rimish were caught in the crossfire. Corwin nearly lost his seat as his horse made an awkward leap over a hole that appeared in the ground before him without warning.

He managed to stick the jump though, and quickly engaged a new enemy. Corwin had lost sight of Kate in the initial attack, but he spotted her now, her gray mare standing out in the sea of dark armor. Although the horse had been bred and trained in Marared, same as his, the mare was fighting like a Norgard warhorse, kicking out and biting at any combatants that came near. Kate must've been using her sway to control the horse, and he hoped she wouldn't deplete her energy too quickly.

Then he no longer had time to worry about her as a new surge of enemies came toward them. These were no mere soldiers, but magists. They hurled spells at the Rimish forces, and whenever magic met magic it dissolved into nothing. At once the damage the wilders had been able to inflict lessened, many of them shifting to hand-to-hand combat.

One of the magists took aim at Corwin, and he raised his buckler just in time to deflect the spell. The enchantment on the shield managed it easily, but it wouldn't last forever. He needed to be careful. He charged the magist, the man's face turning white at the sudden attack. He raised his mace again, a spell already lighting up, but Corwin deflected it with his sword this time. He swung at the magist before he could throw another spell, his sword sinking four inches deep in the man's neck.

But just as Corwin was pulling the blade free once more, his horse stumbled and let out an ear-splintering cry. Corwin tumbled sideways, falling as the horse fell, its weight crushing his leg. His head smacked the ground, knocking off his helmet. Yelping in pain, he managed to pull himself free, his gut twisting as he saw the blood pouring from the deep cut in the horse's neck. The soldier who had done it rushed Corwin, and he raised his sword just in time to block the assault. The Sevan soldier was young, inexperienced, and Corwin parried his next attack easily. Then, pressing his own assault, he cut the young soldier down.

As the boy fell, Corwin blinked sweat from his eyes only to realize it was blood from where his head had hit the ground. Fighting back dizziness now, he scanned the chaos around him, searching for Kate. He spotted Dal a few feet from him. He was bleeding from a cut in his arm, but it didn't slow him down, his dual swords flashing through the air. He'd lost his helmet somewhere along the way, too, but didn't seem to notice. He beheaded his opponent, then immediately swung in search of another.

"Dal!" Corwin shouted. "Where's Kate?"

"Heading for the hole to the west!"

Corwin turned his gaze left, straining to see through the throng of fighting bodies. Then he caught sight of her, battling her way toward the breach. She looked unharmed, no hesitation or doubt in her body as she charged through it. Relief rushed inside Corwin, and he turned back to the fight only to find Dal standing right across from him, swords raised—at Corwin. He only had a moment to react when Dal attacked.

"What—" Corwin raised his buckler just in time to deflect the blow. "Dal!"

He swung at Corwin again, his eyes strangely wide, like a man out of his senses.

"Dal, what are you—" Corwin broke off, realizing the truth. He could see the struggle in Dal's body, the strange jerky motion of his arms and legs as he swung at Corwin again, as if he didn't want to but had no choice. "Who's controlling you?"

"I . . . don't . . . know," Dal said through gritted teeth, even as he swung again. Corwin blocked with his sword this time, but made no move to return the attack.

But Dal didn't stop, despite the hesitation in his body, the strain in his expression. He pressed forward, slashing at Corwin from the right and left and nearly catching him. Corwin's mind raced as he thought about what to do. He couldn't fight him off forever, and he couldn't turn and flee. For a moment he considered giving Dal the vial around his neck, but Dal would cut Corwin down before he even got to him. And whoever was doing this would only seize control of Corwin next.

But he knew who was doing this. There could be only one person, impossible as it was. Corwin's stomach clenched with dread and hate burned through his veins. "Where are you, Gavril?" he screamed, the force of it ripping his lungs.

In answer, three of the Rimish fighters nearest Corwin turned toward him in eerie syncopation, lining up next to Dal to form a wall of bodies. Then, together, all of them answered.

"Right here."

*YOU DON'T SEE ME. You don't see me.*

Kate sent the thought out again and again, touching everyone in range with her magic, and the Sevan soldiers on the wall let her pass by as if she were invisible. She hated leaving so many enemy soldiers standing and able when she could so easily put an end to them—and any chance that they would harm her friends—but she couldn't risk being spotted. And she didn't want to use any more magic than she had to. It wasn't an inexhaustible well, and there was no telling how much more she would need before this day was done.

Once past the crush of bodies, she raced down the nearest street and darted into a dim alley, where she pulled a cloak over her armor and discarded her helmet. The more she could blend in, the better. Not that it took much. As she reemerged on the street, she found the city in chaos, messengers racing by and guards trying in vain to control the riots breaking out. It seemed the citizens of Norgard were in revolt. Seeing ordinary people fighting back lent Kate courage. She must not fail.

Rounding a corner, she ran across a band of women attacking a Sevan guard with brooms and skillets. It was a bludgeoning, slow and cruel, and Kate knew that once the frenzy of the fight passed, these women would remember the suffering they inflicted here forever. Wanting to spare them that pain, Kate reached out to the women with her sway and forced them back. The decision was easier than it might've been, thanks to her brief but intense discussion with Signe before the battle began. Even now Kate felt the swell of relief at having received Signe's forgiveness, and even more—her acceptance. Pushing the feeling aside, she approached the stunned guard, drawing her sword. A moment later she had put an end to him.

"Go," Kate said to the women, "be safe." She resisted using her sway this time. If they wanted to fight, that was their choice, and she wouldn't interfere.

"Thank you," one of them said, patting her arm.

Kate nodded and moved on, deeper into the city. There was only one place Rendborne would be: the castle. She guessed Magnar would be there as well, giving orders on the battlefield from afar, relying on their pages and messengers. They wouldn't risk going into battle themselves.

The panic in the city lessened the closer she drew to the castle. There were fewer guards as well, most of the soldiers called to the battle. Even still, Kate had to use her sway twice more to get through the postern gate. But before long she had made it into the castle. She slowed down, considering what to do next. Getting close to Rendborne wouldn't be easy. She needed to maintain the element of surprise.

A diversion, then.

Reaching into the small satchel hanging at her hip, she pulled out one of the devices Signe had constructed. All she needed was to strike the small piece of flint to the steel at its top and throw it as far as she could, getting herself under cover. The explosion would clear a path the size of a wagon. *Or bigger*, Signe had said. Holding the device lightly in her hand, Kate headed toward the throne room.

Stretching out with her sway, she searched the minds nearest, looking for confirmation of Rendborne's whereabouts, and Magnar's. She would kill them both if given the opportunity. Soon, she made contact with one of the magists keeping watch near Rendborne. She searched the man's thoughts to sense what he could see. Rendborne was indeed in the throne room, along with six guardsmen. It didn't seem like much protection, but Kate knew Rendborne didn't need any at all, not with his magic. There was no sign of Magnar. Kate gently probed the topmost thoughts in the magist's head, but again there was no indication of the Godking's presence. She didn't dare press harder for fear of giving herself away.

Easing out of his mind, she carried on down the corridor toward the door into the throne room. If she could get in the right position, she might be able to take out most of the guards with Signe's device, clearing her path to Rendborne. The armor she wore and weapons she carried had all been enchanted with spells of protection. They should be enough to let her get close to him. He wouldn't fear her, not with the Hellsteel disguised as it was, and that would make him arrogant. She could use it to her advantage.

Wanting to check the perimeter for more guards, Kate reached out with her sway again. But before she could get anywhere, a powerful force seized her mind. It was dark and shadowy, but with brightness leaking out from it, like the sun during a full eclipse. Thoughts and feelings that didn't belong to her filled her mind now. For a moment she was so overwhelmed by it that nothing made sense; it was all noise and chaos. Then the brightness intensified and with it came clarity. This wasn't some force, but a living thing, full of emotion and intelligence.

The uror horse.

It was alive and nearby—and calling out to her for help. *I'm coming*, Kate answered, not hesitating for a moment, even though Rendborne was so near. She couldn't ignore the horse. Its spirit called to her, compelling her forward. She hurried out of the castle and toward the stables. Every person she passed along the way she repelled with a thought. She headed down the aisle where she'd sensed the horse, but it wasn't there. Checking again, she realized it was on the backside of the barn, in a narrow alcove that ran in between the stable and the perimeter wall.

*I'm almost there*, Kate called out to it. *Just a—*

She froze at the sound of a woman's harsh voice. "Come on, you stupid horse, I'm trying to save you."

Kate rounded the corner into the alcove. Ahead the uror horse was pulling back on the lead rope attached to its halter, held by a woman wearing a dress far too fancy and expensive for a stable. Her long brown hair hung nearly to the ground, draped around her body like a silken curtain.

"Stop," Kate shouted, drawing her sword. "Let the horse go."

The woman peered around the horse, a frightened glare on her face as she spotted Kate. "No, I won't let you harm it."

Kate blinked, taken aback by the response. The last thing she intended was to harm the uror horse. Perhaps this woman wasn't an enemy after all, despite her Sevan accent. Kate reached out to the stranger with her sway, curiosity getting the best of her. Something blocked her way, a force like that which had protected Rendborne's thoughts from her so long ago. Like the vial of blood that protected Corwin even now.

"Who are—" Kate began, then broke off as the truth struck her like lightning. Horror slid down her veins. Her blood began to pound in her ears.

This was Eravis Fane. There was no mistaking it. The picture of her in the *Rime Review* had captured her visage adequately, and Corwin's memories filled in the rest. The Sevan princess was beautiful beyond measure, stunning to behold, with impossibly perfect features.

Hatred ignited like wildfire inside Kate. No matter what Corwin said, she was the Sevan princess, as much a threat to Rime as her father or Rendborne or any of them. Mindless with her churning emotions, Kate charged forward, sword at the ready.

A look of terror lit across Eravis's face and clumsily she reached for the ornamental dagger at her side, pulling it free just in time to block Kate's swing. The uror horse shied sideways as steel kissed steel in a shriek of metal. Kate wrenched her sword free with enough force to send Eravis tumbling backward, her other hand letting going of the uror horse's lead as she fought to keep her balance. The horse backed up out of the way, but it didn't flee as any ordinary horse would've done. Kate sensed it there like a hum in the back of her mind.

She advanced on the princess, expecting her to run, but Eravis held her ground, raising the dagger once more. Kate lashed out with her sword, the swing hard and fast. It struck low on Eravis's blade, and with a yelp, the princess lost her grip. The dagger flew out of her hands, crashing against the side of the stable. Kate lunged forward, pressing the tip of her sword to Eravis's chest.

Frantically, Eravis shuffled back, soon tripping over her skirts. She fell, landing hard on her rump. Her teeth caught her bottom lip, and blood blossomed over the side of her mouth. Kate lowered her sword toward Eravis, but the other woman kicked at the blade with one booted foot, knocking the tip of it aside. The sight of those boots took Kate by surprise; she would've expected fancy slippers to go with the fancy dress.

Pushing the thought away, Kate swung again. Eravis deflected it once more with another kick, but she was too slow to stop Kate's counterstrike. The blade slid past her defenses, and Eravis recoiled on instinct, uselessly covering her chest with her hands. Something about her defensive position stopped Kate cold. She could taste the woman's fear on her tongue, and it made her stomach clench.

*Monster.*

*No, she is my enemy. She is Sevan—*

The sound of raised voices nearby drew Kate's attention. Keeping the blade pointed at Eravis's throat, she stopped to listen.

"Where is the horse?" someone shouted in a Sevan accent.

Eravis let out a small cry. "They're coming," she frantically whispered to Kate. "He's going to kill the horse."

Kate stared down at her, confusion clouding her mind. She pushed it away and reached out to the soldier who'd shouted, gleaning his thoughts. He'd been sent by Rendborne to bring the uror horse to the throne room. The soldier didn't know why, but Kate did. And so did Eravis, it seemed. Questions rose up in her, but there wasn't time for any of them as the soldier stepped into the alcove entrance ahead.

"What goes here?" the man said, mouth agape at the sight of Kate and Eravis. He started to shout for help, but Kate grabbed hold of his mind with her sway, and in a second she rendered him unconscious. He fell, just as another guard appeared around the corner.

"Get the uror horse," Kate said to Eravis, and then she rushed the soldier. She cut him down easily, his surprise working to her advantage.

Three more of them followed the first two, and these Kate put to sleep with her magic as well. Then she dispatched them all one by one with her sword, unwilling to risk the possibility that they would wake and warn Rendborne.

"Who are you?" Eravis said from behind Kate, fear palpable in her voice.

Kate turned to face her. Eravis had taken hold of the uror horse's lead once more and had retrieved her dagger. She held it out in front of her in defense. Seeing her that way, willing to defend the uror horse at the risk of her life, eased the tight knot in Kate's heart. Corwin said she had saved him, and that she had given him emotional comfort to survive his ordeal. Kate couldn't hate her, not knowing that.

Then again, she didn't have to like her either.

"My name is Kate Brighton," she said at last.

"Oh." Eravis's mouth fell open in surprise, but she closed it quickly, giving a quick nod. "I know who you are . . . the Wilder Queen . . . and . . . Corwin's true love."

"He told you about me?" Tears pricked Kate's eyes at the realization.

Eravis nodded again, something pinched in her expression. "He thought you were dead, but even so he couldn't stop loving you."

Kate swallowed hard, getting her emotions in check. This wasn't the time or place.

Eravis must've thought the same. "We need to get this horse away from the castle. Will you help me?"

Kate frowned at her. "Why do you care what happens to it?"

The question seemed to take Eravis by surprise. Her brow furrowed in confusion, as if she didn't fully understand her own motivations. "Because it's important, isn't it? To Rime?" She gazed at the uror horse, a look of tenderness crossing her face. "Besides," Eravis said, looking up. "If Rendborne wants it dead, it can't be for anything good. Nothing good comes from that man." Hatred deepened her voice.

*Enemy of my enemy*, Kate thought grimly. "Follow me. I can get the horse out of the city." She turned and headed down the alcove.

"Wait," Eravis called, and with a sigh, Kate turned back to her. Eravis set her lips, a pained look on her face. "Please, will you help me escape as well? Rendborne killed my father. It's only a matter of time before he does the same to me."

Kate's eyes widened in shock. "The Godking is dead?"

"Yes," Eravis replied, a glare darkening her features. "The moment the fighting began, Rendborne killed him. My father's been making trouble for days, ever since he realized that Rendborne stole the protection of our godsblood. Without it, Rendborne was able to force him to sign documents naming him as lord regent of Rime. Rendborne has already blamed Magnar's death on Rimish spies to infuriate the Sevan troops."

It made sense, and Kate had expected such betrayal from him. Still, there were questions she would've liked to ask, but before she could the sound of hurried feet filled the courtyard. "Yes, I'll help, but we need to go. Now."

Kate led them down the alcove the way she'd come. The horse appeared perfectly calm, and when Kate touched it with her sway, she sensed its approving warmth.

As they hurried out of the stable, Kate made up her mind about what to do. Although the last thing she wanted once the battle ended was to have Eravis hanging around for Corwin to find her, she could see no other way to keep her safe. She owed Eravis that safety for what she'd done for Corwin. *And with it the debt will be repaid.*

"The uror horse will carry you safely around the battle to our encampment," Kate said as she darted down an alleyway, one that would lead them straight to Raith's shade door. "You'll be given my protection there."

"How?" Eravis asked, something haughty in the question.

"You're just going to have to take my word for it."

They walked the rest of the way in silence, meeting no one. When they reached the shade door, Kate pressed her hand against the rough stone and whispered the word of invocation. A line of light shone from the wall, drawing the outline of the doorway. It was small, barely wide enough for the horse to fit through. Kate went first, leading the uror horse out onto the field. Distantly, she could hear the sound of the raging battle. The uror horse raised its head and snorted loudly in alarm.

Keeping a tight hold on its lead, Kate closed her eyes and reached out with her sway, searching for Signe. She found her quickly. *Signe,*

Kate thought, sending the word directly into her mind. She felt Signe flinch, but only for a moment. *Help save the uror horse. I'm sending it to you along with Eravis Fane.*

She sensed Signe's confusion at the strange request, but also her quick acceptance. *I . . . I will keep them safe.*

Satisfied, Kate withdrew her magic and turned to Eravis. "I'll help you get on." She stooped down, cupping her hands together to give Eravis a foothold. Then she boosted her up onto the horse's back. Although the princess appeared nervous, she wrapped her fingers through the horse's mane with one hand and accepted the lead rope from Kate with the other, sitting astride like a practiced horsewoman.

Kate faced the uror horse. Holding its head between her hands, palms spread over its cheeks, she touched it with her sway once more. *Go, find Signe Leth. She will keep you safe.* Kate sent the horse an image of who Signe was and where to find her. Kate pressed the urgency on the horse. To her surprise it answered back, a simple *yes* that was more feeling than language.

Letting go of the lead rope, Kate looked up at Eravis. "The horse knows the way. Just stick with it."

Eravis stared back at her with a stunned gaze. "You're like him, aren't you? Lord Gavril?"

"I'm nothing like him." Kate fixed a glare so fierce on Eravis that she flinched.

"Yes, I can see that you're not," Eravis said after a moment. "I owe you my life, Kate Brighton. A debt that I will repay. Whatever I have the power to give you, I shall."

Kate considered the woman's statement carefully. "There is

only one thing I wish from you."

"Say it, and I will make it so," Eravis replied, the haughty princess once more.

"When the battle is over, you are to go home to Seva, and never again return to Rime."

Eravis opened her mouth as if to protest, but then closed it and gave a firm nod. "I swear it on all the gods both living and dead."

Satisfied as well as she could be, Kate stepped back. "Good luck."

"Thank you, Kate. I will never forget you," Eravis said.

"Nor I you," Kate replied, no matter how much she wished she could.

With that, Eravis and the uror horse headed up the hill, soon disappearing from view.

Kate watched them go, her emotions settling inside her, the jealousy and hurt she'd harbored starting to fade.

Grateful for it, she turned back to the mage door with renewed focus, one hand touching the hilt of the Hellsteel still strapped to her hip. It was time to stop Rendborne. Once and for all.

CORWIN STARED AT THE FOUR assailants across from him. He knew them all, called them all friends—Dal his best friend, his shield brother.

Now they were his enemy. Corwin felt his mind split. To fend off four opponents at once, he needed unwavering focus, but he couldn't manage it. Not knowing that Gavril was somewhere nearby.

"Dal, don't do this," Corwin said as Dal raised his sword, preparing to strike. "Fight him."

"I . . . can't." Dal's whole body shook as he spoke, as if he were in the throes of fever tremors.

"Yes you can." It wasn't empty hope. Dal's resistance was palpable, far greater than Corwin had ever seen anyone manage against Gavril. Maybe that meant this wasn't Gavril after all—or if it was, perhaps he wasn't as strong as he used to be, or his attention was divided enough for Dal to break free.

But the other three Rimish soldiers weren't putting up nearly the same amount of fight. The three of them charged Corwin at once, moving to encircle him. Corwin raised both sword and buckler in defense. He blocked the first blow, parried the second, and ducked the third. Coming up from the crouch, he jabbed the hilt of the sword at the first soldier's face, knocking off his helm and smashing his nose. The man stumbled backward with a grunt of pain. If he'd been a true enemy, Corwin would've followed through with a cutting blow to his neck, but this was an ally—no matter what Gavril might force him to do.

Corwin turned to block another blow. This soldier wielded an axe, which hit like a boulder, jamming Corwin's shoulder, pain alighting down his entire right side. It took all his strength to first hold the blow, then deflect it. He followed through with a vicious left hook, the side of his buckler connecting with the man's neck. His helm remained in place but his head snapped sideways, stunning him.

The third soldier advanced now, but he wasn't alone—Dal had lost his struggle, and he came at Corwin at the same time. Corwin danced backward to keep them from surrounding him again. He especially feared Dal. The others were soldiers, but Dal was a warrior. Corwin would've had have a hard time beating him in single combat, let alone two on one.

*Make that four on one.* The others had recovered, and once again were advancing on Corwin. Pushing thoughts of Gavril out of his mind, Corwin focused on the fight before him. He needed to disarm the soldiers as quickly as possible before engaging Dal. Drawing on years of training and a carefully honed instinct, Corwin threw himself into the fight. His whole body became a weapon, his sword an extension of his arm, his buckler an extension of his fist.

The hardest part was fighting to disarm instead of kill. His old arms master taught him that he would fight like he trained and so he trained to deliver killing blows. But he managed to be more precise. The helmetless soldier he rendered unconscious with a blow to the temple with the side of his shield. The man dropped to his knees and tumbled over, landing face-first on the blood-slicked grass. Corwin broke both of the axe-bearer's wrists, rendering him powerless to hold any weapon. To the third soldier, he delivered a vicious kick to the man's knee, dislocating it.

Then Corwin swung and faced Dal, raising his sword just in time to block a dual strike from both of Dal's swords. They fought, trading blow for blow, parry for parry, but Corwin could find no opportunity to disarm or incapacitate his friend. Fatigue tugged at Corwin's arms, and sweat stung his eyes. Around them, the battle raged, but no one moved to intervene; they were all fighting their own battles with the seemingly inexhaustible enemy.

There was no way through Dal's defenses, not without delivering a killing blow. But Corwin refused to do that.

"Corwin," Dal said, panting heavily as he swung his right sword crossways at Corwin's torso in a move meant to confound the opponent and to coax him into leaving himself open for a counter-strike. Corwin knew the move well and didn't fall for it. "Do you remember Belloss?" The strain in Dal's voice made him sound like a stranger.

"Of course I remember." Did Corwin now have to worry that Gavril was exploiting his memories?

"Bait the Drake," Dal said.

*Bait the* . . . Corwin shook his head as understanding struck him. "No. I can't." The move wasn't one taught by any arms master anywhere, but an underhanded tactic that was more at home in a barroom brawl than a formal fight. If done right, the opponent couldn't improvise a way to block it, but it wasn't meant to disarm—it was meant to maim, severing all the tendons in the opponent's hamstrings. If the person didn't bleed out, they would never walk normally again.

"Yes you can. It's the only way."

Corwin shook his head, aware of how strange it was to be having an argument like this in the midst of a fight.

"Please . . . I don't know . . . how much . . . longer . . . I can hold . . . him." It was getting harder for Dal to talk, to maintain control of his own mind. "Kate . . . needs . . . you."

His words struck Corwin like an arrow. How long had it been since she went through the wall? Too long. And he still had Gavril to contend with. Corwin knew that even if he killed Dal, Gavril would just move on to the next available mind, another vessel for him to turn into a weapon.

Corwin didn't answer. He didn't want Gavril to know what he had decided. If Gavril was deep enough into Dal's head, he might know how to anticipate the move and counter it.

Corwin let the fight continue another few moments, and then he went into the Bait the Drake position. Dal recognized it at once, and for a second Corwin saw him start a countermove, but then a tremor spread through his body, and he held back just long enough for Corwin to strike.

The edge of his blade slid in between the folds on the backside of Dal's leg armor, reaching skin and all the precious tendon and muscle beneath. With a cry, Dal fell forward onto his knees, his leg no longer able to support his body.

"Dal!" Corwin reached for him, dread pounding in his temples. His strike had curved wide, cutting through the side of Dal's leg toward the front, dangerously close to major veins.

"Get away!" Dal slashed out with his arm. "He's still here. He's still got me."

Corwin's fingers clenched around Dal's shoulders. He wanted to rip Gavril apart, to make him suffer. This had to end. He would kill Gavril again, and this time he would make sure he was truly dead.

Lurching to his feet, Corwin started to turn, then stumbled as a hand took hold of his ankle and yanked. It was Dal. Still fighting. Still being forced to fight.

"Let him go!" Corwin shouted, trying to pull free of Dal's grip, but Dal held on as if his hand were an iron clamp. The strength was impossible, especially from someone injured and bleeding and fatigued from fighting.

Corwin kicked, yanking and shoving with all his might, but he couldn't break free. He glanced behind him at Dal only to see it wasn't Dal anymore. His features were contorted into a fierce rage, animalistic, like a wounded beast. Dal yanked himself forward, pinning Corwin's leg beneath his body.

With panic clutching at his thoughts, Corwin searched for his sword, but it had fallen out of reach. Cursing, he squirmed back around, working to fight Dal off. They began to grapple; Dal groped for Corwin's throat while Corwin fought to keep him back. They were of a similar weight and height, but whatever Gavril was doing gave Dal unnatural strength. No matter how hard Corwin struggled, he couldn't break free. Desperate, as Dal's fingers sank into his throat, Corwin balled his hand into a fist and struck Dal in the temple. He might as well have been punching a brick wall, for all the effect it had.

Even worse, Dal began to laugh. "Keep fighting me, Corwin," Dal said. "The more you resist, the sweeter my victory." It was Dal's voice, but Gavril's words. Nausea burned through Corwin's gut.

"Let him go, you coward," Corwin said, staring into Dal's eyes, knowing Gavril could see him. "Face me yourself and stop hiding behind—" The words died in Corwin's throat as the pressure on his windpipe built. His panic heightened, blurring his thoughts. Then instinct took over, and Corwin lowered his hand to his waist, where he could feel the small knife he wore pressing into his side. His fingers gripped it, pulled it free.

He raised it, Dal's throat within reach, naked and vulnerable. But he knew he couldn't do this. Couldn't kill his best friend.

"Do it, Corwin," Gavril said in Dal's voice. "Kill him before he kills you."

"No," Corwin croaked, struggling to draw a breath.

"Do it and know that there is nothing you have that I cannot take away."

Corwin pressed the knife to Dal's neck, drawing blood. Dal made no move to stop it, and his grip on Corwin's throat remained steady. This was a stalemate.

"You have no choice," Gavril said through Dal. "To get to me all you must do is kill your best friend."

It was sickening to hear such words come from Dal's mouth, to know that he was being used like a puppet. Corwin had never known such hate before. It was like an all-consuming fire intent on burning him up from the inside until there was nothing left.

"Corwin," Dal said, and this time it was Dal speaking. Blood trickled out from the sides of Dal's eyes, spilling onto his cheeks like crimson tears. More blood flowed from his nose, mouth, and ears. Gavril was killing him, slowing squeezing the life out of Dal with his magic. And yet he was still here, still fighting.

"We can beat this, my friend." Tears burned Corwin's eyes at the sound of misery in Dal's voice. "No one can defeat us. Not when we're together."

"You're right," Dal replied, his gaze hardening. "Tell Signe . . . I love her."

"Noooooooooooooooo!!!" Corwin screamed, but before he could pull back the knife, Dal threw his head forward, jamming his throat against the blade. Blood pooled over Corwin's hand, hot and sticky. Dal remained upright half a moment longer, then he crumpled to the ground, the light in his eyes extinguished.

Corwin fell to his knees beside his friend, his brother. "No, Dal, gods, please, no." He drew him into his arms, his grief like a madness, driving away all sense of the battle, all concern for his own safety even as more Rimish soldiers drew near him, swords ready and minds bent to Gavril's command.

Reaching deep inside himself, Corwin searched for the will to fight, but it wouldn't come. Not with his best friend lying dead in his arms. He tilted his head back, eyes closed against the sun.

A shadow moved across his face, looming over him. Opening his eyes, Corwin saw a horse, one half of it as white as ivory and the other half as black as onyx. The uror horse. With a shrill neigh, it spun about, slamming both back feet into the nearest soldier coming to attack Corwin and sending him flying. Then it turned and struck another soldier with a foreleg. Teeth bared, it spun about several more times, fighting off any who dared draw near until no more did.

Wonderment flooded Corwin's chest as he stared at the uror horse standing over him, nostrils flared and eyes wild, a halter on its face with a lead hanging loose. The horse snorted and stomped its hoof, impatient now, demanding. Somehow, Corwin understood what it wanted and hope gave him the strength to climb to his feet. This wasn't over yet. He had to keep fighting. For Kate. For Dal. For his people.

The uror horse stood still as stone as Corwin climbed up, one hand holding its lead rope. The moment he sat down, the horse leaped forward into the canter and then the gallop, as if certain of the way. Corwin held on, putting his trust in it. This was no ordinary horse, after all, but a being sent from the gods.

The horse rode for a cluster of Sevan soldiers not far from the gate. They were standing in a formation around a single man in their center.

Gavril.

Corwin's heart constricted in his chest, and he forced air into his lungs. "We must end him," he said, shouting against the wind. The horse's ears—one black and one white—flicked back and forward as if in confirmation.

The horse charged into the line of soldiers, rearing up to knock three of them over. Corwin held on, left hand fisted in the horse's mane now and right hand tight on his sword. He swung as the horse came down, felling one of the soldiers in a single blow. In perfect unison with the horse, he shifted his weight and struck the next one. The uror horse handled the final two with hooves and teeth.

Then there was no one left but Gavril, who had retreated as soon as the attack began and now stood several yards away, his back to the wall and with Corwin blocking his escape through the gate. The man raised his hands toward Corwin and the horse, fingers bent as if he sought to pull Corwin down with a thought. But it wouldn't work. Not with the vial around Corwin's neck. He could feel it heating up, reacting to the magic, deflecting it. It was as if Kate herself stood beside him, protecting him. The uror was safe too, its mind unchangeable even for someone with sway.

"You can't get to me anymore, Gavril," Corwin shouted.

"Perhaps not," Gavril replied. "But I can get to them."

Corwin glanced to his right to see that several Rimish soldiers had followed him with the intent of backing up their prince. A dazed look had come over their faces, and Corwin watched in horror as they turned to face one another, weapons held throat to throat.

"Let me go, Corwin, or they all die," Gavril said, already taking a slow, measured step toward the gate, as if certain Corwin would do as he bade.

Corwin looked at the soldiers, seeing the fear in their eyes, the helplessness. Some of them were struggling against Gavril's grip, but he held them tightly. *Stalemate again.*

*No*, Corwin refused to give up, to give in.

Slowly, he slid off the horse's back. "How did you survive the Hellsteel?" Corwin asked, stalling as he racked his brain for a way out of this that didn't involve sacrificing his men. *I will sacrifice no more this day*, he vowed, the loss of Dal burning in his chest.

A dark look crossed Gavril's features. He was thin and haggard, deep dark pits beneath his eyes and his skin bleached white as bone. "The Lord Ascender is powerful. Even death obeys his bidding."

"Rendborne's death is coming for him right now," Corwin said. "But what about the Hellsteel? It should've taken your magic."

Gavril flinched, and his hand rose to his chest automatically. Corwin watched the gesture, and he could now see the shape of something beneath Gavril's tunic, something that wasn't part of his armor. A vial. "This too, the Lord Ascender granted to me again."

Corwin frowned. There was something beneath Gavril's words. He was not being truthful about his restored magic.

*It is borrowed*, a voice spoke inside his mind. *Stolen.*

Corwin blinked in surprise, wondering where the voice had come from. But he didn't doubt the truth of it. This was purloined magic—which meant it could be taken away. If he could just be quick enough.

Corwin could tell at a glance that the armor Gavril wore beneath his clothing had been enchanted by the magists. He would have to be close to penetrate that defense—and the Rimish soldiers would be dead long before he managed it. But he didn't need to penetrate Gavril's armor—he only needed to end the man's magic, and the vial was atop the armor, not beneath it. Without his magic, Gavril was less than nothing, a worm soft and vulnerable and easy to squash.

Slowly, carefully, Corwin shifted his sword to his left hand and reached for the knife at his belt with his right. Across from him, he heard the soldiers groan, still fighting to save themselves and their friends. He had to trust they would hold Gavril's will at bay long enough for Corwin to see this through.

"Rendborne isn't here to save you this time," Corwin said, judging the distance carefully, willing his heartbeat to slow. He drew a breath and held it.

"The Lord Ascender is everywhere at once. He is—"

Corwin raised his hand and launched the knife at Gavril's chest. The man's mouth fell open, but he was too stunned to react in time. The knife struck just as Corwin intended—shattering the crystal vial around the man's neck. Crimson spilled down Gavril's front.

*Kate's blood*. Corwin knew it instinctively, remembering how she'd been so drained when they first escaped Norgard so many weeks ago.

Terror spread over Gavril's face as he realized what had happened, that he was no longer a wilder with the gift of sway—but an ordinary man. A soft one at that, slow and untrained in the art of war.

At once, the soldiers lowered their swords from one another, and before Corwin could even take a step toward Gavril, the soldiers rushed him, surrounding the former wilder, blades up and eyes open.

Gavril lay dead a moment later, beheaded by the last men he'd victimized. A dark pleasure surged through Corwin, but he didn't dwell on it. He refused to let his hatred for Gavril turn him into a monster that celebrated the death of another—no matter how much it was deserved. But Gavril was truly dead this time, and nothing would ever bring him back.

Vowing to forget the man forever, Corwin returned to Dal. Although the urgency to find Kate was blaring inside him, he took the time to drag Dal's body toward the wall, away from the harm of the battle. It was a small thing, but the most he could do for his fallen friend.

Then with tears still burning his eyes, he turned toward the uror horse, which hadn't yet left his side. He quickly mounted and said, "We need to find Kate."

Again, as if the horse understood, it surged forward, darting through the gate, past the few soldiers remaining there and into the city. They raced down the familiar streets to Mirror Castle. As they rode through the opened gates into the bailey, a loud explosion rent the air. The horse shied at the noise and slowly came to a stop in the center of the courtyard. The explosion had come from somewhere ahead.

*Oh gods, Kate!*

Corwin urged the uror horse forward, and it raced up the steps into the castle itself, the doors once again left opened and unguarded. Corwin slid from the horse's back and patted its shoulder.

"You need to get away from here, my friend." He didn't want to know what would happen to it if Kate succeeded in killing Rendborne with the Hellsteel. And if she failed, Corwin would do everything in his power to finish the job.

This time the horse ignored him, standing with all four feet planted and its gaze fixed unerringly toward the throne room ahead.

With an ache squeezing his heart, Corwin turned away from the horse and headed through the entryway and up the stairs into the throne room. Signs of the blast he'd heard were everywhere, the columns charred and some of the plaster crumbling. Half a dozen

Sevan soldiers lay scattered across the floor, their bodies bent at odd angles and their armor charred as well. *One of Signe's explosive devices did this.* Lifting his gaze, Corwin spotted movement ahead.

A few feet in front of the Mirror Throne, which had somehow come through the explosion undamaged, Kate stood across from Rendborne, the trident in her hand. Freed from its disguise, the Hellsteel glowed red. Fear shone in Rendborne's eyes as he held his hands toward Kate, his palms aglow with magic. But Corwin knew the Hellsteel would deflect anything he threw at Kate, and if he'd been armed before, he wasn't now.

"You will never defeat me," Rendborne said, taunting her despite his fear. "You will meet the same end as your father."

"You're thinking of the wrong death," Kate taunted back. "I will kill you same as I killed Vikas."

With his heart climbing his throat, Corwin rushed toward them, his sword at the ready. The very tip of it still glowed with magist enchantment, enough to withstand a single attack. At the sound of his pounding steps, both Kate and Rendborne glanced his way.

Too late, Corwin realized his mistake. In the half second of surprise that had come over Kate at his appearance, Rendborne lunged at her. He yanked the Hellsteel out of her hands, swung in a quick arc—then plunged the three prongs straight into Kate's throat, sinking them all the way through to the other side.

"Kate!!!"

Every part of Corwin screamed out in agony as he watched her fall, same as Dal had fallen. Blood and magic spilled out of her with the Hellsteel still buried deep in her neck, and a black, living shadow rose up from her body as the life left it.

Rendborne turned his eyes onto Corwin now, his gaze triumphant. Although he made no move to retrieve the Hellsteel, no trace of fear showed on his face as the black smoke swept over him . . . and dissipated, with no perceptible effect. Somehow, he'd made himself impervious to the Ruin.

*But he is still a man, still vulnerable to steel.*

Corwin raced forward, sword clutched in both hands. Idly, Rendborne threw a bolt spell at him. Corwin caught it with his blade, deflecting it. It ricocheted up toward the ceiling, and a large chunk of stone crashed to the ground, sending up a cloud of dust.

Still Corwin pressed on, reaching Rendborne just as he unleashed another spell. This one struck him in the shoulder and knocked him off-balance. He spun, just catching himself, then came at Rendborne again.

Rendborne launched a jet of wind at Corwin, the blow sending him backward several feet. He slammed against the ground, starbursts crossing his vision as his lungs seized, robbed of breath and unable to draw another.

Rendborne approached, peering down at Corwin with a broad smile on his face. "Welcome, Corwin, the very last of the Tormanes. May you be forgotten as I was once forgotten. Once, but no more."

With that, Rendborne reached into his pocket and withdrew a crude shiv, a single piece of Hellsteel sharpened enough to stab. Then slowly, suredly, he raised the raw red metal over his head, the tip pointed down toward Corwin, who lay there unable to stop the coming blow.

THIS WAS WHAT IT MEANT to die.

Passing from one world into another, like stepping through a veil. Kate felt her passing this time, the way her soul slid from its body and into something else, a not-body in a not-place.

One she'd visited once before.

Broad, white leaves surrounded her on all sides, bits of black nothingness in between them. Beneath her feet, the limb of that vast, ageless tree held her easily. A light ahead drew her forward. She moved toward it slowly, savoring the weightless feel in her new body, one that seemed to be made of light and air and nothing more. If she wanted, she could float up among the boughs, drifting through the leaves like so many clouds.

But she didn't want it. Not with that light ahead, calling out to her. Singing to her in a voice only she could hear, a song that strummed the cords of her soul until she felt herself singing in return.

Soon she reached the glimmering pool residing in the conflux of leaves. This time, Kate didn't hesitate at the pool's edge. She stepped off it into the light, her heart soaring with no trace of fear. No knowledge of fear anywhere.

The light consumed her. She felt herself being unmade, but it wasn't an undoing; it was a mergence, her soul becoming a part of the light, until she no longer had a sense of self at all, only the expanse of that brightness forever reaching and unending.

An eternity passed.

And then another.

Then finally the pain of her making started again. She felt herself pulled from the light as a baby is pulled from the womb, forced from one world into another. But it wasn't pain as she once knew it—of nerves firing warnings to her brain. This was pain in its primal form: separation from the whole.

Kate felt her new body that was at once her old body, limbs that had belonged to her long ago. She stretched out with them, remembering. She could feel the tug of every bit of sinew, the rush of blood down every vein. Slowly, she became aware of the darkness around her, a void of nothingness. Not the absence of light but true dark itself, a separate, complete thing. She was alone in it, but not afraid. There was nothing to fear here, only to regret and mourn.

The dark lessened, and light slowly took on form, resolving into the shape of a single candle standing on the ground in front of Kate, its flame dancing in an unknown wind. She saw that she was sitting, legs crossed beneath her and nothing but the void all around.

Then the darkness across from her resolved into shadows. They parted, like dark leaves, and a figure stepped through them. She looked like a human woman on the surface, but beneath she was something else, something more. Her appearance kept shifting, the way light plays on water. At one moment her skin was as white as ivory, at the next as dark as onyx, and before long every other color in between.

The only thing that didn't shift in her appearance was her eyes.

These glowed like an animal's at night, steady as stars in the sky. Smiling, the woman sat down across from Kate, the candle flickering between them.

"Who are you?" Kate asked, finding her voice at last. It had been so long since she'd heard it she barely recognized it as her own.

"I am you," the woman replied. "And I am no one and everyone."

Kate blinked. "What do you want from me?"

"To give you a choice." The woman raised her hand, and a slit of brightness appeared to Kate's right. It spread, opening like a tear in a piece of fabric. Through the opening she saw a strange place, a massive room with marbled columns crumbling and charred and a throne made of mirrors. She was seeing it as if from the heavens, looking down at two men, one standing over the other, who lay helpless on the floor. Vaguely, she recognized them both.

She turned back to the woman. "A choice to do what?"

In answer, the woman raised her other hand and another hole in the darkness appeared. Through this one Kate saw only light. It was that place she'd been before, the one of completeness and a peace that was like an unending dream full of every bright memory and hope and yearning, all fulfilled.

Kate turned back to the woman. "This is no choice at all."

"Isn't it?" The woman cocked her head, her long hair rippling from black to white to black again.

Kate returned her gaze to the throne room, seeing the two men once more. This time she focused on the face of the man lying on the floor. An ache spread through her chest as she realized it was Corwin. Memories flooded her, and she gasped at the strength of them. For the first time since entering these other worlds she remembered who she was.

She faced the woman once more. "If I go back, will I be able to save him?"

The woman didn't answer, only stared at Kate, the whisper of a smile on her ever-shifting features.

Kate turned and looked at the light, and the sight of it made her heart ache with yearning. Facing the woman once more, she said, "If Corwin dies, will he join me there?" She motioned to the light.

Again, the woman didn't answer, but Kate knew she could. This woman knew everything, was everything—and yet she was only a part of something greater, something vast and unknowable, other faces and names and beings lingering beyond the void.

Kate closed her eyes, forcing such contemplations away before she was overcome by them. More questions flooded her mind, doubt rising up in her like a tide. There was so much unknown waiting for her through that side of the veil—whether or not she would survive the fight with Rendborne. Suppose Corwin died and she did not; what then? What if they both lived but the love between them continued to wither and die? What if she was left with this gaping hole inside her, an endless yearning that could never be fulfilled? What if she failed at everything she set out to do? What if—

She stopped the questions before another could surface in her mind. There were no answers to them here.

It didn't matter. What did was the things she did know: That there were other people besides Corwin facing danger and death at this very moment. There were people who would suffer if Rendborne succeeded, who would carry on in misery and oppression.

But she could end it.

"You are the only one who can," the woman said, as if hearing her thoughts. "You must ask yourself: What are you willing to lose?"

The truth rose like the sun in Kate's mind. *I would lose it all. To save them.* A great heat filled her heart as a light began to burn from inside her, seeping through the brand on her chest until the scarred skin shone like a star.

Seeing it, the woman's smile widened. She stood and held out her hand. Kate took it, and for a moment she felt that completeness again, that peace like a dream. Then the woman guided her to the awaiting portal, where she could see her own body lying in a halo of blood. The uror horse was there, standing at the doorway, watching these events unfold. She could sense its pain, the wound in its soul, one placed there long ago. This too needed to be corrected, an end made.

And a beginning.

Letting go of the woman's hand, Kate stepped toward the portal. Just before she did, it transformed into a pool of light. Then she was falling through it and rising up again.

But not as Kate Brighton.

As the Paragon.

IN THE NEXT MOMENT, there was light. Only light.

It was so bright, Corwin felt the strength of it sear his vision. But it passed as quickly as it had come, and he blinked the blurriness out of his eyes, realizing belatedly that Rendborne was no longer standing over him—that he hadn't delivered the killing blow Corwin had been certain was coming, helpless to stop it.

But he wasn't helpless anymore. He scrambled to his feet in time to see Rendborne slowly standing up as well, as if he'd been knocked over by the force of the light. But that was impossible. There's been no explosion, no wind, no force at all. And yet—

Something pulled Corwin around, like an invisible hand on his shoulder. Kate stood before him. Alive and whole—the wounds on her neck nothing but white scars, as if they'd healed so long ago they were already fading. There was no trace of the trident anywhere. She was the source of the light. It shone over her left breast, through the hole it had burned in her armor. It shone through her—originating from the Paragon brand over her heart. Somehow, the ritual had worked.

Corwin knew it without asking, could see it in the way her whole body seemed to glow, her face luminescent, dark eyes sparkling like crystal in the sun. Only the longer he stared at her, the less she looked like herself and the more like someone else. A woman with ever-shifting features, her face and hair first black, then white, then black again. It was like the way the light plays on water, at once casting shadows and banishing them in turn. And he understood that this wasn't his Kate any longer, but the Paragon—the vessel for the goddess. His heart ached at the truth, and he felt the pain of her death all over again. There seemed no room for her inside such a being.

The Paragon strode toward Rendborne, her courage unflinching, each step as certain as if she'd seen these events already and knew how they would come to pass. Corwin pulled his gaze away from her and onto Rendborne. He still held the Hellsteel shiv in one hand. In the other he held magic, a spell ready to launch at her. The shock had fled from his face, his expression hard and determined, but with fear lingering in his eyes.

He didn't yet understand that it wasn't Kate standing across from him now.

Pulling back his hand, Rendborne launched the magic at the Paragon. She didn't move to block it, simply walked forward, letting it strike her in the chest, where it dissolved in an instant, swallowed by her light. With his face contorted in anger, Rendborne tried again. He hurled fire this time, and although the heat of it made Corwin shrink away, the Paragon didn't react at all. Once more it struck her, and once more the light swallowed it.

With a scream of frustration, Rendborne raised the Hellsteel shiv this time, both his palms aglow with magic. Corwin sensed what he was about to do and hurled himself forward, trying to block the throw—the Hellsteel was a godslayer, and even though there was no sign of Kate, only the Paragon, her body was still the vessel.

He almost made it, but the Hellsteel soared past him at the last second, driven forward with an unnatural speed by Rendborne's magic. It traveled so fast, no one could've stopped it. With a cry rising in his throat, Corwin turned to the Paragon, certain to find Kate fallen once more. Instead, she'd come to a stop, one hand clutching the Hellsteel shiv, its deadly tip inches from her unprotected face. She lowered the weapon, and with her other hand, cupped the red steel. It melted beneath her touch, dissolving into dust.

"That's impossible!" Rendborne screamed. "What are you?"

The Paragon spoke, the voice still Kate's and yet so much more—as if it were a thousand voices melded into one. "I've come for you, Gershwen Tormane. To restore the life you have stolen."

*Gershwen Tormane. My great-great-granduncle,* Corwin thought, shock ripping through him. Gershwen was his true name. Son of Rowan and brother of Morwen. The Nameless One no more.

At the Paragon's words, Rendborne paled. For a second, Corwin thought he might collapse, but then Rendborne spun and fled. At once, Corwin launched after him, overtaking the older man in just a few strides. He tackled him, and they both tumbled to the ground, skidding through the rubble.

Rendborne let out a grunt of pain, but that was all he had time to do before Corwin was on top of him, fists slamming into his forehead, his cheeks, his nose. All the rage Corwin possessed poured out of him now, his fury a living force inside him. Memories flashed through his mind, of his friends' suffering, his brother's death, Dal's death, Kate's death, his homeland ravished. So much destruction this man had wrought. Corwin would kill this man with his bare hands if he had to. Mindless of the pain in his knuckles, his hands, his arms, he kept at it. Blood splattered from Rendborne's mouth, his eyes rolling into the back of his head as he made no motion to defend himself.

Sensing the end was near, Corwin struck harder than ever, but then a firm hand touched his shoulder and he froze. Sudden warmth spread through his body, and his hatred fled as quickly as it had come. He sagged toward the ground, panting and spent.

The Paragon pulled him into a standing position, then moved him aside, out of the way, as easily as if he were a child. She knelt beside Gershwen Tormane, laying one hand on his red, swollen cheek, the gesture almost a caress, the smile on her face almost loving.

"I don't understand," Corwin said, bloodied fingers clenched. "Why did you stop me? This man deserves death."

The Paragon turned her head toward Corwin, and there was no trace of Kate in her face anywhere. No trace of humanity. "The power of the goddess is not meant to take life, but to give it."

She laid a hand over her left breast, cupping the light there with one palm. When she pulled her hand away a moment later it glowed like a star. Turning back to Gershwen, she placed her glowing hand on his chest, over his heart. His eyes went wide and a groan escaped his throat, a sound of pain and also relief.

The light in the Paragon's hand shifted from brilliant white to a golden hue, lovely to behold and far less blinding than the Paragon's light. She stood, cupping the gold in both hands. Then, raising her gaze, she let out a whistle. The uror horse trotted over to her at once, its neck arched and mismatched eyes wide with wonderment. It stopped before the Paragon and waited, absolutely still.

"What are you—" Corwin broke off as the Paragon placed both her hands against the uror horse's chest. The golden light grew suddenly brighter, and then it exploded, expanding outward in a brilliant wave. It swept over Corwin, and he stumbled sideways. Recovering, he shifted forward and had to brace himself against the uror horse's side to keep his balance. The moment he touched the animal, he felt his mind slip his body. It was like falling into a dream—one moment awake in one place, the next somewhere else entirely.

Someone else entirely. He was the uror, one of many, many of one. He was Kalar, the horse sent to judge the hearts of Edwin and Corwin. He was Murr, the wolf sent to choose between Orwin and Owen. He was Jahara, the bear who judged Borwin over Norwan and Jorwen. He was all of them, so many that had come before, so many yet to be. Uror, one of many, many of one.

And yet one of him was missing, lost a long time ago, leaving the rest broken and incomplete, like a great chain with a missing link.

The eagle, Niv, who had been sent to Morwen and his brother Gershwen. Niv, who had died at Gershwen's hands, and yet had lived on in a wrong vessel, twisted and bent, corrupted by a transformation that never should have been. For years the missing uror had longed to return, the trauma of separation turning into hatred, into madness. Even now, with the Paragon holding its soul cupped in her hand, Niv resisted this rejoining, terrified of what it had once been, so long forgotten. The golden light turned a darker hue, the fear Niv had known as a human trying to overtake it. But the rest of the uror surged brighter, welcoming Niv home, restoring it as part of a whole. One of many, many as one, the chain reforged.

An equine scream rent the air, the sound of it pure joy and elation, a trumpet of victory. At once Corwin felt himself pushed back into his body, the connection he'd momentarily shared with the uror horse severed.

Gasping, he looked up to see the Paragon standing before him. Her gaze shifted to Gershwen, who lay silent and still a few feet from Corwin. Corwin turned to look at the man as well, startled to see he was Rendborne no longer. The severing of his soul from the uror's had left him old, skin yellowed and sagging off brittle bones, hair as white as salt. Deep crevices lined his face, and his body was so thin a strong wind would be his undoing. Yet he wasn't dead. He lingered still, spent and empty. Stripped of magic and purpose, along with everything else. Despite all the man had done, Corwin felt pity swell in his heart for him.

Yet when Gershwen turned his gaze on Corwin, there wasn't despair in his eyes. Only relief. He drew a deep breath, straining from the effort. Then, on a breathless exhale, he said, "Be a good king, Corwin Tormane. As I was the worst of us, may you be the best."

And with that, the life at last passed from Gershwen's body.

Corwin stared at him, waiting for a relief that didn't come. Rendborne was gone, his worst enemy defeated, but at such a price.

*Kate.*

He turned his gaze onto the Paragon. "What happens now?"

"The victory of Rime is certain," she replied. "Magnar Fane is dead and the Sevan forces are retreating."

Corwin blinked in disbelief. Was it truly over? He stared at her face, reading the truth in her eyes. The Paragon would know. In the end, believing in her was easy.

"Yet all is not finished for you, Corwin Tormane." The Paragon motioned to the uror horse—to Kalar. "You must complete the third trial. Only then will Gershwen's corruption be completely undone."

Corwin swallowed, the knowledge of what he would have to do sending a spike of fear through his chest. The third trial had always been the same for every would-be king: to throw himself into the Well of the World. He glanced at the door behind the Mirror Throne, the one that led to the Vault of Souls.

Then he turned back to the Paragon. "What about Kate? Where is she?"

"She is here." The Paragon touched her left breast, where the white light of the brand was already starting to fade.

"What happens when you go? Will she remain? Will I ever see her again?" He couldn't forget the sight of the Hellsteel piercing her throat, the way she'd fallen, the blow surely a mortal wound.

The Paragon didn't answer. Instead she sank to the ground, slowly, like a cat settling down for a nap. "Go now, Corwin. Before it's too late." Her eyes slipped closed, and she lay on her back, hands folded across her stomach. She seemed to fall asleep at once, going as still as death.

SUMMONING ALL THE STRENGTH OF will he possessed, Corwin rose to his feet and turned to the door behind the Mirror Throne. He descended the long, steep steps to the Vault of Souls, carrying one of the torches that were always kept lit in the passageway. His heart was heavy with thoughts of his fallen loved ones. The burden of death seemed to pull him down and down, one slow step after the other.

When he reached the vault, he paused at the threshold, feeling the weight of that great, black eye, the opening to the Well of the World, staring at him once more. For a second he almost turned back, all the fear and doubt he'd known before rising up in him. But then he remembered Kate, the way she had been after the Paragon ritual first failed, and the way she was a few moments ago, vessel for the goddess. Destiny fulfilled. A sacrifice made for the triumph of Rime.

He would do no less.

Steeling his courage, he strode toward the edge and looked down. Warmth seeped up from out of that endless pit, like an exhaled breath. He stared down into its depths, seeing nothing, yet feeling everything. The weight of what he was expected to do pressed down on him. It was so much harder to do this alone, with no one standing beside him, either to encourage or dissuade. This was all on him, a choice to be made, a leap of faith to be taken.

*Faith.* The word resounded inside with the ring of truth, of revelation. He realized that might be the entire point of the trial. To answer the question of if he could step forward in faith. Only it wasn't truly about making an impossible leap into a bottomless hole. It was about whether he could make decisions without knowing for certain what their effects would be but trusting they would be for the good. For every decision made was like jumping into the dark. Nothing could be known for certain beforehand. There was always risk.

Was he wise enough? Brave enough? Did he possess the compassion to think of those he ruled as both equal to and better than himself? Did he have the capacity to listen to them, to learn from them? Could he risk losing himself to the Well of the World, if it meant Rime would be as one? That Rime was more than just a king?

*Yes*, he thought. That was something this long, hard journey had taught him, if nothing else. It was the one thing he knew without doubt.

*Be a good king.*

Setting the torch on the ground, Corwin stepped off the edge and into the pit. He fell and fell—right out of the world itself.

He found himself in a dark place, void of light. For a time he was nothing, not even shadow. Just a mind, a soul adrift. But then a warm, soft light began to grow around him, pushing the shadows back, giving them form.

He saw large, white leaves that must be growing on a tree the size of the universe. A woman appeared from between the leaves. He knew her face, her shape, the feel of her presence. And yet he'd never seen her before, not truly. He didn't think anyone ever had. Her skin shifted from white to black and all the colors between. This was the goddess Noralah. The true sovereign of Norgard, protector of Rime.

Corwin bowed, vaguely aware that he once more possessed a body to do so.

"Arise, Corwin Tormane," the woman said, her voice filled with the sound of a thousand combined into one.

He did so, his limbs trembling from the sheer terror of her awesome presence. The power radiating out from her was the same as the Paragon, only magnified a hundred times. He would've preferred to remain kneeling, but instead he held himself upright, obeying her command.

"You have fought a long, hard fight. A good fight," Noralah said. "You have helped restore the uror, and proven yourself worthy to be king of Norgard and protector of all of Rime. Do you accept this charge?"

The meaning of her words slid through Corwin slowly, the dawning realization that he had the choice to refuse. If he wanted. He searched his heart, but the doubt that had been with him before he stepped into the Well of the World was no longer there. In its place was a quiet certainty. He would face every challenge, conquer every fear, and turn every failure into good. That was what it meant to be a good king.

*No*, he realized. That was what it meant to be the best version of himself. The best anyone could ever be, king or commoner, wilder or magist, man or woman. *We are all the same.*

"Yes," Corwin said, finding his voice at last. "I accept."

The light around the goddess began to grow, until it was bright enough to extinguish all the darkness that had been there before. It enveloped Corwin, consumed him, and returned him to the world—the prince reborn a king.

Corwin found himself lying next to the Well of the World. The torch had long since gone out. But he no longer needed it to see. The uror brand on his palm glowed white, casting long shadows across the vaulted ceiling. Vague memories flitted through his mind. He remembered stepping into the Well of the World and a fall that seemed to go on forever. He remembered a vast, ancient tree, and a woman, but everything else about his time in there was shadowy, like a dream that fades upon waking, remembered later only for the feelings it invoked and none of the details.

In a daze, Corwin climbed the steps back to the throne room. It was full of people, the sound of their voices a low grumble. Most were Rimish soldiers—wilder, magist, and common folk alike, still soiled and bloodied from the battle. They all went silent as he stepped through the door. Familiar faces stared back at him. He saw Lord Jedrek and Lord Felton, Lady Myrrh and Lord Ormand all crowded near the throne. Toward the middle of the room Bonner, Nadira, Signe, Valora, Wen, Harue, and Tira were standing in a semicircle around Kate. She was lying where he'd left her, in the same lifeless pose. The uror horse stood guard over her.

*Kalar,* Corwin thought, and the horse raised its head toward him, its mismatched eyes fixing on his with unspeakable intelligence. A warm glow spread through Corwin as he sensed Kalar's mind. It was like those times when he and Kate had shared thoughts. Only in this, Kalar felt like a part of him, a link from within instead of without. His thoughts were Corwin's thoughts, shared and connected.

*She waits for you to call her back*, Kalar said.

*I know.* Corwin saw that other world again for a moment, however, and wondered if he should. If it was what she would want. He couldn't know. All he knew for certain was that he didn't want to live in any world without her.

He strode into the room, the crowd parting for him. He kept his eyes fixed on Kate, even as he felt everyone else watching him. They didn't matter. Not yet. His friends also parted for him, giving him room to kneel beside Kate. Her skin had turned to gray, and when he laid his left hand on her arm it felt like ice. For a moment, fear held him in its grip. She was gone, truly gone, not a spark of life in her. Belatedly, he realized that Tira and Bonner were both crying, and Signe's cheeks were flushed from the effort of trying not to.

Turning over his hand so the palm faced up, Corwin stared at the uror brand and the light shining through it. It was so bright the others pulled back from him, shielding their eyes, but Corwin didn't look away. He stared at it, waiting for it to grow brighter yet. Finally, when it seemed to reach its peak, he turned his hand down and pressed his uror brand against Kate's chest, atop the Paragon brand over her heart. Heat burned through him, and he watched the light blaze through Kate. It slid through her veins, turning them into golden rivers beneath her skin—they flowed down her arms, up her neck, and across her face. Everywhere.

A moment later, Kate's mouth opened, and she drew a breath, her chest rising and falling beneath Corwin's hand. Then her eyes slid open, finding his at once. Like always.

"Corwin," she said, and the rest of the room broke into cheers.

He barely heard them, barely sensed anyone else around save Kate. He stared down at her, unable to keep the smile from spreading over his face, the joy filling him up like air in his lungs. For a moment he felt the same connection to her that he felt with Kalar, as if they were one and the same, the light they shared binding them together.

When she returned his smile, one half of her lip curling up, it was like a shared secret between them. Corwin grasped her hands and pulled her into a sitting position. She went willingly, face turned toward his. Their lips met in a kiss. Corwin breathed her in like life and she did the same. The things that had been between them seemed far away, banished forever by the sacrifices—and choices—they had made.

"I love you, Kate," Corwin said against her lips.

"And I you," she replied, her mouth brushing against his. "You have always been my friend, my love, my prince . . ." She pulled back from him. "And now my king."

"All hail Corwin Tormane!" Valora shouted, her voice echoing through the throne room as loud as a trumpet call. "High King of Rime!"

Applause broke out anew, and this time Corwin registered it. He glanced down at his palm to see the light in the uror brand was already faded. But it didn't matter. Everyone in the room had seen it, and they'd witnessed the way it had pulled Kate back from death.

With a firm grip on Kate's hand, Corwin rose to his feet, pulling her up beside him. One by one the people began to bow, the motion spreading out like a wave. When it reached the lords of Rime near the throne, they too bowed—even Jedrek, although he was the last.

Corwin felt the weight of his new title already pressing down on him, but he turned his gaze to Kate, knowing he could bear it all, bear anything, with her beside him.

"And you have always been my queen," he said, loud enough for all to hear. Then he kissed her again. A promise of many more to come.

THE DAYS THAT FOLLOWED WERE filled with both great joy and great sadness.

War, regardless of how necessary, was always a dark endeavor, but never more so than at the end of it. For even at the lowest points during the fighting, there was also the hope of victory, the sense of purpose to save what can be saved, no matter what the cost. Afterward, however, those debts came due. There were so many dead to see to. Hundreds, maybe even thousands. Kate felt the loss of each one, but none more so than Dal.

Thinking about it now sent a wave of despair through her. Not just for the loss of her friend, but for the horrible weight of her actions as she saw them now through the foil that was Gavril. He had orchestrated Dal's death with sway, the same as she had done with so many others. She'd learned many things in her time in that other world, and during her journey as the Paragon, and one of them was the certainty that she never should have used her power to kill. Just because something could be done didn't make doing so right. Sometimes the opposite was true—not doing something that could be done was what made it right. But she'd gotten so wrapped up in the need to win, to end the war, to fulfill her duty, that she'd failed to weigh the cost of her actions against her very soul. She understood now that how the battle was won was equally as important as the winning itself. Losing herself along the way would've made the victory a defeat. She needed to maintain a good heart, not just to win at any cost.

A part of her wondered why, when the goddess restored the life to her body, she hadn't stripped her of her sway. Noralah could've, if she'd chosen. But Kate had a feeling she could guess the reason: because she needed to come to terms with her power, to live with it, to constantly be making the choice of how to use it. To take away the temptation to use it entirely would be too easy.

*And nothing in this world is meant to be easy*, Kate thought.

That, she believed, was for the next one.

Valora oversaw the preparation of Dal's body with Signe helping beside her. It was unusual for a foreigner to be allowed to help with such a ritual in Rime, but the rules about these sorts of things, it seemed, were going to change. And besides, no one was going to argue with Signe about it. Her grief was like the tide—nothing could hold it back. Kate's heart ached for her friend, and worry for her consumed her thoughts. She'd lost so much, too much—her mother, her love, her health. Kate knew even someone as fierce and strong as Signe could still break.

Corwin, too, was taking the death hard, although he did his best to keep his grief hidden. His official coronation wasn't to take place for another few weeks—not until most of the rebuilding of Norgard had gotten under way, a process quickened by the help of wilders—but he'd been declared high king across all of Rime, the remaining lords swearing fealty in writing. As high king, he needed to be strong for his people. There were many hurting, many afraid both about what had happened and by all the changes coming now.

From the beginning Corwin made it clear that the persecution of wilders was over, but it would take time for the hatred and prejudice to die. Decades, perhaps, Kate thought, if not centuries. They would have to remain vigilant.

They were off to a good start, however. Yaron had been elected head of the Mage League, which, moving forward, would be known only as the League, as wilders were soon to be joining their ranks. Grand Master Storr had survived the battle of Norgard; the moment the Rimish forces invaded, he'd immediately surrendered, and just as quickly proclaimed his innocence by insisting that Gavril had been controlling him. It seemed a valid excuse, but Kate quickly determined he was lying. He'd sworn fealty to the Godking for the same reason he'd done everything else—the desire to maintain his power. In the end his lying about being forced only made the case against him all the stronger. He was awaiting trial, one that, for the first time, would include the high king and his councilors alongside the leaders of the League. No longer was the League going to be given the autonomy they'd known in the past. Corwin declared they were to be a part of Rime, never separate. And in return, magists and wilders both were to be given a seat in the high king's court.

"We are all Rimish," Corwin said over and over again. Eventually the rest of Rime would start to believe it—and even if they didn't, they'd have to live with it anyway.

Once Dal's body had been prepared, Corwin and Bonner, along with the help of a few others, carried him up the Steps of Sorrows on Goddess Tor all the way to the Asterion itself, where they laid him atop a funeral pyre. Valora prayed over his body, speaking all the ancient rituals that would send his spirit through the veil and into the beyond. Once done, Valora lit the torch and handed it to Corwin. As high king, it was his right to set the fire for his best friend. With tears falling freely from his face, Corwin accepted the torch, then turned and handed it to Signe.

"Dal would've wanted you to do it," Corwin said, his voice thick with emotions. For a moment, Kate thought Signe would refuse. Eshians buried their dead.

But after a moment, she took it from Corwin and said, "He loved us both." Then she turned and walked toward the pyre, a slight tremble in her arms. The fuel on the pyre caught at once, the fire quickly rising up to consume the body offered to it. As Signe stepped back from the building heat, Kate heard her whispering in her native tongue. A prayer spoken to her own gods.

Dal's fire burned all through the night. Kate could see its chaotic glow from atop the battlements as she went out that night in search of Signe. In the hectic days that had followed the battle, they'd had little time to talk, a problem Kate sought to rectify now. She could sense Signe's pain from afar, feeling it without her magic. Kate found her easily, standing atop the battlements with her gaze fixed on Dal's funeral pyre in the distance. Her cheeks glistened in the moonlight, evidence of her silent tears.

Kate stood next to her, then slid an arm around Signe's shoulder. "I'm sorry, my friend. I've never been so sorry before."

A sob racked Signe's body, and she turned her head toward Kate, burying her face in Kate's shoulder. Kate hugged her more tightly, saying nothing, doing nothing other than letting her grief flow unhindered. Sometimes a purging was the only answer.

At last, Signe raised her head again, and Kate released her

shoulders, letting her arm fall to her side. But at once, Signe took her hand and held it.

"You've nothing to be sorry for, Kate," Signe said. "The sacrifices we made were worth it, all of them. No great thing can be accomplished without great sacrifice. Such is the way of things in this life."

"You've always been wise beyond your years," Kate said, smiling.

Signe returned the smile, her grief retreating from her expression, for the time being. "We are both wise now, I do believe." She paused, her head cocking to the side, birdlike. "Becoming the Paragon has changed you."

Kate nodded. It had indeed. A change that went far deeper than the brand on her chest. The star emblem had faded to white, same as the scars on her neck where Rendborne had struck her with the Hellsteel.

"We both have changed," Signe said, her gazed fixed on the funeral pyre once more. "With more to come soon, I'm afraid."

Sudden dread spread through Kate at Signe's words. She drew a deep breath, trying to quell it. "What do you mean?"

After a pause, Signe turned back to her. "I'm leaving. As soon as the coronation and wedding are over."

"Why?" Kate didn't bother asking her where she was going, the answer obvious.

"Do you remember what I told my mother that day in the dungeon?"

Kate thought about it a moment, soon recalling the strange word. "Kaiolah. You said it was the secret to your black powder. But what is it?"

"It's a prophecy. Like Seva, there used to be magic in the Esh Islands as well, but it vanished many years ago. Until now. Until me."

Kate's eyebrows climbed her forehead in surprise. "You have magic?"

"Yes. Or at least, I believe that's what it is. It's the only explanation." Signe sighed and rubbed her cheek; weariness had painted dark lines beneath her eyes. "The black powder I mixed for Bonner's revolvers was never the same as what the Furen Mag makes and sells. Theirs is similar, yes, but there is an ingredient in the making that can only be found in the Esh Islands, and the Furen Mag never allow it to be exported anywhere else. It is our most highly guarded secret."

Kate's throat tightened at her choice of words. Already Signe was counting herself among the sisterhood. "Then how were you able to make it?"

"By adding an ingredient of my own. One that comes from me. A drop of my tears or sweat is the key."

Now Kate blinked, her mind unable to comprehend the magnitude of Signe's claims. "You mean you put a part of yourself in every batch?" But she'd made so much, an unfathomable amount.

"A single drop goes a long way." Signe grimaced. "But that is why no matter the circumstance, it wasn't a secret I would ever share."

"Except with me." Kate was awed by the gift, her chest swelling with the pleasure of it.

"You are my sister, Kate, and my friend. I trust you with my life."

Kate bowed her head to her. "And you, mine."

An awkward moment passed between them, neither of them comfortable with voicing such sentiments, despite how true they were. Or maybe because of how true they were.

After a while, Signe let out a sigh. "I should've returned to the islands the moment I realized I was the kaiolah. The prophecy says that the person born with this ability will one day restore magic to the Esh Islands."

Goose bumps sprouted down Kate's arms, not in doubt of Signe's claims but in certainty of them. Like the godtears in Seva, magic was returning to the rest of the world. And with it would come change—both good and bad. She considered for a moment what might have happened if she'd succeeded in killing Rendborne with the Hellsteel, and she'd never been so glad of failure.

"And with my mother dead," Signe continued, "I must go back. I'll be needed more than ever, and . . . and I need to make amends for the damage I did when I left."

"Does this have to do with the man in the ruby-buttoned doublet? And the secret you shared with him?" Kate recalled the conversation well, the day Signe had convinced her to tell Corwin the truth about her magic. And yet it seemed so long ago now.

"Yes," Signe replied, and Kate could tell by the sharpness in her voice that she didn't want to say more.

Kate sighed, unable to help her disappointment. "Will you ever tell me that story?"

Signe smiled. "One day. When we're both old and hideous and our adventures are far behind us."

"I hope mine are already behind me," Kate said.

"Perhaps they are," replied Signe, but then she shrugged, both of them knowing the possibility remained open.

Throwing out her arms, Kate pulled Signe into a hug. "I will miss you." The words were an understatement, but the feelings that passed between them as they embraced spoke for the rest.

Corwin's coronation was a grand affair.

Like most grand affairs, Kate could hardly remember it afterward, the details blurred into one long and dazzling haze. Every lord of every Rimish city traveled to Norgard to attend it. Usually, the farthest cities only sent ambassadors to represent them during such events. Not this time. It seemed all the cities had been shaken by the Sevan invasion. They were ready to strengthen the union between the cities and with the League, as well—to ensure an invasion never happened again. Kate didn't think they needed to worry, though. Eravis had come safely through the battle, as Kate had promised her, and not long after she'd been sent home, taking with her the remnants of the Sevan soldiers who had surrendered. A sign of good faith between the two countries. Mazen Fane had been crowned king in his father's place, and he had already expressed gratitude for his sister's safe return. It wasn't a true treaty, but the option seemed open to it. One day.

All Kate truly remembered afterward was the way Corwin had looked, handsome and regal and entirely kingly. Seeing him like that sent a thrill of wonder through her. She'd always known he was born to rule, but witnessing it come to fruition was a different thing entirely.

If her memory on the coronation was vague, her recollection of their wedding the following week was even more so. In many ways, it was an even grander affair. Certainly for her, at least. The dress, the jewels, the holy words spoken in the temple with the high priestess presiding, and the seven-hour banquet afterward were all like a long and blurred dream. A good one, but yet she was eager for it to end so that she could be alone with Corwin, both as themselves again and not the new king and queen, objects of celebration and scrutiny.

The moment they could, they slipped away from the banquet to their new rooms, shedding their fancy clothes the moment the door was closed and locked. They stayed awake the whole night through, savoring each other and marveling at this dream that had come true, despite the impossibilities, odds that had once been so stacked against them. They explored each other again, reacquainting and learning the stories told in their scars. His, the ones on his back and wrists from his time spent in the mines. Hers, the ones on her chest and throat, and the tattoos on her arms.

But the best part of the night, the one Kate would forever remember the most clearly, was when they snuck out of their rooms and out onto the cavalry fields, like they used to do when they were children. They brought a blanket with them and spread it out in the middle of the quiet, empty field. Ahead, the moon and its ring were full, the field below awash in silvery light. They lay on their backs side by side, staring up at it.

"The servants will talk if we're found out here," Kate said after a while.

Corwin rolled on his side toward her, propping his head on one hand. "Good. The chance of getting caught was always half the fun." He leaned toward her, one hand cupping her hip, fingers pressing on her moonbelt, as he kissed her long and deep, a moment to savor.

Sighing as he pulled away, Kate grinned. "So it was. I suppose we must make this a regular activity, then. For as long as we're able to." She could see a time when she would no longer wear the moonbelt. The thought scared her but also thrilled her—another adventure they would experience together someday. But not now. Now was a time just for them.

"Indeed." Corwin lay back down again. "You know, I always knew we were destined for this."

"For what?" Kate turned to him now, mirroring his pose from a moment before.

"This." He gestured with his hand, as if to indicate everything—the cavalry field, the moon above, Rime itself. "To be husband and wife, king and queen."

Kate made a face. "No you didn't. There were whole years when you never would've dreamed we'd have an end like this."

"It's not an end, Kate. This is a beginning."

"You know what I mean." She rolled her eyes. Then, unable to help herself, she ran a hand down the side of his face, savoring the rough feel of his skin against her fingers where his shaved beard was already trying to grow back again. If she were a man, she would ask one of the magists to enchant the hair away rather than have to shave so often, she thought.

Corwin closed his eyes, leaning into her touch, and when her fingers grazed his lips he kissed them. "I mean it, though," he said, opening his eyes again. "I always did know. If not here, then at least here." He touched his forehead first and then his heart.

Warmth spread through Kate at the sincerity she sensed in him—and not with her magic. Around his neck he still wore the crystal vial. It had been at her insistence—the king more than anyone needed protection against the power of sway—but even with it there, she believed him fully. It was a wondrous feeling to have no way to be sure, but to believe so completely.

"Me too." Kate placed a hand across her heart. "Even when I tried to hate you, I never could."

Corwin laughed. "Thank the gods for that."

Thrilled by his laughter, Kate lay down again, tucking her hands under her head. "But you know, if this king and queen business doesn't work out, we should seriously reconsider joining the circus. What do you think?"

Corwin rolled onto his side again and then gently slid on top of her, trapping her between his arms. He slid his hands down the sides of her face, smoothing back her hair. Then he kissed her, leaving her breathless when he pulled away a moment later. "So long as I'm with you, Kate, I shall be happy. Be it as king or pauper. Just you is what matters."

Kate ran her hands up and down his back. "Just us, you mean," she said, and then she kissed him again. Once. A hundred times.

Forever.

# ACKNOWLEDGMENTS

In the years since I started writing books, I've come to understand what an honor, privilege, and tremendous responsibility it is to be a storyteller. Time is our most precious possession as human beings, and the fact that you, dear reader, have spent your time here, with these characters, means the world to me. So first and foremost, my thanks go to you. I hope your time here counted for something good.

I also owe a huge debt of gratitude to Fairyloot for bestowing your special magic on *Onyx & Ivory*. Thank you, thank you, thank you! Also a huge thanks to LitJoy, Spearcraft, Wanderlust Reader, Pop Reads, and the Book Quay. Loot crates for books are the most amazing invention ever. You all are like fairy godmothers, spreading story magic to readers all over the world.

Another thank-you to every bookstagramer who posted a pic of *Onyx & Ivory*. I'm in awe of your talent with these photos.

A big round of applause for the amazing team at Balzer+Bray for your ongoing support: Alessandra Balzer, Donna Bray, Renée Cafiero, Michael D'Angelo, and Mitch Thorpe, as well as art director Alison Donalty, designer Molly Fehr, and artist ilovedust for another epic cover.

Thank you to the New Leaf team: Joanna Volpe, Kathleen Ortiz, Pouya Shahbazian, Mia Roman, and Veronica Grijalva.

Now on to my personal army of wilders and magists. First up, thanks again to my editor, Jordan Brown, for believing in me and my stories. You're my Raith in so many ways.

Same goes for my agent, Suzie Townsend, although you're also my Signe. So fierce and brilliant and always the person I want guarding my back. And to Cassandra Baim—with your unflappable assistance and friendly guidance, you've been my Bonner.

To my friends and critique partners, who keep me sane and grounded: Lori M. Lee, Kristen Simmons, Lorie Langdon, Kristina McBride, and Liz Coley. I couldn't do this without your support.

To my wonderful and supportive family: Adam, Inara, Tanner, Betty, Phil, Debra, Krystal, Vicki, Jay, Amanda, Evie, Elaina, and Weston.

And lastly, thanks to God and his son, Jesus, who reigns with love and justice both.